T0196365

BABTOO

AND THE
LEGEND OF THE SPOTTED ZEBRA

J. D. KIBLER

authorHOUSE®

AuthorHouse™
1663 Liberty Drive
Bloomington, IN 47403
www.authorhouse.com
Phone: 1-800-839-8640

Published by AuthorHouse 10/17/2013

ISBN: 978-1-4918-2500-6 (sc)
ISBN: 978-1-4918-2498-6 (hc)
ISBN: 978-1-4918-2499-3 (e)

Library of Congress Control Number: 2013917998

PROLOGUE

A long, long, time ago in the outer fringes of the African grasslands, lived a small tribe of tall, nut-brown people called the Watinkees. The Watinkees were a proud and peaceful nomadic tribe, following the herds of zebra, giraffe, wildebeest and gazelle as they migrated across the plains.

Living on the grasslands was often harsh and dangerous for the Watinkees. Predators like lions, spotted panthers and hyenas, which followed the herds, often stalked the tribe and preyed on any unsuspecting tribesmen. In spring, sudden, violent storms produced swift waters that often raced through the camp, washing out their temporarily erected tents causing chaos among the tribe. In the summer months, the sun would be so hot that waves of heat would sweep the land, drying up and shrinking the life-giving watering holes leaving huge cavernous cracks in the thirsty earth.

The life of one member of a Watinkee tribe probably would have never changed had it not been for one such sudden and particularly violent storm arriving at the coast of Africa near one of the tribe's hunting camps.

Chapter 1

The Drought

The story begins with the worst drought in fifty years. The once succulent grass had slowly lost all color, turning from a pale green to a crisp brown. Village crops dried out and withered to blackened husks. They stood as scorched reminders of past famine and hardship instead of becoming plentiful harvests. Foraging for nuts, berries and roots became increasingly difficult. Dust filled the air, choking all color from the horizon and leaving a hazy mirage of the once picturesque landscape. Small tree leaves hung withered and limp, rustling listlessly in the stagnant air.

Only the strong, leafy domes of the giant Baobab trees, with their deep penetrating roots, were still green and able to withstand the oppressive heat, which gave some shady refuge to weary animals and natives. Like a mother welcoming home orphans, the large branches became home to prey and predator alike.

The drought had taken its toll on the Watinkee tribesmen. Food and water became scarce as they and other nomadic tribes moved even more frequently to provide for their clans. Many of the old and very young had already perished. The remaining people struggled desperately to sustain themselves on the open savanna, praying for relief and rain. The fight for survival was particularly devastating for a young warrior with his wife and child.

A fat termite on the well-worn path to the once majestic monkey-bread tree suddenly stopped, waving its antennae in a whirl of

4

motion as if sensing impending doom. With a shake of its blind head, it hurried along with the rest of the colony to its home inside the tree.

The ancient monkey-bread tree stood as a lone sentinel in the middle of a desolate petrified forest. A century ago, it had been alive with life and home to generations of birds, butterflies, and monkeys. It had provided shelter to countless herds of antelope, gazelle, and the occasional tribesmen.

Today, the tree was only a shell of the majesty and beauty it had once been. The bark had long since peeled off, exposing long used highways for termites and other insects. The old tree's limbs were crooked and bent, rising toward the sky in a silent prayer for rain. At the base of the tree, scattered like small children, dry saplings also struggled for life in the drought. As if in answer to the prayer, black clouds were forming across the heat-oppressed plains, blocking out the stifling heat of the day.

Thunder rumbled in dark clouds that rolled swiftly across the sky, anxious to release their pent up power. Tentacles of lightening snaked through the evening sky, revealing the moving silhouettes of animals desperately searching for shelter from the impending storm. The jagged flashes of light in the darkening sky seemed to search for unwary targets, constantly probing the earth.

A lone branch on the monkey-bread tree seemingly reached out and grabbed at an elusive bolt of lightning. Electricity crackled and charged the air as the limb exploded, sounding as if a thousand thundering drums were beating at once. Sparks flew from the branch and ignited the dry kindling and saplings around the tree. The once proud tree became a funeral pyre as its branches waved in the air frantically. Smoke and ash filled the sky as the fire burned everything it touched and spread quickly into the savanna.

Thick black smoke rolled ahead of the raging fire, sometimes shifting directions at a moment's notice or the slightest change in wind direction. Animals scattered, not knowing how to escape the tongues of living flame. Desperately trying to outrun the intense heat of the blaze, gazelles and wildebeests ran with their mortal enemies the lions, hyenas, and cheetahs.

Already fighting nearly impossible odds, many of the savanna tribes faced certain demise. The all-encompassing inferno gave little clue as to where they could safely hide. Scattering into the night, people separated and became lost from one another in the ensuing chaos.

Darkness covered the sky as the heavy rain-filled clouds blotted out the sun, turning the oppressive heat of the day into a choking humid night. Thunder rumbled like a huge hungry belly as the clouds suddenly burst, releasing torrents of rain.

The flames battled the thunderstorm and like two titans fought for supremacy over the savanna. The resounding thunder competed with the roar of the blaze as the clash for dominance raged on. After what seemed like days, but was actually only a matter of a few hours, the rain finally subdued the fire. Small sheltered areas hidden from the storm contained embers that sent out envoys of blackened cinders that sizzled and popped, only to fall back to the damp earth, smothered and quiet.

The following morning the sun struggled to chase the remnants of the storm away. As it slowly rose above the horizon, it burned away the remaining black clouds revealing the devastation left by the rampaging fire. Pockets of steam and smoke rose like wraiths in the air, only to disappear as the sun quickly dried all remaining moisture from the soil. Blackened husks of what once were proud animals that had been just a step too slow, lay in poses of heartbreaking death.

The once picturesque landscape, now a barren desert, held the shocked remains of people and animals struggling to survive the devastation. Dusk finally cooled the savanna as the sun's rays lost their fury for the day, bringing some relief. Stars were beginning to appear like bright jewels on the empty canvas of the sky and for a moment, brought hope for the future. Then, as if in mockery to the struggles below, thin wispy clouds scuttled across the night sky, draping the moon and stars in a mosaic pattern of light and dark.

Moments of hope faded when the light gave way to darkness, giving the savanna an eerie, forlorn feeling of despair.

The scattered moonlight gave barely enough illumination for the retreating man and woman to see as they wearily made their way across the plain. The woman stumbled and struggled to keep her balance as she clutched a small child in her arms. The child, unaware of their plight, cooed softly in his mother's embrace.

The tall dark man, accompanied by the young woman with unusually white hair, helped her to move forward, gently taking her arm. They were alone and desperate to find friends, family or any other survivors from other tribes. If their enemies or predators caught them in the open savanna, it would invite injury or death, even for an experienced warrior, as he was. Exhausted, they staggered toward a huge tree standing in the distance. The women had wrapped the child in soft leopard skin with an eagle feather by his head, as if he was a prince of a tribe.

The child, weary and hungry, whimpered only slightly as he gazed into his mother's eyes. She lovingly caressed his cheek, trying to comfort the small child. Looking up, she peered into the darkness fearfully, searching for any sign of movement.

The man, spent and bleeding, stood defiant. He proudly carried the only weapon he had used to defend his family. The spear stood six feet tall, topped by a long sharp metal tip stained red with blood.

The previous night, a group of hyenas had attacked the couple at their camp. Though suffering from serious wounds, they managed to escape with their lives. Fatigued from pain and loss of blood, they desperately hoped to find a safe place to rest for the night. Feeling as though they played a cat and mouse game, they had the uncanny feeling of an unseen foe stalking them.

Suddenly, sounds like hysterical laughing split the night air. The relentless hyenas had pursued and finally found them once again. The man quickly turned, his eyes scanning the dark horizon for movement. With a quiet word to his wife and a loving touch to her hand, they turned and hobbled hurriedly toward the protection of the giant tree.

Huge ragged heads with red, unblinking eyes and massive slathering jaws parted the tall grass and sniffed the night air hungrily. Low growls and mewling noises from parched throats and skeletal corpse-like bodies filled the air. Spotting their quarry moving toward a tree, the hyenas quickly fanned out for the ambush.

Out of breath and barely able to stand, the warrior and his wife turned to face the emerging beasts. The woman turned and ran desperately to reach the tall tree and placed the infant onto a large branch that jutted out like an island. High enough to be out of the reach of the ravenous hyenas, she lashed the baby to the branch. Her hand then reached for the small knife she carried at her hip.

The hyenas attacked without warning. Screams and growls filled the night air as they leaped toward their quarry. The man, possessed as if by demons, thrust and slashed at the oncoming horde. Blood spilled on the thirsty ground making their footing wet and slippery.

A beast attacked from behind as if sensing a frontal attack was certain death. The man spun around to meet this new threat, but tripped over the body of a wounded hyena as it snapped at his legs. The woman lunged with her knife and quickly put an end to its savage life. She looked up into the night for her husband and watched as he drew the starving animals further from her. He desperately fought on, a lone hero only the gods would witness. She loved her husband and could not let him fight this lopsided battle alone.

Too many to fight, he soon became overwhelmed. He tripped and fell to the ground and became instantly mobbed by the vicious animals. A particularly nasty beast latched onto his back, pinning him to the ground. With an insane scream of desperation, the woman threw herself into the fray, stabbing and biting like a wild thing, only in the end to succumb to the uneven battle. The sounds of the fight diminished as the beasts slowly slunk off into the night.

The cool night air turned into a hot humid morning. A lone hyena returned to the tree looking for food from last night's battle. An interesting scent caught his keen senses. His dry, cracked black nose twitched back and forth testing the light gust of wind leading him to the large tree. The sound of a crying baby caught his sizable ears as he looked up toward the large branch.

Pacing back and forth with eager anticipation, he leapt for the blanket in the tree. Barely catching the corner, he exposed a small leg. With the second leap, the snapping jaws closed on the dangling leg, ripping the flesh to the bone. The baby screamed in agony as the branch shook from the force of the impact. Tasting blood excited the hyena. Running in circles under the tree to gain some momentum, he gathered his legs underneath him for the final leap.

The hyena's full attention was on the defenseless child and he did not notice the Watinkee warriors running toward the tree. As his jaws started to close on the small dangling foot, the spear found its mark in his chest. The hyena felt a blast of pain before he fell to the ground, narrowly missing the exposed leg. His breathing came in gasps as he snapped at the massive spear embedded in his chest. As his eyes dimmed, a Watinkee warrior placed his foot on his head and yanked the spear from his body.

Reaching up, the warrior carefully dislodged the small infant from the branch. Strange, he thought, as he looked into the eyes of the infant that were as grey as the clouds in the sky and with hair as white as an old man's beard.

Dread rippled through the band of warriors as they searched for signs of his mother and father. They saw from the tracks and half-eaten corpses of some of the hyena that a great battle had taken place. A few hundred yards away the gristly remains of the two proud warriors lay together. Scattered around them like leaves in a forest, were several dead hyenas. Beside the warriors was a spear of great artisanship with a golden eagle feather attached to it. This they took to give to the boy when he grew up as a reminder of how his parents sacrificed their lives for him.

CHAPTER 2

THE PERFECT STORM

Eighteen years later a cargo ship with four large triangular sails was heading around the coast of Africa. The captain was a small, rotund man with eyes the color of jade and bright red hair that hung to his shoulders. His long flowing beard, streaked with grey and braided into two strands, tucked into his belt that held a ponderous belly.

He frowned at what he saw as his teeth ground into the small tobacco pipe, furiously puffing the dark red ember. Smoke circled his head clinging to his brow like a fluffy hat before disappearing into the air.

His bright green eyes gazed across the ocean at large rolling black clouds that grew and swelled with every passing moment. The large rectangular sails flapped listlessly against the masts. The still ocean, unusually calm, spelled trouble.

In the cargo bay was the treasure the captain was trying to protect. A stallion with unusual large spots marking his body kicked at the stall, as if sensing the impending storm. A mare and her 3-year-old colt whinnied excitedly, aware of the stallion's uneasiness.

The King of Spain had given Captain Morgan the task of transporting the highly prized stallion, mare and her colt around the Cape of Good Hope to South Africa. The horses were a gift to the governor of the colony.

A raindrop splashed on Captain Morgan's bulbous red nose. At that moment, he awoke from his reverie. The wind howled from the heavens and seemed to assail him from all directions at once. Tearing his hat from his head and flinging his ruffled shirt wide open, the gale pummeled his burly chest and portly stomach like a boxer in a ring.

Captain Morgan pointed a stubby finger at the first mate, yelling at the top of his lungs, "Man the sails! Turn to starboard! ALL HANDS ON DECK!" The wind tore the words from his mouth and they were almost lost in the torrent of rain and thunder.

The swarthy man standing next to him, terrified at the suddenness of the storm, turned to relay the orders to the crew. At that moment, a giant wave crashed into the ship and like a giant fist drove the man into the mast with the force of a hammer on an anvil. Like grasping fingers the wave swirled and receded, slowly dragging his lifeless, broken body overboard to disappear forever into the dark depths.

The crew scrambled out of their quarters, rushing to their assigned tasks. All were experienced crewmen and they knew this was no ordinary storm. Praying to their pagan gods, they worked side by side to steady the tossing ship and knew that it would take extraordinary effort and all of their skills. Struggling against the wrath of the storm, each man desperately tried to do the work of two. The deafening noise of the thunder drowned out their frantic screams of terror. Jagged streaks of lightening lit up the sky for only fractions of an instant, but were enough for the men to see fear clearly etched on each of their faces.

The second mate clutched the wheel of the ship with a vise-like grip as wave after wave of salt water pounded over him. He fought desperately to keep the ship upright. His strength was waning and his muscles became rigid with fatigue. He slowly began to lose the battle with the storm as his fingers loosened and slid off the wheel.

The captain grabbed a skinny man with terror-filled eyes and a wispy beard plastered to his pointed chin. Grimacing against the onslaught, Captain Morgan's two front gold teeth reflected the man's fear as he bellowed, "Get down to the hold. Throw out anything of weight that we don't need. Go now. Hurry! Take whoever you can find to help!"

The man screamed at two stalwart men as he headed toward

the hold. Working furiously, they tied down the main mast with ropes already slick with blood from their frantic hands. The three crewmembers staggered through the swinging doors like drunken sailors after a night of revelry. Stumbling down the stairs, the three men were tossed about like rag dolls while fighting the listing ship.

The horses, mad with terror, shrieked ear-piercing squeals, kicking their stalls to break free. The ship groaned and creaked, testing the strength of the seams and rivets. Muscles strained with desperate urgency as the men dragged crate after crate through the hold and unceremoniously tossed them in the churning ocean. Water cascaded and funneled down the slippery steps making the work harder still. The ankle-deep water rose quickly around their legs in frothy swirls threatening to drown the exhausted crewmen.

The ocean tossed the ship around like a cork in a bottle. Wind whistled through portholes, sounding like drowning seamen screaming defiant curses. Bolts of lightning split the sky in a jagged cadence around the ship. The masts rocked back and forth, straining to stay upright, dodging the electrically charged blue streaks that seemed to get closer with every strike.

Captain Morgan glared fiercely into the face of the storm. Rain pelted his heaving chest and winds tore at his body, trying to dislodge him from his perch on the deck. He raised a beefy, scarred fist and shook it furiously to the heavens.

He bellowed, "Why are you taking this ship from me? I pray to thee every night. I now curse you then and am damned!"

Suddenly, as if the gods had heard, it became eerily calm. The rain fell more softly and the ocean seemed to lay in wait. All eyes looked skyward. A low rumble of thunder echoed in the rolling black mass of clouds. The air felt supercharged as hairs stood up on the crew's skin like tiny armies of soldiers.

Lightning split the darkness, turning night into day. It snaked its way down seemingly in slow motion toward the swaying mast like a finger chastising a child. Eyes looked on in horror as the white light found its mark and shattered the mast into a thousand pieces.

Splinters showered down among the men, striking their exposed skin and creating fresh cuts. Blue fire erupted from the broken remains of the mast, setting the sails ablaze. The ship floundered like a giant wounded bird. The storm's fury continued to grow with frightening strength. The men knew then that the ship was lost but they continued to fight valiantly on against all hope.

Captain Morgan worked desperately with his men, trying to save the sinking ship. Leaks appeared as rivets started to pop. Boards protested under the tremendous strain as pressure from the pounding storm grew to a crescendo. The ship seemed to groan and scream, reminiscent of a tortured soul gasping for its last breath.

A large hole appeared in the hull, as the ocean punched through like a giant fist, ripping through the boards and washing them away. The damage was too great for the ship to sustain.

Despite the best efforts of the crew, the ship, with a final shudder, split apart. The raging sea tossed the crew around like rag dolls as they descended down into their watery grave. Lifeless eyes stared upward as their bodies slowly sank to their final resting place.

The horses, suddenly freed from their confines in the bowels of the ship, bobbed to the surface. Terribly confused and distressed, they swam furiously to save their lives. Despite their best efforts, they too were slowly losing the battle to the violent sea.

CHAPTER 3

BABTOO

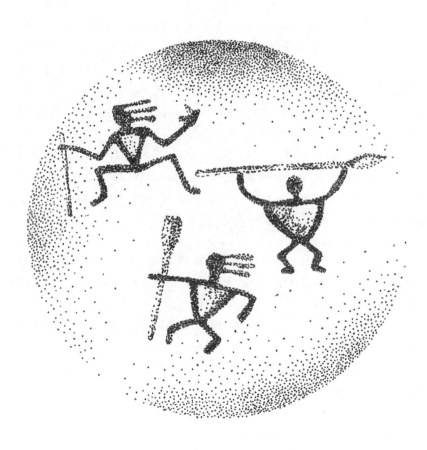

A tall, muscular, bronze-skinned boy stood beneath a cliff overhang, gazing over the hot burning sand at the still waters of the ocean. He was a head taller than his fellow tribesmen were and had white curly hair that hung down his broad back in waves. His features were those of his mother, a slave from a distant land. With high cheekbones and almond shaped eyes that smoldered with intelligence, he stood apart from the rest of his tribe.

The sky was blue with not a cloud anywhere. The breeze was very slight, cooling the sheen of sweat off his brow. His muscular chest rose and fell easily as he breathed in the air, smelling the impending storm. He shifted his broad shoulders slightly to look for shelter. This was his first hunt in his quest to become a warrior. He carried a six-foot spear topped by a razor sharp steel tip, adorned with an eagle feather. He had fallen behind the hunting party, and now was on his own.

Babtoo looked with disdain at the twisted foot that caused his delay. The elder members of his tribe had told him that as a small child hyenas had twice attacked his family. The first attack had caused grave injuries to his parents. Overwhelmed by the second assault, they had sacrificed their lives to save his. The elders also told Babtoo how a Watinkee search party had found him still lashed to the branch where his mother had left him and how they rescued him from the hyena that injured his foot.

During his youth, the crooked foot had caused Babtoo to be much slower in games compared with the other young warriors; however, his quick wit and strength often saved him from defeat. Growing up without parents and having only a few friends in the Watinkee tribe had tested Babtoo's character and steeled his determination.

Knowing his physical limitations, the boys of the tribe had often played cruel tricks on him. The spirited Babtoo quickly learned that no one would shelter or protect him. These were lessons that only hardened his resolve to prevail. He became smarter and more innovative, often reversing the tricks played on him by his insensitive tribesmen. His skills were honed and very acute, alerting him to danger.

The tribe's shaman had looked after Babtoo during his youth and had treated him as a son. A group of warriors known as the Mautuks had killed the shaman's own son in a raid and so the child was a welcome addition to their family. The Mautuks were an ancient enemy of the Watinkee tribesmen that lived in the jungles of Africa.

The shaman, whose name was Wattus, and his wife had been excited to raise this unusual looking boy. After examining the spear found with the boy, Wattus had known that this child was far from ordinary. Would his leg ever heal enough for him to fulfill his destiny, he had wondered. Wattus had taken destiny bones and after rattling them in the palm of his hand, had thrown them on the sacred shield. He gasped when he had seen what the bones revealed. He and his wife died shortly after, never telling anybody what he had seen.

Looking up at the darkening sky, Babtoo felt the heavy hot air and the sudden stillness of nature around him. He knew something menacing was on the way and had to find shelter. Scanning the landscape with his sharp eyes, he found what he was looking for. In the distance, overlooking a shallow inlet, the dark opening of a large cave beckoned him. He hurriedly limped toward it hoping it would be deep enough to shelter him from the impending storm. The cave Babtoo discovered opened into a shallow inlet, surrounded by jagged rocks that had stood for a millennium as if ancient warriors guarded the entrance. The ocean was dark and restless, pounding the stone guardians with increasing fury. White, frothy caps appeared as the waves reached with outstretched fingers, clawing further onto the sandy beach.

Darkness quickly approached as the storm neared the shore. Streaks of lightning illuminated the beach, helping the struggling Babtoo find the cave's well-camouflaged entrance. The howling of the wind soon rose to a deafening roar. He had barely entered the cave when huge raindrops splattered across the beach with such force that miniature craters pockmarked the sand.

Babtoo's feet bled from shell fragments scattered on the beach. He lurched into the cave entrance, tripping on driftwood hidden in the sand. The pungent odor of rotting seaweed assailed his nose as he picked himself up off the ground. Standing up, he brushed the sand and dirt off his clothes and took in his surroundings.

The cave was dark and damp from the tides. As his eyes adjusted to the darkness, he saw that farther back the cavern opened up into a giant, domed grotto. Through several crevices high in its rocky ceiling, streams of dim light infiltrated the area below, giving it an eerie appearance. The light was enough to enable Babtoo to see the enormous amount of driftwood that had accumulated from storms of years past. He picked up a small amount of dry wood and started a fire to ward off the damp cold.

Babtoo had learned long ago how to work quickly with his flint and stone to create a fire. In no time, the parched kindling ignited into a small, dancing flame. He quickly fed the fire with bigger pieces of wood, and joyfully watched the fire grow, softly illuminating most of his temporary refuge.

Shivering from the dampness of his clothes, he carefully removed them, spreading them around the fire to dry. His crippled leg ached in the dampness as he stretched out. Babtoo lightly massaged the long deep scars that had formed where flesh should have been.

Moving closer to the fire, Babtoo fumbled in a small leather pouch made of jaguar skin containing dried meat. Chewing the meat thoughtfully, he inspected his surroundings as the fire reflected off the dank walls of the cave. Looking more closely, he discovered bones scattered among the driftwood in a shadowy corner of the cave.

Curious, Babtoo rose from the fire to take a closer look. A human skull lay half buried in the debris. Using his spear, he poked at the bones, hoping to find the reason why they were here without a proper burial. In the flickering firelight, the skull leered at him with empty eye sockets causing a shiver to run up his spine.

After closer examination, Babtoo noticed that the whole top of the skull was gone, making it appear like an upside-down bowl. Jumping back, Babtoo tripped over another set of bones causing him to fall backwards. These bones did not seem as old as the first skeleton. Bits of flesh still clung to fragmented pieces of bone. Upon closer examination, Babtoo found the skull decapitated in an identical manner as the first body's remains. Pieces of clothing that resembled an outfit a Watinkee warrior would have worn lay torn and burned in the fire pit. A feeling of apprehension sent a trickle of sweat slowly down the back of Babtoo's neck.

Suddenly, a thunderous boom sounded and a lightning streak lit the cave with a flash of brilliance. Feeling great horror, Babtoo saw cryptic signs painted in red on the walls in a language he did not recognize.

A numbing fear started to creep into his mind. Images of nightmarish figures dancing in the night stemming from superstitious tales at bedtime many years ago now became very real. Babtoo fought to control his fear. He quickly backed out of the cave, turning into the squall of wind and rain outside.

The storm whipped his hair around with such force it momentarily blinded him. Sand stung his face and body, tearing into his skin. With reluctance and great trepidation, he returned to his small fire, watching the cryptic shadows float across the cave walls. He flattened himself against a wall, placing his spear protectively in front of his body to wait out the storm.

Flashes of lightning continued to reveal the terrifying inscriptions written on the walls inside the cave. The rocky cavern surrounding Babtoo suddenly became a mystical and hostile world.

Misty wraiths seemed to float into the cave from the sea. Babtoo imagined an army of undead souls marching in to claim the living inside the cave. The terrible images in the cavern came alive as the wind whistled through the cracks sounding like pleas for mercy or screams of pain.

Fear kept Babtoo alert for most of the long night as his eyes darted from one image to the next until exhaustion finally took its toll. He drifted into an uneasy sleep dreaming of nightmarish warriors with pointed teeth. They chased him through the savanna, always one-step behind and just out of reach. The storm outside finally subsided as it moved out to sea. The cave became deathly quiet once again.

Babtoo awoke with a start. Even though the storm had moved out to sea, defiant rumbles of distant thunder remained and greeted the faint glow of dawn. Recollections of the previous night flooded his mind with frightening clarity. Struggling with a fear that was gripping his very soul, he forced himself to re-enter the back of the cave. He had to assure himself that the visions his mind held from the night before were real, not just a bad dream or figments of his imagination.

Slowly, he stepped back to the still smoldering fire. Carefully, he blew the embers into a small blaze. He picked out a large piece of driftwood that had remained only partly burned and moved it back into the glowing embers. After waiting for it to catch fire, he picked up the makeshift torch, and gritting his teeth, moved forward to better explore the rear of the cave.

In the dim light, grisly details started to take on a life of their own. He cautiously proceeded to work his way around the piles of bones, which seemed randomly scattered. Babtoo felt sure that marauding animals caused the bone's erratic pattern. He sensed as if the skull's sightless eyes were pleading with him to find their killers as he made his way toward the back wall.

The torch illuminated and brought the cave writings to life. Reaching out and touching the inscriptions, Babtoo's throat tightened. His stomach lurched as his breath caught in his throat. The sudden revelation that the pictures were outlined in red blood gave him caution. He looked over his shoulder to see more images of human sacrifices reveal themselves in the flickering light.

The crude drawings depicted a violent tribe of people with short spears and small oval shields. They told a story of how they captured their victims and made them into slaves. Further illustrations portrayed forced marches by the enslaved people to a forested land, where sacrifice and certain death awaited them.

They also depicted a large triangular structure made of square stones, higher than two tall trees, with wide step that led to a slab platform. On this platform, muscular warriors restrained captives, as a man dressed in animal skins and feathers performed a brutal ritual before they viciously sacrificed the helpless slaves.

The last sketch on the wall was the most gruesome that Babtoo had ever seen. It demonstrated the depravity of this evil tribe, showing warriors sitting around a large fire pit, cold-bloodedly devouring the victim's flesh. Babtoo gasped in horror as he comprehended the fact that he was looking at scenes painted by a horde of cannibals.

Babtoo remotely recalled that many years ago he had heard of a vicious tribe called the Mautuks. As a child, Babtoo remembered stories of the Mautuk's sadistic and brutal nature and that they came from the jungle to raid and plunder native villages.

Recalling the story, it had been a tale of how the Watinkees, surprised by an attack of the ferocious cannibals, had repelled them in a hard-fought battle. The fleeing Mautuks fought to get back to their jungle home, but the Watinkee warriors fiercely pursued them. Catching them in the open savanna, all the invading Mautuk warriors died in battle. The massacre should have ended the reign of the cannibals. Yet years later, could other members of their tribe have returned to the Watinkee's land?

Panicky, Babtoo ran to the front of the cave, discarding the torch.

Suddenly, he had the feeling of foreboding. He had to get back to the hunting party to warn them! As he stepped into the light of the approaching day, the glare from the sun blinded him as he covered his eyes with his hand.

Finally able to focus on the landscape that surrounded him, Babtoo could not believe what he saw. He rubbed his eyes several times to comprehend the dismal view that greeted him.

The sun rising from the eastern horizon cast long straight, searching shafts over the ocean, revealing the devastation the storm had dealt the land. The ocean, calm now, licked at the beach with a steady rhythm. The waves pushed in upon each other only to fall back and disappear into the sand.

The huge rocks that stood like protective sentries around the bay now had bobbing pieces of splintered wood and other materials surrounding them. The once sparkling beach now looked ominously like a graveyard at the bottom of the ocean. Seaweed draped across driftwood. Broken boards were scattered in all directions and lay half buried in the sand. Long ropes, twisted by the storm, lay curled up among the thick layer of shells, resembling dead sea snakes. Torn sailcloth clung to the shattered remains of a ship mast floating forlornly in the surf.

Babtoo breathed in the air, now filled with the smell of rotting fish and other sea creatures baking in the sun. Seabirds, welcoming the plentiful meal awaiting them on the beach, circled overhead with raucous squawks. Babtoo walked towards the surf, weaving in and out of the wrecked ship's carnage.

Scanning the beach, he saw a large, bloated body, rolling back and forth in the surf. As he approached the man, he could see he was shirtless and wearing colorful, baggy pants. The man's red hair and white skin gleamed strangely in the foaming water. Babtoo noticed gold hoops adorning the dead man's ears. Using his spear, Babtoo cautiously rolled the body over to look in the corpse's face. He peered into features that stared back at him with dead, terror filled eyes. The man's mouth, pulled into an alarming grimace, expressed the dread he had experienced the last minutes before his death. Babtoo jumped back from the unexpected visage.

Slowly, he pulled the heavy man ashore into the soft sand, and looked out into the bay once more. As he had expected, more bodies floated in the surf, rocking back and forth, slowly making their way toward shore with each passing wave.

An occasional fin circled menacingly around the bodies, only to disappear with a splash and reappear somewhere else. Babtoo looked for any sign of human life in the vast ocean before him, but saw none. He wondered how many poor souls had lost their lives, either to the sea or to the sharks. Revulsion sent a shiver through his body as the repulsiveness of the situation gripped him.

CHAPTER 4

THE GIFT FROM THE SEA

The young horse struggled hard to keep his head above water. The previous night's storm had sapped his strength almost to exhaustion. His nostrils, caked with salt, huffed in air as he valiantly struggled to swim toward land. He could already smell the beach and the grasslands that lay beyond.

Gray, sandpaper-like skin bumped into his flank, and an ominous fin flashed close behind. As the shark circled, the yearling kicked out. A hoof smashed into a mouth full of sharp, jagged teeth. Blood spurted as part of the hoof snagged on a serrated tooth.

Surprised by the blow to his mouth, the shark turned away, looking at the horse with black, soulless eyes. Courage and determination coupled with fear spurred the colt on. The battle was one sided and the struggle would soon be over.

One hoof reached the sea-bottom, digging in for extra traction. The second hoof caught the bottom in an explosion of sand and mud. The horse was no longer swimming, but labored to gain footing in the shallows. The gray predator, excited by the blood, launched his body and opened his mouth for his final attempt. The horse whinnied in desperation, sensing the final attack.

The horse's struggle did not go unnoticed. Babtoo shaded his eyes from the rising sun to see the wild skirmish that was taking place in the shallows of the sea. In disbelief, he saw what looked to be a spotted zebra fending off a shark while attempting to reach the nearby land. A look of awe appeared on his face, for he had never seen a spotted zebra, let alone one swimming in the ocean. He admired the animal's courage, but was also very much aware that the animal was fighting a losing battle.

Babtoo's decision came easily, and he knew instantly what he had to do. He made the choice to save the creature without any conscious thought for his own safety.

Shifting his spear to his right hand, Babtoo sprinted into the surf, ignoring the pain in his leg. The sand sucked at his feet, and the waves pushed and pulled his body relentlessly and for every two steps he took forward, he was thrown back one.

Saltwater filtered into his nose and mouth. Coughing and spitting the water out, Babtoo concentrated on the area where the shark's fin had last been visible. He caught a glimpse of the grey fin cutting the surface of the sea as it slowly sank from sight.

Thinking quickly, he tried to place himself between the animal and the shark. The horse stumbled into the shallow water, exhaustion finally taking its toll. It barely flinched as Babtoo splashed toward it in the chest-high water.

Diving into the cloudy water, Babtoo looked for the shark to appear once more. The pounding surf agitated the ocean floor, infusing the water with floating particles of seaweed, sponge, coral, and sediment dislodged by the storm. His eyes grew accustomed to the murky water as the fast-moving silhouette took shape in front of him. He quickly stood up, and with a thrust of his spear, stabbed the large fish in its side. A jagged cut followed the spear point tracing a path along the flank of the shark. Spinning away from the attack, blood trailed the wounded creature like a red scarf fluttering in the wind.

A wave knocked Babtoo back into deeper water while he still grasped his spear, ready to strike again. He kicked strongly to fight the current while searching the cloudy water for the elusive enemy. Fighting to get back to the shallows, he wondered if he had seen the last of the shark.

In the dimness of the ocean, he suddenly saw a dark shadow coming directly at him. As the shark rapidly closed the distance,

Babtoo realized the water surrounding him was red with blood. He understood immediately that the injury had made the shark crazed with pain, and especially dangerous.

This time, Babtoo was better prepared. Knowing the water would slow his thrust, he waited until the shark came closer to the surface. Poised to strike, he ferociously shoved the spear's steel tip into the gaping jaws of the monster. The spear found its mark, pricking the small nut-sized brain. As Babtoo drove the point deeper, the shark's thrashing body continued forward, further impaling itself on the spear's shaft. Its black eyes rolled back in terror, while its wide-open jaws lined with razor-sharp teeth still tried to reach Babtoo. Hanging on to the spear with powerful forearms, the shark drove him back into the shallows. His feet dug into the sand until the shark's final death throes subsided. The spear lodged deeply into the shark's body and Babtoo was unable to remove it in the water.

Looking at the growing pool of blood surrounding him, Babtoo knew other sharks would be attracted to it. Digging his feet into the sand, he pulled the massive shark toward the shallows. He completed his efforts just in time. Scanning the surface of the inlet, several fins were already visible in the bloodied shallow water.

Babtoo successfully extracted his spear from the shark's still twitching body with his hunting knife. Worn-out, but happy, he sank into the warm sand of the beach. He looked at the carnage around him and wondered who had brought the wrath of the gods down on them. The strange spotted zebra he had so bravely saved stood in exhaustion, bleeding from its rear leg. Too fatigued to stand any longer, the animal collapsed and sank to its knees.

Babtoo stood up and put his knife back into the sheath at his waist. He grabbed his spear and walked over to take a closer look at the pitiable creature resting in the sand. He stared in confusion as he took in the differences that were unusual for a zebra.

The animal was white and black like a zebra, but instead of stripes, it had black spots of various sizes covering most of its body. With the warm wind drying its hair, Babtoo noticed that the mane and tail of this strange creature was much longer than any zebra he had ever encountered.

He knew that nobody in his tribe had ever seen a zebra with spots, nor had they ever heard of one to exist. What type of mystical creature was this? Could a zebra swim in the ocean and gallantly fight off sharks?

Babtoo was convinced that the gods had sent him a sign. What kind of sign could it be? Deep in thought, he squatted in front of the strange zebra, reached out, and gently touched its forehead. To his delight and astonishment, the animal did not draw back at his touch but instead gently nuzzled his forearm. It seemed to be tame. Babtoo felt a rush of excitement surge through his body. Would the animal let him treat the injured leg?

The rear leg revealed a jagged slash down to the hoof. With each beat of the animal's heart, blood pumped down in small rivulets and dripped slowly into the sand. A small fragment of pale bone showed through the bleeding flesh. Looking around for something to dress the wound, Babtoo remembered the pieces of sailcloth he had seen still clinging to the ship's mast. Slowly getting up so as not to startle the animal, he ran back to the battered mast where the sail still clung.

With his hunting knife, he cut out a large section of the heavy fabric to bind the wound and make a temporary shelter. Then, using the last of his drinking water, he gently cleaned the animal's wound and bound the leg tightly to stem the bleeding. The animal, comforted by the human's tender care, slowly rolled over to lie on its side and relaxed.

Babtoo then built a tent-like structure with pieces of wood and sailcloth to protect the zebra from the sweltering sun. Still concerned over the animal's condition, Babtoo knew he had to find food and water to assure his survival. Gathering up his empty water bag and spear, he sprinted past the debris on the beach to the grasslands above. He knew of a hidden animal trail that led to a shallow depression, which he expected to be full of water after last night's storm.

Once he reached the small water hole, he was elated to see that he had guessed correctly. He quickly filled his water bag and glanced at his surroundings noticing the grass crushed and trampled. Unusual footprints were scattered around the water hole that were unfamiliar to Babtoo. He had a tingling sense of fear that somebody was watching him since the memories of the cave were still fresh in his mind. Hurriedly, he pulled up some grass and swiftly returned to the spotted zebra.

The animal still rested in the same position in the coolness of the shelter. At Babtoo's approach, the creature lifted his head and gave him a meek nicker. Babtoo checked the injured leg, and with satisfaction, noted that the heavy bleeding had stopped.

He knelt next to the zebra's head and poured some of the water into his cupped palm, offering it to the animal. Babtoo's hand was thirstily licked dry and so he repeated the process several times until most of his water was gone.

Babtoo realized that tomorrow he would need to find a bigger water container for the animal. He put his water bag aside and placed a small amount of the fresh grass in front of the animal's soft muzzle. To his delight, the zebra readily took a few blades and chewed slowly, looking at him with large, soulful eyes.

Babtoo looked at the sun and knew it would not be long before dusk. He had made the tent large enough for both of them to share for the night. He cleared an area under the textile roof from rocks and debris and then stretched out close to the animal's head. He was in dire need of sleep and the bizarre events of the last twenty-four hours had exhausted him.

Babtoo's last thoughts turned to the hunting party and the beautiful creature beside him. Before the animal came out of the sea, he had planned to warn his tribe of the possibility that cannibals were in the area. If he did, he would have to leave the miraculous zebra sent by the gods. He knew that the injured animal would not be able to survive without his help.

Babtoo felt torn between his allegiance to his tribe and his obligation to the wonderful creature the gods had sent him that now depended on him. How could he possibly make the right decision? He decided that he would ask the gods guidance in the morning.

He took one more look at the extraordinary animal resting peacefully next to him, and smiled with contentment. Reassured that the animal was comfortable, Babtoo closed his eyes and drifted into a deep sleep.

A stubby finger with dark, curled nails scratched absentmindedly at the bone in his nose. The nose clung to a face that sported heavy, shaggy brows and a sloping forehead. Hair, short and curly, matted his head. Eyes the color of the blackest coal peered out with cruel wit. With a shake of his head, bone earrings jingled faintly.

The warrior stood up, revealing a black layer of hair clinging to his small body like a wild animal. He did not stand over five feet tall, yet every movement was as calculated and cunning as a wild cat.

The Mautuk was on his way to the cave near the beach when the storm surprised him. Having to find shelter fast, he made camp under an umbrella of dense trees. Wet and miserable, he built a fire and waited out the storm.

The next morning, he continued on his way to the cave. His surprise at what he saw saved Babtoo's life. All day long, the warrior hid in the cliffs and observed the unusual events unfolding before him on the beach. Unsure of what to do, he picked up his small shield and short spear, and loped with an easy stride toward the west and his tribe. He was a scout for the Mautuks.

Crinkling his nose in disgust, Babtoo awoke to the smell of rotting fish and sea creatures slowly roasting on the beach in the warm sun. Immediately, memories of the previous day's events flashed through his mind.

Babtoo stood up too quickly, and felt a sharp pain in his crippled foot. Ignoring the ache, he turned to the animal he had saved from the shark. The creature was now standing, slightly favoring the injured leg.

"A good sign," Babtoo thought. Approaching the young animal, Babtoo patted the animal's neck, and ran his hand down its flank toward the wounded back leg. Shivering slightly under the unfamiliar touch, the creature stood patiently and allowed the native boy to examine his wounded foot.

As Babtoo looked down at his own crippled foot, he felt a powerful connection with the creature. Cleaning the wound and re-wrapping the leg, Babtoo knew he had to make a decision regarding his future with the animal.

Walking around the scattered debris from the ship, Babtoo spotted the lifeless shark's body rolling back and forth in the surf. Even in death, the shark seemed to grin back at him in sheer defiance.

Babtoo removed his knife from its casing and pried open the monster's enormous jaws. He had never seen the inside of a shark's mouth, and stared down in astonishment at the three rows of sharp serrated teeth.

Working quickly, he painstakingly dislodged about thirty of the largest teeth. He would make a victory necklace for himself and the zebra. The rest he would use as an offering for the gods. He knew that they would be very pleased to receive his gift and planned to consult them for guidance in a prayer ceremony that morning.

Babtoo started a small fire and knelt down in the sand, spreading the teeth out in front of him. Raising his eyes and hands to the sky, Babtoo's voice was clear and strong. He sang about the strength of the spotted zebra, the fierceness of the shark, and the bravery he was able to display in the recent struggle for life.

His young, clear voice carried upward as he asked the gods to give him guidance to solve his dilemma. All he needed was a small sign to point him in the right direction. Babtoo waited, but no sign appeared above him. He only saw the ever-present seagulls flying close over his head, screeching to claim the rotting sea creatures on shore. He watched them keenly as they circled in quest of the ample fare below.

A thought crossed his mind. Maybe the gods were trying to give him a sign at another location. Raising up from his haunches and grabbing his spear, he walked over to an area where the sea gulls seemed to be forming a ring.

Babtoo's anguish turned into jubilation when he saw that the gods had not deserted him after all. Directly before him in the wet sand, he found a large seahorse with a piece of small twine entangled around its neck. The twine connected to the arm of a starfish. On the opposite arm of the starfish, lay a pointed stick. Incredibly, the sea horse, the starfish and the stick had formed a constellation in the sand. Footprints of a bird led away from the stick to a shallow pool of water.

Babtoo suddenly knew his destiny. The gods had given him the magnificent animal to keep. Now he had to find a name for the wonderful creature. He sat and pondered many names, but none seemed to fit. The animal had come from the sea under mysterious circumstances.

Eno Bi Mas meant 'mysterious creature from the sea' in the Watinkee language. Babtoo mused that he did not really think that the creature had belonged to the sea, but had mysteriously appeared from a faraway place. Maybe the gods sent him from the heavens. *Eno Bi*, meaning 'mysterious creature' seemed more appropriate.

Unexpectedly, Babtoo slapped his forehead. That was it! He jumped up with unbounded excitement. The Gods had guided him to choose a name. He would call the animal **"Enobi"**. It would be a great and noble name, known by his children and their children, and warriors would mention it only in awe and reverence around their campfires. Babtoo paused in his thoughts in wonderment. He had seen the future and now was certain of it.

Knowing now what direction to take, Babtoo immediately went to work. Chasing the screaming gulls away, he turned to look for any remaining rope from the mast. Spotting a length of line half buried in the sand, Babtoo cut a lengthy piece to lead the animal to water and food.

Babtoo wondered, "Will this magnificent animal let me lead him to the grasslands? A zebra with spots, and yet he was so much more beautiful and wonderful! He was a gift from the gods themselves!" An excitement welled up deep inside him as he approached the animal with reverence.

Talking softly as he approached, the animal's ears swiveled back and forth at the sound of Babtoo's voice. He reached out and gently rubbed its head and neck, calming the powerful creature. The unusual blue eyes never left him, following his every move.

Slowly making a large loop, Babtoo slipped the rope over the animal's head. Still tossing his head slightly and snorting uneasily, Enobi followed Babtoo's every move. The rope fell easily around the muscular neck while Babtoo's gentle voice calmed the big animal.

Babtoo squared his shoulders and leaned lightly on his long spear. He needed to lead the creature to water and safety. Giving the rope a firm tug, he walked forward, leading the horse along toward the distant grasslands. He felt by the resistance of the lead in his hand that the zebra with spots was limping behind him, trying to keep up.

The sand was deep and progress was slow. Gradually, the terrain changed from dry sand into lush, green grasslands. Babtoo searched for the almost invisible trail that had led him toward the shallow water hole. He hoped that there would still be enough water left to quench his and this animal's thirst.

Remembering the strange tracks he had seen the previous afternoon at the water hole, Babtoo approached the area with extreme caution. Smelling the water, the thirsty animal suddenly stumbled past Babtoo while the rope slipped from his sweating hands. Enobi gulped the coveted liquid noisily, trying to satisfy his thirst.

Babtoo stopped and scouted the area around him. He sensed that someone was watching him. Dropping down to a crouch and holding his spear in front of him, Babtoo scanned the expansive plains ahead for any visible movement. He saw none.

CHAPTER 5

CHINTOOK THE LION MASTER

The wind whispered through the grasslands, gently pushing the plants back and forth, carrying sounds and scents of the savannah. Enobi suddenly became very alert. With his ears twitching back and forth, the large animal tried to locate the sound or scent that alerted him to danger.

Babtoo instantly tensed as he noticed Enobi's uneasiness. He held his spear in front of him in defense, sensing an impending threat. Stalks of grass parted slightly, revealing four Watinkee tribesmen's silent approach. Relieved, Babtoo lowered his spear.

Surprised by the sudden appearance of the unfamiliar beings, Enobi reared up on his hind legs, wildly pawing the air. Babtoo frantically clung to the rope, trying desperately to calm the big animal. The tribesmen aimed their spears at the strange animal, ready to throw them if anything were to happen to Babtoo.

Desperate with determination, Babtoo finally brought Enobi back under his control. The animal responded to his calm voice and firm hands, trusting the man that had gently cared for him and settled down to an uneasy truce with the four tribesmen.

Chintook, the leader of the Watinkee hunting party, stepped forward, obviously impressed at what he had just seen. He was a lean, grizzled man with scars crisscrossing his chest from a hunt that had gone terribly wrong. On his head was the mantle of the lion he had killed that had given him those horrific scars.

Chintook had been young when he lost his father to a Mautuk raiding party. The responsibility of hunting for his family had come at an early age. He had been stalking a gazelle that he had wounded earlier that fateful day and he had readied himself for the final kill. Little did he know that a lion had also been stalking the same gazelle.

Chintook had spotted the animal and had been ready to dispatch it when the lion had charged through the underbrush with a terrifying roar. Surprised, Chintook had had to spin around quickly and in desperation had planted his spear in the dirt. The lion had catapulted through the air with great speed and impaled itself on the weapon. Struggling to get at Chintook, the lion had ripped into his body, gouging him with sharp nails and jagged fangs. In panic, Chintook had drawn his hunting knife and had frantically stabbed the lion repeatedly.

The life had faded from the lion in only a few seconds but it had felt like hours to Chintook. He was in shock when he had finally dragged himself out from under the beast. He had lain in the bush for hours, hovering between life and death.

A rescue party had found him barely clinging to life and had been amazed at what they observed. Chintook was barely alive, still clutching his spear, the body of the rogue lion next to him, now stiff from death. After they had skinned the mane from the dead beast, the warriors had transported Chintook back to safety. It had taken him months to recover from his wounds. Since the near-death experience with the lion, Chintook felt invulnerable.

Chintook had made a headdress out of the lion's mane during his lengthy recovery and now wore it whenever he was leading his men on a hunt or in battle. Considered as one of the Watinkee's greatest warriors and hunters, Chintook had taught Babtoo much in his young life.

With an upraised fist and in a strong voice, Chintook bellowed, "Well met Babtoo! We thought you were lost in the storm and I am glad we have finally found you. It was difficult finding you after that downpour washed out your tracks." Chintook paused, not able to take his eyes off Enobi. After a moment, Chintook asked, "What kind of creature do we have here? I have never seen a zebra with such markings. Is this a magical beast? Where did you find such a beautiful animal? Power and beauty combined into one creature." Chintook looked hard at Babtoo before continuing, as if he were talking to a high priest, "How do you speak to it? It seems to listen to your command."

Babtoo was immensely proud of Enobi and exclaimed with great enthusiasm, "Well met Chintook. This truly is a mysterious creature. His name is Enobi. He came out of the sea and fought off a huge shark." Babtoo pointed at Enobi's wounded leg, "Enobi suffered a wound in his rear leg before I was able to kill the shark. I believe this is my totem, like your lion mane cape!"

Chintook was very impressed at the control Babtoo had over the powerful beast. He glanced back at the other three warriors, who remained standing uncertainly, still pointing their spears in Enobi's direction. Chintook gave the command to lower their weapons.

Babtoo excitedly interrupted his order and warned them about the strange tracks he had seen at the water hole. "Chintook, I have discovered a great cave down by the beach where I took shelter from the storm. There are strange drawings and human bones in the cave. I remember stories of a tribe of cannibals told to me as a youth called the Mautuks."

He continued to tell them about the bizarre cave he had spent the night in. He stood straight and tall as he related to Chintook and the men what he had seen. The drawings painted in blood and skeletons of humans lying haphazardly throughout the cavern still sent a shiver through his young body.

Chintook listened to Babtoo with intense interest. He remembered that as a young warrior, he had lost his father to a clan of people known for their practice of torturing and eating their captives. The tribe's name was the Mautuks, a brutal, uncivilized people with a taste for blood - human blood. Instinctively, Chintook's hand reached down, touching the shank of his long skinning knife.

Turning toward the other warriors, Chintook gave a sign with his hand for his men to scout the area for Mautuk tracks. With a sharp motion and chop of his hand, the warriors obeyed Chintook's command and cautiously melted back into the grasslands. Chintook decided that the cave would have to wait. He hated the Mautuks with every fiber of his body and with good reason.

His father had died when he had fallen prey to an ambush by a Mautuk raiding party. Three Mautuks had died by his father's hand before the evil tribe's warriors finally overcame him. They desecrated his father's body leaving a grisly sight for the Watinkee search party that later found him.

Chintook knew that his father had died well and that his spirit was in the Watinkee warrior's star formation in the sky. They were reserved for only the best and bravest Watinkee warriors. Revenge was never far from his mind but the safety of his hunting party would always come first.

Chintook and Babtoo waited for the warriors to return from their scouting expedition. Whispering a silent prayer to his father's spirit, Chintook appealed to the gods to help him find the Mautuk scout before he reached the safety of his tribe.

The first to reappear as silently as he had left was Ohat. He was a head shorter than Babtoo, but built like a powerful wrestler. His long powerful arms and huge hands gripped his spear, making it appear like a toothpick. Grinning, he lifted his hands in sign language to indicate that there were tracks. He motioned for Chintook to follow him to a large grove of trees that he pointed to in the distance.

Moving like a phantom, Chintook faded quickly into the grasslands with Ohat. Babtoo, caught up in the moment, swiftly turned to join his tribesmen. Enobi, sensing the warrior's excitement, gathered his strength and trotted after Babtoo.

The warriors moved like shadows, barely disturbing even the smallest blade of grass. Carefully, they trailed the faint tracks to the trees. Puku and Ukup, the other two tribesmen, were already exploring the well-concealed site of an extinguished campfire. Although they were brothers, they were as different from each other as the change of seasons.

Puku, a tall gangly warrior with hair the color of ash, leaned on a spear and pointed at the blackened patch of earth. "He camped here, Chintook, to wait out the storm."

Ukup, squatting on the ground with his fat, stubby body, poked through the cold remnants of the fire searching for any evidence that could divulge the identity of the intruder. Chintook, already familiar with a Mautuk camp, studied the campsite and knew immediately what kind of warrior it had been.

Babtoo slid down beside Ukup and Chintook to look at the cold clumps of charcoal on the ground. He suddenly felt the same ominous feeling that had bothered him the night before while in the cave. Enobi, seemingly sensing Babtoo's uneasiness, nuzzled him from behind. With a bold snort and a spirited shake of its head, the animal's flared nostrils inquisitively tested the air.

Chintook scanned the campsite with eyes that missed nothing, looking for anything that would give him a clue as to how big the scouting party actually had been. Bent blades of grass and only one set of footprints was all he could find. From the campfire site, Ukup dug out small bones the size of monkey fingers scorched by the fire.

Puku carefully held a small arrowhead in his hand. The tip was dark and gleaming, as if dipped into something wet. "Ukup found this by the fire under some leaves. The arrowhead looks wet."

Chintook took a close look at the arrowhead's point and somberly motioned for the warriors to gather around. Speaking in a hushed voice, Chintook whispered, "Poison! This is a Mautuk arrowhead. These people use the poison from the mamba snake or dart frog to kill their enemies. They are a cowardly tribe and may now be invading our land. A cannibal drinks human blood and will eat human flesh. He must be found before he gets away. We don't know what he has learned and whether there are more of them. We can't let him get back to his tribe. Who is with me?"

Looking questioningly into the eyes of each of his warriors, Chintook saw only loyalty and determination staring back at him. He nodded with satisfaction.

Puku said, "I'll go with Ukup to trail the Mautuk. We can find out where he's going and maybe we can cut him off."

Chintook's brow knotted in thought as he peered at them. "Only find out in what direction he is going. They rarely go out on their own and he might meet up with others of their kind. We'll travel together for strength in numbers."

Nodding their heads in unison, Puku and Ukup scanned the horizon, and slowly fanned out in quest of additional signs or tracks. Both expert trackers, Chintook knew they would not be long finding the Mautuk.

Chintook took Ohat and Babtoo aside. A powerful hand settled on Babtoo's shoulder, almost spinning him around. Chintook's dark eyes bored into Babtoo's young gray eyes, and then glanced down at his lame foot. "This is going to be dangerous. You don't have to come with us. Go back to the tribe and tell them of what we are about to do."

Babtoo was stunned. He was not about to be left behind. This was his time to become a recognized warrior. Excitement surged through him as he quickly shook his head and raised his spear. "Do not send me back and do not worry about me! I'll keep up." He glanced at Enobi, "Me and my magical beast." He puffed out his bronzed, young chest in pride.

Ohat looked at the powerful looking creature and silently wondered what this beast could do. Looking at Babtoo and Enobi, both were lame and he hoped they could keep up.

Chintook frowned, but understood Babtoo's reluctance to go back. Babtoo had a spirit that reminded him of himself when he was younger. Shaking his head, Chintook said, "If you fall behind, we cannot wait for you."

The small monkey hid among the branches of the strand of Balboa trees. He had strayed a little too far from his troop and was now alone. He peered furtively between the leaves, looking for the movement that alarmed him only a moment ago. Too late, he realized the danger when the arrow buried itself in his leg. Screeching in pain and surprise, the monkey jumped to the next higher branch. The poison, which took effect almost immediately, slowed his reflexes. The jump was far too short, and, as darkness overtook it, the monkey tumbled to the ground.

The almost invisible black man stepped from behind the termite mound, never taking his ferret-like eyes off the fallen monkey. He absentmindedly scratched a termite bite on his ankle.

With a slight grimace and shake of his ugly head, the Mautuk scout thought, "Monkey again. Ugh. Soon it will be Watinkee tribesmen." He had had a successful scouting mission and he was intent on getting back to his fellow tribesmen.

In another couple of days, he hoped to join with the other Mautuk scouts and warriors. Skinning the monkey with practiced ease, the Mautuk tribesmen wondered about the boy he had seen with a strange beast. Could this be a bad omen? With a shrug, he put the skinned monkey on the spit and started a small fire. Anticipation of battle with the Watinkees quickly put the boy and beast out of his mind.

Chapter 6

The Chase

The sun's oppressive heat beat down on the savannah. Sweat trickled slowly down Babtoo's back as he tightly clutched his spear. His other hand expertly held a filing stone. With practiced care, he slowly filed his spear-point to razor sharpness. Looking into the distance, Babtoo could only imagine at what was to come. He completely trusted Chintook and the other warriors.

He wondered about how he would prove himself. Gripping his spear, his muscular arms rippled with youthful strength. Quickly rising and taking quick aim, Babtoo tossed the weapon toward a small, fleeing lizard. A slight smile crossed his face as the spear easily found its mark. He imagined that this could have been a Mautuk warrior.

Retrieving his spear, Babtoo thought about his injured foot, "Can I keep up with these noble warriors? I'll have to. This is my chance to prove that I can be a great warrior too!"

Enobi was close by, grazing on the succulent grass. Babtoo thought, "This wonderful animal, what can it do? Why did the gods present this gift to me?"

Puku and Ukup returned after a few minutes, having discovered the almost invisible path the Mautuk warrior had taken. Approaching Babtoo, Puku said, "You were very lucky, Babtoo. We tracked the Mautuk back to the water hole. It seems he spent some time there. The view he had was of the area you said you found the Enobi. You were lucky. You could have been a meal for a Mautuk."

Insulted by the comment, Babtoo quickly replied, "I would have welcomed the challenge!"

Puku admired the spirit the boy had, but looked sternly at Babtoo. "Do not be overconfident, young buck, and do not under estimate these people. I have seen firsthand what they can do. They are cunning and vicious and do not attack unless they are sure they can win. If they kill you while your back is turned, that is all the better for them."

Babtoo nodded and acknowledged the advice. Puku was a seasoned warrior warning him to be careful. He quickly swallowed his pride. "Thank you for the lesson. I won't underestimate these people again."

Chintook knelt on the ground and started a small fire. Several pouches lay scattered around his body. A small bowl with a mixing stick lay near the open flame. Lifting the bowl with the palms of his hands and raising it to the sun, Chintook uttered words of prayer.

Carefully taking small amounts of herbs from the different pouches, Chintook cautiously mixed a concoction that was both colorful and pungent. Still mumbling prayers and going into a trance, he threw some powder in the fire. A brilliant puff of red smoke appeared in a flash and disappeared just as quickly. Recovering from the self-induced trance, Chintook took his index finger and started painting symbols on his body and face, preparing for the upcoming battle.

Babtoo watched as Ohat, Puku, and Ukup traced signs and symbols over their faces and body with the paint. They quickly transformed themselves from simple tribesmen to fearsome warriors. When they all were finished with the ritual, Chintook took the remaining paint and applied it to Babtoo's head and torso.

With gruff words, Chintook said, "Babtoo, these symbols will protect you. Remember, we fight for the lives of our people. Stay close to me and you will live to see another day!"

"Make me look fearsome, Chintook" replied Babtoo.

Chintook responded with a slight smile. "This is for protection

Babtoo, not for you to scare your enemies! Your spear thrust will do that!"

Sitting quietly while Chintook applied the war paint, Babtoo thought, "I have learned a great deal already and welcome this challenge. I will prove to them I am ready to be a man."

With the confidence of youth, Babtoo looked toward Enobi and thought, "With you at my side, how can we lose?"

The sun appeared to streak across the sky. The day was getting late. Wind swirled the grass gently like the nod of an old man's sleepy head. Grains of dust and dirt slowly filled in the slight depression left by the Mautuk warrior's foot. Further on, a bent blade of grass was slowly straightening from a toe print. These were the only signs left by the passage of the warrior. Ukup and Puku zigzagged across the path searching for these small, almost invisible tracks left by the diminutive man.

The going was slow but steady as the day quickly turned into night. Despite his crippled foot, Babtoo easily kept pace while leading Enobi.

Chintook called a halt beside a small stand of trees. The fading light made it more and more difficult for Ukup and Puku to track. Predatory animal calls were beginning to fill the night air. A scream cut short by ravenous roars and growls silenced the night for only a few moments before animals continued their life and death struggle on the savanna.

Ohat built a small fire to keep wild animals at bay. Gathering his warriors around him, Chintook's formidable presence demanded respect. The lion mane surrounding his broad shoulders had fallen across his back and shimmered in the fading light.

He said, "We are gaining on him. The signs are getting fresher. With luck, we should be closing in on him by tomorrow. However, we need to be extra vigilant. We don't know if he's alone or meeting with other warriors. Those of us on watch must be extra careful and alert in case he doubles back."

Chintook posted Ohat for the first watch. Grabbing his spear,

Ohat quickly ran his thumb over the edge checking the sharpness of the point and then disappeared into the night. A look of eagerness crossed his painted face.

Enobi limped into the firelight unsure of the different calls and sounds but found comfort in Babtoo's presence. Taking Enobi's lead, Babtoo traced his hand along his back to the injured foot. Enobi gently nuzzled him, enjoying Babtoo's gentle touch. Quickly changing the dressing on his leg, Babtoo noticed in the firelight the wound looked much better. Enobi seemed to be limping less and was more alert.

The hoof would never be perfect again, and the fleeting thought of his own injured foot compared to Enobi's foot brought a tear to his eye.

Whispering gently in Enobi's ear, Babtoo breathed, "You and I have a warrior's heart. I know our brothers do not yet see this. We will prove our courage to them. Then everyone will tell stories of us around the camp fire like they tell of our Chintook and the great lion."

CHAPTER 7

ETTAR THE MAUTUK

Ettar, the Mautuk warrior, marched toward the sea, eager to rejoin his Mautuk brothers. An annoying feeling of somebody watching or following him was nagging on his subconscious. Constantly looking back and seeing nothing did little to ease his mind.

As dusk was falling, Ettar looked for a likely spot to make camp. A small outcrop of rocks and brush made an excellent campsite. After evicting a small wart hog from his hole, Ettar settled down for the night.

Rummaging around in his bag for food, Ettar pulled what was left of the monkey he had killed the night before. Picking off a maggot and squeezing it with grubby blackened fingers, he popped the rotting meat into strong, apelike jaws.

Chewing absentmindedly, crunching through bones and flesh with equal ease, a thought entered his devious mind. A cloud covered the moon and in that instant, Ettar was gone from the relative safety of his camp. The only evidence of his presence was an arrow head that had slipped out of his bag unnoticed when he ate.

The cloud passed over the moon and found Ettar standing outside the rocky outcropping, staring into the night. Shadows crisscrossed the night while luminescent eyes shone in the darkness, blinking, and then reappearing somewhere else. Muffled growls and woofs faded in and out of the darkness.

Ettar was far from frightened. He was little more than a beast himself. Tired as he was, Ettar glanced back from where he had come. With a shrug of his hairy shoulders, he loped off into the night, blending in as a specter fades from view.

The full moon rose steadily in the sky among the stars and looked like a one eyed man with a freckled face. It bathed the savanna in a soft light and reflected off the yellow glow of the big cat's eyes.

It had been three days without a kill and the grumbling in her stomach was unbearable. She was desperate to feed her cubs that trailed slowly behind her. Twice that night she had stalked her prey only to have them spot her easily in the moon light.

A different scent assailed her nostrils. The pungent smell washed over her senses with a suddenness that stopped her in her tracks. Before she could move a muscle, the Mautuk warrior stepped out from behind the rock.

Ettar looked up from the ground and stared face to face with the lioness. He was no coward but cold fear churned in his belly with only twenty yards separating the hunters. How could he have been so careless? The big cat growled a warning sound deep from within her throat. Eyes that glowered with a deep and instinctive hatred for all human kind stared unblinking at the Mautuk warrior.

Slowly, Ettar raised his spear and took a step backward snapping a twig with a loud popping sound. In that instant, the lioness charged toward him with a savage roar breaking the trance that had made each hunter immobile.

Ettar hastily threw his spear and drew his knife knowing this could be his last fight. The wart hog that he had expelled from the small hollow earlier in the evening lost its nerve and made a mad dash from the safety of its hiding place. Confused and scared, the pig ran in between the two contestants.

The lioness leaped toward Ettar then, with an acrobatic move in midair, turned and caught the pig as it ran by. The spear thudded harmlessly in the ground where the lioness had been, quivering from the impact.

The squeal of the warthog was cut short as the lioness clamped down on its neck, snapping bones as if they were dry twigs. With a shake of her head, the fight was over. The warthog hung limply in her mouth, a meal for her starving cubs. She cast a backward glance toward Ettar, and stalked into the tall grass with her hungry cubs eagerly following close behind.

The night was relatively cool, yet Ettar, with a shaky hand, wiped sweat off his low, hairy brow. On legs that felt like rubber, he quickly retrieved his spear. Peering cautiously into the night and paying extra special attention to the direction the lioness went, he listened for danger.

Ettar whispered a quick prayer of thanks in his deep guttural language using obscene gestures with his hands to his dark and sadistic god. Satisfied with the atonement, he quickly jogged into the savanna, making a large detour around the muffled growls and whines of the feeding lioness and her cubs.

The rest of the night passed uneventfully for Ettar. He quickly retraced his steps back the way he had come. On a low rise, he stooped to get a closer look at the well- hidden Watinkee camp.

A look of surprise crossed his apelike features at what he saw. The same boy and mystical creature from the beach stood guard over a small camp of warriors. He had to get closer for a better look.

An evil glint shone in his eyes as he thought, "Maybe I can take a trophy home to my brothers." He crept closer to the boy, knife out and ready.

Puku gently nudged Babtoo with his big toe. Babtoo instantly came awake, excited to take on a warrior's task.

"You have the final watch little brother." Ukup whispered quietly.

Babtoo rubbed the sleep from his eyes with the back of his hand and quickly searched for the rope to Enobi. Speaking quietly, Babtoo asked, "How has the night been? Are things quiet?"

In the same quiet whisper Puku replied, "Nothing stirs tonight. Even the beasts are quiet. It will be dawn soon. Stay alert for any changes in the cricket's song or small animal movement. That will signal you to be extra wary. Listen to the animals. They will also guard you!"

With a nod of his head, Babtoo headed out for the final watch. Sitting on a rock, he listened intently trying to become in tune with the night sounds. The long spear held out in front on his lap gave him courage. His skill with the spear was unrivaled.

Enobi stood quietly to the side, grazing on the rich grassland. Babtoo cast his eyes on the big animal and quickly got lost in thought. Enobi's leg would never be the same again as he hobbled over the ground. Yet as he watched, the strange zebra kept testing the leg, trying to make it stronger, much as Babtoo had done when he was younger. He saw the strength of spirit in his every movement. "Yes," Babtoo thought, "we are a lot alike." The breeze played across the savanna, gently moving the grass back and forth like an unseen hand.

Babtoo, still deep in thought, studied Enobi as he grazed, forgetting the advice Puku gave him. His thoughts continued to wander, "All that has happened so far, was it by chance? Were the gods picking him for some great deed?"

Looking up into the early morning sky, a star streaked across the heavens with a fiery tail of light. The crickets had stopped chirping. The small animals had stopped scurrying around as if waiting for an upcoming event. Babtoo, too engrossed in his own thoughts, never noticed.

Ettar, eager with anticipation, crept closer. His black hairy paw clutched a short stabbing knife. The silhouette of the boy was just over the rise. His low brow furrowed in concentration. The cool night breeze quickly dried the sweat off his black hairy body that blended into the night like a wraith.

His toes dug into the ground for the final rush. A stalking cat could not be quieter. Twenty feet separated him from his quarry. A quick stab to the heart was all he had to do. The wind picked up ever so slightly and with a final deep breath, he charged.

Enobi jerked his head up from grazing, startled by a foul stench in the air. His ears quickly swiveled to catch the charging warrior. His shrill whinny shocked Babtoo out of his reverie. Turning quickly to where the Enobi was looking, Babtoo caught sight of the charging warrior.

Ettar hesitated just long enough at the sudden commotion of the strange animal for Babtoo to ready his spear. A deep guttural cry rumbled from Ettar that he hoped would frighten the boy. Babtoo never hesitated, but stood firm, spear in hand and now ready.

Babtoo thrust his spear before him to impale the small warrior. Shifting at the last moment, Ettar leapt onto Babtoo with his slashing knife. Babtoo grabbed his knife hand and punched Ettar into his large nose, flattening it across his face, stunning the cannibal.

The strength of the boy was much more than Ettar had expected and small tendrils of fear were taking root in his belly. Babtoo threw his weight into a wrestling move to throw the Mautuk's body away from him to enable him to use the length of his spear. Ettar, no slouch to fighting moves, suddenly found his body sailing through the air and under the hooves of the spotted beast.

The giant animal reared up on its hind legs and came smashing down so near his face that dust and dirt blinded him. Suddenly he felt a tremendous crushing pain in his ribs. Rolling away from under the hooves of the animal a spear thudded, digging into the ground where he had just been, shivering with energy.

The camp was suddenly alive with activity. Injured and in pain, Ettar had to get out of there fast. Disengaging from the fight and fleeing into the night, he could barely breathe through his smashed nose and broken ribs. The pain was almost unbearable.

"How could this have happened? How could a boy be so strong? Now I am running for my life." Ettar thought through gasps of pain. Licking his lips and tasting blood, his nose ran in gory rivulets. Fractured bones in his chest made it difficult to breathe as he looked into the slowly brightening sky. He hoped to be able to warn his Mautuk brothers of the power of their enemies. Breathing heavily, Ettar stumbled into the savanna.

Ohat was the first to burst on the scene following the fight. Babtoo quickly went to Enobi and tried to settle him down. Pawing the ground and digging up huge clumps of dirt, Enobi snorted with excitement.

Shaking from the exhilaration of the fight or fear, Babtoo could not say. He was certain, however, if not for Enobi, he would have been dead. Stroking his neck gratefully and whispering, Babtoo quickly put his savior at ease.

Ohat surveyed the scene of the fight and knew without asking what had happened. Chintook materialized out of the tall grass with spear in hand, lion's mane blazing with the first rays of the sun, ready for battle. With a quick word to Puku and Ukup, the two tribesmen circled the camp to be sure that no one else was there.

Babtoo stood on shaky legs. Chintook strode over and asked, "Are you all right?"

Babtoo took a deep breath. "He came out of nowhere. If not for Enobi, things may have turned out differently."

Chintook put a hand on his shoulder. "Your time has not yet come Babtoo. Your magical animal, Enobi, was put in your life perhaps just for this. Learn from it and remain alert. This is dangerous business and is not over yet!"

Babtoo replied, "I think he is wounded. He may not get far."

Chintook said, "Let Puku and Ukup find him. They are very skilled at tracking. They'll find him when the sun rises. I am proud of you Babtoo. This could have turned out badly for all of us!

The dew on the grass glittered like a field of diamonds as they caught the rays of light from the breaking dawn. The sunrise found a small hairy man stumbling across the savanna on weary legs. Like a raging fire, each breath he took was agony. His swollen nose no longer bled, yet it throbbed with a constant ache and felt three sizes too big, making it difficult to breathe.

Ettar zigzagged across the savanna like a drunken man, tripping on small mounds of dirt. He had to find a place to hide. The trail he left behind was so obvious a small child could follow his tracks. His beady black eyes searched the horizon. He knew if he did not get far enough away, the Watinkees would find and kill him. He would have done the same to any one of them.

By mid-afternoon, Ettar could go no further. In the shimmering haze he saw a small rise with a rock outcropping. "Is this a good place for my final stand?" He pondered.

Ettar reasoned, "I can signal my brothers and hope they come to my aid. The Watinkee tribesmen will also see the signal, but I have no choice. I can go no further and have to take the chance."

The hunter had turned into the hunted and he began to panic as his fear continued to grow. Looking back at his own trail, Ettar knew there was no choice. They could easily find him by his tracks.

Exhausted and weak, he hobbled to the rock outcropping, too tortured with pain to hide his tracks. With a final gasp, Ettar reached the rocks and sat down heavily, wheezing with shallow breaths. For a moment, his vision swam and he was nauseous. The sun seemed dimmer and the sounds of the savanna seemed very far away.

Gathering his remaining strength, Ettar reached down with feeble fingers that shook to grasp clumps of dry grass. Groping in his pack, he found a flint and stone. He laid several different colored powders out in a row. His hands were clumsy and weak as he struck flint to stone.

A tiny spark leapt from the stone to the grass, hungry for something to burn. At first, nothing was visible. Ettar, with labored breath, blew life into the spark to ignite the grass. A tendril of smoke curled into the air as a glow started to form. Within moments, the small amount of grass started to burn. Ettar continued to feed the flame until exhaustion was upon him.

Shading his eyes, Ettar gazed across the savanna. Tiny dots were slowly moving in his direction. He knew little time remained before the Watinkees discovered his hiding place. Leaning on the rock, hot from the sun, he reached for his colored powders.

The different colored powders were for signals to his Mautuk brothers. Green meant to continue to follow, the yellow was to proceed with extreme caution, and the red was for an emergency.

Taking the red pouch and pouring the contents in his hand, he slowly blew it into the flame.

A bright red plume took shape drifting slowly into the sky. The powder continued to burn eventually smothering the tiny flame. Ettar could do no more. Leaning back on the rock, he slowly closed his eyes. His vision swam with terrible memories of a fierce boy and spotted zebra trampling him underfoot.

At first, the pursuing Watinkees saw the ruby like spots glistening on the bent blades of grass. They appeared in the middle of a track with the impression of long curled nails. In that slight depression, a small bristled black hair stood straight up as if planted. The congealing blood spot and hair were not alone. Five sets of eyes scanned the small, seemingly insignificant depression to see what else they could learn.

Chintook looked beyond the track and followed the erratic footprints as far as his eyes could see. He was the first to speak. "Babtoo, you and Enobi must have wounded him badly. He's not trying to conceal his tracks and is bleeding freely. It won't be hard to find him."

Babtoo puffed out his chest with pride. "Enobi is a great warrior. We make a good team. Together we fought and wounded our first enemy." Confident with youth and his recent success, Babtoo felt like he was invincible.

Looking down at Enobi's hoof, a wave of concern overshadowed his confidence. The cut on Enobi's leg had reopened and blood trickled down into a puddle, slowly disappearing into the parched earth. Chintook followed Babtoo's eyes and knew the leg needed rewrapped.

The warriors understood Enobi had a played a huge part in the safety of their band and waited patiently for Babtoo to rewrap the injured leg. Time was still on their side to catch the Mautuk warrior judging by the look of his tracks drunkenly crisscrossing the plain.

Chintook called Ukup and Puku to his side. Looking across the savanna at the disappearing tracks, Chintook said, "Follow the trail closely. Be sure the Mautuk is not meeting with anybody and stay out of sight until we catch up. If there is any trouble, or you see anything strange, then send Puku back and warn us."

With a nod of their heads, Puku and Ukup slipped into the savanna without a word.

Ohat watched Puku and Ukup disappear into the savanna. Each warrior blended into to the grasslands with ease, following the trail like hungry jackals. Excitement and the need for revenge were palpable in every move they made. Ohat knew that Puku and Ukup were the best trackers the Watinkees had and hoped they would quickly find the wounded Mautuk warrior before he signaled other Mautuks.

Looking back to Babtoo as he applied a grass and mud bandage on the injured animal's leg, Ohat wondered how the boy had developed a relationship with this amazing animal. The boy was different, a head taller than even the tallest Watinkee, and much broader in the shoulders with unusual blond hair. The bravery he had shown in the face of danger was like that of a seasoned warrior. Ohat wondered if he was the son of a chief. He heard the story of how they had found Babtoo and the great spear he carried, but never knew his parents before the great fire.

Chintook also watched as Babtoo applied the dressing to Enobi's leg. A sense of respect for this orphan boy was beginning to grow in his mind. Babtoo reminded him of his own childhood. His gaze shifted to the rising sun as he waited impatiently to be on the way.

Mautuk warriors rarely traveled alone. This was only supposed to be a hunting expedition and now was turning into a war party. He worried about the safety and inexperience of his fellow tribesmen. They needed to dispatch this scout soon before he joined with other Mautuk warriors.

Squinting into the sun, Chintook saw a thin red line of smoke curl into the air. His chest tightened with anxiety with the urgent need to go. He knew a smoke signal was as good as a conversation to a Mautuk warrior.

Puku and Ukup moved silently into the savanna. Following the tracks left by the Mautuk warrior was no great feat. Although the tracks zigzagged across the grasslands, the warrior was heading toward a hill. Spots of blood clung to small bushes and grass plants as he had staggered by.

Ukup was the first to speak. "Puku, this trail is too obvious. We should already be upon him."

Puku squinted in the morning sunlight, taking in the savanna. A pencil thin red line appeared from a small outcropping about a mile away.

Puku pointed with his spear at the red smoke and whispered to his brother, "We are not alone. Our Mautuk enemy is signaling for his tribesmen. We need to be extra careful from here on out. No doubt, Chintook has seen the smoke. We know where he is, but now, so do his brothers. I wonder how many Mautuk warriors are around to see the signal."

Ukup said emphatically, "We must hurry and kill him before his Mautuk brothers see the signal. The tracks lead in that direction. If we are quick, we can be in and out before the other Mautuk warriors arrive."

Puku slammed the butt of his spear into the ground to grab Ukup's attention, "NO! Chintook said only to follow the Mautuk. We will wait for the others to see if the smoke attracted other Mautuk warriors. If we have seen the signal, so have his tribesmen. They may be there already! Before we charge in, Chintook, Ohat and Babtoo should be here."

Ukup was not thoroughly convinced, but respected his brother's advice and silently agreed. Like phantoms in a ghost story, they broke away from the trail and started to circle the rocky outcrop.

The sun slowly rose into the morning sky, baking everything that touched its path. Chintook could wait no longer.

Gruffly he spoke, "Babtoo, we must be on our way. We cannot leave Ukup and Puku out in the savanna for long. That thin trail of smoke in the distance is signaling other Mautuk warriors. There are only six of us and there may be many more Mautuk. I fear not for myself but for the safety of this hunting party." Chintook looked closely as Babtoo put the final wraps around Enobi's leg.

If that spotted zebra had not warned them of the Mautuk warrior, Babtoo, and perhaps others of his hunting party may not have lived through the night. The only reason he had stayed was to be sure that Babtoo and his magical creature would not lag far behind. Babtoo had proven to be a worthy warrior, but he was still young and Chintook feared for his safety

Babtoo looked up from what he was doing and could almost read Chinook's thoughts. With a piercing gaze, he shook the hair out of his eyes and said with the confidence of a man, "I will not let you down. I will be there before the battle starts. Strength will guide my spear to its mark."

With those strong words, Chintook could only nod. Saying a small prayer under his breath for the safety of his little hunting party, he glided into the brush with Ohat.

CHAPTER 8

SQUANTO
THE MAUTUK LEADER

Squanto, the skeletal thin Mautuk warrior chief, searched the sky. His watery brown eyes drooped, making him look like a starving jackal. A hand as hairy as a monkey's paw shaded his tearing eyes from the sun.

Peering intently at the small red smudge in the sky, Squanto shivered slightly. He was not an overly brave warrior, preferring to attack when the odds were overwhelmingly in his favor. He had not lived as long as he did by being brave.

Ettar was a good tracker and they could ill afford to lose him. The red smoke in the sky meant only one thing, danger. It was not like Ettar to be late for a rendezvous.

Small shrunken heads rattled together on his belt as he turned toward four other Mautuk warriors. His brown eyes searched their faces for courage, but as if rats caught in the open, none volunteered to go. Should he send a scout to look things over before he committed his warriors? Each man was a veteran fighter, and yet, Squanto knew that if the odds were stacked against them, his warriors would disappear from the fight.

Ettar was far too important to him. The high priest would not be happy if the scouting trip was not a success. The high priest would want to know what Ettar had discovered about the Watinkee tribe. Shivering slightly, Squanto knew the high priest had little tolerance for failure.

Shaking his head, Squanto's mind whirled with battle plans. Far more important to him was to keep himself alive during this upcoming battle. He turned to each warrior, evaluating them silently. Putpow was the most experienced warrior. He had taken many enemy scalps and seemed to lead a charmed life. Putpow was a master with the short spear. Yet, even he did not volunteer to rescue Ettar.

Ottorhut was Ettar's friend. His eyes darted from one warrior to another looking for support of Ettar, but not wanting to go by himself to scout. He nervously fingered his long knife, waiting to hear what Squanto's decision would be. Nunten and Haehoe both looked at one another, wondering if they too, would be chosen to go.

Devious and crafty, the warrior chief sat down and scribbled in the sand. His long black nail scratched the earth as his idea came together. Each warrior nodded and knew what he had to do. As the plan came together, devious smiles showed sharpened, blackened teeth.

The first to leave was Ottorhut. Hefting his short spear and slowly fingering the shrunken heads on his belt, Ottorhut left without a word. The grass seemed to wither under his feet as if not wanting to touch such a foul thing.

Nunten and Haehoe followed closely behind, but on a parallel course to the outcropping where Ettar's signal smoke had been seen last. Shadowing Ottorhut and keeping him safe from ambush was their responsibility.

The final to leave were Squanto and Putpow. Squanto was taking the bravest and most fierce warrior with him to ensure his own safety. Looking down at his plan in the dirt, Squanto practically guaranteed his success. With an apelike foot, he brushed the sketch away.

Babtoo slowly rose from dressing Enobi's leg and ran his hand across the animal's back to his finely sculpted head. Enobi quivered at the touch and shook his head as if to say, "Let's get going." Babtoo admired the spirit of the spotted zebra and it gave him strength.

With a small tug on his rope, Enobi and Babtoo moved into the brush. Babtoo walked alongside, studying the trail. He could see where the Mautuk warrior had gone. The erratic trail was speckled with blood. Alongside, the faint footprints of Puku and Ukup shadowed the obvious path of the wounded warrior.

He really did not have to follow the trail. The smoke from Ettar's fire could have guided him. Learning a lesson from last night, he would be vigilant and never again underestimate his enemy.

Puku and Ukup could get no closer. They found a shallow ravine with small bushy trees. From a hundred yards they could see the outcropping where Ettar was slowly fanning the fire to keep the smoke alive. There they stayed, not moving a muscle until Chintook and Ohat appeared.

Small beads of sweat covered their bodies until a breeze kicked up to dry the perspiration, covering them with dust. They blended into the landscape like two tall termite mounds. Chintook and Ohat would have walked right by them if not for their blinking eyes.

Chintook followed the slight depression and stepped over a small dry branch, careful not to break it, with Ohat following closely behind. Hiding behind a scrub thicket with leaves that hung limp and dry from lack of moisture, Chintook settled into place, watching the thin line of smoke curl into the sky. His lion's mane blended in perfectly with the surroundings.

He did not have to wait long. A furtive movement by the rock outcropping grabbed his attention. At first, he thought it was his imagination, staring at the same place in the shimmering heat. Rubbing his eyes and squinting, the movement became a small hairy man. A ripple of hatred went through his body.

Each warrior flexed fingers ever so slightly on their spears. They waited for other members of the Mautuk tribe to show up. After what seemed like hours, but was only minutes, and seeing nothing more, Chintook gave Puku and Ukup the sign to go.

Blending into the savanna, the two tribesmen gripped their spears tightly. Using shrubs, tall patches of grass, and depressions made by animals, they advanced to the rocky outcrop. Chintook followed their every movement. Waiting in the ravine, he was better able to see if there were any other Mautuks about. Perspiration dripped from his forehead into his eyes, giving the illusion the savanna swam in front of him.

Not daring to move to give away his position, Chintook spotted two other Mautuk warriors circling the outcrop. Puku and Ukup were not aware of the danger yet. He had to act quickly. Motioning to Ohat with the tip of his spear, they advanced toward the two Mautuks, sacrificing stealth for speed.

Squanto's plan was coming together. He and Putpow had slowly made it to the outcropping undetected. From his vantage point, he could see Nunten and Haehoe slinking up on the two Watinkee tribesmen. He raised his eyebrow in silent admiration of the stealth of the Watinkee tribesmen but reveled in the fact that they soon would be dead.

Raising his head above the grass, Squanto could see two other Watinkee tribesmen closing in on Nunten and Haehoe, "This is going to be a massacre." Squanto chuckled. Slowly crawling to the next rock, he and Putpow moved closer to the ambush.

Babtoo and Enobi used all available cover as they warily approached the outcrop. Suddenly Enobi started to twitch his ears and his nostrils flared, testing the air, and like an arrow looked in the direction of the outcrop alerting Babtoo to the danger. Enobi's ears swiveled back and forth trying to catch the almost silent progress of Chief Squanto and Putpow.

Dropping the rope, Babtoo crouched down and looked upon the start of a battle. Squanto and Putpow had not seen him. They were too busy focusing on Chintook and Ohat. He had to get there fast before the Mautuk warriors ambushed them. Ignoring the pain in his foot, Babtoo hastily melted into the savanna and advanced upon the enemy warriors.

Babtoo realized he was not scared for himself. He was more afraid of being too late to save his friends. The scene was playing out all too quickly and yet it seemed as if time was standing still. He heard every cricket chirp, every rustle of scampering small animals, and the low cough of a hidden jaguar. Babtoo focused on only one thing....stop the Mautuk from hurting his friends.

He pictured himself like a jaguar, sleek, quiet, and blending into his surroundings. He had played and excelled with other Watinkee children at this game. He was in his element. His crippled leg gave him a disadvantage for speed, but it taught him that speed did not take the place of stealth. Enobi, sensing the mood of Babtoo, followed slowly behind, ears pricked for danger.

The sun beat down mercilessly in its uncaring glare, watching as the scene unfolded before it. Shimmering heat waves waltzed across the savanna in anticipation of what was about to become. Shadows followed their human counterparts, matching their every move.

For a moment, time did stand still. There were no birdcalls, no animal movement, and there was no breeze. It was if the entire savanna held its breath. Then, things happened in an explosion of violent movement leaving no time to think, only act.

Chintook and Ohat were running toward the battle hoping they could stop the ambush on Puku and Ukup. Spears raised and ready to throw at their targets, they rounded a bend in the trail and passed a termite mound perched precariously on a small hill. They were so intent on saving Puku and Ukup that they failed to notice the movement behind the mound. Clumps of grass slowly rose from the ground taking on the shape of men. So well concealed were the two Mautuks, Chintook and Ohat never saw Squanto and Putpow raise their weapons. This was the typical Mautuk way, ambush from the rear.

Spears cocked and ready to throw, Putpow and Squanto became

startled when a blood-curdling scream broke the silence. It sounded like it was everywhere around them. They froze for just a split second trying to find this new threat when a spear sprouted from Putpow's chest. Turning and clutching at his wound and trying to stop the flow of blood, he slowly sank to his knees and died.

Squanto whirled around to face this new threat only to find a boy with a hunting knife. Out of nowhere came Enobi, rearing on his hind legs. Squanto hastily threw his spear at the boy only to miss him and land in the dirt with a dull thud. Babtoo was on him in an instant slashing at his chest and face.

A long red line suddenly appeared down his cheek as the knife bit deeply in his face. Pointed, sharp teeth shattered on the blade of the hunting knife as it traced its way through flesh and bone. Squanto panicked at the strength and ferocity of the boy and looked for an avenue of escape. With an extraordinary effort born of fear, he threw Babtoo off and ran into the bush, abandoning his fellow tribesmen. Babtoo limped after him but could not catch him.

Chintook stared in amazement at the courage of the boy. With a shake of his lion's mane, he nodded his thanks and shouted a "Well done Babtoo" before quickly turning away. Ohat threw his spear at the retreating Mautuk only to fall short of the mark. Retrieving his spear, he gave Babtoo a silent salute.

Nunten and Haehoe saw that the ambush had failed. Quickly turning they tried to slink back into the bush unnoticed.

Chintook and Ohat followed them into the grasslands. Ukup and Puku scampered quickly behind, forgetting that two other Mautuks were on the rocky outcrop.

Babtoo retrieved his spear and wiped it clean on the dead Mautuk's black fur. Hobbling over to Enobi, he quietly settled the big animal down.

A scream erupted, cut short with a suddenness that made Babtoo shiver. Then, howls of pain, followed by garbled pleas of mercy, before they too, were silenced. A lion's mane, tinged with blood, outlining Chintook's face, appeared out of the swaying grass moments later. Ohat trailed behind with a spear, the tip colored red.

Ettar and Ottorhut looked upon the shocking scene. Their whole scouting party was dead, and soon they would be too. Ettar struggled to stand. His ribs burned with each breath he took. Ottorhut watched as pain washed over Ettar's face as he struggled to stand.

They were not brave men, but anger and hatred took the place of fear. If they were lucky, maybe they could escape this trap.

Ottorhut helped Ettar down the rock before the Watinkees could trap them on the face of the hill. Hiding behind a rock sheltered by a small tree, they waited patiently for the Watinkee tribesmen.

The sun glinted crimson off the blade of Chintook's hunting knife. Blood slowly ran down the hilt of the blade as he shook the few remaining drops free. This did not go unnoticed by the two remaining Mautuk warriors. Shivers of fear passed through their bodies as they gripped their weapons tightly.

The thin line of red smoke wavered in the slight breeze as it gradually ran out of fuel. Chintook motioned for them to fan out as he glanced up at the rocky escarpment. Moving cautiously, the tribesmen were not yet aware of the danger behind the rocky outcrop. Babtoo fell in behind Chintook with his lion's mane and the two blended into the background.

Despite his crippled leg, Babtoo was a master of stealth and deception and could move quickly. Chintook taught Babtoo much as a child and he was an able student. The Mautuk warriors never saw him.

Ottorhut screamed as he leaped from behind the small tree. Startled, Chintook and Ohat froze for a split second before jumping out of the way. The quick move from Chintook saved his life as the spear flew past his shoulder and skidded on the ground. Ottorhut drew his knife and fell on Ohat, slashing at his head, trying to kill him quickly, before Chintook could recover.

Puku and Ukup quickly ran back down the hill, but were too late as Ettar threw his spear at Chintook. The poorly thrown weapon at such close range pierced Chintook in the shoulder. Pain etched his face as he spun around and fell to the ground. Ettar stumbled after him with a drawn knife.

Babtoo braced himself for the long throw as the battle quickly unfolded around him. Unleashing the powerful throw, his spear arced into the air to lose itself in the bright sunlight. The polished point arced down to earth past Chintook with such force that it pinned Ettar to the termite mound. Ettar's eyes dimmed as he tried feebly to clutch at the spear. Looking up, Ettar saw Babtoo standing over him. With his last seconds of life, he wondered why he had ever chosen to attack a boy with a magical beast.

Puku reached Ohat and quickly drove his spear into the remaining Mautuk. Ottorhut died without ever seeing the spear thrust. Ohat rolled over on his knees, gasping for air and crawled toward Chintook.

Chintook was writhing in pain clutching the spear in his shoulder. Ohat drew near on unsteady feet and took Chintook's head in his arms. Whispering in his ear, he said, "Chintook, we need to remove this spear. It may be poisoned."

Chintook nodded, but said nothing. His teeth gritted in pain as his hands clenched the ground. Ohat called, "Puku and Ukup, get over here and hold Chintook down." Puku said, "That could kill him. It's in deep."

Ohat glared at Puku. "We have no choice. It could be poisoned."

Quickly Puku and Ukup grabbed Chintook's arms and held them tightly. Ohat reached for the end of the spear. "Are you ready Chintook?"

Before Chintook could nod his head, Ohat wrenched the spear out of his body and threw it away. Not a sound came from their leader. A moment of clarity came to him. He felt no pain as his body started to relax before he lost consciousness.

Rummaging around in his leather pouch, Ohat took out some dressing and some black powder. Sprinkling the powder over the wound to help stop the bleeding, Ohat prayed this would work.

Striking flint to stone, the black powder caught fire cauterizing the wound. He then wrapped it with a tight dressing to keep it clean

Babtoo retrieved the spear and examined it closely. Puku came over to look at the markings and tip. Glancing worriedly at Babtoo, he said, "Look closely, Babtoo. This spear is poisoned. That black tip is from the venom of the Mamba snake. Chintook has to get to the medicine man soon or we will be praising his spirit form. Go get some strong limbs and make a litter." Babtoo quickly disappeared into the brush, cutting limbs with his knife.

Slowly, Puku walked back to Chintook and Ohat. "The spear is poisoned. Babtoo is making a litter. We have only one chance to save Chintook and that is to move fast."

Ohat, realizing the trip would take too long, grabbed Ukup. "You go to the tribe now. Tell them what has happened and get the medicine man to meet us. We will be behind you. Follow the dry streambed back to the main camp. That will be the safest way."

Ukup motioned back toward Chintook. "You will need help with the litter. There is only you and Puku. Babtoo cannot drag the litter."

Ohat said, his tone allowing no argument, "Do not question me. Go now and go fast. Chintook's life depends on you."

Ukup looked at Chintook's still form. Beads of sweat already were forming on his forehead. Without a word, Ukup grabbed his spear and dashed out into the savanna.

Ohat helped Puku lash the branches together to form a litter. Using the lion's mane as a bed, Puku and Ohat placed Chintook's still form on the litter. His breathing was shallow and labored while sweat quickly soaked into the cape.

Grabbing the ends of the litter, Puku and Ohat started walking back to camp. Babtoo dislodged his spear from the Mautuk warrior as his limp form slid down the termite mound to land in a heap. Angry termites were already swarming over his still body. Without a backward glance, Babtoo followed Puku and Ohat.

Drool and blood dribbled out of Squanto's mouth as he watched his fellow tribesmen fall to the Watinkee warriors. Choking on the blood from his wound, a piece of rotten tooth dislodged from his mouth. The gaping wound on his face flapped like a wounded bird whenever he turned his head.

A look of utter hatred crossed his features. He had lost good friends he had known since childhood. Squanto's mind whirled with bitter thoughts of revenge, but right now, he had to get back to the remaining scouts by the ocean.

Turning back across the savanna, Squanto gathered his weapons and hastily hobbled toward the trees. Finding a small shelter, Squanto took out the tiny monkey bone finger. Sharpening it with his knife, he attached a piece of sinew to it. Without the benefit of a medicine man, Squanto tried sewing the piece of skin back himself. He let out a primordial scream as the first prick of his crudely made needle pierced his skin. Clamping his mouth shut from the pain, his eyes rolled back into his skull as he fell into the sweet blackness of unconsciousness.

Ohat, Puku, and Babtoo all turned at the frightening scream. It seemed as if it was all around them. The hair on each man's neck stood in fear listening to the savagery of the cannibal's cry. They all turned to look into the distance, searching across the savanna where they thought the scream had come. Seeing nothing, they stood uncertainly, waiting for Ohat to make a decision.

Ohat knew one Mautuk had gotten away in the fray but that they could not spare a man to go after him. Contemplating only for a moment, he said to the other two, "Let's go. We don't know how many more of them there are and Chintook needs to get to the medicine man. Babtoo, scout for us while we carry the litter."

Feeling more and more like an equal, Babtoo took the lead into the brush, trying to find the easiest path to take and watching for enemy warriors.

❖❖❖

Squanto recovered from the comforting darkness of unconsciousness and finally was able to keep his cheek from flapping down. Tasting blood, he hobbled toward the ocean. He had seen enough. Revenge was a seed planted and savored. He would bring a large force of warriors and crush the Watinkees.

Talking to himself, Squanto said, "I want this boy called Babtoo. He is a powerful warrior with strong magic and I will to be the first to taste his flesh and gain his courage!" Thinking of how he would kill the boy gave him strength as he disappeared in the brush.

CHAPTER 9

HOMEWARD BOUND

The bright orb in the sky seemed to scorch the battlefield. Shimmering waves of mirages chased each other across the savanna in the suffocating heat.

Puku and Ohat carried the litter with Chintook for miles. Their bodies were drenched in sweat and still they stumbled on. Their mouths dry and tongues swollen, each breath felt like a kiss of fire. Babtoo scouted the terrain ahead to watch for enemies and guide them to the easiest paths. Still their progress seemed very slow.

Small ravines became great canyons to navigate. Large open areas seemed impossibly long to cross. Chintook tossed and turned on the litter making it difficult to control. His movements were becoming increasingly erratic. One thing for certain, he was getting weaker. Concern for their chief drove them past the point of exhaustion.

Babtoo saw the strain on Puku and Ohat. They would never make it until nightfall. He wished he could help, but looking down at his crippled leg and knew he would be of little use.

Watching Enobi make his way through the savanna gave Babtoo an idea. The animal seemed to move with ease through the brush, even with his injured foot.

A thought entered his mind, "What if they could attach the litter to Enobi? He is much stronger and faster than even Puku and Ohat combined, even with an injured foot. He seems to have the strength of ten warriors. I wonder if Enobi would allow me to attach the litter to him."

Turning around, Babtoo raised his hand. "Halt!" Startled, Puku and Ohat looked around, trying to find an enemy or a place to run.

Ohat was the first to recover and shouted, "Why do you stop us?" They stumbled to a halt, quivering with fatigue.

Babtoo quickly ran back and helped settle the chief to the ground. Turning to Ohat, Babtoo pointed to Enobi. "I believe we have another warrior to help us."

Ohat quickly looked around and could see nobody. "Where do you see this warrior? I do not see anybody coming to help. Ukup could not have possibly gone to the tribe and gotten the medicine man this fast."

Nodding in agreement Puku said, "This is true, Ohat, but let's see what the young warrior has to say." The compliment of 'young warrior' was not lost on Babtoo. He felt an overwhelming sense of pride.

He quickly laid out his plan. "Enobi is also a warrior. I believe he is stronger, even with his injured foot. He can drag the litter further and faster than we can by ourselves. If Enobi will allow it, I think we can attach the litter and he can drag it for us."

Both warriors focused on Enobi, sizing him up, wondering if the magical animal could do this.

Ohat reached over to Babtoo. "Will he allow us to attach the litter to him? Can you keep him from running away?"

Babtoo, not knowing for sure he could do this, but now committed to his plan, stared hard at Ohat and said grimly, "I will ask him and see if he will have the honor to pull Chintook."

Babtoo got up and walked quietly to Enobi, putting his hand around his neck. A slight quiver rippled through the animal's body as he nuzzled Babtoo in greeting. Quietly he whispered in Enobi's ear, "This is a great honor to carry Chintook to safety. I will be with you every step of the way. You have been at my side since the beginning and we now need your great strength." Babtoo stroked his neck and fondled his ears.

Enobi looked at him with large saucer-like eyes as if to say, "I will do as you ask if you are there at my side."

Babtoo stepped back and waved toward Ohat and Puku. "We must construct leather straps to hold the litter so Enobi can drag him."

Babtoo cut two sticks and fastened them together with straps. Quickly, the two warriors tied the leather straps to the litter and then attached them to the sticks.

Gently Babtoo laid the sticks across Enobi's back so they could fasten the litter to them. Enobi's withers quivered at the touch, but he stayed still. Babtoo talked to him all the while, telling him what he was doing.

With the final leather strap attached to the litter, the warriors stepped back to inspect the work. Enobi looked back at the contraption he was dragging and snorted uncomfortably. Babtoo touched his face and whispered that his people would sing songs about him around the campfire. The touch and gentle words calmed the big animal. With a gentle tug on his leash, Babtoo and Enobi started walking forward, slowly at first, but then more quickly as he became used to the weight he was dragging. Ohat and Puku looked on in amazement, grateful for the reprieve.

The hours dragged on throughout the day. The sun seemed to linger in the sky longer than it should. The heat seemed hotter than usual.

A pack of hungry lions watched disinterestedly in the heat as the small band of Watinkee warriors trudged by. Small clouds of dust exploded in the air with each step Enobi took, only to dissipate as suddenly as they were made.

Babtoo's foot began to throb painfully, but he only became more resolved, thinking, "I cannot let Chintook down. I must go forward and ignore this pain. They look to me to get Chintook to safety."

Holding his head high and squaring his shoulders, the pain became a badge of honor. It reminded him that he was somebody whom they could depend on. This was more important than anything he had ever done.

Enobi pulled the litter with little effort. The extra weight made little difference with his great strength. Small bits of blood leaked through the makeshift bandage around his leg, dotting the grass like sprinkles of rubies scattered haphazardly across the plain. The blood quickly dried, turning a reddish brown and leaving a trail easily followed.

This did not go unnoticed by the big black cat, trailing behind, slinking in and out of the shadows. He was a master of disguise and stealth and went from bush, to tree, to ravine, back to the grasslands. At times, the big cat concealed himself only a few feet away undetected. The warriors, too fatigued, did not notice the danger.

Enobi did not recognize the panther smell, but instinctually started to get nervous from the pungent odor. Babtoo turned around and soothed the animal, encouraging Enobi to continue to go forward, unaware of the danger.

The day finally ended and the last of the sun's rays disappeared over the horizon as the darkness brought relief from the heat. Stars appeared slowly at first, like scouts looking to see if it was safe to come out. Then moments later, the sky blossomed with stars of heroic constellations immortalized by the Watinkee tribesmen.

Black clouds raced across the sky, concealing the constellations one by one, making it impossible to see. Thunder rumbled and shook the earth like a drum, and yet no rain fell.

Ohat stumbled head long into a thorny bush, pricking and scratching himself with long needle-like thorns. With a curse, he held up his hand and called a halt. Babtoo stopped suddenly, the pain in his foot almost unbearable. Enobi, not recognizing the command, continued to walk and pushed Babtoo into Ohat. Stumbling forward and off balance, Babtoo fell into Ohat in a heap. Both men, weary from the day, laughed aloud-startling Puku. Puku emerged from the savanna chuckling to himself at the tangle of arms and legs as Ohat and Babtoo tried to disengage themselves from one another.

Puku stepped carefully around the two warriors to reach Chintook's still form. Breathing raggedly and glistening with sweat, Chintook looked upon Puku with glazed eyes. Snatching a water skin from his waist, he gently tried to force water between Chintook's clenched jaws. Water dribbled into his mouth and down his chin as he gulped the water greedily.

Moaning softly, Chintook placed his fevered hand on Puku. His voice sounded faint and far away. "Where am I? How did I get here? Where am I going? I see the great- spirit and he beckons toward me." His grip tightened on Puku's arm with surprising strength and he whispered, "Do not let me die from a Mautuk spear. I have much to do still, in this life."

Ohat and Babtoo crowded close behind, listening intently to their chief's words. Puku clenched Chintook's hand tightly to get his attention and spoke urgently, "We will not let you die. Enobi and Babtoo are carrying you to the village. We have made good time and will be there soon. Ukup is fetching Whutknot and they'll meet us somewhere between here and the village. If not for Babtoo and Enobi, we wouldn't have made it this far."

Babtoo, embarrassed by the compliment, yet intensely proud, stroked Enobi's side and wiped sweat from him. Chintook's gaze fell on Babtoo and without a spoken word, Babtoo knew how proud the fearless warrior was of him. Then, Chintook collapsed, his eyes fluttered closed, not to open again that night.

Babtoo was relieved that Chintook appeared strong enough to talk as he continued brushing the sweat from Enobi with clumps of grass. Working his way down the leg, he carefully cleaned and rewrapped the wound. The bleeding had stopped, but Enobi would never be able to outrun a racing lion.

Looking down at his own throbbing leg, Babtoo could understand the significance of being disadvantaged. Animals and people did not last too long in the bush when they were injured. It was nature's way of ensuring that only the strong survive. Yet, he knew deep inside him that the two of them together would be formidable and that they made a powerful team. Turning away and rubbing his own leg, Babtoo gathered his belongings and limped to a small tree. Leaning against the trunk as it bent back from his broad shoulders, Babtoo massaged his leg.

They made camp without much talk as the clouds blotted out the stars making their mood very somber. Each man settled into a spot around the small fire.

Ohat said, "I'll take the first watch, then Puku, and Babtoo last. I know your foot is hurting you, little brother, so try to get some sleep first and recover your strength. Tomorrow, with the help of your Enobi, we should be able to get close to our village. I hope that Ukup has make it back safely and already on his way back with Whutknot."

Babtoo raised his spear high. "Let me take the first watch. I can't sleep until my foot stops aching. We have all worked hard today. I will wake Puku when I get tired."

Puku nodded in agreement, leaned back into his makeshift bed and fell quickly asleep snoring gently.

Ohat walked over to the litter that held the chief to see if he was sleeping. Chintook was restless. Muttering unintelligible words, he fought to stay alive, fighting unknown demons. Lying close to Chintook, Ohat laid his spear down within easy reach. He would be Chintook's personal guard tonight.

Babtoo walked over to where Enobi was grazing, still favoring his back leg. Staring into the night, Babtoo stroked the big animal's neck. The rumbling thunder had faded into the distance yet the clouds still blanketed the stars. Heat lightning still lit the sky with some regularity.

Thinking through the events of the last couple of days, Babtoo realized how close he had come several times to losing his friends, or dying himself. Glancing back at Chintook, he knew just as well that it could have been him. Yet strangely, he was not afraid. It was as if his destiny was starting to unfold before him. An excitement welled deep within his breast as he breathed the night air.

Over the course of just a few days, he had come to rely on Enobi. The animal had keener senses than even the most gifted Watinkee tribesmen did. A barely heard cough caught Enobi's ears and he lifted his head and tested the air. His flaring nostrils quivered in the hot night as he turned toward the faint sound.

Babtoo now trusted the strange spotted zebra's instincts and knew something was wrong. His eyes strained into the darkness, looking for movements, shadows, or another sound to give away the intruder. He glanced back at his two friends and did not want to alarm them if nothing was there.

Enobi stamped his foot and snorted softly. Babtoo put his hand over his great nose to soothe him as he searched the gloomy night for movement.

For a split second, heat lightning erupted from the heavens in a dazzling display of brilliance. That was all the time Babtoo needed to see the black panther sneaking up on them only a few yards away. For a moment, they both stared at one another. In the enormous cat's head, two eyes glowed like white-hot embers. Babtoo was mesmerized for an instant and felt as if he could lose his way in their unfathomable depths. The pads of the cat were huge, silently stalking closer, flexing his great claws in the dirt.

His black coat blended into the background, making the cat almost invisible. When the lightning moved off into the night, only the luminescent glow of his eyes let Babtoo know it was no apparition.

The blink of his eyes was the only warning Babtoo had of the silent charge. Slapping Enobi on the rump sent him running to the side. With spear raised, Babtoo threw hurriedly into the dark, hoping it would hit the almost invisible silhouette of the panther.

A scream that sounded like a thousand banshees split the air as the spear creased the panthers hide and thudded harmlessly into the ground, skidding to a stop in the root of a nearby tree. Babtoo drew his knife just when the big cat struck.

Five hundred pounds of solid muscle crashed into his chest with such force, two ribs snapped like dry twigs. The big cat's claws, which were as big as a human hand, gripped and slashed at Babtoo's chest and back while teeth searched for his neck and face.

Grunting from the impact, Babtoo fell backward onto the ground. Shielding his face with one hand from the panther, his other hand desperately stabbed upward trying to dislodge the beast clinging to him. The snapping jaws and suffocating breath were inching closer to his head. Babtoo's breath was coming in short agonizing gasps as his broken ribs interfered with his desperate attempt to get air.

The earth shook with hoof beats and then the sound of a meaty thud and grunt sent the big cat flying. Babtoo inhaled sharply, the pain in his ribs sharp. Enobi had kicked the panther off with hooves as hard as granite and with such force, it stunned the great beast.

Rolling to his side, Babtoo retrieved his spear in time to see the panther charge toward Enobi. Getting to his feet and gasping in pain from the effort, Babtoo threw the spear.

The weapon was lost in the darkness when it hit the big cat. Stumbling from the impact of the heavy spear, the big cat dropped to the ground howling as two other spears drove into his body. Snapping and growling, the cat tried to run, but his strength quickly ebbed from the wounds inflicted by the two Watinkee warriors. With a final shudder, the black cat died.

Babtoo swayed on uncertain feet, surveying the scene, before he collapsed on the ground. Enobi had saved his life again. Blood flowed from a dozen cuts. His ribs were on fire and breathing deeply was painful.

Puku was the first to reach Babtoo. Helping Babtoo sit next to a tree, Puku did a quick examination of him. What had seemed like hours to Babtoo was only seconds. If the fight had lasted much longer, Babtoo was sure he would have died; a sobering thought Babtoo wished he had not had. Ohat drove the spears deeper in the big cat's twitching body just to be sure it was dead.

Long deep scratches that crisscrossed Babtoo's chest and back bled profusely. Puku quickly bound his wounds and ribs, grimacing at the sight, while Babtoo pursed his lips to stifle groans of pain.

Babtoo struggled to hold onto consciousness as his vision swam in and out of darkness. Gripping Puku on the arm, Babtoo, wincing, asked, "Is Enobi all right? I threw my spear but am not sure I stopped him."

Ohat squatted down close to Babtoo and whispered, "Enobi is fine, thanks to you. Babtoo, your spear did find its mark. This skin is now your totem. You will wear it as Chintook wears his lion's mane. You are truly blessed, Babtoo, to have two powerful totems. Enobi and a black panther are very powerful."

As if in answer to that question, Ohat dropped the ebony skin of the panther by his side.

Puku gruffly spoke, "You are meant for great things, Babtoo." New respect for Babtoo resonated in his voice.

Knowing that Enobi was not hurt, Babtoo let the darkness overtake him.

The first rays of pink light peeked over the horizon, but seemed smothered by the darkness. At first, it appeared in the predawn hours that darkness would win, and then more rays appeared and chased the night away. Babtoo, exhausted from the previous days, was still dreaming. He dreamt his foot was not crippled and that he could run. He could run, and run, and run. His breath came in ragged gasps, when suddenly he woke up, gasping in pain.

Babtoo twisted to the side, trying to relieve the pressure on his fractured ribs. The events of the previous night were not a nightmare, but reality. Looking around, Babtoo looked at the folded panther skin. An uncontrolled shiver passed through his body as he became aware of the size of the beast he had killed.

Reaching for his spear, Babtoo tried to use it as a crutch to get up. Wincing in pain, a barely concealed groan escaped his lips. The exertion was almost too much for him as he took his first step. He was determined to get Chintook back to the village, and he would not fail.

Puku was the first to help him get up. "Babtoo let me help you."

White as a sheet, Babtoo leaned against the tree, trying to catch his breath. "I can do it. Let me rest for just a moment."

Puku looked at him doubtfully as fresh blood dotted his bandages. Leaning heavily on his spear, Babtoo limped over to where Chintook's litter rested on the ground. Ohat stood to the side, ready to help if needed. The effort was almost too great.

Ohat watched, concern on his face, "Babtoo, you are too weak to go on. Puku and I will carry Chintook the rest of the way."

Babtoo gazed on Chintook's still form. The chief was pale and breathing rapidly with shallow quick breaths. Sweat beaded his face, and yet the morning sun had just barely kissed his cheek.

Resolve to succeed only hardened Babtoo. "I can do this." He emphasized it with such conviction, Puku and Ohat stepped out of the way. Taking a shaky breath, Babtoo took hold of Enobi's rope. Talking softly, Babtoo led him back to the chief. Holding him still, Ohat and Puku hooked up the litter. Enobi snorted as if to say, "Are you ready?"

Babtoo took his first shaky step forward. His wounds itched from scabs that had formed during the night. His breath came in short gasps as he strained to breathe. His crippled leg throbbed from overexertion and he badly needed more rest. Still, he trudged on with his shoulders back and his head held high. Pride was the only thing keeping him on his feet. The cool morning sun had long since disappeared, turning into an angry red ball in the sky, and still he trudged on. In the distance, Ohat and Puku navigated the terrain for the easiest path.

A tree in the distance swayed like a Watinkee dancer. The heat dried the sweat off his body before it was able to cool him. Babtoo's breathing was becoming ragged and hoarse. The bandages covering his body were turning a deep crimson. Ohat and Puku seemed to be getting further and further ahead and yet the tree remained just as far as when he noticed it the first time.

Babtoo had stopped walking and did not realize it. He clung to Enobi for support and watched the hazy outlines of Puku and Ohat getting further ahead. In his mind, he continued to walk. No matter how fast he walked, he could not keep up.

Puku looked back from the trail ahead. He quickly flagged Ohat. "We're traveling too fast. Babtoo can't keep the pace. It's a wonder he made it this far."

Ohat glanced back at Babtoo and alarm creased his rugged features. Quickly they ran back to the struggling warrior.

Babtoo in a daze, waved them away mumbling, "I am fine, I can see the village from here."

Ohat and Puku both looked at each other with worry. Babtoo could go no further. He slowly slid to the ground and whispered, "I am very tired. They will come for us. We are not far away, I see. Look, I see them coming for us now."

At that moment, small swirls of dust danced across the plains to disappear behind the tall grass. Ohat noticed the fresh blood on the bandages and knew Babtoo could not continue. If not for his courage and heart, they would have never made it this far. They would not leave their little brother behind.

Helping Babtoo up carefully so not to hurt his fractured ribs, Ohat said, "Yes Babtoo, we are almost home. We have to ask your magical beast if it can do us one more favor. He has dragged Chintook with bravery and strength. Can we ask him to carry you too? The village will know what a great warrior you are with this last great feat."

Babtoo stood on unsteady legs. His vision and mind cleared as pain shot through his body. Gripping the rope and putting his face close to Enobi's ear, Babtoo whispered his request. The big brown eyes looked at Babtoo with intelligence. The ears swiveled back and forth as if to say, "I would carry you to the ends of the earth."

Babtoo leaned into Enobi, his strength almost gone. Ohat caught

Babtoo before he slid back down to the ground. Motioning to Puku, they carefully gathered up Babtoo and placed him on Enobi.

At first, the extra weight made the big animal shy away. Babtoo clung to him like a monkey, talking to him all the while. Enobi quickly settled down and snorted a challenge. His big head shook up and down as if to say, "Yes, let's get going."

Puku and Ohat quickly backed away, not knowing what to expect. Yet it seemed like the strange zebra knew what to do.

Puku and Ohat started walking, looking back to see if the animal would follow them. Enobi had no trouble keeping up. Babtoo continued to whisper to Enobi, encouraging him to keep up. He moved forward, careful not to dislodge his precious cargo.

As the sun travelled across the sky, a jackal awoke from a sound sleep. Unfamiliar hoof beats were approaching his hiding place. Looking out from his burrow, he saw an odd sight. What looked like a zebra, but was much bigger, with spots, came very close to his home. What was most unusual was an odd growth on his back. Upon closer inspection, he saw a man on top of this beast. With a twitch of his jackal nose, he scurried back into his hole, hoping never to see that thing again.

Babtoo saw the furry tail disappear into his hiding place. He was feeling a little stronger and more alert with the rest . His ribs hurt with each step Enobi took, and yet his breathing came a little easier. Testing his strength with his legs, Babtoo noticed his knees could guide Enobi. Gentle pressure with his left made him go right. Gentle pressure with his right made Enobi go left. He felt the power of Enobi obeying his commands. A surge of excitement filled his chest at the possibilities. Looking ahead, Ohat and Puku continued to forge ahead.

CHAPTER 10

SQUANTO'S JOURNEY

A fly buzzed lazily over the ragged flap of skin. Yellow puss leaked out from between the makeshift stitches. The ragged red line on his face gave off a putrid smell of dying flesh. Skin around the wound was grey and mottled, turning black and blue in some spots. Squanto's face had swelled to twice its normal size, squeezing one eye completely shut. A fly landed on a particularly juicy spot when suddenly a hairy hand smashed it against the cheek. Wincing in pain, Squanto rolled the fly between his fingers and sucked it between his large dark lips.

Fever was coursing through his body. His one good eye glared at the surrounding savanna as if to dare the gods to strike him down. Hatred spurred him on. Gulping the last of his water, Squanto trotted out from his hiding place. Looking toward the meeting place where he would find his tribesmen, Squanto knew a war party would be there.

He thought, "They had to wipe out the Watinkee tribesmen for good. How were they to do that, especially since he was so easily beaten? Is it because of the beast and the boy? The Mautuks had powerful gods too. Perhaps they needed to sacrifice more slaves!" That thought sent a shiver of pleasure coursing through his body.

His erratic walking attracted little attention from the predators today. The midday sun beat down on the savanna relentlessly. A group of lions clearly saw him stumbling along an animal trail they frequently hunted, but they could only muster a barely heard growl. Squanto passed a short distance from a pack of wild dogs that only had energy for the nursing puppies clinging and suckling on their mother. Laughing hyenas gazed in his direction, saliva forming on their sharp fangs, and yet a short chuckle was all Squanto heard. His luck holding so far, the chief headed for the confines of the trees.

As his strength finally gave out, Squanto found a tree he could climb to get a look at the surrounding territory. The constant pain in his face would not let him rest. A cool breeze told him he was getting close to the ocean. Sniffing the crisp clean ocean air gave him hope of reuniting with his tribe.

Scanning the distant horizon, a thin black line of smoke wavered and swayed in the air like a cobra. The rest of the scouts would be there. They would not wait long for him, nor would they send anybody out to look for him.

He was tired and had traveled a long way from the battle. His energy sapped from the flight, Squanto laid his head down against his chest. Closing his one good eye, he fell asleep, dreaming of the sacrifices yet to come.

The evening turned into night and still Squanto slept. Blackness blanketed the savanna making it hard for even the nighttime dwellers to see. The tree Squanto was in was neither very large nor tall. The redeeming characteristic of this tree was the large branch he was able to rest on without falling off.

The sound of claws scrabbling on bark was the only thing that saved his life. His good eye snapped open. Looking down, a large hyena that had showed no interest during the day now was trying to jump on the large flat branch. Whines of excitement filled the air as Squanto looked down in horror at how close the hyena was getting to his branch before falling back down to earth.

Scrambling up on his feet, Squanto clutched his spear and looked for a higher perch. As suddenly as the hyena was there, it was gone. The night air was perfectly still. Silence filled the emptiness of the plains. Peering into the night, Squanto searched for signs of what kind of beast could scare the hyena off. The minutes ticked by. Sweat popped out on his forehead. He was holding his breath without knowing it. "Breathe, Squanto, breathe." He whispered to himself.

. Just when he started to relax and thought he was safe, out of the darkness an apparition appeared so suddenly that Squanto froze in fear. A huge head with fangs bared and a long thick black mane blotted out the savanna behind him as it leapt for the limb where he was sitting.

Red eyes glared with hatred, born into the big cat from a millennium of transgressions committed by ancient man on his species. He wanted only one thing, and that was to rend this pitiful excuse for a human into a thousand pieces. Catching the limb with a paw, the big cat hooked the other leg around and hung there for a moment, growling and roaring as his back legs frantically pedaled, searching for a hold.

Squanto stood with his back against the tree. A demon would be no less frightening. Looking at his pitifully small spear and the large male lion, Squanto wanted to do what his body told him to do. "RUN!" his body screamed, but there was nowhere to go but up, so he climbed.

Catching the next higher limb with scrabbling fingers, Squanto climbed. He shot up the tree like someone possessed. Strangled cries of fear escaped his ruined face. Balancing on one of the tree's top branches, thin even for a small man, Squanto watched in disbelief as the lion slowly levered itself up to stand where he had just been.

Balancing itself on the limb with his hind legs, the lion stretched out to reach Squanto. The massive weight of the beast shook the top branches, showering dry leaves on the beast. Squanto clutched the branch and swayed back and forth like an over-ripe fruit waiting to fall.

The lion roared hungrily, reaching with razor sharp claws. With a final leap to catch Squanto's quivering body, the branch cracked, and then snapped off at the base of the tree. The heavy cat let out a strangled growl as he tumbled to the ground entangled in the broken limb. He fell with a heavy thud, knocking the air from his body. Stunned, he rolled back on his feet, shaking leaves and grass from his body. Glaring up at Squanto and roaring his impotence, he sauntered off into the bush with a flick of his tail. Squanto, frozen with fear, dared not leave the safety of the tree until the relative safety of the morning.

The light breeze weaved itself in and out of the leaves, gently making them dance on their short stems. A small leaf fluttered from the tree, twisting and turning in its descent, catching the morning light with shades of green and brown. The breeze caught the leaf and like a butterfly, it landed several yards from the tree. Birds began chirping in the morning to welcome the new day.

Squanto clutched his small branch with fingertips rubbed raw from shifting his grip on the rough bark. A bloodshot eye peered into the dawn, searching for any enemy that walked on four legs. The branch creaked ominously under his weight as the tree swayed back and forth with the breeze. Glancing down, Squanto saw the branch broken by the big male lion the night before. He noticed the claw marks just inches from his perch. As a rabbit conceals itself from a hunting hawk, Squanto had not moved a muscle through the night.

With the dawn came fresh hope. The scary noises that had surrounded his perch throughout the night were gone. All that remained were tracks and a broken branch as if mocking him to come down.

Fear slowly subsided in proportion to the advancing dawn. Shaking his head, Squanto tried to get his wits about him. Listening intently to the morning noises that surrounded him, he tried to identify each sound and put them in their place.

One particular sound caught his attention. A female bird had a nest just a few feet below him. She was singing a beautiful song, dancing around her nest with four brown eggs arranged in a circle, not realizing the danger above her.

Listening to the bird sing, Squanto realized how hungry he was, and as if to answer that question, his belly rumbled long and loud. Shifting his grip to rub his stomach, Squanto looked hungrily at the bird and her nest. Slowly stretching his cramped legs, Squanto tried to unfold himself from the branch. Stiff and sore, his movements were jerky and uncontrolled. His legs felt like a thousand needles were pricking him all at once, as the blood flowed back into them.

Shifting slightly to accommodate his cramped legs, the branch suddenly gave away. Clutching frantically at the trunk of the tree with flailing legs and arms, Squanto slid down the tree to the next branch were the bird was nesting. Frightened, the bird flew into the air, circling around to see what had shaken the branch where she sat. Breathing heavily, Squanto wrapped his legs and arms around the trunk. Looking intently at the nest, he contemplated his next move.

The branch was too small and thin for him to crawl out on. The bird was bigger than he thought and its mate was answering her calls for help. Now there were two large birds screaming at him. This could attract the attention of predators. He had to think of something fast. Using his spear, Squanto pushed the nest off its precarious perch and it landed with a gentle bounce on the ground. Satisfied, he began his descent.

Angered at the loss of their nest, the two birds continued to scream in frustration and dove at him relentlessly. Gripping the tree with one hand, Squanto waved the other around his head trying to keep the birds away from his damaged face. His toes were searching for the next perch when his grip slipped.

Tumbling to the ground, Squanto landed with a thud in the thick grass. Stunned, he lay there for a few minutes collecting his wits. Looking over to his side, the nest laid upside down, the unbroken eggs spilled on the ground. Reaching over with his finger, Squanto poked the eggs back in the nest. Sitting up against the trunk, he greedily sucked the contents of the eggs.

Standing on unsteady legs, Squanto sucked the remaining fluid from the last egg with a satisfied smack of his lips. Still hungry, but refreshed, he glance at the sky to pinpoint where he last saw the smoke from the night before to help guide him to his fellow tribesmen. Satisfied, he crushed the eggshells with his heel, grinding them into the ground with disdain.

Venturing out from the stand of trees, Squanto loped toward the ocean. Hoping they were not far off, he faced the rising sun. His strength would not hold for long and his face was in desperate need of attention. Blinking in the morning glare, his eye felt like boulders were rolling around under the lid. He knew if he kept the ocean breeze in his face, he would find his brothers.

The heat of the day had finally sapped the last of Squanto's strength. He stopped sweating hours ago as chills racked his body. He could no longer swallow as his tongue swelled and dried, tasting like old leather. Putting one foot in front of the next, Squanto dragged his spear on the ground. A lone tree shimmered in the distance, slowly getting larger and larger. Upon reaching the tree, Squanto fell into a heap, delirious with thirst. He desperately needed to rest as exhaustion finally took its toll.

Two hundred feet in the air, the huge bird flapped lazily around on the drafts and currents of air, expending as little energy as possible. Its beady black eyes could follow an animal as small as a mouse as it scurried from one tuft of grass to another.

Today, something else caught the big bird's interest. He had spotted a much larger and more unusual prey. The animal had two legs and wandered in the savanna erratically. Sometimes it would stop and look around, peering into the sun. Other times it would stumble and catch itself before it fell. Soon, other birds of his kind had noticed this creature and were flying in circles, waiting for him to fall for the last time. Movement had at last ceased and the buzzard spiraled in slow circles down to the tree to wait.

The rock was hard and uncomfortable. It was Quid's turn to be a lookout for the other Mautuk warriors. Getting off the rock and sitting on the ground, Quid enjoyed the last of the warthog they cooked yesterday. Laying his spear on the ground, he chewed noisily, spitting out any bones that he could not eat. They were waiting for Squanto to report with his scouts. Squanto was late and time was getting short for them to return to their people. Quid settled down and got comfortable, quickly falling asleep in the midday sun.

The ant waved his tiny feelers in the air. He had discovered that not far from his nest were some discarded bones and meat. Hurrying back to the colony, the message went out that food was just a short distance away. Soon, thousands of ants converged on the food and surrounding vegetation.

Quid awoke from a dream of a hundred spear tips pricking him. Looking down, thousands of ants were everywhere, biting and stinging him. Quid jumped up and down trying to brush the ants off, killing as many as he could with his feet. Overwhelmed, he ran a short distance away, brushing himself off vigorously.

Looking up, Quid saw buzzards slowly circling not far away. Wondering what could be dying, Quid followed the slow descent of the birds to a lone tree not far off. Stalking toward the tree, he did not know what to expect. He was hoping for something that they could eat without having to kill it. Slowly approaching the tree, Quid saw the first buzzard hop off the branch to the ground.

Quid approached the tree cautiously, using every bit of cover he could find. Peeking around a small sapling and parting the clumps of grass, he got a shocking surprise. A Mautuk warrior was leaning against the tree, too weak to fight off the vulture. The big bird was eye to eye with the warrior as it prepared to take its first bite. Jumping up and waving his hands, Quid ran for the bird, throwing his spear to scare it.

The big bird spread its great wings to fly, flapping furiously to get off the ground. Frustrated by a stolen meal, the vulture landed in a branch close by and waited to see if he would get another chance.

Quid quickly ran to the tree and looked down at the fallen warrior. He could barely recognize Squanto's features. Swollen and purple, his face was almost unidentifiable. His breathing was harsh and ragged. Reaching for his water bottle, Quid tried to give Squanto a drink. Water trickled down his throat. His eye opened for a brief moment looking past Quid.

Mumbling incoherently, Squanto kept repeating, "Spotted Zebra, great power, Spotted Zebra, great power, too much for us, too much for us! Everyone lost."

Quid didn't know what to make of this. He knew he had to get Squanto back to the others where they would figure out his delusions. In the meantime, he could not leave Squanto here. The vulture did not go far and would be back as soon as he was gone. Grabbing the injured warrior under his arms, he boosted him up. Squanto leaned heavily on him as they made their way back to the beach.

Restlessness and fever racked his body for two days. Quid and the other warriors gathered strange herbs to help bring quell the infection and rattled old bones over his quivering body. They applied saltwater compresses over his wounded face to bring the swelling down. They chanted to their evil gods and danced around the campfire in immoral ways to appease the evil spirits locked in Squanto's body.

Squanto would scream in hatred about some sort of Spotted Zebra god. He flailed around, dreaming of the relentless attack of a tall Watinkee warrior with broad shoulders and flashing grey eyes.

Quid looked down on Squanto, not much caring whether he lived or died. He knew Squanto had been defeated and had lost some of his friends. He just hoped he would live long enough to tell everybody what had happened.

On the third day, Squanto became conscious. He looked around the dark confines of the cave and felt safe. He wondered if his memories were just a bad dream. When he touched his face, he knew those memories were a reality. The wounds on his face were puffy and red, but with time, would heal, leaving a long jagged scar. Testing his limbs, he climbed out of bed. Stumbling to the cave opening, bright light stabbed at his eyes. Blinking for several seconds, Squanto was finally able to see.

Grabbing Quid he said, "Gather the scouts. I have valuable news. In the meantime, I need food."

Quid shook off Squanto's grip and pointed to the cold cook pot of yesterday's meal. Leaving Squanto to fend for himself, Quid gathered the warriors.

They built a large fire for the anticipated news from Squanto. Fifteen warriors gathered to hear what he had to say. The night hid the degenerate warriors as the fire light reflected off fifteen hairy faces waiting eagerly to hear Squanto's news.

They sat in a large semicircle around the fire waiting for Squanto to make an appearance, whispering among them as to what could have happened. Silenced reigned as Squanto entered the circle of light. He looked diminutive and weak as the light bathed his small frame. Raising his skeletal arms over his head, Squanto recited a guttural prayer to their dark gods. All fifteen warriors chanted with him, eager to hear his tale.

Squanto lowered his arms and silently looked at each warrior in turn. With a voice starting out small, Squanto gained momentum as the story unfolded. He told of great tales of bravery and the ensuing battle. He told them how the evil Watinkees in great numbers had ambushed their scouting party. Squanto went on to say how he was lucky to get out alive. He reenacted the battle telling how he had killed at least three Watinkee tribesmen, but that they finally were able to overpower him. Pointing to his wound, Squanto touched his face to emphasize his point.

Most of all, he told of a spotted zebra and a warrior with grey eyes. He talked of how this magical beast protected the warrior, throwing off his aim with a spear. The fight with the Watinkee tribesmen was desperate. He alone was able to get away, while the rest died under Watinkee spears.

After the speech, the warriors talked excitedly among themselves.

Squanto, exhausted after the lie, knew he had done his part. He would return a hero and started back toward the cave.

Thinking his lie had worked, Squanto smiled. His foul plan to wipe out the Watinkee tribesmen was going very well. He had a debt to pay to that young warrior with the fierce grey eyes. There would be time for revenge. He had planted the seed and savored his perceived outcome. They could return with more warriors to handle this upstart tribe.

The next morning, the Mautuks were gone. A charred fire pit with burned bones scattered around was all the evidence that remained. The wind erased the ashes across the beach and soon covered the bones in a sandy grave. A short spear thrust into the ground was a warning to any Watinkee tribesmen that the Mautuks were here and would return.

CHAPTER 11

THE WELCOMING PARTY

Babtoo, still weak from the panther attack, patted Enobi on the neck. Leaning down, Babtoo whispered in his ear. "We have come far, my friend."

Enobi shook his head and nickered in response. Peering into the distance, Babtoo could make out the two warriors, Puku and Ohat. They looked for the shortest path with the least obstacles and wove back and forth, disappearing and reappearing in the grasslands.

Sitting on the back of the horse, Babtoo could see more of the savanna clearly. He noticed the lions stalking their prey with each individual lion having a role in the kill. The baboons were scattered over a large area, yet Babtoo spotted them all, including the scouts. Fleet footed gazelles smelled the cheetahs and were moving away from them to a small hill with a copse of trees. He saw a bigger picture of the savanna as the life in it flowed around him.

It was no surprise that he was the first to spot Ukup with Whutknot, the medicine man, and two other warriors. Whistling to catch the attention of Puku and Ohat, Babtoo pointed in the direction of the approaching tribesmen. Puku and Ohat both looked up at once and turned in the direction he pointed. Fading into the brush, not sure who it was, they waited in hiding.

Babtoo saw them clearly and yelled a greeting. "Hey, over here, we have come far and need your help!" Babtoo forgot that Ukup had not seen him on the magical beast yet and might be wary.

Ukup and the medicine man both stood in disbelief. The other two warriors stood defensively, not sure what to do. Puku and Ohat stepped out of their hiding places with looks of relief on their faces.

Puku clasped the hand of Ukup and said with a huge smile, "Well met brother. I'm glad you were so swift. You are a welcome sight. Chintook needs Whutknot's skills. He is very weak."

Ukup, elated at finding his brother safe, said, "Whutknot brought powerful medicine. He knows the poison of the Mautuks." Glancing at Babtoo, Ukup asked, "How did Babtoo get on the magical beast? What about you, brother, was your journey uneventful?"

Clasping his brother on the shoulder, Puku replied, "So many questions, where do I start? I think Babtoo needs to tell his own story. We don't know how he talks to his totem, but are grateful he can!"

The medicine man quickly crossed the space to get to Chintook, ignoring the brother's greeting. Edging around Enobi, not knowing what to expect, he knelt down by the litter. Taking the blood soaked bandage from around Chintook's body, a grimace crossed his features. The wound had festered and puckered with a reddish black discharge.

Whutknot motioned for Ohat to come over. "Quickly, boil some water and I need some fresh mud from that termite mound."

Throwing a water skin at Ohat, Whutknot turned back to Chintook's shivering body. Placing his fingers over his body and using gentle hands, Whutknot searched for broken bones and other injuries.

Ohat motioned for the other two warriors to help as he cleared an area for a small fire. Breathing life into the small flame, Ohat fanned the fire to get it large enough for their use. Whutknot glanced up and yelled at the other two warriors to hurry up. Pouring water into a bowl, Ohat placed it over the fire to heat it.

Babtoo almost went unnoticed as Whutknot quickly took charge and started issuing orders. Sitting on Enobi's back, Babtoo felt a bit lightheaded. Grabbing Enobi's mane, Babtoo slid to the ground.

Puku noticed first and raced over, reaching for his friend before he fell. Cradling his head in his hands, Puku produced a water sack to give to Babtoo. Ukup fished in his pockets for a small vile and after breaking the seal, he mixed it in the water. Dribbling water into his mouth, Babtoo reached for the pouch and drank greedily.

Ukup grabbed the skin. "Whoa, little brother. This is strong medicine. I brought this just in case Whutknot did not have enough. This will give you energy and revive you. It is only temporary until we can get you back to the village."

Babtoo shook his head, grateful for the drink, still clutching the skin. He took one more swallow before giving it back to Ohat.

The water had started to boil giving Whutknot the opportunity to mix his medicine. Taking the hard-packed termite mound mud, he threw it into the water to let it thicken. Mumbling a strange incantation, even to the surrounding Watinkee tribesmen, he threw in a mixture of herbs. Steam the color of blood rose from the pot that smelled a lot like buffalo dung. Scooping it up in his hand, Whutknot pressed it into Chintook's wound. Chintook's eyes opened wide with surprise, but slowly his body relaxed as a slow smile played across his face and he drifted off to sleep.

Turning, Whutknot saw Puku and Ukup cradling Babtoo in their arms. Babtoo saw the medicine man coming and tried to wave him off. "I'm fine Whutknot. You need not work on me. I am just a little tired."

Whutknot strode over and gruffly waved Puku and Ukup away, saying, "Let me be the judge, warrior. You have fought in a battle with the Mautuks. They use poison on their spear tips. Let me at least check for injuries."

Babtoo shifted to allow the medicine man to look at his wounds. Peeling off the bandages revealed the claw marks from the big cat.

Whutknot's eyes widened in surprise. "What happened here Babtoo? These are not injuries caused by Mautuks. Looks like you fought a devil and came out the loser. I have some herbs to help the infection and dull the pain. What happened?"

Babtoo could only point to the black panther skin folded on the rump of the spotted zebra. "He tried to kill Enobi. I could not let that happen."

Whutknot glanced at the strange animal with wonder in his old eyes. "Truly there's a story everybody wants to hear."

Puku and Ohat could only nod in agreement.

Babtoo recovered enough strength to boost himself back on Enobi. All the warriors gaped in openmouthed amazement. Sitting as straight as he could, proud to have the respect of a warrior held in high regard, Babtoo's heart felt good. He no longer felt they considered him less than a warrior because of his foot. He was proud the warriors held him as an equal. Ignoring the pain in his body, Babtoo tried hard to remain strong and stoic.

The trip to the village was wearisome. In a few hours, smoke from cooking fires could be seen curling up over the trees. The two scouts had been sent ahead to prepare a place for Chintook. News of the magical beast drew people out from their huts to get a glimpse of this unusual animal. From far off, they were able to see Babtoo sitting on a spotted zebra even before they were able to spot the accompanying warriors.

Young boys were eager to be the first to run and greet the entourage. They stared in awe at Babtoo and the magical beast. The young children chattered all the way back to the village and bragged who had gotten the closest to the large beast. Counsel elders looked with respect at Babtoo as he rode into the village. Women clutched their children in fear, never seeing a sight so great.

Babtoo looked down on all the upturned faces and felt a mixture of pride and honor. A cheer started from one small voice and rose to a deafening roar. Warriors danced around him and boys shouted their joy. The hunting party was back and they were all alive. Babtoo was a hero!

Everybody was glad except one Watinkee warrior watching a short distance away. He stared at Babtoo with eyes full of hatred and jealousy. Hohumph was a little older than Babtoo by a couple of years with a husky build and large nose flattened to one side.

Babtoo was not of the Watinkee tribe and Hohumph would not let him forget it. He hated him for his crippled leg and the extra time Chintook always gave him. The long white curly hair and aristocratic features were unusual for any tribe in the area, so Hohumph targeted Babtoo with his cruel nature.

As youngsters, Hohumph would try to make an example out of Babtoo by embarrassing him whenever he could. He would take Babtoo far out on the savanna hoping he would get lost and not live to return home. Yet Hohumph always found Babtoo the next morning in camp. He would often hide and then maliciously trip Babtoo whenever he walked by, laughing as he fell to the ground. However, what hurt Babtoo the most was the constant name-calling and heartless jokes about his lame foot.

Hohumph took great pleasure in bullying the young warrior, until one day when Babtoo's patience had run out. Fighting back, Babtoo struck Hohumph on the nose so hard as to permanently flatten it to one side. Whutknot, the medicine man, could do nothing to repair the broken stub on his face.

Hohumph had few friends. He had proved himself an adequate hunter, but not overly brave. A large wild dog had chased him on his first hunt where he found refuge in a tree. Puku found him a day later in the same tree where he had stayed all night. Hohumph had never lived that down and so his nickname, whispered in warrior circles, was 'Hohumph doggone', although nobody ever said it to his face.

A beautiful girl stood in the shadows. She was approaching womanhood. Her long dark hair flowed past her shoulders to the middle of her back accentuating her tall and shapely form. The nut-brown eyes danced with excitement and intelligence as she watched Babtoo ride in. Her mahogany colored skin glowed with radiance. She was attractive even for a Watinkee. Her name was Monbeem and she was Chintook's daughter.

After the devastating fire eighteen years ago, many Watinkee men and women had lost their people but had united in other, newly formed or established tribes. Monbeem's mother had been one of the many people lost and had become separated from her family and tribe. She had never known what had happened to them, as smoldering huts and scattered belongings were all that the fire had left.

Chintook had found her wandering on the grasslands, lost and disheveled. Captivated by her beauty, he had taken her for his wife. Soon after, Chintook had been devastated when she had died giving birth to his daughter, whom he named Monbeem.

Hohumph also loved Monbeem and stood close by her, watching her eyes follow Babtoo. Jealousy flared in his chest as he gritted his teeth. He spent all of his free time around her, trying to convince her of his worthiness as a husband. He had proven he could be a good hunter, yet she did not want anything to do with him. He had hoped to talk to Chintook about his daughter, but how was he going to get rid of Babtoo?

Babtoo searched the crowd milling about hoping to see Monbeem. He loved her, but knew he could never marry her. After all, he was lame and not a fully-fledged blood member of the tribe. Babtoo knew he was different. Hohumph had made sure that he and the tribe would never forget.

However, like a moth to a flame, he could not help wanting to be around her. Her smile was infectious and her touch sent tingles up and down his spine. When she talked, it was like listening to music. What would she want with half a warrior, was all he could think.

Monbeem had grown up with Babtoo. She did not see the cripple that Hohumph saw and was sorry for the tricks the young warriors played on him. Through those trials, Babtoo would always find a way to win anyway.

What she saw was a gentle young man with a beautiful smile. She saw intelligence flash in his smoldering grey eyes. His shoulders were broad and the white curly hair that fell to his shoulders was unusual. He had strength no Watinkee tribesmen could match. She was in love with him and could not understand why she could not make him see that.

Hohumph stood behind Monbeem and poked her in the ribs saying, "Looks like they have returned. Seems that Babtoo must have fallen behind and the beast had to carry him. I wonder if he is not the reason Chintook is on the litter. They did have a fight with the Mautuks you know."

Monbeem gave him a scathing look while moving away from him. "I bet he is the hero and I bet he is the one that saved Chintook's life. You are so eaten up with jealousy that the truth hides from you."

With that said Hohumph backed away and slid around another hut for a better view.

Babtoo fought to stay on Enobi. The drink that had revived him before was fading. They had stopped by Chintook's tent among a crowd of followers to lay him in his bed. Whutknot stayed by his side the whole time to be sure that everything went smoothly.

After disconnecting the litter, Babtoo pointed Enobi towards his tent. Tired and hurting, he slid off the horse and stood on uncertain feet. Holding his ribs, and looking around, he saw a ring of children standing around them in awe.

Kneeling down to the children, Babtoo said, "This wonderful beast has carried me far. Could you be so kind as to get him some fresh grass and water?"

The children, excited about doing something for Babtoo and the mighty beast, scattered like leaves in a storm, eager to be the first one back with grass. Leaning heavily on Enobi, Babtoo traced his way back to the wounded leg. The injury was red and swollen, but time and rest would help heal the wound. Bone tired and hurting, Babtoo redressed Enobi's wound. Enobi, sensing Babtoo was there to help, turned his head and whickered.

Soon the children started coming back with bunches of grass and containers of water. Babtoo thanked them for it and brushed Enobi down with some old straw by his tent. Removing the black panther skin off his flank, Babtoo went in to lie down.

The commotion and excitement would not die down. Children danced outside his tent and villagers stopped to look at the magical spotted zebra. All this Babtoo missed as he fell into a deep sleep. The people of the village were anxious to hear what had happened in Babtoo's own words, but would have to wait until he awoke.

Babtoo dreamed of being a strong and able warrior. He dreamed of having two strong legs where he was the fastest runner and strongest member of his tribe. He dreamed of being a leader where people would look up to him. However, most of all he dreamed of being with Monbeem. He dreamed she loved him and thought of him being a great warrior protecting her from harm. His sleep turned into nightmares of Mautuk warriors escaping with Monbeem and he was too slow to follow. He kept running but could not catch up.

He felt like he was tumbling down into a hole, never to get out. Puku gently shook Babtoo carefully so as not to reinjure his cracked ribs. Babtoo woke with a start, grabbing Puku before he was fully awake and twisting his arm in a painful, viselike grip.

"Oh, wake up Babtoo, wake up!" Puku howled.

Babtoo gasped in pain as he inhaled a lung full of air, straining his broken ribs. Sweat soaked his body.

Quickly letting go of Puku, he mumbled, "Sorry, Puku. You startled me. I was having some bad dreams."

Puku took his hand back, rubbing his wrist where Babtoo had squeezed it. "You have been sleeping for two days now. Whutknot has checked in on you from time to time to see how you were doing. He says you will be fine in a few days. Your ribs will heal, but you will be sore. The claw marks will be permanent, but the scars do not run as deep as Chintook's did after he killed the lion. You'll have to keep these bandages on for a while, but he said you came out pretty good and were lucky against the big cat."

Babtoo smiled weakly, careful to control his breathing. His eyes traveled the tent looking for the black cat's hide. A look of alarm crossed his features for a moment before Puku spoke with a chuckle, "Monbeem took your hide. She is curing it now as we speak. She would let no one else touch it. Of course, we could do nothing. We hope it will take her mind off Chintook."

Babtoo frowned at the memory of Chintook. Holding his side, Babtoo spoke with concern, "How is Chintook? Is he any better? Has Whutknot been able to get the poison out?"

Puku's eyes dropped for a moment, "No, Chintook is not getting better. He had gone a long time without proper medicine. He is still in the land of dreams and his fever has not gone down much. Whutknot is working hard to save his life. If not for you, little brother, we may have lost him on the savanna. When Monbeem is not working on the hide, she is with Whutknot trying to help. Whutknot chases her away after a while."

Babtoo shifted a little to get more comfortable, and looked up at Puku. "How is Enobi?" he asked.

Puku chuckled. "You need not worry about Enobi. The children around here have given him more water and grass than he can eat in a week. His back leg no longer bleeds and seems to be healing. He still limps a little though. Perhaps it will take some time to heal, like your wounds."

Babtoo shook his head, hoping the damage would not be permanent like his own leg. Unconsciously he glanced down at his own crippled foot.

Puku followed his gaze and quickly said, "Chief Bowhut asked me to wake you. He's eager to hear your story. Everybody wants to hear your story. The tribe needs some good news with Chintook injured. Chief Bowhut thinks tonight would be good if you are well enough to talk."

Babtoo inhaled with great discomfort, but knew what an honor it would be to talk in front of the tribe. Scratching at the bandages where his ribs ached, Babtoo nodded. "It would be an honor to talk about what I have seen. The Mautuks are here and have to be stopped!"

Puku helped Babtoo to his feet, careful not to reinjure his ribs. Walking toward the tent door, Babtoo opened the flap as the sunlight assailed his eyes. He could not see for a moment and stumbled back into his tent. Puku caught him before he went down. Shaking his head to clear his senses, Babtoo approached the door again.

Opening the tent flap a little so his eyes could adjust, Babtoo saw the usual activity of the tribe. People were walking back and forth, children were playing, and older boys were practicing with their spears. Cooking fires blazed and the smell of food filled the air. His stomach rumbled with hunger.

Pushing the flap aside, he glanced in the direction of Monbeem's fire pit, hoping to see her. Not far away, a small fire danced under a roasting spit where she hovered over a piece of rabbit. She slowly turned the meat as the juices sizzled on the fire. Hohumph stood over her shoulder touching and talking to her. His heart sank as he watched the two of them for a few minutes.

Hohumph had just killed a rabbit and was holding it up for her to see. Babtoo watched as he beat his chest and made a big show of the spear throw that killed the rabbit. Monbeem smiled and nodded her head as Hohumph's story continued to grow. He watched as he put his arm around her and stole a quick kiss. She pushed him away, but he laughed at his own brashness.

Babtoo had seen enough. Walking over to Monbeem, he asked, "Hi Monbeem! Is there anything on that spit you can spare for me?"

Monbeem smiled and all the pain he was feeling disappeared. She pointed to the food. "Take whatever you want. If you're still hungry, I will make more."

A frown creased Hohumph's features. He started to shake and then burst out saying, "So, you have come back from the dead. I heard you could not keep up in the hunt and they had to find you! Did Chintook take a spear because you were too slow and couldn't keep up?"

Babtoo's smile faded from his face as anger slowly took hold. A look of shock crossed Monbeem's face.

"You were not there, Hohumph. It was not like that." Babtoo said as he shifted to take on the burly man.

Hohumph took a step closer to Babtoo as if to push him down, when suddenly, Puku stepped between them. "That's enough, Hohumph! He's no coward. If you strike him, I will personally challenge you in front of the whole tribe. Without Babtoo and the magical beast, we may not have made it out alive!"

Hohumph threw the rabbit down as he walked away, snarling an angry retort, "Another time, Babtoo."

Babtoo gazed after Hohumph, knowing the feud would not end. He sighed and looked at Puku. "Thank you, but I could have handled that myself. Since he's such a coward, he would not strike me down."

"Maybe, little brother, maybe, but he does not like you and I fear there will be a day when he finds the courage to do something about it." Puku admonished.

Monbeem glanced his way. "I thought you were very brave to stand up to him with all that has happened to you. Take this meat and sit and tell me about your adventures."

Babtoo slowly sat down, suddenly very tired. "Perhaps that can wait until tonight when we are gathered. Tell me how Chintook fares."

A worried look crossed her face. Tears welled in her eyes as she spoke in almost a whisper, "Whutknot has done all he can. He is with him all day. He is weak and not getting much better. His fever is high and he does not eat much. He speaks in his sleep of terrible things. Whutknot says if he can't break his fever, he will die."

Babtoo listened with a heavy heart. He wished he could do something to help. Putting his arm around her, he gently caressed her arm and asked her about the news of the tribe during the hunt hoping to take her mind off Chintook.

Babtoo gazed into her eyes and listened as she told him of tribal events during his hunting trip. Listening to the rise and fall of her voice was like a soft melody playing in his mind.

That abruptly ended when he learned how Hohumph was visiting her every day and was planning to ask for her hand in marriage as soon as Chintook felt stronger. Monbeem did not notice his frown when she told him how Hohumph brought food every day to her tent.

Babtoo heard nothing after that. If Chintook died, Hohumph would have a clear path for her hand in marriage. Monbeem would need a warrior to take care of her. In the middle of a story of how Windsaloft had her baby, Babtoo abruptly stood up stiffly, "I must go now. I'll see you in a little bit."

Monbeem was startled at the sudden change in his demeanor. She reached for him and asked what she had said to upset him. He glanced at her with an expression of hurt and pain on his face and said, "Nothing, I am glad Hohumph is so generous." Leaning heavily on his spear, Babtoo walked painfully back to his tent to rest for the upcoming meeting.

CHAPTER 12

MONBEEM

The firefly flew lazily around the tree, blinking, looking for a mate. It seemed as if he was the only firefly under the tree tonight. He flew to a higher branch when he noticed a huge bright light in the middle of the savanna. Above the light, bright sparks shot into the air, twisting and turning, blinking red, then yellow, before disappearing into the night. This must be where he needed to go. Wings lifted in the air to catch the cool breeze as he flew toward the light.

The blaze was huge. It captured the excitement of the Watinkee gathering. Elders threw special powders on the fire, painting the flame different shades of colors. This was a celebration of thanks to the warrior gods for bringing the hunters home alive. Young warriors danced to the beating drums while girls gathered in groups wearing their celebration dresses. Hohumph danced with his jiggling belly especially close to Monbeem.

Older warriors sat in a circle, passing a tobacco pipe around and retold stories of their youth. With each telling, the stories became more and more embellished. Older wives sat and listened to their husbands, nodding their heads with pride at their husband's bravery and hunting skills.

Babtoo wore his best clothes for the meeting. He would have had trouble getting into his shirt if Ohat had not stopped to check in on him. Standing next to Enobi, Babtoo stroked his neck waiting for his time to speak.

Chief Bowhut stepped into the light and waved his arms for silence. The ostrich feathers that adorned his head fell cascading toward the ground. A falcon feather attached to his spear seemed to have a life of its own as it fluttered in the breeze.

All eyes fell on Chief Bowhut. Raising his voice so all could hear he recited an ancient Watinkee prayer:

"We praise thee oh great one.
"Lead us to great hunts so we may not go hungry.
"Let there be rain for our crops so they do not wither.
"Protect us from our enemies as they tremble before you.
"Keep our spear arms strong and hearts without fear.
"Let us prosper in peace under your blanket of strength."

Chief Bowhut almost whispered the last part of the prayer. People leaned forward to hear him speak over the crackling fire. Searching the sky for a sign, Bowhut had his arms outstretched, fingers grasping, as if reaching for a star.

Chief Bowhut fell silent looking at the assembled tribe. He was chief of a great Watinkee tribe. They had lived in peace for many years under his rule. Times were changing with the Mautuk's presence in his land. Listening to the returning hunters, he knew the time of peace was over. Chintook, a close friend and advisor, lay close to death from a Mautuk spear.

He slowly gazed at the warriors around the campfire. People he had watched grow into men looked to him for guidance. The Mautuks were a fierce and terrible enemy. He wondered if there would be war how many of his old friends he would never see again. He was not afraid for himself, but knew there was no good end to this invasion.

Shaking himself free from that thought, Chief Bowhut again became the natural leader of the tribe as strength flowed back into his voice. He once again was a warrior they looked to for guidance from the gods.

Raising his strong baritone voice, Chief Bowhut said, "We have an unwelcomed presence in our home. Our land has been defiled by Mautuk blood. Chintook's hunting party had fought with Mautuk warriors. They killed four of the cannibals, but during the battle, Chintook took a poisoned spear and is now near death. This is not the last we will see of them. It is fortunate that Chintook was able to hunt them down. Let this be known that his bravery, and the hunting party's bravery, is beyond question."

"Speaking with Ohat, Puku and Ukup, they tell me one of the cannibals Babtoo wounded has gotten away. If the Mautuk lives, he'll tell his people our strengths and also our weaknesses. We must prepare ourselves for this! We can't now let our guard down! Babtoo found the first sign of their foul presence in our land. Let him tell his story for all to hear."

Bowhut pointed with his spear for Babtoo to come forward. Still weak from the big cat's attack, Babtoo limped into the firelight, his head high and shoulders back as he led Enobi into the light.

People gasped as Enobi entered the circle of light. Everybody started talking at once. Somewhere a drum started to pound to silence the tribe. Chief Bowhut nodded for Babtoo to start his narrative on the events of the hunt.

Somebody threw a log on the fire. Sparks showered the air as the fire greedily engulfed the log. The orange, yellow and red of the flame danced across the shadows of Babtoo's face. The strength of a man appeared before the tribe, yet the fears of a boy remained locked in his heart.

Looking out at the faces of warriors, he wondered who would judge his actions. Would he show them courage? Would he be a good example for the younger warriors? Would Monbeem look at him as more than just half a man? Could he have done more? Brushing those uncertainties away, Babtoo thought of all the good he had done.

Stroking Enobi's nose, Babtoo gathered his strength to tell his story. He started out slowly, and then picked up momentum as the excitement of the story unfolded before the tribe.

He began, "I had fallen behind in the hunt. My leg ached with the coming of the storm. I found myself by the ocean where I discovered a large cave. Inside this cave were drawings of death I did not understand. There were partially burned bones and skulls that looked human. My dreams were filled with nightmares of a strange people killing Watinkee tribesmen."

Grumbling was heard from the older warriors who had fought the Mautuks before and who understood what the signs meant.

Bowhut held his hand up, "Let Babtoo finish the story. There is much more to hear!"

Babtoo began again, "The next day the storm was gone. In the water floated bodies of people wearing strange clothes. On the beach were large pieces of cloth with rope and wood. Dead fish and crabs were scattered everywhere dying in the sun. Out in the distance I saw something struggling to get to shore, and swimming around it was a grey fin. I knew it would never make it to the beach without my help so I swam out there with my spear. Before I could get there, the shark had attacked this wonderful creature." Babtoo continued to stroke Enobi's nose.

"I used my spear to kill the shark, but not before it had injured Enobi's leg. I wrapped it like I was taught from watching Whutknot to stop the bleeding."

A nod of approval from Whutknot when their eyes met was all the support Babtoo needed to continue.

"Enobi was weak and needed water. I went up the ridge from the beach to get water from a shallow hole when I noticed unusual human tracks. I was not sure what, or who they were. That is when Chintook came upon me. I told him of the cave and tracks. He knew right away that they were Mautuk warriors. He had Puku and Ukup track the prints to see where they would go. He said we needed to take his life so he would not return with others, and so we followed. I had this magical beast and wondered if he could help."

"On the second night, it was my turn to watch. I was looking away when Enobi warned me of an attack. The Mautuk had doubled back and surprised me. He would have killed me if not for this great beast. I turned in time and threw my spear. I missed and we wrestled with his knife. I threw him away from me and into Enobi." Babtoo sighed as he stroked the horse's nose. "Enobi kicked him hard and wounded him, drawing blood. He ran into the night."

The older warriors nodded but looked hard at him for not being more vigilant.

"Chintook is a great leader. We followed, knowing the Mautuk was badly injured. The cannibal found a rocky outcrop and sent up a smoke signal to call for help. We didn't know how many Mautuks would respond to the signal and so we had to be extra wary."

"Everybody had a great part in the battle. I was following from behind when I saw two Mautuk warriors getting ready to ambush Chintook and Ohat. I threw my spear and killed one Mautuk before he could attack them."

"Then things happened so fast. I wrestled with a Mautuk warrior and wounded him, but he was able to get away. We stalked up the hill to capture the scout, but they had already come down and ambushed us. That is when Chintook took a spear in the shoulder. I threw my spear and killed that warrior while Ohat killed the last Mautuk. The one I wounded escaped."

"We had to get Chintook back to the village fast before the poison took his life. Ohat did the best he could with treating the wound and sent Ukup back to get help. I was able to get Enobi to help drag the litter, which saved us time because he is much stronger and faster. In the middle of the night on my watch, a black panther attacked me. I was prepared this time."

The older warriors nodded in approval as smiles played across their faces.

"The panther was quick and dodged my first spear throw but then before I knew it, the cat jumped on me, trying to claw my face. He knocked me to the ground and I stabbed at it with my knife before Enobi kicked it away from me. It turned to attack Enobi when I found my spear and threw again. I did not miss this time. My ribs are cracked and have I wounds from his claws, but if not for Enobi, I could have been gravely injured."

A long collective sigh sounded from the people of the tribe as if they all had held their breath.

"We continued on until we met Whutknot and Ukup a short distance from the village."

Babtoo stopped talking and silence followed. Everybody was waiting for an ending that did not come. The fire had burned down to just a few red embers. The coals blinked red and black giving enough light to show the eager faces of the tribe. People began cheering him for his bravery in battle and his resourcefulness with Enobi.

Turning away, Babtoo left the circle to hover on the outskirts of the firelight. Everybody talked at once.

Chief Bowhut again raised his hands for silence. He spoke, "Listen, everyone! Babtoo had a big part in the battle and is the reason everybody came back alive. Chintook lives because of his bravery and ingenuity. Babtoo has given us valuable information about our enemy. We give thanks to the hunting party of Chintook, Ohat, Puku, Ukup and Babtoo. I would be proud to go into battle with these brave warriors."

Babtoo felt tremendous pride, though he did not feel like a great warrior. There were times he had been afraid. There were times he had put his friends at risk because he could not keep up or was not diligent. It was true he had done some things to help, but he had a lot to learn. A look of confusion crossed his face.

Ohat came by his side and saw his confused expression, said, "Babtoo, you are still young, and yet you have done great things. I think you will do more great things. It is true; Chintook tested you beyond your experience in battle, only because he had no choice. You have proven your skill and worth, not just in battle, but also in getting us home alive. I would be proud to fight by your side if the Mautuks come back."

Monbeem joined Ohat and Babtoo. Putting her hand on his

shoulder, she said, "You were very brave. I knew you had greatness in you." A shy smile formed on her lips as she spoke.

Babtoo glanced down at her and his heart almost stopped. Unconsciously he put his hand in hers, "I was trained by the best. I consider Chintook as my father also."

Monbeem blushed with the compliment. Ohat watched the way they looked into each other's eyes and slipped quietly away.

Unnoticed in the background, Hohumph watched Monbeem approach Babtoo. He saw them clasp hands and whisper to one another, holding each other closely. He seethed in anger and wondered how he was going to get rid of the cripple when suddenly his opportunity presented itself.

Bowhut called upon Whutknot to speak to the tribe about Chintook. Whutknot walked slowly into the fading light of the fire. His shoulders slumped down and the light made his face look long and drawn out. He stood there for a time contemplating what to say as he gazed across at the sea of faces. People waited expectantly, hoping for good news. Chintook was well liked by the people in the tribe.

Whutknot almost whispered the bad news. People strained to hear and moved closer to the dying fire to hear more clearly.

"Chintook is dying. I have used all my powders and my supply of herbs to heal him. It stops the fever for a short while and then it comes back. We have been keeping him cool, but he steadily grows weaker. There is only one hope for him, if we can get it in time. On Mount Kikyomanjaro, there is a purple flower. It grows on the mountain by cool springs. I need the root of the flower to combat the fever. Somebody has to gather a supply of this root before I can no longer control his fever. The journey is long and dangerous, but the choice is clear. It must be done to save Chintook from joining the spirit world with his father."

After hearing of the attack of the Mautuk warriors, nobody was quick to volunteer. Finally, Hohumph yelled, "Babtoo should go. He has the magical beast. Only he can get back quickly. The warriors here need to prepare for an attack if it comes."

Everybody turned toward Babtoo. His ribs ached and the claw marks over his body had not yet healed. He looked across at the expectant faces of the tribe and said simply, "I will go."

A cheer went up for Babtoo as a nasty sneer played across Hohumph's mouth. This would get rid of Babtoo so he could have Monbeem all to himself. It was a good day to be Hohumph.

Monbeem gripped his hand tightly, "You are not healed. You cannot make the journey."

Babtoo released her hand and whispered, "I cannot have Chintook die because I would not go. Perhaps Enobi and I are the only hope. Pray to the gods for me."

Babtoo slowly walked back to his tent to get ready for the next day's journey. Monbeem gazed after him, wondering when she would ever see this great warrior again.

CHAPTER 13

THE JOURNEY

The moon shone down on the savanna as a mother looks down at a child. Dawn was quickly approaching. Nocturnal animals made their way toward their burrows, dens, and trees to escape the heat of the upcoming day. Stars winked out as the first rays of the sun crept over the horizon. The moon could not hold the sun at bay much longer and was slowly fading from sight.

The breeze was still cool as it meandered in and out of the tents of the Watinkee village, carrying the sounds and scents of the sleeping tribesmen. Embers from cooking fires flared back to life briefly, as the breeze passed over them, only to die out again when it was gone.

Babtoo awoke to the sound of the corner flap lazily waving back and forth like a tired flag. It was still dark as he collected his supplies from the previous night. Still very sore and stiff, Babtoo carried his pack toward the tent flap. Thinking about his quest, he hoped Enobi had recovered enough for the journey. He did not know how long he would be gone, but hoped he would be back in enough time for Chintook to benefit from the herbs he would be getting. He could not fail.

Lifting the tent flap aside, Babtoo took his first step on his quest and bumped into Monbeem. She had been waiting patiently for him outside his tent. Stunned that anybody would be awake at this hour, Babtoo asked in amazement, "What brings you here at this early hour?"

Monbeem looked him square in the eye, "You are not going to

leave without saying 'goodbye.'" A tear had formed in the corner of her eye, which she quickly wiped away. Holding a small leather pouch, Monbeem untied it and reached inside. She pulled out a leather thong strung with a single shark's tooth.

Almost embarrassed, she held it out for Babtoo and said softly, "Babtoo, I made this for you. I know you wanted a necklace made out of all the shark teeth but I had only time to string just this one. It was the biggest one. Come back swiftly and I will finish it for you."

Babtoo took the necklace gratefully and put it around his neck. "Thank you. I will wear this with honor."

Puffing his chest out with the confidence of a warrior, he said, "I will be back before the new moon rises. You need not worry about me." Inside he was not as sure of his success as many things could happen on the savanna to a lone warrior. Smiling and squeezing her hand, Babtoo walked past her to get to Enobi. He did not look back, afraid he would run back and kiss her.

Enobi was awake and waiting for him. He came trotting over when Babtoo approached. Looking back at the village, he saw the silhouette of Monbeem standing in the darkness. Reaching for Enobi, Babtoo whispered in his ear, "We need to be swift. This quest is dangerous and the quicker we can do this and come back the better it will be."

A stab of pain in his ribs made him gasp as he leapt on Enobi. For a second, Enobi balked and backed up, but quickly settled down under Babtoo's gentle touch and voice.

Still standing next to Babtoo's tent, Monbeem watched him go as he vanished in the early morning darkness. She continued to watch long after he was gone, still savoring the touch of his hand. Casually wiping a tear from her face, she whispered after his retreating form, "I will pray you are safe and swift, Babtoo. You don't have to prove anything more to me. I love you."

Dawn was peeking over the horizon. Birds were waking up and starting to sing their praises to the new day. Small animals scurried across their path startled by the hoof beats as Enobi approached.

Babtoo pointed Enobi north, in the direction Whutknot had told him to go. He said the mountain would come into view in a few days. There he would find the flower and root needed to help Chintook.

Babtoo was alone with his thoughts and his mind kept drifting back to Monbeem. He wondered, "Did she have feelings for him like he had for her? Was Hohumph going to marry her? Chintook was his mentor; would he survive long enough for him to get this precious root? What if he failed? What if he did not come back?" Confidence in his newly found abilities once again began to grow as he thought, "I can do all of this. After all, I am Babtoo." With that last thought, a smile creased his face.

Pushing all the negative thoughts out of his mind, Babtoo decided to concentrate on the mission at hand. Focusing on ways to secure the root quickly, Babtoo scanned the horizon. Enobi was trotting at a comfortable ground-eating pace. From his vantage point on Enobi's back, he could guide him away from danger. He could not see everything, but was aware of the favorite haunts of the lion, jackal, hyena, and panther. Laying his spear across Enobi's back gave him the assurance he needed that everything would be all right.

As the day wore on, the sun beat down mercilessly on the two travelers. Sweat ran down Babtoo, stinging the cuts on his body. The strain on Enobi's leg started to hamper his gait. Babtoo slowed him to just a fast walk. They were learning to work together and he would not cause harm to this wonderful gift from the ocean.

Sliding off, he examined the back leg. It was healing very well. Whutknot gave him a salve to put on his leg to help mend the wound and stave off infection. Applying the salve and looking up into the sun, Babtoo led Enobi to a nearby grove of trees to wait out the hottest part of the day. They would resume later on when it was cooler.

As a precaution, Babtoo climbed a tree to look across the savanna for danger. His ribs ached as he struggled to climb high enough to scan the horizon. Shielding his eyes from the intense sunlight, Babtoo scoured the plains for any kind of menace. Looking in the distance, he searched for the peak of Mount Kikyomanjaro.

In the expanse of the grasslands, he saw what looked like a skinny little monkey standing upright in the shimmering waste. Rubbing his eyes and looking again, the figure disappeared. Focusing on that spot to see if it would reappear, Babtoo convinced himself it was only a figment of his imagination. That strange image would not leave his mind, however, as he sidled back down the tree.

By late afternoon, it had cooled enough to continue their journey. Animals started to mill about in search of food as the day waned. Babtoo climbed back on Enobi to continue their journey. Refreshed from the rest, Enobi started out quickly, enjoying the freedom to move at his own pace. Babtoo concentrated on the terrain around him, paying close attention to any unusual movement. He constantly looked back over his shoulder to try to catch the image that was nagging on his mind. The figure did not show itself for the rest of the day.

The light quickly faded over the horizon. Babtoo spotted a large watering hole up ahead. Approaching the water cautiously, Babtoo looked around for big cats. Seeing none, Babtoo led Enobi toward the water, guarding him as he drank his fill. A log in the middle of the pond was drifting toward them. Babtoo watched the floating log curiously and thought, "What was a log doing out in the middle of the savanna in a pond?" As he wrestled with the question, it soon became apparent as to why. It was no log.

It had ruled this waterhole for decades. The tail was long and powerful. Unblinking eyes stared at Enobi with an insatiable hunger. Large teeth the size of a Watinkee spearhead gleamed dully in the dimming light as it floated closer to the unsuspecting animal. Moving quickly, Babtoo ushered Enobi away from the waterhole.

Breathing heavily from the exertion, Babtoo looked back to watch the big crocodile sink from site, leaving a barely noticeable wake behind. "That was a close call," he thought. It was time to try to find a safe place to settle for the night before the predators started to hunt.

Babtoo found an outcrop not too far away. It sheltered him from the weather and nothing could ambush him from behind. Tying Enobi to a small sapling so he could not go far, Babtoo settled in for the night. From his vantage point, Babtoo could see the watering hole and everything that approached it. Even in the night, the large black log remained visible, swallowing the blackness around it. Floating from one side of the pond to the next, the crocodile patiently waited to waylay its next meal.

CHAPTER 14

CASTEEL

The night sky was bright and clear and constellations of heroic warriors that lived in the stars for eternity shown down on the young tribesman. Babtoo wondered if someday he would be among the great heroes of his tribe. Stars blinked in a hypnotic way and he quickly fell asleep.

It was midnight when Babtoo came instantly awake. The hairs on the back of his neck prickled and rose. Looking around, everything appeared to be normal. Enobi was grazing a short distance away, the night sounds of the crickets had not changed their cadence. Something was amiss but he did not know what. Standing up to get a better view, Babtoo scanned the night hoping to catch what had disrupted his sleep.

Peering at the watering hole, Babtoo spotted what had awakened him. At the water's edge, the spindly looking monkey was getting something to drink. "Odd," he thought, "that monkey almost looks human. But what would a small human be doing out here?"

Unconsciously he grabbed his spear and started walking toward the water to get a better look when he recognized the figure.

It was a Watinkee child. Glancing back at the water, he caught the crocodile drifting closer to the boy. Yelling at the top of his lungs, Babtoo ran as fast as his legs would carry him.

Startled, the child looked his way and froze in place, watching Babtoo's stumbling run down the hill. Picking up his tiny spear, the boy stood there defiantly, not knowing who it was. The big crocodile submerged for the final lunge as it sank below the surface marking the spot where the boy stood.

Babtoo leapt for the boy. The child, in his fright, threw his spear, narrowly missing Babtoo as he dodged the small missile. Grabbing the boy, he rolled out of the way, as the creature propelled itself out of the water to snap at only empty air. Hitting the ground heavily, the ancient creature looked around to find his prey. Instead of a helpless creature, the crocodile found Babtoo standing with a large spear pointed facing him. Angry at missing his victim, the crocodile closed on Babtoo and the boy as it leveraged itself out of the water.

Babtoo thrust the boy behind him knowing he could not outrun the crocodile. The powerful creature rumbled toward him with a roar and with surprising speed. Water dripped from his gaping jaws, making him appear rabid that sent a shiver up his spine.

Without thinking, Babtoo went on the attack, trying to keep the boy behind him. He thrust with his spear and it glanced off the hard reptilian head. Snapping at the spear, the crocodile slowly forced him back. Babtoo quickly thrust again into the less protected body. It became a dance of thrust, shift, and thrust again.

All of a sudden, a small spear arced through the air and stuck in the big crocodile's body. Startled by this new attack, the crocodile turned to face this new adversary, snapping the spear out from his body. The boy stood there stunned that the small weapon had little impact on the creature.

This was the opening Babtoo needed. A final thrust into the soft tissue under his head was enough for the crocodile. Turning quickly toward the water and with a final slap of his tail, he lumbered back toward the safety of his pond and disappeared into the black waters.

Babtoo stood there for a moment gasping for air as sweat poured off his body from the exertion. Glancing at the boy in curiosity, he recognized him from his own Watinkee tribe.

The boy was only ten years old. He was skinny and small for his age. Often times the young children picked on him because he was undersized, and so they never took him seriously. That, however, did nothing to dampen his spirit. Every day he went back out to prove he was just as skilled as the bigger kids were.

At that moment, Babtoo realized they were kindred spirits. He was not alone in his quest for respect. The boy's name was Casteel.

Casteel stood there for a moment shaking like a leaf in high winds. His eyes were like saucers as he stared at the receding form of the crocodile. A tear appeared that he quickly wiped away, not wanting Babtoo to see it. He did not speak as Babtoo approached him, fearing a lecture for following him.

Instead, Babtoo put his arm around him, "Thanks for throwing that spear when you did. I was having a little trouble with him before then."

The ice was broken between them as Casteel fell against him sobbing and shaking, "I'm sorry, Babtoo. I only wanted to help. I did not want you to go looking for the healing root all by yourself. I am big now and can help."

Babtoo looked down on the child with compassion, "What about your mother and father? Won't they be worried about you?"

Casteel big eyes stared upward, "Why would they be worried? I am with Babtoo and the magical beast. What could go wrong?"

Babtoo disengaged himself from the boy and thought, "I can't go back to take Casteel home. Obtaining the flower is too important. His parents will have to wait. Time is everything here. I hope he does not hold me back."

Looking down at Casteel, Babtoo grabbed his arm, "You must do everything I say, if you are to help me."

Casteel nodded his head vigorously, "I will do everything you ask. Just name it."

Babtoo took Casteel's hand and walked back to his campsite. Dawn was approaching and the pink glow on the horizon indicated he had better be on his way. Looking at his new partner, Babtoo asked, "Have you eaten anything, Casteel? I have some supplies for breakfast, but we need to be on our way soon."

Casteel gave him a sideways glance, "You don't have to worry about me. I'm okay." At that moment, a loud grumbling sound was heard from his stomach. "Well, if you insist Babtoo, we can eat first." Casteel said with a lop-sided grin on his young face.

Babtoo pulled out his supplies and shared his breakfast of berries and jerky with his little friend. They ate in silence, chewing thoughtfully on their food. Babtoo could not understand how Casteel gotten this far. He had passed many predators along the way that would have made an easy meal out of the diminutive boy. Only a skillful warrior would have been able to go undetected. He would ask him later on how he was able to find him. For now, it was good to have company, even if it was a little boy.

When they were finished, Babtoo glanced at Casteel and said, "Quickly now, we must be on our way. We have a lot of ground to cover."

Casteel stood up, "I am ready Babtoo" as a big yawn stretched across his young face. "Do you want me to scout ahead?"

Another big yawn stretched his small brown face, as he had not slept in a full day.

Babtoo stood and looked down sternly at the boy and, trying not to chuckle said, "No, you need to ride with me on Enobi. I want you to watch everything behind me so we do not get surprised by any Mautuk warriors."

Casteel glanced at the strange zebra, "Do you think he will let me on his back like he lets you?"

Babtoo walked over to Enobi, "Let's ask him." Stroking Enobi's nose, Babtoo whispered in his ear, "Enobi, I must ask of you another favor. A small child joins our quest. He is too small to walk very far. Will you carry me and the child to Mount Kikyomanjaro?"

Enobi's ears twitched back and forth at the soft touch of Babtoo's hand and gentle voice. Babtoo took that as a yes

Using a rock to help him mount, Babtoo sat down with a grunt. Holding his hand out, he said, "Come on Casteel. It is time to get going. Remember to watch out for Mautuks back there."

Casteel grabbed Babtoo's hand and, with a little trepidation, leaped on Enobi's back. Enobi, a little startled by the extra weight looked back as if to say, "Is that all it is?"

Casteel grabbed Babtoo around the waist as he tried to get comfortable, shifting this way and that. When the little boy finally settled, Babtoo encouraged Enobi to start moving.

The day was beautiful and the experience of the crocodile quickly faded from their memories. They had not traveled far when Babtoo heard a soft snoring. Exhaustion finally had overtaken Casteel and he could no longer stay awake. Smiling to himself, Babtoo glanced back at the tiny warrior.

Enobi kept up a good pace throughout the morning as Babtoo gazed at the surrounding wildlife in wonder. It was amazing to him to see all the different kinds of animals that lived together on the plain. The gazelles, giraffes, Cape buffalo, and wildebeests all seemed to get along and watch out for each other. He noticed that when predators captured an animal, it was usually weak or old. He surmised that tactic must keep the herds healthy.

Midday was approaching and Babtoo scanned the horizon for a place to rest. One lone tree stood out from the savanna as if beckoning him with a chance for some shade. "This would be another good place to get my bearings for Mount Kikyomanjaro," Babtoo thought.

Behind him little Casteel was stirring. With a loud yawn and stretching his limbs in the air, Casteel awoke to find them in a very different place. The terrain was a little rockier with boulders strewn about in haphazard places. The grass was a little shorter and with fewer trees.

Babtoo glanced back at him and casually asked, "Casteel, have you seen any Mautuks following us?"

Casteel was instantly alert and turned to look knowing he had fallen asleep on the important job Babtoo had given him. Embarrassed, he looked down contritely and mumbled, "I am sorry, Babtoo. I fell asleep, but I will not let that happen again. I see nothing now."

Babtoo cracked a smile, knowing he could never have stayed awake and said, "Casteel, I will give you another chance. If you are to help me, you need to be diligent and do what I ask."

"Thank you Babtoo. I will not let you down. I really only slept for a moment you know!" Casteel said jubilantly.

Babtoo could not suppress the laugh that bubbled out of him. The enthusiasm of little Casteel reminded him of himself when he was a boy. He could not help but to admire this little warrior who had greatness written all over him

Babtoo guided Enobi toward the tree, scaring a couple of warthogs away from their burrow. There he slid off and helped Casteel down. Leaning against the tree, Babtoo looked upwards in the branches. Babtoo took his shirt off to fan himself and did not realize Casteel had not seen the panther wounds that crisscrossed his body. Red and still puckered from the attack, the scars would be noticeable for the rest of his life.

Casteel looked upon the wounds in admiration, "I'll bet that hurt. They say you killed the panther by yourself. That must have been a great spear throw. I wish I could kill a panther." Casteel waved his little spear around as if being attacked.

Babtoo winced as Casteel moved about. A little embarrassed by the compliment, Babtoo reached over and put his arm on Casteel's shoulder, "You will get your chance. But let's get through this adventure together first before we take on another panther."

Pointing up the tree, Babtoo asked, "How fast can you climb this tree? We need to see how far Mount Kikyomanjaro is."

Casteel looked up, and before Babtoo could say another word, climbed faster than a chimpanzee. Shading his eyes, Casteel looked into the distance. Impressed, Babtoo asked, "Can you see it from there?"

Casteel looked down from the branches and said excitedly, "I see it! I see it! It's over there! It has many clouds around it. It must reach all the way up to the heavens!"

Babtoo considered and wondered about that.

Dropping to the ground, Casteel could barely contain himself. His eyes danced with the exuberance of youth. Hopping around Babtoo like a wild child, Casteel shouted, "I am ready to go! I have seen the big mountain!"

Babtoo, equally excited, lifted the small child onto the back of Enobi, grunting from the pain in his bruised ribs. Grabbing the mane, he swung himself up carefully and sat down heavily. Once they settled, Enobi trotted out into the blazing sun. Casteel remembered his duty and looked back intently to watch for any Mautuk warriors following them. He was happy Babtoo still had faith in him after he had fallen asleep the first time. He vowed it would not happen again.

The long wrinkled nose hung down in search of young succulent plants in the drying sun. Finding a clump of young green grass, the articulating nose reached out and grabbed the lush growth, tearing it up from the ground. Coiling her trunk around the clump of vegetation like a gigantic snake, she inserted it into her large mouth. Chewing contentedly, she absently looked around for her trailing family.

She was the matriarch of a large elephant herd. She had been matriarch for forty years and what caught her eye this day was something she had never seen in all her long life.

A large spotted zebra was trotting by with two growths on its back that turned this way and that. They made strange sounds and carried long sticks. The larger growth seemed to be dominant and carried the scent of man.

Bewildered by what she saw, her large ears flapped back and forth while trying to decide if they were enemies. The sensitive trunk rose in the air and swiveled toward them attempting to catch a recognizable scent.

Gathering courage, she issued a loud challenge and charged a short way even though fear churned in her belly. Dating back to the wooly mammoths, man had always hunted them. Born with that memory from ancient times, she quickly stepped back and gathered her family to disappear into the brush.

Babtoo's heart was racing. That was a narrow escape. He knew Enobi could outrun the elephant if he was healthy and only carried him on his back. Fortunately, for all of them, they did not have to find out if he could.

Casteel's fear turned into excitement and he said proudly, "I told you there were elephants around. I saw them following us after we left the tree!"

Babtoo turned and gave Casteel an approving look, "Yes, little warrior, you have redeemed yourself in my eyes."

Casteel looked as if he would burst from the compliment. Hugging Babtoo from behind, his smile stretched from ear to ear. He redoubled his efforts to be sure he missed nothing. Traveling with Babtoo made him feel like he could do anything. Babtoo was the only person that had faith in him and he would not let him down!

Topping a small rise, Babtoo could at last see what Casteel had seen in the tree. In the distance, clouds swirled around the peak of the mountain. The clouds draped over mountaintop, shrouding it in mystery. The top of the peak was white and seemed to push itself up and over the swirling haze. They could now see how vast Mount Kikyomanjaro was.

Babtoo was excited, but soon his heart sank. He thought, "How am I going to find a blue flower in something so large?" Daunted by the task, he rode closer and closer to the mountain. It soon seemed to cover the entire landscape and he wondered why they had not seen it before now.

Casteel, however, did not feel the same way. Shouting with youthful anticipation, Casteel pointed with his little spear, "We have found it and our journey is almost ended. All we have to do is find the flower and go home." A note of homesickness was in his voice.

Babtoo pushed his doubts aside. "You're right little one. We are well on our way to finding that flower. We'll get there by tomorrow and then can start searching. But look, the sun sinks behind the mountain. Let's start hunting for a place to spend the night. They watched in awe as the sun turned the sky surrounding the mountain red, then orange, then yellow as it slowly disappeared from sight. Babtoo turned Enobi toward a stunted tree on a hill to make camp.

Collecting a little bit of wood, they risked a small fire. They had covered a lot of ground quickly and both of them needed rest. Babtoo thought a warm meal so near their goal would keep their spirits up. Watching Casteel busy himself around the fire, Babtoo finally asked him about his journey across the savanna. "Casteel, you had traveled far to find me. How did you do it? The journey had to be dangerous. Were you not afraid?"

Casteel looked down on the ground and traced a figure in the dirt that resembled Enobi. At last, he spoke as he collected his thoughts. "I tried to get up with the sun to ask if I could go with you, but I had overslept," he began. "When I did wake up, I rushed outside to find you, but you had already left. I saw Monbeem staring off in the distance and so thought that was a good direction to go. It was not hard at first to track you. Your magical beast leaves large deep prints. But, it got harder to track the deeper into the plains you went. I could tell I was not going to catch you after a while. But I had come too far to turn back and I wanted to help you!" he said defiantly.

Continuing on when Babtoo said nothing, "I noticed your path was not straight but curved around many times. I only know this from the sun. I found out why when I heard lions roaring or the cackling of the hyena in the distance. Many times, I lost your track. I was scared I would not find you and it was getting dark. I could only go on and then I saw eyes following me, blinking here and there in the starlight. Sometimes they were in front of me and other times behind me. I started to run when I could no longer follow your trail. It seemed I ran forever when I came upon the lake. I had not brought any water and was very thirsty."

As if reliving the story, Casteel took a long drink out of Babtoo's water skin. When he continued, he shook off the nightmare and continued, "That's when you showed up out of nowhere. It was amazing how you dodged my perfectly aimed spear and saved me from that crocodile."

Babtoo shifted to hide the smile on his face at that last remark, trying not to mock the ten-year-olds bravado.

Peering at him through the crackling flames, Babtoo said with a seriousness that caught the boy's attention, "You should not have come after me. It was a dangerous and stupid thing to do. If you had died out there, the guilt I would have felt may have been too much." A look of discouragement swept over Casteel's face.

"Your parents will be very worried. However, you have shown outstanding bravery and courage and I commend you on your tracking skills. I shall not forget this. I am glad you're here with me today, little brother." The last thing Babtoo said picked up Casteel's spirits and gave him confidence once again. He knew he was wrong, but the call for adventure was too strong for his young spirit to ignore. After all, he was Casteel, and he was with Babtoo, a great a strong warrior.

The next day was bright and clear. They were able to see the mountain for the first time in all its glory. It was a little overwhelming at first as the two of them stared at the grandeur in front of them. Clouds ringing the mountain seemed ripe with moisture. Gauging the distance, Babtoo picked a path that would lead them to the base of the mountain where he thought would be a good place to start their exploration for the root.

Enobi picked his way through the terrain at a snail's pace. Rocks were scattered about the plain in a haphazard manner. Some were very large boulders and others the size of a man's fist. Ravines cut deeply into the plain, slicing through the landscape and feathering out into lush green patches of grass with an occasional tree.

The abundance of small animals astonished Babtoo. Rabbits raced away hearing Enobi's approaching steps. Small mice and ground squirrels scurried into their burrows only to reappear again after they had passed. The absence of larger game surprised Babtoo.

Perhaps, he thought, it was because the terrain was rough and rocky which prevented them from moving quickly.

The day faded into dusk when they found a particularly wide, but shallow ravine carved at the base of the mountain. The ravine ran up the mountain and was lost from sight as it curved to the other side. Darkness hid the deep shadows and crevices that crisscrossed the ravine from all sides.

Looking up, Babtoo saw a slight resemblance the mountain had to Whutknot's old and deeply lined face. Chuckling at the thought, Babtoo wondered what Whutknot would say if he knew what he was thinking.

The terrain was too steep for Enobi to continue and Babtoo thought this would be a good spot for him to get food and rest. Dismounting, Babtoo looked at Casteel. "How good are you at throwing that spear?" he asked. "I will make a small fire if you can catch a rabbit to eat."

Casteel looked up with conviction. "You will have your rabbit tonight. I saw several coming out to feed on the grass while I was watching for Mautuks. You will see! We will not go hungry!"

Babtoo watched as Casteel scampered around the bend. He had no doubt Casteel would catch a rabbit or some other small game. A Watinkee child is born with a spear in his hand and taught how to use it effectively at a young age.

Babtoo started the fire and let Enobi graze. The small fire reflected off the nearby stone face distorting his shadow as it played along the cliff face. The ravine's inky blackness seemed to absorb the little flame as it flickered weakly. Babtoo peered up the ravine hoping to see a trail or path in the murky darkness. This would be a challenge for him, he knew, as he looked down at his crippled leg.

Before long, Casteel ran around the corner holding up two large rabbits for Babtoo to see. He said proudly, "Look, one for you and one for me."

Babtoo, admiring the two rabbits said, "Nice job, Casteel. That takes the skill of a warrior to hunt not just one rabbit, but two in the small amount of time it took you. Let's eat. We have a big day tomorrow and will need our strength."

Casteel beamed from the compliment and started skinning the rabbits. After their meal, Babtoo and Casteel got comfortable and fell into a deep sleep. Dreams of the elusive root just out of reach made sleeping restless for Babtoo.

Babtoo awoke later in the morning than expected while Casteel still slept comfortably. The mountain shaded them from the morning sun, keeping the ravine cloaked in darkness.

Babtoo nudged Casteel gently awake with his toe. The sleepy child yawned and stretched, looking expectantly at Babtoo for guidance. Making a hasty breakfast, the two gazed up the treacherous mountain path. The task seemed overwhelming, but Babtoo showed confidence and would not be daunted. Casteel was in high spirits and almost pulled Babtoo forward on the quest for the purple flower. They left Enobi grazing comfortably in the relative safety of the ravine until their return.

The shadows never receded far and only lightened a shade or two as the morning progressed. The two warriors worked their way up the ravine as the sunlight gathered strength. The climb was hard and perilous with large boulders deposited in the middle of the path that had to be gone around. Rockslides had caved in partial areas of the ravine that needed climbed over or another route found. Each obstruction was exhausting work for Babtoo.

The ravine never seemed to run out of obstacles. Babtoo's foot ached and his ribs hurt, yet he could not stop or give up. Chintook's life was far too important. Casteel was looking for him to lead the way. An inner voice kept him focused to push forward and a vision of Monbeem waiting for him when he returned hardened his resolve.

Casteel saw the look of determination on Babtoo's face as they worked their way toward the top of the crevice and was determined not to slow Babtoo down. He saw Babtoo's limp, but pretended not to notice.

Babtoo's aching ribs heaved as they reached the top of the ravine in the late morning. The air seemed thin making breathing even more difficult. Sweat poured off their bodies and yet, it was not hot.

A look of disappointment crossed Babtoo's face as he wiped the perspiration from his forehead. The distance they had traveled was not far and they could still see Enobi grazing peacefully in the ravine below. Babtoo looked at the climb ahead and saw small animal trails that ran erratically up the mountain.

Taking the lead, Babtoo said, "Casteel, we must go on. It's almost noon and we have to find Chintook's medicine quickly before it gets dark. Climbing in the day is bad enough, but if we have to go back in the dark, it will be very dangerous."

Casteel stood, and said with the confidence, "Let's go, Babtoo. Where do we go from here?"

Looking intently at the ground, Babtoo had an idea. His eyes traced the animal trails and followed the largest and widest one as it disappeared in the distance.

"Casteel, we'll follow the largest animal tracks. All animals need water. They should lead us to a watering hole and that's where we should find the flower."

Casteel nodded his head vigorously and said, "I can track Babtoo. Let me go first."

Babtoo looked at the youngster as he hopped from one foot to the other, his face beaming with excitement. Perhaps he should go first and then he could better keep an eye on him. With a nod, Babtoo agreed, "O.K., Casteel. You have proven you are a good hunter. Follow the tracks that lead to the largest trail. With luck, they in turn will lead to water and that's where we will find the flower."

Leaping forward like a hound on a scent, little Casteel started forward. Babtoo smiled inwardly. He liked Casteel and secretly was glad he was with him. He would make a fine warrior someday. Hurrying along, Babtoo quickly followed.

The trail only proved to be more difficult. The terrain was hard and rocky. At times Casteel lost the trail in the hard packed soil. Babtoo would then retrace their steps to search beyond the path in the adjacent landscape. Adept at seeking out clues on where to pick the best direction , Babtoo would locate the trail further up the mountain.

Trained by Chintook, Babtoo was an excellent tracker and enjoyed teaching Casteel the little tidbits of information that would make him into a great tracker too. Casteel was more than a willing student. Traversing a particular narrow and steep ledge, Casteel found a large pit with water in the center. There, a large number of trails converged down to the watering hole.

The water was clear and fed from inside the mountain. Water trickled down a rocky embankment and fell several feet into the pond, sounding like a soft rainfall in spring. Small fernlike plants dotted the banks, curling their broad leaf-like fronds toward the water, brushing the surface lazily in the breeze.

On the far side of the pond in the dappled sunlight grew the purple flower for which they were desperately searching. The plants grew in the water on tall stalks, sinking their roots into the soft mud like water lilies. Swaying gently in the breeze, they beckoned the two travelers to come closer.

Before Babtoo could stop Casteel, the boy ran and leaped over rocks and a rather large limb half in and half out of the water to get to the mesmerizing plants. Still not convinced everything was safe, he watched the boy wade into the water to reach the purple flowers.

Babtoo started to walk toward the water hole when the large limb started to move. Frozen for a second, he watched as a large python snake slithered toward Casteel. It lifted its head like a periscope above the fronds and flicked its tongue in and out, closing in on the unsuspecting Casteel.

Babtoo let out a yell and threw his spear trying to hit the serpent in the concealing foliage, hoping it would be enough to give Casteel a chance get away. The spear flew harmlessly in the fronds surrounding the snake. Startled, Casteel looked up as Babtoo yelled. Staring into the python's hypnotic eyes, Casteel stood as if in a trance, powerless to move. Slithering closer, the snake raised its head above the fronds, swaying back and forth as it coiled for a strike.

Babtoo drew his knife and in a stumbling run leapt for the head of the snake. Grabbing it by the neck and forcing it down, they rolled on the ground. Surprised at the serpent's strength, Babtoo stabbed downward, losing his knife as the coils quickly wrapped around his body. His muscles heaved as he forced the snake from his chest, freeing an arm. For only a moment, Babtoo took in a deep lung full of air before it again started to tighten. Casteel stood motionless, too shocked to do anything but gape at the fierce battle.

Out of the corner of his eye, Babtoo saw a large boulder with sharp edges. His muscles protested with the attempt to get to his knees and he struggled to stand on shaky legs. The immense weight of the snake sapped his strength. His breaths came in shallow gasps as bright spots swirled around his darkening vision.

Desperate for oxygen, Babtoo crashed into the jagged rock, banging the constrictor's head on the unyielding surface. Stunned, the snake relaxed enough at the shock of the blow allowing Babtoo to take a deep breath. Rolling to where he dropped his knife before the monster could start crushing again, Babtoo stabbed downward into the muscular body. In an instant, he could breathe again as the large snake dropped to the ground. Wounded, the boa constrictor slithered its broken body awkwardly toward the water and disappeared down a dark hole.

Gulping huge amounts of air, Babtoo fell to his knees as his battered ribs screamed in agony. With each breath he took, his ribs protested from the effort.

Casteel ran up to him and embraced him. The howl of pain that greeted him made him quickly let go and step back. Casteel, scared and unsure, mumbled, "What can I do?"

Babtoo said nothing for a long time, waiting for the pain to subside. Casteel stood there wringing his hands, watching Babtoo struggle to breathe. Once he caught his breath and the pain subsided,

Babtoo looked at Casteel and said, "Finish getting those plants. Let's get out of here before that snake decides he's hungry again."

Casteel, spurred into action, raced over to pick as many of the plants as he could carry. Babtoo sat up and examined his body. His ribs were turning black and blue already. He had a few minor cuts, but those would heal.

Casteel returned with a bunch of plants under his arms and stood waiting obediently.

Struggling to get to his feet, Babtoo groaned and said, "Do you remember the way back little one?"

Casteel nodded, not able to speak. This was the second time Babtoo had saved his life. Perhaps he was not ready to be a warrior after all.

"Lead on then and don't go too fast." Babtoo said

They got back to camp well after dusk as the oncoming darkness made it difficult to navigate the steep ravine. More than once, loosened pebbles turned into small landslides making their footing hazardous.

Arriving back at camp, Babtoo checked on Enobi. The animal was well rested and he whinnied excitedly when he saw Babtoo. Exhausted and hurting, Babtoo rolled into his bedroll and fell into a deep sleep. Casteel looked on at his hero. Truly, this was a great man. Nobody in his short life has ever beaten a serpent constrictor. Not even the great stories around the campfire told of such great feats. Casteel remained on guard as long as he could before his eyes became too heavy to stay open. Then he too fell into a deep sleep dreaming of giant crocodiles and huge snakes.

CHAPTER 15

THE PLAN

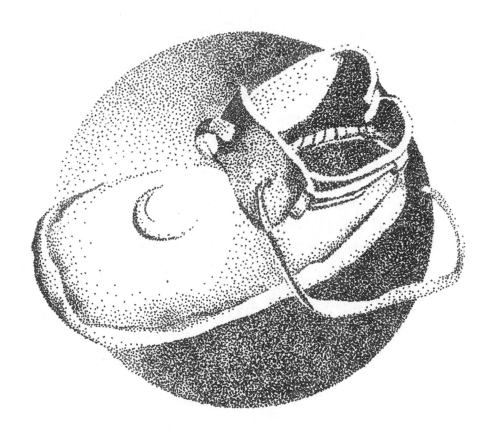

The long spear was not impressive. The metal tip was dull and jagged from lack of care and a single crow's feather hung listlessly in the slight breeze. Bright colors of red and green sloppily applied down the length of the spear had long since faded into dull shades of copper and brown.

A plump, grimy hand gripped the spear loosely while the other hand clenched and unclenched spasmodically. He had a paunch that he tried to cover with an overly large shirt that was greasy and dirty that matched the care of his spear.

The face looked brutish with a large nose turned to one side and small eyes that squinted into the sun. Lips the size of monkey's thumbs were chapped and drawn down in a scowl. His brow was always furrowed and wrinkled, as if thinking deep thoughts, but people knew him more for his devious actions and strong opinions.

Hohumph sat and brooded over Monbeem's affection for Babtoo. He thought, "I was lucky to convince the Watinkee tribe to have Babtoo retrieve the healing root for Whutknot's treatment of Chintook. I'm also glad I didn't have to go with Babtoo. I know the trip will be dangerous and hope Babtoo does not return. But with that magical beast he controls, I'm not so certain Babtoo will fail, and that is my problem."

Scratching his nose, Hohumph thought, "If Chintook dies, Monbeem will have nobody to look after her. I've been hunting for her when Chintook is away and even now while he lays wounded. My chances are pretty good to ask for her hand in marriage. The counsel elders would grant me that because of all that I have done for her. Marrying Monbeem would increase my status in the tribe!"

"But if Babtoo were to come back, she might not agree to marry me, then. On the other hand, if Babtoo didn't come back, or was unsuccessful getting the flower, Monbeem would have to marry me. I wonder if I would be able to control the magical beast. It would go a long way to impress Monbeem. How can I get Babtoo to leave and never return?" A devilish smile formed on his face as the beginning of a plan formed in his mind.

It was dusk and rabbits were coming out of their holes. Hohumph had waited patiently for several hours to get one. He was sick of rabbits. Nobody wanted him to go on a big hunt, which was O.K. with him. It was too much effort and too dangerous to go after bigger game. He would be content with what he could kill by himself and carry back to Monbeem. Even she started looking at other cooking pots to see what they had. Shrugging his shoulders at the thought, she would have to get used to it for now. A skinny rabbit twitched its nose as it hopped from behind a bush.

The stars were out in force when Hohumph started back to the village. It had not been a good day for hunting. He fiddled with the one skinny rabbit on his belt and wondered if it was because he had a lot on his mind. He was sure of one thing and that was he was going to see Monbeem again. Looking down at his rabbit, he knew this would be no prize, but it was something to offer her. They would not go hungry tonight. His mood changed at the thought of seeing her smiling face again.

Approaching the village from the grasslands, Hohumph slowed down and did not want to seem overeager. Negotiating the maze of tents and huts, Hohumph skirted some of the more prominent warrior's huts to escape embarrassment for today's small catch. Stepping from behind a tent, Hohumph caught Monbeem tanning the large black panther skin Babtoo had killed.

Uncontrolled anger erupted from him as he kicked a small stone into the fire, creating a shower of sparks. Throwing the rabbit down, he said, "Monbeem! Why do you do this? The skin will wait until he gets home. I have brought you another rabbit to cook. I am hungry."

Monbeem turned her head to look at him. Her eyes glinted with unconcealed loathing. "I am proud to do this for Babtoo. I want it to be ready when he returns. He deserves your respect at least. You did not have to go on that dangerous journey that you volunteered him to do. He was man enough to know Chintook's life was at stake."

Hohumph backed up and said, "I would have gone but was afraid I would have slowed him down. I bring you food instead. Who has hunted for you when nobody would? It is I, Hohumph that shares everything with you."

Glancing down at the scrawny rabbit, Monbeem sighed, "Yes, you have brought us food. Chintook is grateful you have hunted for us. I will tell him of all the wild beasts you have brought back for food."

Ignoring the gibe, Hohumph accepted her statement as a truce. Watching Monbeem skinning the rabbit, he imagined what life would be like if she were his. Sprinkling the rabbit with a few herbs she had found, she began cooking the meat. It was not long before the scent of rabbit filled the air. Hohumph could hardly wait.

Reaching over Monbeem to get the meat, Hohumph brushed up against her. The smell of his clothes was offensive and she almost gagged. Turning away in anger, Monbeem said, "Hohumph! Can you not wait until I have finished cooking it? It is still not done!"

Hohumph bit a huge piece from the small rabbit and said, "I will save you some. After all, I need my strength to go hunting."

With that, he tore off a leg and handed it to Monbeem. "See, I am most generous," he said as he rubbed his belly. "If we were to be married, you would get more. Have you thought about it much?"

Monbeem looked straight at him and glowered, saying, "Hohumph, I am grateful for all that you do for me and Chintook. We will pay you somehow, but I will not marry you!"

Hohumph peered at her through hooded eyes and said, "Maybe

you will change your mind. You will see. I am a great warrior. You don't know all the things I can do."

With that, he pounded on his chest.

After gulping down his meal, Hohumph decided to go back to his tent. He took a circuitous route so he could hear all the gossip of the camp. People were sitting around campfires, talking about Chintook's health, and if Babtoo would be back in time. The warrior's life was slowly slipping away. Whutknot had done all that he could and hoped Babtoo would return in time.

Hohumph thought, "Good, if Babtoo is late, and he dies, I will have a better chance with Monbeem. She will need me to be a provider and protector. I hope he fails in his quest and is too late to save Chintook. Then I wonder what the village will say about him."

Continuing on, he stopped by one of the outer tents and heard Casteel's mother crying. Casteel had been missing for two days, now. His father, Norbuck, had taken some of the tribe's best trackers and scoured the land around the village looking for some sign of the boy. They had found a small set of boy's tracks that could have been Casteel's, but lost them in a wildebeest herd that covered miles on the open plain. As the days went by, she was losing hope of finding him.

Norbuck stood stoically with the trackers and his friends. He placed his hand on his wife's shoulder to lend his strength and support. Nevertheless, he too was upset. His shoulders slumped down and his head turned toward the side as he quickly wiped a tear from his face. Kneeling down, he hugged his wife and ushered her into their tent.

The warriors who had helped track Casteel whispered in low voices about their futile efforts to find the small boy. Hohumph leaned a little closer and pretended to be polishing his spear. He found they had gone north when they lost his tracks. He knew the boy was smaller and weaker than other children his age were. He often thought, "Oh well. He would have been no good anyway. He probably would not have amounted to much because he is so weak and small. Only the strong become Watinkee warriors."

Unconcerned, Hohumph shrugged his shoulders and continued on his way. His mind was busy calculating a way to increase his stature in the tribe and look good in Monbeem's eyes. Deep in thought and not paying attention, he stubbed his toe on a tent stake. His spear went flying as he crashed to the ground. Sprawled on the hard packed earth like a giant toad, Hohumph heard an explosion of laughter at his expense. Grabbing his spear and using it as a cane, Hohumph hopped on one foot toward his tent, growling at their mirth and silencing even the boldest one, "I will show them. They will not laugh at me anymore."

Once back at his tent, Hohumph threw his spear in the corner and flopped down on some animal skins. Seething at his bad luck, he massaged his stubbed toe. He knew it would not take long before the whole village was laughing at his misstep. Perhaps he could redeem himself and save what little respect he had.

Thinking back to the little boy, Casteel, Hohumph grasped on to a despicable thought, "What if I go searching for the little kid? I know he went north. Maybe I could find him. Better yet, maybe I could pretend to look for him. He is probably dead by now anyway. I'll tell Monbeem that I intend to find him. She'll think I'm brave and noble, and then I'll ask her to help me. She knows Casteel's family and will do everything she can to help find him. Then I can have her all to myself and she will see that I am a great warrior once we're out on the savannah."

With a self-satisfied smile, he laid his head down to sleep on the musty, dirty skins thinking of Monbeem and the glory he would receive from finding the child. Satisfied, he fell asleep almost instantly; his loud snores could be heard five huts down.

Waking up the next morning, Hohumph felt refreshed. His plan was beginning to form as to what he would do. He thought to himself, "I want everybody to know what I'll be doing. First, I need to do is talk to Chief Bowhut and get his blessing for the journey. I'll leave out the part about taking Monbeem. They'll find out later that she decided to go and think she wants to help me on her own. Chief Bowhut will tell the village what I am about to do and this will get me the respect I deserve. Before I go, though, I will steal some of Casteel's clothes and hide them out on the savanna ahead of time. When we find them, this will show Monbeem what a good tracker I am."

He smiled broadly, as his plan came together. Standing up, he forgot about his stubbed toe and howled in pain as he tried to walk. Looking down at his swollen toe, a frown replaced the smile. He would wait for the swelling to go down before he could execute his plan.

Limping out of his hut, he went toward Casteel's tent. Hohumph found a spot where he could watch the activity there and be unobserved. He hung around the tent waiting for Floret, Norbuck's wife to leave. The sun was climbing into the sky and she had not appeared out of her tent. Anxious to proceed with his plan, he dumped the water pot on the ground when nobody was looking.

Calling softly, Hohumph said, "Floret, it is I, Hohumph. I have come to ask you if there is any news about Casteel. I am very worried and want to help."

Floret peeked out of the tent flap. Her eyes were teary and swollen from crying and her hands shook from worry. She peered at him with doubt, but was desperate for somebody to help find her son. Stepping out into the bright sun, she wiped the tears from her eyes with shaky hands and said in an agonized whisper, "We don't know where he is. Norbuck sent the out the best hunters to find him and they lost his tracks in a herd of wildebeest. Around the wildebeest were lion track." She paused as she wiped a tear form her face, "We fear the worst."

She hung her head in her hands and started crying once again. Hohumph had little sympathy and no patience for her weeping, "Maybe I can help. I will look for your boy now. Perhaps I can get lucky and find him."

Floret peeked behind tear-stained eyes and looked at him queerly. This was not the Hohumph she knew. Fresh tears began to flow as she stepped up and hugged him saying, "We would be grateful for anything you can do to find him." Looking down at the empty water pot, Floret picked it up and said, "Now I must go. Norbuck likes fresh water when he comes home." She scurried off to fill the jug.

Hohumph had his chance. Looking casually around to see if anybody was looking, he quickly stepped into the tent. Rummaging around, he found a small shirt and pair of Casteel's moccasins. Taking these items and stuffing them in his shirt, Hohumph slipped from the tent and proceeded to limp toward Chief Bowhut's tent.

Chief Bowhut was talking to Puku. The concerns of a Mautuk attack overshadowed his usual jovial demeanor. Extra scouts searched the trail that Chintook and his hunters had taken hoping for more clues to their activity.

Puku had led a band of hunters to scout for any signs of the crafty Mautuks in the area. They returned and searched the cave Babtoo discovered and found the remains of past sacrifices. Chief Bowhut looked grim as they reported what they had seen.

Chief Bowhut asked gravely, "How goes it with your scouting, Puku? Did you find the cave that Babtoo had discovered and was it as bad as he said? He is young, and young warriors could be prone to exaggeration. I was hoping it could have been just some animal bones and a healthy imagination."

"I wish I could say it was his imagination," Puku responded. "In fact, it was just as he had said and more. There was recent use in that cave by the Mautuks. I found several human bones and skulls in a fire pit. I don't know what tribe they were from, or if they brought their prisoners with them to sacrifice for their scouting mission. The paintings are still fresh on the wall and drawn in blood."

Puku paused before going on, "I saw evidence of about a dozen Mautuk scouts in and around the cave. Babtoo must have wounded the one that escaped pretty badly because I found partially burned and bloody bandages in the fire pit. As a warning, they left a spear in the ground. I scouted around the cave, but they must not have left a rear guard behind to watch. We were lucky to have fought only a small number of their scouting party. Maybe they had enough and won't come back."

Bowhut nodded and said, "I thought when we had beaten them before that they would never return. We should have chased them into the sea. We lost many brothers to their spears and arrows that day. They are a dark stain on our land and if it is a scouting force as you say, then they have gotten what they came for to take back to their homeland. If you saw a spear, it could be that they will return."

Hohumph sidled up to the tent to listen in on the conversation, trying to stay invisible. If the Mautuks were in the area, he would go the opposite way to look for Casteel. Hohumph knew he was not a brave man. "Better to run today to be better able to run tomorrow is my motto," he thought.

Ohat rounded the corner and almost bumped into Hohumph. He looked oddly at Hohumph as he passed, wondering what he was up to. Overhearing the conversation Chief Bowhut was having with Puku, Ohat said, "We have killed four of their scouts. They will retaliate. Do not be lulled into thinking they will not return. They intend to do us harm. We should bring the fight to them instead of waiting for them to attack us."

Chief Bowhut retorted, "No, we'll not take the fight to them. We will protect our land, but we can't follow them into the forest. We know nothing of what to expect in that dark place. I have sent warriors to scout the forest only to have them never return. I won't sacrifice my friends and warriors with the limited knowledge of their land. If I could unite the other Watinkee tribes for this single cause, then maybe we could make the attempt." Turning toward Ukup, Chief Bowhut asked, "What did you see, Ukup?"

Ukup listened intently as the conversation got a little heated and said, "I went to the coast to search for Mautuks. I did find old campfires and discarded gear. Several trails were leading to our village. I think they plan to single out our village, and so we must be wary. They cannot fight all the combined Watinkee tribes, but they can defeat us one tribe at a time. Once they establish themselves here, we will never be at peace."

Bowhut could only agree. Shaking his head, he said, "We'll continue to scout the area. If they attack, it will be before the great wildebeest migration that we follow. If they have not attacked by the start of the migration, then they'll probably wait until next year."

Hohumph shivered at this news. This was no time to be out looking for a lost boy. He was probably already dead. He hoped to travel in the opposite direction of where the Mautuks were seen last. Losing his nerve to talk to Chief Bowhut, Hohumph slunk back to his tent to think.

Once there, Hohumph took out Casteel's clothes that he had stolen. Taking his hunting knife out, he cut the shirt into strips, tearing it where he could. Looking at his handiwork, a sick smile crossed his face. Hohumph thought, "When I go out hunting, I'll soak some of these strips in blood. Wherever I place these strips, it will appear that beasts attacked him. Then everybody will know that is why he is still missing, maybe never to return. The village will be glad that we found something." His mind shifted to Monbeem, "I'll lead Monbeem to these bloody rags once we're on the trail. She'll think I am a great tracker. People will congratulate us on finding the clothes and I will become a hero in everybody's eyes.'"

Hohumph's idea had finally come together. He would wait until evening to hunt and soak some of the strips of clothes in rabbit's blood. Tomorrow he would inform Chief Bowhut of his plans.

The moon was the only light in the sky for Hohumph to see as he smeared rabbit's blood on Casteel's clothes. As if knowing his plans, a cloud passed over the moon, concealing his cowardly act in darkness. Placing the small moccasins and shirt in a leather pouch, Hohumph started back toward the village.

Walking directly to Monbeem's fire, Hohumph threw down his three rabbits. With a sideways glance, Hohumph said, "I have brought you three rabbits instead of one. I was hoping you would help me with something."

Monbeem looked directly at him and said, "What do you want Hohumph? If it is to cook these rabbits tonight, it is late."

"No, no, that is not it. Although I am hungry," he said slyly. He continued, "You know that Casteel is missing. I am worried for him and so I stopped by his family's tent. Floret cries big tears and has little hope. Chief Bowhut has sent out some trackers but they lost his tracks in a wildebeest herd. The main scouting party is out hunting for food or searching for the whereabouts of the Mautuks and they have not seen him." Hohumph paused to see what her reaction would be.

Monbeem looked at him with tears at the corner of her eyes. She tried to wipe the tears away, but they slid down her face like raindrops, leaving a glistening trail.

Hohumph had hoped that would be her reaction. Before she could speak, he grabbed her hands in his and said with as much sincerity as he could muster, "I feel the same way too. I want to go out and look for him. However, it is too dangerous to go out by myself and I don't think Chief Bowhut has anybody to spare. Would you go out with me to help find Casteel?"

Before she had a chance to think it through, Monbeem extracted her hands from Hohumph and said, "Of course I'll come. I'm good with a spear and am a fine tracker. Chintook has taught me much. Sometimes I think he wishes I were a boy. I can do nothing more for Chintook with Whutknot there. Whutknot is doing all he can and I just seem to get in the way. I just hope Babtoo gets back in time." She said with a sad smile.

Hohumph quickly hid the frown that was beginning to form on his face at the mention of Babtoo's name. Standing up, he said, "Yes, I hope so too. I would like to see Chintook stand one more time in the sun laughing with you. However, I am hungry, let us cook these rabbits and eat. We need a good meal for our journey tomorrow!"

A little warning bell in Monbeem's head gave her some

trepidation. She ignored it, and thought, "Is it because I dislike Hohumph so much? This is a very brave thing for him to do and I want to help Casteel's family. How can I refuse to aid Hohumph in this? I cannot let my dislike for him get in the way of helping to find little Casteel."

With that last argument put to rest, she became at peace with herself. Cooking the rabbits, Hohumph and Monbeem talked about where they would start looking first and what supplies they would need.

First thing tomorrow, Hohumph would tell the chief of their plans. He got up to leave and tried to kiss her, but Monbeem turned away and said, "Hohumph, we are not married."

He turned to go and a devious smile formed on his face. "We shall see Monbeem what you think of me when this is over." With that thought, Hohumph fairly skipped home thinking how well his plan was coming together.

At first light, Hohumph gathered supplies for their journey. Stuffing Casteel's bloodstained clothes in a leather pouch, Hohumph tucked it away inside his sweat stained shirt. The dawn brought the bustle of early morning activities when he stepped out of his tent. Walking briskly toward Monbeem's tent, Hohumph listened to the awakening tribesmen, thinking, "Soon they will be talking about me and Monbeem on our epic journey to find Casteel. They will be saying Hohumph's name along with Monbeem's in the same breath."

Upon arriving at Monbeem's tent, Hohumph waited impatiently outside. Not hearing anything, he decided to risk going inside. Pushing the flap aside, he saw that Monbeem was still sleeping. She was so beautiful with a look of peace on her gentle face. Her lips parted slightly as her chest rose and fell with each breath.

Hohumph stood over her for a full minute before her eyes fluttered open. Looking startled, she said, "Hohumph, what are you doing in here?" as she clutched the blanket around her more closely.

Hohumph whispered, "I called for you to come out, but you did not answer. It's time to go."

"I'll be out in a minute. Please leave while I get ready." Monbeem said.

Hohumph turned slowly, enjoying every minute. "We'll have to hurry. Chief Bowhut needs to know we are going." With that, he turned to leave. Taking a deep breath of fresh air, Hohumph sighed.

A short time later, Monbeem pushed the flap of her tent aside and found Hohumph sitting by the cooking fire. He looked up as she approached, and she said, "I'm ready to go. Let's tell Chief Bowhut and be on our way. I'm eager to see if we can find Casteel. I still have hope that he is alive!"

Grinning slyly, Hohumph said, "Yes, I also have high hopes. I too would like to find him quickly."

Walking together, they navigated their way through the village and approached Chief Bowhut's tent. He was sitting outside his tent picking at his breakfast. He had not expected Monbeem and Hohumph to be together so early and thought it very strange.

Hohumph was the first to speak. "Chief Bowhut, you know that Casteel has not returned home yet. I know you have sent trackers out and have not been able to find him. I also know you cannot spare other warriors because of the threat of war with the Mautuks returning. I have taken it upon myself to look for him with the help of Monbeem. We leave today and should be gone no more than a quarter moon's turn."

Chief Bowhut looked at them very curiously. He wondered why Monbeem leave with Hohumph. For a full minute, he said nothing, trying to think of what was really going on. He could come up with no real reason other than what Hohumph said.

Looking out at them through bushy brows, he said, "I give you a week, no more. Do not make me waste valuable time looking for you too. If Monbeem wants to go with you, I give her my blessing." With those parting words, Chief Bowhut waved them on as scouts were arriving with fresh reports on the Mautuks' whereabouts.

CHAPTER 16

THE MAUTUK VILLAGE

The spider monkey reached with long delicate fingers to grasp the fruit just out of its reach. The shifting weight of the clumsy monkey finally broke the fruit free. Slipping through his outstretched hands, the fruit fell precipitously to earth. Bouncing from branch to branch on its descent, the bruised and battered fruit smashed to the ground, splitting open to reveal the meat and seeds inside.

The rain forest went on forever and it was a natural barrier to the plains people. Inside the jungle, dangers lurked everywhere. Carnivorous plants seemed to reach out and grab at their victims. Poisonous spiders and snakes hid in the leafy vegetation, well camouflaged to strike any unsuspecting tribesman.

Sunlight rarely made it down past the canopy and the unpleasant smell of rotting vegetation filled the air. Blotches of light only seemed to deepen the gloomy atmosphere. During the day, the darkness was only a few shades lighter than the night. Dark imaginations of specters and wraiths hiding in the gloomy interior came to life. They were believed to be undead spirits unable to find their way to the underworld.

Squanto breathed the decaying air deep into his lungs. This was his native land. Slipping through the forest like animals, the hunters had finally made it home. Picking the fruit up with his hand, Squanto took a large bite, spitting the seeds to the ground. Looking around at the chattering monkeys, too far out of reach to hunt, he motioned for the others to go ahead.

The puckered scar on his face was still very painful. He thought of Babtoo with hatred every time he tried to chew. The wound had scabbed over, but constantly itched and bled when he tried to eat. The gash gave his mouth a permanent frown, making him look mean and irritated.

Squanto's mood matched the disfigurement on his face. They were approaching the village and had nothing to offer the priests in the way of slaves. Their scouting mission would be a failure no matter what kind of news he gave. How could he turn this failure around to make it into a success?

Leaning against a tree, Squanto's hand unconsciously went to his scar and started picking at the scab. Finally getting it to bleed, he sucked on his finger, tasting the coppery blood. It reminded him of previous sacrifices and helped him to think.

Sucking on his fingers, Squanto thought, "How can I make myself look good through this disastrous raid? The Watinkee warriors were ferocious. The boy on that huge animal was relentless. Did he have some power over animals? Can I find some way to capture him and release his power to me?"

"I'll tell the high priest they have powerful magic to control huge beasts. One had a lion's mane on his head. I wonder if that is all part of their magic." Smiling crookedly, the thought of more sacrifices pleased him. This would make him strong, he thought. Leaping to his feet, Squanto hurried to catch up with the rest of the hunters.

The stone pyramid was ancient beyond even the first Mautuk's memory. Basalt stones weighing tens of tons were stacked upon one another with great precision. No tool that the Mautuks had could replicate the cuts or find a way to move the basalt rock to the middle of the jungle.

Curling vines had dug their roots deep into the stone, snaking upwards to appear like pulsating veins, giving the pyramid life in the stagnant air. Black smoke from the cooking fires curled lazily upward toward the triangular top where it seemed to collect in a permanent hazy cloud. The shadows of the pyramid absorbed what little light filtered through the trees and clouds, keeping the village in constant darkness.

Carvings of an ancient race of people etched in the stone base depicted strange rituals. Kings and queens, warriors, slaves and workers, all told of a culture long since passed. Nobody really knew what the depictions meant or who they were. Those earlier memories having been lost centuries ago were now the reality of the Mautuks.

A small inscription on one cornerstone of the pyramid was almost unrecognizable. It was the figure of a priest holding a knife. The sacrifice was on a table with blood pooling on the stone. The priest had a heart in his hand, holding it above his head, offering it to the gods. In the air, a large head with a crown on it was smiling. This faint, depraved inscription was the only thing the Mautuks were able to understand and incorporate into their own religious beliefs.

Squanto stepped out into the clearing with his warriors only to find there was no celebration for the returning scouts. Mautuk women and children looked up from their labors briefly, only to continue working at their appointed tasks. They worked like zombies, mindlessly, without joy or spirit. No children ran and played and no Mautuk women ran to see their warrior husbands.

The high priest considered joy and happiness a weakness and so disapproved of anything that did not revolve around worshipping them. People only came alive when they performed their ritual sacrifices to their savage gods.

Slaves from different tribes and regions performed the hardest work. Taskmasters with whips and canes kept close guard on the slaves as they moved through the camp. Many had backs scarred and bleeding from the constant abuse. The sounds of their misery only seemed to excite the guards more as whips cracked on exposed flesh.

Broken of spirit and the will to live, many only barely felt the sting of the lash or the pounding of the cane. They looked eagerly to the day when they would no longer have to suffer the brutal existence the Mautuks offered.

Squanto walked boldly with the remaining warriors to the pyramid entrance horrifically decorated with human bones and skulls. Silent screams from gaping jaws seemed to echo in their heads as they passed through the door into the lightless interior. Each warrior shivered as the imagined scream slowly died, leaving them dreading the darkness like small children.

From inside the pyramid, the high priest took charge of the tribe. Like a phantom spirit materializing out of the gloom, the high priest slowly took on form. Silently, he approached his throne to sit down. Accompanying him on both sides were two huge warriors that looked like an altered cross of a mountain gorilla and Mautuk warrior.

His black cape of crow's feathers fluttered as he moved to sit down. On his shoulders, two leering skulls made the priest appear to have three heads. His own head had been painted white, matching the bone white color of the skulls on his shoulders. The only bright color was the red parrot feathers attached to his ceremonial knife.

Squanto and his fellow warriors immediately prostrated themselves on the floor, groveling and praying to the high priest. After what seemed like minutes, the priest raised his ceremonial knife and bid them to rise. Each warrior looked up hesitantly before jumping to his feet, waiting for the next order.

The high priest looked at them with inky, soulless black eyes that swam with an evil glint. An involuntary shiver rode up and down Squanto's spine.

A voice that seemed to come from everywhere but where the priest was sitting boomed, "Squanto, you bring me no slaves to sacrifice and you have lost four of your men."

This was no question but a statement of fact. It was as if the priest knew beforehand of the past events.

"Why have you come back without those gifts for me?" the priest asked in a terrible voice that sounded like the hiss of a snake. Immediately the rest of the warriors got back on their knees and started groveling once again for mercy.

Squanto had to choose his words carefully. He glanced up

through hooded eyes and said, "Master, they have strong magic and they control beasts. They defeated our powerful magic. We fought bravely and killed many, but could not bring back prisoners. I have been wounded and was lucky to escape, only to have my brothers' die by Watinkee spears." Playing along, the warriors all nodded in agreement.

The priest looked down with dispassion and hissed, "I do not know of Watinkee magic that can control beasts. You are lying, Squanto."

Squanto was trembling in fear and said, "No, I do not lie. A Watinkee warrior sat on a large beast that spit fire at us. He saw where we lay in ambush to attack. There was no warning, just fire and spears. One warrior was a lion and fought with great strength. He seemed to be everywhere at once. Then this beast man attacked me with such speed, I barely had enough time to defend myself. My magic was strong and able to fend him off but I received this as a parting gift." Squanto touched the puffy red wound on his face.

Mixing a lie with the truth seemed to be a good idea, but thinking back to the battle, Squanto was not so sure if he lied much at all. It was a terrifying ordeal and things did happen fast. "Maybe the beast did spit fire? Who was to say if it did not? I am the only survivor," he thought.

Convincing himself that it was the truth, Squanto waited to hear how the priest was going to respond. To doubt the priest's high magic could get you killed, or sacrificed, both of which would be terrible ways to die.

A deathly silence filled the chamber for several minutes. The sound of their own hearts beating furiously as if trying to escape from their ribcage was all that they heard. Each man held his breath, afraid to breathe.

The priest ignored the tension in the air. He appeared to be having a conversation with the skulls on his shoulders. Eerily, the mouths seemed to move as if alive. The priest's head swiveled from side to side as if conferring with them, and yet, there was no sound in the still air.

Finally, the high priest reached a decision. His gaze immobilized them with fear. Pointing at four of the warriors with his knife, he said, "You four. Go back and find out more about these beast people. I want slaves brought back this time. Do not come back without them."

The four men jumped up quickly and bolted out the door. Squanto's eye narrowed to hear what would happen next.

"Squanto, you have fought bravely. You may go and see your wife. The other remaining scouts will be punished for their lack of gifts."

The huge warriors on either side of the priest moved forward to round up the rest of the Mautuk scouts.

Squanto breathed a sigh of relief and quickly exited the lightless chamber into the dim light of day. Ignoring their screams for mercy, Squanto headed for his tent where his wife was busy cooking food.

There was no love between them. It had been a pre-arranged marriage from the high priest. She was an adequate cook, but not very beautiful, even for a Mautuk. However as the years went by, their relationship had developed into a very functional one. Both knew what their obligations were and performed them as if on cue.

Squanto sat down heavily and leaned against an old stump he used for a backrest. Glancing casually at his wife, a bowl of stew suddenly appeared before him. No words needed to be spoken between the two as he slurped his stew noisily, grimacing at the pain in his face. Before he knew it, she had provided a cold damp rag and applied it to his wound. As gently as she could, she washed the infected cut. When she became careless and caused him pain, Squanto grabbed her hand, "Careful, woman."

Cowering under his touch, she continued to wash the wound. Squanto felt no remorse about what he had done. He alone was the master of his tent. He was cruel and demanded respect from his wife.

CHAPTER 17

RETURN FOR SLAVES

The four banished Mautuk warriors sent back to Watinkee land breathed deeply of the dank forest air. Both relieved and anxious, they stopped to regroup. Looking back to see if they were followed, the four stood uncertainly.

There was not a leader among them. Quid, the young Mautuk who found Squanto by the tree dying, gripped his spear defiantly and looked at his fellow tribesmen. He was young, but not short on confidence.

Wiping his brow from perspiration he said, "We have run far enough. It is time for a plan. We can't go back now without slaves. Squanto failed, but we will not. Our high priest's magic is strong and that makes us strong!" He pounded his chest.

The other three warriors pounded their chests also, the fear of the High Priest slowly draining from their exhausted bodies. Already, the other three were looking to Quid for leadership.

Monchu, a short hairy Mautuk with arms that almost reached his ankles, said, "What can we do? There are only four of us. If Squanto's right and the Watinkee magic is stronger than ours, how are we to succeed?"

Stuffe, the largest of the warriors, but slow-witted said, "There is no stronger magic than the high priest's. What you say can get us killed. He can strike us down anywhere." He looked up into the trees as if to emphasize the point and flinched at the sudden call of a crow.

Harroot, the blackest and hairiest of them all, peered over to

Quid and growled, "Who put you in charge, Quid? I say I am the leader. I am older and smarter than you!"

Quid bristled at this last statement. Hefting his spear, he said, "Let's see who will be the leader then. There is only one way to settle this."

Harroot was no coward but could see this was quickly getting out of hand. Quid was an expert knife fighter and fearless in battle. Harroot was no match for the young warrior's skills. For now, he decided to follow Quid.

Harroot threw up his hands and said, "No need for this. You can lead, Quid. We all need to work together. It won't be easy with just the four of us and fighting between us will not help."

Quid visibly relaxed as they sat down in a circle to talk about their plans.

The morning was beautiful. The blue sky was clear with small puffy clouds carelessly floating by, and with little imagination, created shifting images of many different animals. Birds sang and crickets chirped. Small animals scurried by in their never-ending search for food as Monbeem and Hohumph started on their journey to find Casteel.

Monbeem was happy and her spirits were high. She felt good about the journey and hopeful in finding Casteel. With each step she took away from the village, Monbeem envisioned herself with Babtoo instead of Hohumph.

She was an accomplished tracker and hunter. Chintook had taught her all the skills she needed to survive if anything were to have happened to him. She could do nothing at home but sit and worry until Babtoo got back with the healing plant. Helping Hohumph look for Casteel gave her something worthwhile to do and took her mind off the failing health of her father.

Hohumph was happy, but for different reasons. He had reason

to believe Casteel was already dead and that they were not really going to find him. He lightly touched the small pouch around his chest containing the bloody strips of Casteel's shirt and the pair of moccasins. Their journey would end when Monbeem found the evidence he planned to use. They would come back as heroes with the new knowledge of Casteel's fate. Hohumph's gaze shifted to Monbeem's lithe form. Her grace and balance amazed him as she stepped lightly over and around objects. She moved quickly over the rough terrain, scanning the ground for tracks.

The pace had Hohumph out of breath in the first mile. He could barely keep up and his breath came in rasping gasps. Finally, shouting as he fell behind, Hohumph declared, "Hey, Monbeem. This pace is too fast. We might miss something."

Monbeem turned to look at the wheezing form of Hohumph with disgust. She yelled back and said, "Come on, Hohumph. Casteel needs our help. We have to find where the other scouts had left off. Then we'll cross the wildebeest herd tracks to see if Casteel has gotten that far."

Hohumph finally caught up and almost collapsed. Tossing his spear to the side, he put his hands on his knees gasping for air. "Yes, Monbeem, we will do that, but we should still search for his tracks in the wildebeests' crossing. It is possible the trackers missed something there. They said they only looked up to the herd." Hohumph said, thinking this would be a good excuse to rest.

Monbeem shook her head and said, "Yes, but that's a couple of days away. We need to get there first to search."

"Monbeem, we will get there in plenty of time. If you get too far ahead, I won't be able to help you if you get into trouble." Hohumph huffed, as he was recovering from the run.

Looking down at Hohumph, Monbeem thought, "I should have done this alone. I can take care of myself. I don't need this warthog of a pig slowing me down. Nevertheless, to be in the bush alone is very dangerous. I hope he proves better at tracking than running."

Monbeem said quietly, "Perhaps you're right, Hohumph. I will slow down a little and pay closer attention to what's around me."

Hohumph stood up, puffing his chest out and said, "If we work together, the better our chances of finding Casteel. He may have doubled back and the trackers missed it." Glancing around as if looking for some sort of clue, Hohumph drove his point home.

The pace Monbeem now set was considerably slower. Taking Hohumph's advice, despite her better judgment, was difficult. She knew in her heart Casteel was far from this place and that Hohumph would only move at a snail's pace to waste time.

She busied herself memorizing every detail she could about the passing terrain. Monbeem pinpointed where a pride of lions was and wondered if these were the lions the trackers were talking about. She spotted the hyena pack following the lions at a safe distance, chuckling, growling, and fighting with each other. Up ahead, wild dogs were barking as they chased a rabbit down a hole. All this and more she observed throughout the day.

This was unfamiliar territory to Hohumph. The lions seemed very close and so he gave them a wide berth. A hyena laughed, startling him as he looked for the nearest tree to climb. Gripping his spear with sweating hands, Hohumph stared into the savanna with fear, trying to locate the pack of wild dogs barking nearby. Touching the pouch around his neck, he thought, "We'll go on a little further. It's too soon for Monbeem to find this yet. She'll wonder why the trackers had not found it sooner."

Monbeem also noticed the startled reaction of Hohumph at every noise and shadow. The way he held his spear, always on the defensive, made her laugh at his cowardice. "Perhaps," she thought a little more kindly, "it is wise to have a little fear. Warriors have died out on the plains for being careless. Mautuks were seen around here and maybe they still could be. Hohumph may just be aware of the dangers more than I." Nevertheless, in her heart, she knew differently.

The day progressed without incident. The sun had completed its long journey in the sky to sit on the horizon as if deep in thought, before finally sinking out of sight. Monbeem stood, watching the sunset, mesmerized by the sight. It always made her feel close to mother earth.

Hohumph stood next to Monbeem thinking completely different thoughts. The rays of the sun seemed to reach for his eyes with glaring brightness, temporarily blinding him. Turning away, he gently tapped Monbeem's shoulder, "Let's find a place to camp. It's late and I don't want to be caught on the open savanna. We have seen many things today that will hunt us now that it is dark."

For the first time, Hohumph made good sense. Turning away, she allowed Hohumph to lead them to a good campsite. It was a rocky outcrop with a stunted tree just barely growing in the depleted soil.

Hohumph struck flint to tinder to start a small fire. There they sat and cooked the rabbit Hohumph had killed, outwitting the wild dogs that had chased it.

Monbeem sat across from Hohumph as he turned the rabbit over the small fire. Hunched over the spit and staring into the fire made him appear like a pregnant warthog. He glanced furtively into the night for phantom enemies keeping him uneasy and on edge.

The fire kept most of the big cats away, but the smell of food was powerful. Eyes appeared as globes of luminescent light as they reflected off the fire. They stared unblinkingly at them before suddenly winking out and reappearing somewhere else. The bush was alive with scampering feet and whines of hunger.

Monbeem was not used to the open savanna and shifted closer to Hohumph. A shiver of fear swept through her before she could control it. Disgusted with herself, she volunteered to take first watch, "Hohumph, you have done much today. I will take first watch after we eat. You look exhausted and can use the sleep more than I could. I am not as tired."

Hohumph glanced at Monbeem to try to detect any mockery in her voice. He was glad she had moved closer to him. Perhaps she feared being out on the savanna more than being with him. "It's true,

I am tired, Monbeem. I have done much on this journey so far and we have traveled a great distance. Wake me when the moon reaches half way. But first, let's share this meal."

Taking the rabbit off the spit, Hohumph split it in half and chewed noisily. Monbeem watched as he sucked the meat off the bones and threw them into the bush. A scurry of activity, with growls and whines, over the bones quickly followed. Wiping his hands on his shirt, Hohumph rolled into a blanket and quickly fell asleep. Snoring loudly, many of the animals retreated to a safe distance, afraid of the unusually loud noise.

Monbeem finished with her rabbit and deftly threw the bones into the fire. Looking around, many of the eyes had long since disappeared since the promise of more food was gone. She got up and walked to the edge of the fire's flickering light to gaze into the stars. She longed for Babtoo. He was a hero in everybody's eyes except his own. He thought his leg was a disability that held him back, and yet he had accomplished more than most other warriors had in his young life with both legs. He didn't realize how special he was. Suddenly a low "woof" nearby startled her and sent her scrambling next to the fire and closer to Hohumph.

Hohumph felt the gentle nudge of Monbeem's hand as he struggled to wake himself. Yawning like a big baboon and cracking his knuckles, he looked sleepily at Monbeem. "Is it my turn to watch already? I feel like I just fell asleep." Looking at the moon to observe its position in the sky, Hohumph noticed it was past his time to take the second watch. Getting to his feet and dragging his spear, Hohumph took a position next to the small stunted tree.

Monbeem quickly rolled into a ball and fell asleep almost instantly. Hohumph noticed how tired she was and how her gentle breathing sounded like a lullaby to him. It was not long before his eyes became heavy and he too, fell asleep.

The moon slipped behind the horizon and gave way to the rising sun. Hohumph became unbalanced as the tree branch he was leaning on suddenly broke. Instantly awake, he looked around guiltily, hoping Monbeem had not noticed he had fallen asleep. The noise had awakened her and she scanned the brush for intruders.

Hohumph yawned and said, "How did you sleep?"

Monbeem looked at him with sleep-filled eyes and said, "I slept very well, thank you. What was that noise?"

Hohumph breathed a sigh of relief knowing she did not know he had fallen asleep on his watch and said, "I broke this branch to put on the fire."

Looking at Hohumph queerly, Monbeem noticed the fire had long since been out. Dismissing the branch, they quickly ate breakfast of dried meat and continued on their way. Monbeem glanced down at the tracks surrounding their campsite and was startled at how close the beasts had come. Stepping over the tracks as if they were alive, Monbeem quickly put that thought out of her mind to focus on finding Casteel.

The day progressed without incident. Monbeem had slowed to accommodate Hohumph's shuffling gait. She was anxious to go faster but could not get Hohumph to pick up his pace. She knew it would be too dangerous to go on alone. Becoming separated for any length of time left a warrior vulnerable. Too much could happen to anyone alone on the savanna.

The sun beat down unmercifully on the two travelers. Hohumph searched for shade so they could rest until the day cooled. "Come on Monbeem. I have found that small tree over there to sit under until the heat of the day passes."

Monbeem, agitated because the pace was already too slow, insisted, "No, we have to keep going. I hoped to make it to the wildebeest crossing before nightfall. At this pace, we'll not make it until tomorrow. Casteel may be dying and every minute we waste is lost to him."

Hohumph looked like a puddle of water as his clothes clung to him in a sweat soaked mess. "Monbeem, we do no good to Casteel if we die before we make it to the crossing. It is hot and we should get out of the sun for a short time. We will make it to the wildebeest crossing by nightfall. I promise."

Looking doubtfully at Hohumph, Monbeem said, "Alright, just for a short time. I think we're close to the spot where they lost his tracks."

Hohumph, with a sly smile said, "Yes, I think we're closer than you think."

Spotting a small tree, they headed in that direction. Crashing through the brush noisily and waving his spear around as if fending off evil spirits, Hohumph blazed a path to the tree. Upon arriving, a look of horror transformed his unsuspecting face. Monbeem followed close behind and stopped abruptly, eyeing the awakening giant.

The black mane bristled at the interruption of its nap. The golden eyes were instantly alert as it gazed at the two tribesmen, piercing their souls as if speared. A roar of defiance accompanied by a yawn showed long yellow teeth. Standing up suddenly, his muscles rippled as he moved, the black tip of his tail twitched this way and that. The lion, agitated at the disturbance by the two humans, only heightened his aggressive behavior. Taking in a deep lung full of air, the lion sniffed to determine what was before him, then eyed them dubiously. Smelling fear, he took a step forward.

Hohumph had seen enough. Yelling at the top of his lungs, he ran back down the trail to find a large tree to climb. All the weariness he felt before left him in a rush of adrenaline. Forgetting about Monbeem, he sprinted to the next nearest tree and threw down his spear to climb faster, looking like a fat, clumsy chimpanzee.

The sight would have been comical had Monbeem not now faced the beast by herself. Slowly backing away with her spear held out in front, Monbeem watched the lion intently.

The yell Hohumph had made startled the lion. Looking around for other surprises, the lion flicked its tail and disappeared in the bush leaving Monbeem trembling from the strain. Backing slowly to the tree Hohumph was in, she melted to the ground, suddenly very exhausted. Hohumph reached down and grabbed her hoisting her into the tree. Saying nothing to one another, they stared out into the savanna, trying to penetrate the dense bush, looking for the king of beasts.

An hour passed, then two, and still they sat in the tree trembling, wondering if it was safe to come down. Finally, their fear dissipated and they both looked at one another sheepishly. Monbeem wasn't sure if she should have run with Hohumph, or if Hohumph should not have left her. She looked at him with a growing sense of loathing. Her life had been in peril, and leaving her to the lion to save himself was an act of cowardice. She was sure she would never have him accompany her again.

Climbing down the tree, Hohumph retrieved his spear. With false bravado he said, "Wow! That was close. If I hadn't yelled, you would have been dead. I tried to distract him so he would chase me. I think it worked because he left you alone. I saved your life."

Monbeem could not believe what she was hearing. Glaring at him for his faint-heartedness, she said sarcastically, "Yes, you did startle the lion, how very brave of you."

Turning her back on him, she thought, "I can only hope to find Casteel fast. I don't know if our luck will hold due to his spineless, selfish actions." Shrugging her shoulders, she knew she was doing the right thing and would not let Hohumph get in the way.

Evening was approaching and the wildebeest crossing was just up ahead. The two settled on a safe place to spend the night. They started a small fire to keep the larger predators at bay. Monbeem was not in the mood for conversation and chose to sleep first.

Hohumph did not argue and waited for her to settle into a rhythmic breathing pattern. After waiting a little longer and stirring the fire to see if she would wake, Hohumph slunk out of the camp. Breathing the night air, he looked back to see if she had moved. The glowing, blinking orbs surrounding their campsite scattered as he made his way toward the wildebeest crossing.

The moon was just a sliver in the sky, but the night was clear and the stars were out in number. Dim as it was, Hohumph was able to make his way deeper into the crossing. Here the terrain was relatively flat with the vegetation eaten lower to the ground by the grazing wildebeests. He could hear the grunts and bellows of the sleeping herd not far away.

Fingering the pouch around his neck, he pulled out the small moccasins. Rolling one into a ball, he threw it as far into the brush as he could. Moving further out, he tossed the other one some distance away.

Smiling slyly to himself, he thought, "Enough of being out here. This trip has been long enough and I am already weary of it. Tomorrow we'll find these moccasins and the next day I'll hide the bloody shirt pieces. After she finds these things, we can head back home. Besides, it's dangerous out here so far from the village."

Taking a final look at where he threw the shoes, he turned to walk back to camp. Stumbling on a root that seemed to snake out of the ground before returning to the confines of the earth, Hohumph fell in a pile of wildebeest dung. Angry with himself, he trudged back to camp, brushing the dung off his clothes.

The moon was high when he got back to camp. Stepping out from the darkness into the campfire light, Hohumph looked down at Monbeem to see if she still slept. For a moment, he could only stare at her beauty. Then he bent down to nudge her awake.

Monbeem awoke instantly. At once, her nose wrinkled and she asked, "What is that awful smell, Hohumph?"

Turning away a little embarrassed he answered, "Well, I went to relieve myself and fell into a pile of wildebeest dung. I'll clean myself off in the morning."

Monbeem looked a little puzzled. "The wildebeest crossing was still a little bit of a walk away," she thought to herself as she shrugged her shoulders. "Leave it to Hohumph to find the only dung pile left by a stray wildebeest this close to camp."

The night ended and the pink dawn of day greeted her eyes. Monbeem was getting used to the small animal noises and glowing eyes curious about their campsite. The sun's rays were growing bright when she woke up Hohumph.

Tired and grouchy, Hohumph rolled over for more sleep. Monbeem, a little more insistent, shook him harder and said. "Let's go, Hohumph. We have a lot of ground to cover today."

Hohumph rolled over and brushed dried dung off his clothes. Smiling to himself, he knew they would find something today. Monbeem would have a different opinion of him by the end of today. Monbeem wrinkled her nose at the foul smell and chose to sit on the opposite side of the camp, up wind from Hohumph. Eating a quick breakfast in silence, the two then proceeded into the wildebeest crossing.

Like coursing hounds, the two tribesmen searched this way and that, looking for any clue of the missing boy. Hohumph was careful to search in the direction he went the night before. His tracks were obvious to the trained eye. Nonchalantly he started to make his way to the first moccasin.

Monbeem was also an expert tracker trained by her father. She tried to remember everything he taught her, but rarely had the need to use those skills, though she did have a keen eye for detail. A large set of tracks that were deeper than the rest looked a lot like the ones that Babtoo's magical beast made. She wondered aloud and called to Hohumph, "Hey, Hohumph. I think I found something. I think Babtoo came this way also. These could be the tracks of his magical beast. I wish I would have paid more attention to that."

Startled, Hohumph looked all around at the surrounding plain expecting to see Babtoo come riding down on them. Relieved that Babtoo was nowhere around, Hohumph sprinted over to Monbeem to have a closer look at the deep imprints.

Squinting down at the old tracks, a look of mock concentration crossed his features. Poking with his finger to dislodge some of the loose dirt and grass, he said, "Monbeem, that looks like a water buffalo track. That couldn't be Babtoo and his magical beast."

Looking at him in doubt, she said, "I wonder what a water buffalo would be doing this far from water?"

Glancing up at her he said, "Could be water around. We would not know it. Let's continue to look up ahead."

Brushing the track away in the dirt, Hohumph stood up and pointed, "I may have found something over there in the bush."

Dismissing the track, she followed Hohumph to the area where he had tossed the moccasin the night before. Hohumph turned and said, "If Casteel came this way, it is possible he rested in this thicket. Let's search over there."

Monbeem nodded at the possibility and started to scan the ground. Odd, she thought, "How many times has Hohumph been over here? There is another set of his tracks going in the direction of camp. No, that can't be," she thought, shaking her head. "It must be him just circling around aimlessly."

All of a sudden Hohumph yelled in a booming voice that interrupted her train of thought, "Over here, I have found something. Hurry!"

Monbeem forgot what she was thinking and raced over to where Hohumph was standing. On the ground was a small crumpled up moccasin. Carefully, she picked it up and examined it. A tear formed in one of her eyes. She held the moccasin as if it was a child close to her heart.

Smiling from ear to ear, Hohumph said, "I told you he came this way. Let's look for more. Maybe he's around here." Hohumph took off in the direction he thought he threw the second moccasin. However, it was dark when he did it and all the bushes looked the same.

Monbeem nodded, clutching the small moccasin close to her as hope of finding the small boy slowly faded. Walking as if in a trance, she tried to focus on the ground and look for tracks or other pieces of clothing. Spotting an irregular shape in a bush, Monbeem went over for a closer look. There, on the bush about three feet in the air, the other moccasin hung on a branch.

Picking it up and matching it to the other one, Monbeem called Hohumph over. "Come over here Hohumph! I've found the other moccasin!"

Hohumph, aggravated for not finding it first, hustled over to Monbeem. Peering at the moccasins and turning them over in his hands, Hohumph said, "No doubt, these are the same. Let's start calling for him. He must be around here somewhere."

Hohumph and Monbeem started to shout Casteel's name. They searched everywhere in the area around where the moccasins were found. Their loud voices startled gazelle and zebra, and the occasional warthog. Finding nothing, the two headed toward camp. Monbeem unknowingly was following Hohumph's tracks from the night before. He was busy chattering away at their incredible luck and did not notice how they were coming back to camp.

They were still about an hour from camp and the sun was starting to set. Monbeem looked down at a faint set of tracks and stepped over a curling root that concealed a smashed pile of dried dung. Thinking only of Casteel, she continued walking and did not give the tracks a second thought.

Once at camp, Monbeem busied herself getting ready for the evening meal. Hohumph had not been able to hunt today and so they ate dried rabbit that she had brought. Hohumph sat next to her and looked like a proud peacock. He was so full of himself with the find of the moccasins.

Hohumph proudly said for the tenth time, "I found Casteel's moccasin. I knew he would have been there. Tomorrow we will find him for sure. I have other ideas where we might search."

Monbeem was tired of the constant bragging. The fate of Casteel weighed heavily on her mind. Gently rubbing the soles of Casteel's moccasins and listening to Hohumph brag, she tried to put the events of the day together. Trying to shut him up, Monbeem finally acknowledged his greatness and said, "Hohumph, without your skillful knowledge on tracking, we would never have found these moccasins. You truly are an impressive warrior. I am sure we'll find Casteel tomorrow because of your extraordinary ability to find things."

Hohumph, satisfied he received his rightfully deserved recognition, said, "How could you have ever doubted me?"

Monbeem just looked at him with half closed eyes and said, "Could you take the first watch? I am very tired."

Hohumph was more than glad to comply and said, "You rest now. We will find him tomorrow. You'll see."

Grinning to himself, he thought, "This is coming together better than I hoped. We'll be on our way home tomorrow afternoon.'

Monbeem rolled up in her blanket with her back to Hohumph and tried to get some sleep. Tired as she was, sleep eluded her. Her mind wrestled with little events that by themselves probably meant nothing, but added together became a perplexing puzzle.

She thought, "How odd it was that Hohumph seemed to know exactly where the first moccasin was. What was even stranger was why one moccasin was high on a bush three feet in the air? Why were there no signs of Casteel's footprints anywhere around and why would he take them off?"

The smell from Hohumph's ripe clothes still hung in the air when Monbeem thought, "That smell? I wonder if the dung pile Hohumph fell in was the one we saw closer to the wildebeest herd. What was he doing that far from camp in the middle of the night? I also wonder about his tracks leading into camp. That wasn't the way we left camp. How could he have been so sure we would find something of Casteel's? How could Hohumph know all these things when he barely leaves camp, even to hunt?"

Monbeem tried to think of explanations for all these oddities but one thing kept coming to the forefront. "Could he have known? Could he somehow be responsible for Casteel's disappearance?" That thought made the hairs on the back of her neck stand up.

Her body became rigid as Hohumph moved closer to her and cocked his head, listening to her breathing. Pretending to be asleep, she listened to his raspy breathing. His breath was like a foul smelling dense fog that clung tenaciously and would not let go. It was all she could do to not wrinkle her nose and gag before he moved away.

All was quiet except for the scurrying of little feet in the bush. She waited a few minutes before rolling over and searching for Hohumph's large, ungainly silhouette.

Softly calling his name and getting no response, Monbeem sat up. Letting her eyes adjust to the darkness, she got up and walked around the camp, whispering his name quietly, hoping he would not answer.

Satisfied he was no longer around, she started to search for him. She was not afraid for his safety but wondered where he had gone. In the distance, a black outline was quickly disappearing into the night. Gathering her spear, Monbeem swiftly pursued the retreating form of Hohumph. It was not a great feat to follow the stumbling, cursing Watinkee, even though the moon was not out and the stars were dim.

Hohumph cursed his luck as he tried following an animal trail to the wildebeest crossing. Kicking an ant pile with his foot, hundreds swarmed out of their broken home to attack his huge clumsy foot. Large dark ants, with huge pincer beaks swarmed under his pant leg to bite his bare skin. Hopping around like a wounded ostrich, arms and hands slapping his legs, he tried to run from the teeming army.

Monbeem silently chuckled at the sight. Watching him limp away in a broken run, she followed hastily behind.

Hohumph continued deeper into the wildebeest crossing, moving quickly at a trot. Monbeem had no trouble keeping up, however in the dim light found she was struggling to see the clumsy figure as he zigzagged through the plains. She had to follow closer than she wanted in the darkness, but remained undetected.

Hohumph stopped by a small ravine with small bushes clinging to the side. Roots crisscrossed the ravine, exposed to the elements, trying to hold back the dirt from the infrequent flooding. Hohumph peered down the ravine and thought, "This is a great place to put one of these torn shirt strips."

Hearing a rustling of grass not far off, Hohumph glanced back furtively. Seeing nothing but empty darkness, he threw a strip of shirt into the ravine where it snagged on a root. Satisfied, he continued forward. Looking for trees in the distance, he headed there at a quick jog. Rummaging around in his leather pouch, he produced another torn shirt piece and tossed it into the copse of trees.

Puzzled at this, Monbeem watched impatiently, hoping he would move on. Not far from where the ravine cut into the dry earth stood a small stand of stunted trees. Hohumph headed in that direction. Monbeem waited until he reached the trees to investigate what he had thrown into the ravine. Slipping toward the ditch and blending into the shadows, she approached the edge where Hohumph had been.

At first, she saw nothing but blackness. A light breeze sprang up breathing life into the ravine, rustling the leaves of the bushes. The piece of cloth caught the breeze and fluttered slightly in the gentle wind like the wing of a bird.

Reaching down toward the root to grab at the cloth, the ravine suddenly gave away. Stifling a yelp, she rolled down the hill clutching the piece of cloth as she slid past. A small landslide followed with dust flying in the air. Lying on her back, she gazed at the top of the ravine. Gasping for breath, she still clutched the cloth as if were a treasure.

As the dust settled, she peered closely at the fabric. The fabric consisted of small lacings down the front and it was covered in dried blood. This looked like it could be Casteel's shirt. Realization of what this meant sent shivers down her spine.

Staring at the cloth in shock, the puzzle pieces she had been wrestling with were all falling into place. The moccasin in the tree, the tracks back to the camp, the squashed dung pile now all fell into place. Tears started to well in her eyes and she started to cry. She realized the only plausible explanation was that Hohumph had killed Casteel to become a hero in the eyes of the tribe. She suddenly realized she had been asked to accompany him in order to provide testimony of his bravery and excellent tracking. Of course, they would never find the boy, but they would have found bits and pieces of his clothing.

She had not even finished the thought when a familiar face leered out of the dust cloud. A sickly smile appeared on Hohumph's face, knowing he had been caught. Scrambling to her feet Monbeem yelled, "Hohumph, how could you do this to Casteel? He was just a young boy. Why did you kill him?"

Hohumph, startled by this accusation, had a look of confusion cross his ugly face. He cried, "I may be guilty of planting evidence as a ruse to impress you, but I never killed Casteel. How could you think that?"

Hohumph reached his hand down to Monbeem and said as softly as he could, "Monbeem, you know that is not true. I could have never killed little Casteel. Please believe poor old Hohumph!"

Monbeem shrank from his hand and scrambled out of the ravine to retrieve her spear. Pointing it at Hohumph she screamed, "Get out of my way, Hohumph. You are nothing in my eyes. The whole tribe will know of your cowardice. Let them decide whether you killed him. You will pay for this."

Hohumph produced his spear out of nowhere and was now pointing it at Monbeem, the crow's feather fluttering on the spear. He said, "Monbeem, we don't have to do this. I did not murder Casteel. Just listen to poor Hohumph!"

They stood looking at one another, spears poised, sizing each other up.

Chapter 18

The Capture

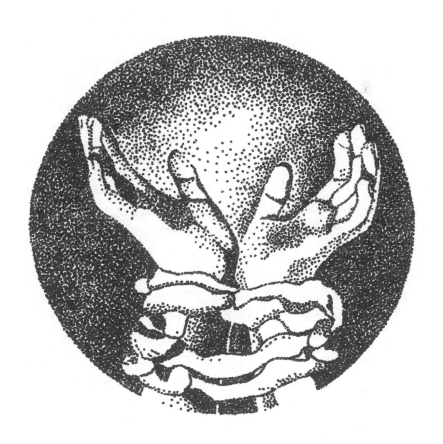

The clear raindrop fell from the heavens above, striking the bright green young leaf that reached for the sun. Landing on the leaf with a splash, the raindrop joined countless others creating a miniature emerald reflecting pool. Too heavy, the leaf tilted, pouring the rain down the tree, like a tiny, cascading waterfall. The small puddle broke apart as some soaked into the living tissue, bringing life to the majestic tree, while others continued on their journey to the forest floor.

The Mautuk warrior looked up in discomfort. His war paint running down his face looked comical instead of the fearsome visage he tried to create. The raindrop hit his upturned face and quickly turned from crystal clear to a dirty black smudge as it mixed with the dirt.

Looking up into the dense canopy, hoping for some relief from the rain, Quid turned toward the others. Stuffe was dejected and hopelessly looked for a place to stay dry. Monchu, the short hairy Mautuk, seemed perfectly happy in the downpour. The black oily hair on his skin looked to be water repellant. Harroot walked by his side without a word, his war paint streaked and unrecognizable.

The four Mautuks finally came upon a cave tucked away in a hill. Exploring the interior, Quid made his first decision as a leader to stop there until the rain subsided. Pushing and shoving, the four scrambled into the dry cave. Huddling at the entrance, they peered out at the dreary forest.

Quid pulled out his sharpening stone and started to file his spear.

His eyes darted from one warrior to another, wondering if it was possible to push his warriors further. Looking at their down turned eyes, Quid sat back and said, "We'll stay here for the night. We have traveled far today and deserve rest."

The others looked at him with relief. Monchu pulled out flint and stone to start a small fire. Gathering small grass and twigs in the cave, he expertly started the tiny blaze. Pointing at Stuffe, Monchu said, "Stuffe, I need more wood and grass for the fire. You go find some while I keep this fire burning?"

Stuffe grunted and got up to leave. Looking at the soaking rain, Stuffe turned around and said, "No, you go out and get it."

Monchu tensed for a moment and said, "You want to dry off, don't you Stuffe?"

Stuffe opened his mouth to argue but caught the look Quid gave him and decided it was easier to get the wood. Disappearing from the cave, Stuffe stumbled out into the rain.

Quid stared into the small flame and said, "Harroot, we need to scout ahead. Once the rain stops, you'll search the fringe of the forest. I don't want any surprises. We'll stay here until you know where will be the safest course to follow."

Harroot glanced over to Quid and said, "Let me take Stuffe. If I run into any trouble, he would be a great help."

Quid thought about that for a second before nodding his head yes.

Monchu continued to baby the fire and said, "If Squanto told even a little bit of truth, we need to be extra careful. Capturing Watinkee warriors is no easy task. They have strong magic."

Quid glared over at Monchu and said with a bitter retort, "Are you saying we're not as strong as Watinkee tribesmen? Squanto is old and slow. We are younger and faster. What is it that you are afraid of Monchu?"

Monchu reeled back as if slapped. "Nothing! Only that Squanto did have younger Mautuk warriors with him and they didn't come back alive. Don't discount Squanto. He is as wily as a fox."

At that moment, Stuffe entered the cave with damp twigs and branches. Throwing the kindling down by the fire pit, he surveyed his clansmen. The atmosphere was thick with tension. He wondered how they could be out of sorts sitting in a dry cave when he was out getting soaked in the rain.

He mumbled, "Everything is wet. These are the only things I could find that might burn." Sitting down heavily by the fire pit, he poked Monchu and said, "Well, get going and build this fire. You said you would build it so I can dry out."

Monchu shook himself free from the insulting accusation from Quid and got busy with the fire. Smoke from the wet branches filled the air, but they were in no immediate danger of detection. Watinkee tribesmen never enter the forest.

The morning brought a dense fog that curled around the base of the trees and spiraled up toward the canopy. Patches of fog clung to small clearings that resembled congregating lost souls who had forgotten their way to the underworld. Sounds of their moans were not lost to the tribesmen as the wind navigated through the jungle.

Quid leaned against the side of the cave and looked out into the roiling mist. This was a bad omen. He felt oppressed with a sense of impending doom. Shaking the superstitious thoughts from his head, Quid looked back and motioned for Harroot. Quid thought, "This is a dangerous scouting mission. Maybe something bad will happen to Harroot. Then he won't be around to challenge me for leadership." A slow smile formed on his face.

Quid looked toward Harroot and gruffly said, "Time to go. Get Stuffe and report back as soon as you have something!"

Harroot stood up and said, "But the spirits are still out!"

Quid just pointed outside with his spear and said, "You must fear them more than you fear our high priest."

Harroot smiled grimly at Quid and said dejectedly, "Come on Stuffe. It's time to go."

Stuffe approached the entrance, shuffling his feet. Looking outside, a frown creased his face. His eyes questioned Harroot, but with Quid's threatening glare, he knew there was no choice. Raising his hands in the air, Stuffe traced an unholy gesture to his god before stepping into the thick concealing mist. Harroot followed close behind as they disappeared into the steamy forest.

Harroot led the way as Stuffe tailed behind. Stuffe was the most superstitious of the four Mautuks and peered into the mist with trepidation. Constantly tripping over Harroot's heel, Stuffe slammed into an overhanging branch. Lying on the ground for a moment, stunned, he wanted to go no further.

Harroot looked back at the big Mautuk lying prostrate on the ground and could not contain a fit of laughter. Stuffe looked up and noticed the mist was slowly burning away. The dim jungle was getting brighter and they were close to the jungle edge. A sheepish smile crossed his face as he scrambled to stand up.

Harroot said, "Look Stuffe, a good sign. Soon the mist will disappear. The lost spirits will once again be gone and we can continue our search without fear."

Stuffe nodded his head in agreement, eager to be on the way.

As they continued, the damp forest floor gave way to drier conditions. The trees got smaller and the open areas got larger. Approaching the forest edge, tendrils of bright light filtering through the thinning canopy hurt their sensitive eyes. Under a leafy frond, they sat and rested and contemplating their next move.

While they relaxed under a large crooked tree that resembled an umbrella, they pulled out some uncooked monkey meat. Chewing in silence, the two Mautuks were lost in their own private thoughts.

Harroot knew why Quid sent him out here. He was sure he wanted him killed to prevent him from challenging his leadership. He thought, "Quid is a hot head and he will get us killed. I won't die because of his pride. I know Stuffe is loyal to me if Quid is dead. Who knows what will happen out in the savanna."

Stuffe thought only of the quest at hand. "I hope we can get home quickly. The spirits did not seem happy when we left this morning. Maybe we can appease them with a sacrifice of our first captives."

The sun was hot and for two warriors used to the cool confines of the forest, both felt uncomfortable. They moved away from the shade and out into the open savanna, keeping the tree line in sight.

They soon spotted a large herd of wildebeest and decided to get a better look. Moving cautiously into the open, they approached the nervous herd whose grunts and bellows were deafening as they crept slowly on.

Harroot and Stuffe circled behind them as they went past. As the animals trotted by, the savanna was quiet for a moment. In the distance, a barely discernible yell echoed across the plain. Listening closely, two voices were calling a single name.

Instantly they were on guard as they melted back into the savanna. The voices would get loud, and then would fade away, only to get closer again. Confused as to how many there were, Harroot and Stuffe found a small termite mound in a copse of trees and hid behind it to watch the open plain. What they saw both astonished and delighted them.

Monbeem and Hohumph continued to call Casteel's name as they searched for any place a boy might hide, oblivious to the danger it attracted. They were so intent on their hunt that they were not aware of the Mautuk warriors watching them.

Harroot and Stuffe continued to monitor this unusual activity to see if there were any other Watinkee tribesmen in the area. They shrugged their shoulders in puzzlement as to why anybody would yell and scream in the middle of the savanna.

Harroot and Stuffe were nearly discovered as the two Watinkee tribesmen abruptly changed directions and headed toward the small copse where they were hiding. They readied their spears when Hohumph and Monbeem passed within only a few feet of them. Luck was on Hohumph and Monbeem's side, however, as Harroot waited to be sure there were only two of them, much to the chagrin of Stuffe.

Harroot also noticed one of the warriors had a black feather on his spear. He wondered, "Does our high priest have power out here? Is that just a black feather on the end of his spear or a high priest's crow feather?" Without a closer look, it was impossible to tell.

As the two Watinkee tribesmen moved away, Harroot whispered, "Stuffe, go back and get Quid and Monchu. I think we have found our gifts to the high priest. If we're all here at the same time, we'll be able to take them alive. Now go. I'll see where they're camped and meet you here tomorrow."

Stuffe looked hungrily at the two Watinkee, nodded his head, and then disappeared without a sound.

Quid was elated. Capturing two Watinkee warriors out on the open plain should be easy. They seemed to have lost something or someone. He watched them through the whole afternoon as they looked under every bush, down every ravine and all the outcrops in the area. Still they shouted one lone name. "Casteel! Casteel!" Quid did not know whom or what the name meant, only that they could not find it or him.

Stuffe found his way back to the cave without incident. Light was fading fast as he entered his jungle domain. The canopy allowed very little light to filter down to the forest floor causing shadows to blend in with the gloom surrounding the trees. He waited a moment for his eyes to adjust to the forest dimness before stepping into the duskiness beyond.

Disappearing into the jungle, squabbling monkeys never saw him. Birds continued to sing without noticing his fleeting form. Small animals scurried almost underfoot as Stuffe raced to the cave. Even a stalking tiger was startled as the big Mautuk appeared out of nowhere only to disappear again as quickly.

Approaching the cave, Stuffe noticed Quid standing at the entrance looking out into the jungle. Quid was both surprised and excited at Stuffe's quick return without Harroot.

Quid waved at Stuffe and asked, "Any news my big friend? You have come back sooner than expected. Have you found something we can use? Is Harroot alright?"

Secretly he wished Harroot were dead.

Stuffe, out of breathe said between gasps, "We have found two stupid Watinkee tribesmen wandering around lost. Harroot didn't want to attack them without you. He thinks we can take them alive."

Quid excitedly asked, "How far away are they? Can we get to them tonight?"

Stuffe, finally able to get his breath under control said, "Yes, tonight would be good!"

Monchu appeared in the entrance beside Quid, eating a monkey on a stick. Waving the food in front of Stuffe he said, "Eat, Stuffe. We need your strength when we capture the Watinkees".

Without formality, Stuffe grabbed the meat and chewed absent-mindedly, thinking of the two vulnerable Watinkee tribesmen. He thought, "Soon we will be eating people again instead of monkey meat." A satisfied smile crossed his face.

The three Mautuks quickly assembled their war paint designed to strike fear in their enemy's hearts. Painting their faces white to look like skulls, they applied black to form gap toothed grins, eyeless sockets, and sunken cheeks. Gathering up their spears, they headed out the cave entrance.

The darkness was complete. The only thing they could see were the few misty wraiths floating ominously through the air. Moving cautiously out into the forest, they travelled with pure animal instinct born from the savagery of their lives. Their eyes seemed to glow in the dark from their unnatural heritage.

Stuffe, like a hound on a scent, led them unerringly toward the forest edge. Stepping over fallen branches and moving around dark, dank water holes with practiced ease, the three Mautuks slipped through the forest. Stuffe hesitated only once when the wind howled through the boles of the trees sounding like a cacophony of undead spirits. Quid jabbed him with his finger to get the superstitious Mautuk moving again.

They reached the savanna well before midnight. The moon gave off little light and the stars seemed hesitant to shine. To the Mautuks, it could have been just a cloudy day. They missed very little.

Stuffe led them to the sleeping wildebeest herd. Like ghosts in the night, they passed by without even a bellow or grunt from the sleepy animals. Slowing down, they materialized out of the night like phantoms, finding Harroot in the shelter of some trees.

Harroot turned around, startled by the sudden appearance of his tribesmen. Three leering faces stared at him with eager anticipation.

Quid was the first to speak, "Harroot, do you know where their camp is?"

"Yes, Quid. They are about an hour from here. It is a man and a woman. They don't appear to be warriors. They're looking for someone or something. I don't know why the two are so far from home making so much noise."

Quid snorted and said, "Have you scouted the area for other warriors?"

Harroot, tired of the badgering questions, answered, "Yes, yes, they have nobody. They are alone. We can capture them easily!"

Quid thought for a moment and said, "Monchu, help Harroot with his war paint. I expect to be back in the jungle before day break."

Before long, the four frightening looking Mautuks emerged from the copse of trees. Slowly they headed toward the Watinkee's camp. In the distance, the warriors heard fragments of conversation. One was crying, the other pleading for something. Abandoning the route to the Watinkee camp, the warriors switched direction and headed for the unknown voices. Keeping low, they came upon an unusual sight. Spreading out, they watched in disbelief at what they saw before them.

Two Watinkee tribesmen were pointing spears at one another. The woman was crying and yet seemed ready to fight. The other, larger Watinkee appeared to be a warrior but seemed to be afraid, pleading for his life. They were so absorbed in their standoff that they did not notice the four Mautuk warriors materialize out of the darkness. The four Mautuks stood for several minutes, waiting for the two Watinkee tribesmen to notice them. Finally, Quid had enough. With a loud yell, they surrounded Hohumph and Monbeem.

Caught completely by surprise and paralyzed with fear, the two Watinkees dropped their weapons. Quid quickly tied up the stunned couple and marched them down to a nearby water hole.

CHAPTER 19

THE RESCUE

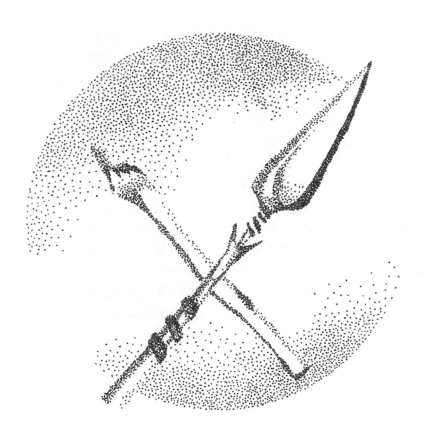

The warm African night seemed cold and uncaring. Monbeem felt isolated, without hope of rescue. Surrounded by the four Mautuk warriors, she became lost in despair. Poked and prodded, Monbeem stumbled toward the nearby water hole. Glaring at Hohumph through down cast eyes, she blamed him for their capture. She looked for avenues of escape and met with disappointment and fear at the hopelessness of their situation.

The grim visage of the Mautuks inspired terror beyond anything she had ever known. This journey gave her insight into Hohumph's cowardice and she now knew not to depend on him for an escape plan.

Hohumph appeared like a giant to the smaller Mautuks. He walked slowly like a beaten man. His shoulders slumped forward while his eyes darted from one warrior to another, looking for some sort of compassion. He saw none and was very afraid for his life. He had heard stories of captured victims and tried hard not to shudder. His devious mind continued to work through the nightmare of horror for some way out. Coward that he was made him all the more crafty.

Thoughts ran through his mind only to be rejected. "Perhaps I can barter with them. I wonder what they need. Can I exchange Monbeem's life for my own? If she gets back to the tribe knowing what I did, she will have me exiled anyway. No! Better to be exiled than to do anything to help this barbaric tribe and hurt Monbeem." Shaking his head at the terrible notion earned him a poke in the back with a spear.

Upon reaching the watering hole, Monbeem and Hohumph were led to a tree and were snugly tied to the trunk. Their bonds were tight, cutting off the circulation in their hands. Looking dejected, they waited to see what was going to happen next.

Hohumph tried to speak to Monbeem and whispered under his breath, "Any ideas on how to get out of this?"

Monbeem looked at him incredulously and said, "Hohumph, you killed Casteel. Do not speak to me. You got us into this mess. Now we will die because of your actions."

Hohumph spoke a little louder, aggravated she would not listen to him. "I told you I did not kill Casteel. I wanted you to think I am a great warrior and tracker. I wanted to be more in your eyes."

Hohumph yelled the last sentence to the disbelieving Monbeem. A cold stare greeted him sending shivers up his spine. He was not sure what to be more terrified of, the Mautuks or Monbeem's disgust for him. Stuffe got up and casually backhanded Hohumph across the face, knocking a tooth out of his mouth. Spitting blood through smashed lips, Hohumph tried to shrink away.

Stuffe, satisfied with the result of his slap, licked the blood from the back of his hand. A smile creased his evil face in anticipation of the coming sacrifice. Sitting down with the rest of the Mautuks, Stuffe had not felt this good for a long time.

Stuffe was the first to speak of the two Watinkee prisoners, "I think we need to sacrifice the woman now to thank the gods for a successful capture."

Monchu nodded in agreement, "I agree with Stuffe. A sacrifice would be welcome to the gods."

Harroot spoke for the first time upon hearing Stuffe and Monchu, "Now is not the time for a sacrifice. We are still in Watinkee territory and vulnerable to attack. Let's wait at least until we get back to the cave to sacrifice the woman. Then we have only one prisoner to take back to the temple. That should be enough."

Quid listened to Harroot and said, "Yes, I agree. Getting out of

Watinkee land alive is good. We have been lucky so far. We can take our time with the woman later at the cave."

Quid motioned for Stuffe to get the spears of Hohumph and Monbeem. He got up and retrieved the spears where he had carelessly thrown them on the ground. Walking toward the light of the small fire, he noticed one spear had a crow's feather hanging limply on the shaft.

"Aghhhhhhh!" Stuffe yelled, throwing the spears down by the fire as if he had burned himself.

Quid, startled, looked at the big Mautuk strangely and asked, "What's wrong Stuffe?"

Stuffe could only point at the crow's feather attached to the spear shaft in the grass. Suddenly, they all jumped to their feet and signed to their gods, mumbling prayers of forgiveness. Stumbling around the fire, they bumped into each other in their haste to appease the gods. Fear and superstition trickled into their minds and suddenly the four warriors were not as confident as before.

Quid kicked the spear with his toe revealing the crow feather. The black feather absorbed the fire light and seemed to multiply before their superstitious eyes, taking on a life of its own. Quid wanted no part of the spear and its powers.

Congregating away from the fire and spear, the four Mautuks looked over at Hohumph. The fear became contagious and now gnawed at their bellies in waves. Nobody can carry a crow's feather besides the high priest. Was this a message of some sort? Stuffe looked down at his hand by the light of the fire and cringed, visibly shaken with delusions of angry gods for slapping the fat Watinkee.

Hohumph noticed the odd behavior of the warriors after examining his spear. Leaning over to Monbeem, he whispered, "We may have a chance. They're fearful of my spear. I think it's the feather of the raven on it. I heard somewhere where their high priest has a cloak made of raven feathers."

Monbeem just looked at him with cold brown eyes and said

bitterly, "I hope you're right, Hohumph, for both our sakes. Maybe you can convince them of your fearlessness."

Watching the gathering closely, Hohumph wondered when to make his move.

Quid swallowed hard before he said, "Harroot, this is your fault. You are the one that spotted these two tribesmen. You should have seen the crow's feather on his spear. This is a bad omen. Maybe he was marked to be left alone."

Harroot stepped back a little and said with a threatening voice, "You asked for prisoners and now you have them. Don't blame this on me."

Monchu chimed in and yelled, "You have cursed us Harroot. You and Stuffe both have cursed us!"

Stuffe sidled alongside Harroot and said, "I stand by Harroot."

Quid and Monchu stood on one side as Harroot and Stuffe took several steps back with spears raised. The glint of the cold metal spear tips poised in his direction brought reason to Quid and he quickly realized the futility of the argument. Raising his hands in the air to get everybody's attention, he relented, "What is done, cannot be undone. Let's decide what to do now."

The spears tips slowly lowered as the four Mautuks stood uncertainly, glancing furtively back at Hohumph and Monbeem.

The sun was hot. The blazing orb withered everything in sight. Plants erupted in smoke and turned to ash as the fiery sphere passed overhead. Animals staggered across the sand with tongues hanging limply from open mouths. Watering holes long dried up with ancient crocodile bones that had turned to dust were only depressions in the parched, cracked earth.

Babtoo saw all of this and more as he and Enobi stumbled across the sand.

Wind from the arid plains kicked up sand monsters that swirled around like cyclones, engulfing anything still tenaciously clinging to life. They chased anything that still moved and covered the ones that had fallen, never to get up again.

One such cyclone finally caught up with Babtoo and Enobi. It circled around them, lashing their bodies with dirt and grit. It slowly squeezed the life from their bodies as they tried to gulp the arid air.

A giant head of a serpent formed at the top of the cyclone and seemed to laugh at their misfortune. The head poised as if to strike...

Babtoo lurched out of the dream, sitting straight up from his makeshift bed to blink into the midday sun. His mouth was parched and his lips were dry and cracked. A strangled croak burst from his mouth as he struggled to break away from the nightmare.

Looking around him, Enobi grazed peacefully nearby. Casteel sat on a small rock nearby, whittling on a stick, waiting for Babtoo to awake. The breeze was pleasant, though hot and dusty, as the terrifying dream faded from his memory.

Casteel, instantly alert, ran over to Babtoo and said excitedly, "You're finally awake. You seemed exhausted after the battle with the snake. However, you did not have to worry. I was here watching over you and Enobi. Nothing was going to get by me!" Proudly he displayed his little spear and the sharp point glinted brightly in the sunlight.

Babtoo looked at him and smiled, slurring the words with a tongue thick and slow, "Casteel, get me some water. I had no fear you would not watch over us."

Casteel beamed at the compliment and ran to fetch water. Taking a deep breath and gasping from the pain, Babtoo pulled his shirt up to examine his ribs. A black and blue ribbon traced its way around his body and ribs ending by his neck.

"That was a close call," he thought.

Casteel ran as fast as he could with a skin full of water, almost tripping on stones to get to back quickly. Slowing, and out of breath, Casteel handed him a sloshing bag of water.

Grateful, Babtoo drank greedily as the water dribbled from his mouth and traced a pattern in the dust that stuck to his face. Babtoo glanced at the sky and realized how far up the sun was in the sky. Looking questioningly at Casteel, he asked, "How long have I been out?"

Casteel's face became serious when he said, "A full day at least."

Babtoo, shocked at how long he had slept, struggled to regain his feet. His vision swam briefly as he tried to control his breathing. He felt the pain in his chest ebb to a dull ache as he swayed from the exertion. Standing there, strength slowly began to flow back through his limbs and body and his mind became clear and focused.

Grabbing Casteel he said, "Let's go! I have slept far too long! Gather up the medicine and we'll ride into the night if we have to. These flowers have to get back to Whutknot in time. Chintook's life depends on it. I won't forgive myself if we are too late!"

Together, Casteel and Babtoo raced over to where Enobi was grazing. Casteel ran ahead while Babtoo limped painfully behind. Lifting his head, Enobi's ears swiveled back and forth as the two approached.

Stopping just short of Enobi, Casteel looked back as Babtoo caught up. Walking up to the horse and stroking his long graceful neck, Babtoo tangled his fingers in his mane. Whispering gently, Babtoo said, "My big friend, it is time to go. I hope you have rested well. We'll need your speed and strength to carry Casteel and me. Let's get back to the tribe in time to save Chintook's life."

As if in response, Enobi shook his head up and down vigorously with a snort of pleasure. Climbing gingerly on his back, Babtoo reached down to give Casteel his hand.

"Remember what your job is, Casteel. Be alert and carefully watch our back trail. There could be Mautuks about and we need to make haste. I'm counting on you to be my eyes behind us. Can you do that?"

Casteel was elated that he was trusted with such an important task and said proudly, "I will be your eyes. Nothing will get by me. I watched over you so nothing would bother you. I even chased a lizard from your head while you slept!" Casteel brandished his small spear over his head making Babtoo laugh for the first time in weeks. He liked this plucky little warrior and was glad he had him by his side.

The terrain was rocky and interspersed with ravines. Babtoo tried to follow the same trail that led them to the mountain but found going back to be a bit more tricky. They did not come out in the same place as when they started and soon found themselves taking more time to get past the base of the uneven ground. Finally approaching the savanna, both Babtoo and Casteel heaved a sigh of relief.

Enobi was at his best in the open savanna. Trotting along with only a slight limp, he still could cover a lot of ground, even in the heat of the day. Sweat glistened on his coat, but Enobi seemed tireless and forged ahead.

Casteel, true to his word, scanned the horizon for any sign of Mautuks. They passed herds of zebra, wildebeest and gazelle. A giraffe stopped eating to gaze in their direction as the odd figure of an animal with two riders trotting past. Babtoo continued to guide Enobi with his knees, becoming more and more confident in their ability to work together. Evening was approaching and still they continued to ride into the dusk.

As twilight fell, Babtoo slowed their pace. Enobi was tired and his limp became more pronounced. Darkness was a dangerous time. Predators hunted unsuspecting or careless prey and they would not be one of those.

Poking Casteel, Babtoo said, "I know you're tired little brother, but now you need to be especially alert. We are the hunted now. Take care and listen, for we are vulnerable in the dark. We can't see in the dark like the big cats."

Casteel nodded, his eyes as big as saucers.

Following the teachings of Chintook, Babtoo relied on the stars for guidance. His goal was to get to the watering hole by midnight. They would rest there until dawn, and then continue refreshed for the rest of their journey.

Babtoo understood the limp Enobi had and knew that even one night of rest would greatly improve his leg. Thoughts of his own crippled leg swirled around in his mind. He would not let his leg be an excuse anymore. The spotted zebra had gone all day with little rest and never once slowed down. Enobi is an amazing gift and one I could learn from!

Casteel saw the flickering light first. The small campfire seemed to struggle in the vastness of the savanna. Pointing Enobi in that direction, the two tribesmen went for a closer look. It was the same waterhole with the big crocodile where Babtoo had first found Casteel. Perhaps it was a Watinkee scouting party.

The flame never seemed to grow larger the closer they came. It did throw off enough light, though, to guide Babtoo and Casteel through the dark savanna.

Not knowing what to expect, they kept to the ravines and trees or tall grass to keep hidden as much as possible. Alert for trouble, but hoping there would be none, Babtoo leaned back and whispered to Casteel, "We're going to approach the campfire from the back. Remember where we had our camp?"

Casteel nodded vigorously.

"That's where we're going. We'll have a good view of the lake and of whoever made the campfire. Don't make a sound. It might be our fellow tribesmen or it could also be Mautuks. After the last battle, I don't expect them back so soon, but we have to be certain. They are fearsome warriors and do just what we don't expect."

Casteel whispered back, "I'm not afraid. I'm with Babtoo who tamed a magical beast. You have fought Mautuks and won. I am proud to be by your side."

Babtoo smiled grimly hoping he would not have to prove himself to Casteel. Without the help of experienced warriors, Babtoo knew his chances would be small if they ran into a Mautuk war party.

Approaching the watering hole from behind, Babtoo spotted his old camp, although little evidence of it remained. Sliding off Enobi, Babtoo helped Casteel down. Tying Enobi to a small shrub, the two crawled on their bellies to the edge of the hill for a look down at the camp.

What they saw stunned them. Casteel was about to shout when a big hand clamped over his face. Looking down at Casteel with eyes that smoldered, Babtoo put his finger to his mouth and whispered, "Shhhhhh! We need a plan! Do not worry little brother, we will find a way to set them free."

Casteel shrank from the intensity of his gaze and nodded his head up and down.

Seeing the Mautuk warriors in full war paint frightened little Casteel to the core. All the stories he had heard paled to what he now witnessed. The skull faces seem to leer up at him as if searching for his hiding place behind the rock.

The worst part was Babtoo knew both captives well. Monbeem leaned forward with her hands tied to a tree. Her head hung down in limp strands around her face. She appeared listless, with no spirit, as hopelessness had finally eaten its way into her soul. Hohumph looked no better, although his hands were free, and it appeared he was talking with four Mautuk warriors.

The stories they told of Mautuk warriors at bedtime to get children to obey were true and not exaggerated. Uncertainty gnawed at Babtoo as he slid back down the hill. Catching his breath, he watched Casteel struggle with the fear that grew with every minute that passed. From birth, Watinkee tribesmen learned early on to fight and hunt. No one would have expected Casteel to battle Mautuks at his young age.

Looking over at Babtoo, Casteel saw a stoic, grim faced warrior. The man was determined and his eyes showed no fear. He watched as Babtoo calmly grabbed his spear and examined it as if he were trying to breathe life into it. Lifting the spear with both hands, Babtoo prayed for protection. What Casteel overheard was protection for him, Monbeem and Hohumph. Babtoo only asked for strength and courage for himself.

A sense of calm settled over Casteel. He would follow Babtoo unquestioningly. Lifting up his own small spear, Casteel tried to emulate the man he admired. Tears ran down his face as he too prayed.

Babtoo looked steadily at Casteel as if weighing his measure. Reaching over, he pulled Casteel closer to him. Whispering into his ear, Babtoo breathed, "I have a plan, but I need you to........"

Casteel nodded, a thin smile spread across his face. He was going to help save Monbeem!

CHAPTER 20

HOHUMPH'S LAST ACT

The four Mautuks stood in a circle by the fire glancing furtively at Hohumph. The crow's feather attached to the spear reflected the firelight as it danced across its inky blackness. Superstition paralyzed them as they argued about what to do with the prisoners.

The enigmatic Quid said, "Let's just take the girl. Leave the big one there. If he dies by an animal it will not be on our hands."

Harroot shook his head and said, "If he is a man of the priest, we have to let him go. He may have powers beyond what we know. That crow's feather could be a way for him to communicate with our high priest."

Stuffe, holding his head in his hands cringed and quietly said, "I am dead. I hit him. I am dead. I hit him." Stuffe repeated this same thing over and over again.

Quid slapped Stuffe in the face as he bemoaned his fate. "Shut up Stuffe!" He yelled.

Stuffe backed up, looking for a place to hide.

Monchu said, "I agree with Harroot. Let him go and see what he does. If he acts as if he could be a vessel for the high priest, we let him live. If not, we kill him and burn the spear."

Quid was unconvinced, but Harroot and Monchu made sense. They had to do something to find out who Hohumph really was. Reflecting on what the others said, Quid agreed, "O.K. let's let him go. We'll see if he is the high priest's dog. If not, we'll kill him where he stands for the blasphemy of carrying a holy feather."

Monchu and Harroot nodded in agreement. Stuffe looked

apprehensively toward the other three and said, "You have killed me!"

Exasperated, Quid said, "Shut up, Stuffe. Just shut up!"

Quid noticed all eyes were on him. They were looking for him to release the big fat Watinkee warrior. Quid looked directly in each warriors face as their eyes darted from his to Hohumph's slouching form. Realizing he was going to have to do this himself, Quid gathered the courage to walk over to the tree. Hohumph and Monbeem looked on with great trepidation as he approached.

Hohumph watched the erratic behavior of the Mautuks. The argument took some time to finish and it appeared they had made a decision. The leader shuffled toward him cautiously. Hohumph cringed as Quid stepped in front of him with his spear raised. The other three warriors followed closely behind, flinching at Hohumph's every move. Extending his spear, Quid slipped the point in between Hohumph's bonds cutting them off his wrists.

Leaping back, the Mautuks waited to see what would happen. Hohumph sat unmoving for a full minute. His eyes were searching for an avenue of escape, but fear prevented him from getting up. The Mautuks were nervous and getting a little anxious. Finally, Monbeem glanced at him wondering why he had not moved.

Leaning over to him so the Mautuks could not see her talking, she whispered, "Get up you big oaf! This is your chance to get us out of here. Do not be a coward. Show them what a real Watinkee warrior is!"

Hohumph inched his way up the tree to stand. His clothes were soaked as sweat trickled down his body. His mind, numb from fear, screamed, "Run! Run! Run! Do not look back! Escape! Find a way out!"

The Mautuks were nervous and starting to point the wicked looking spears in his direction.

Monbeem screamed, "They will kill us! Do something!"

Quid aimed a spear in her direction, poised to throw.

Hohumph finally reacted and screamed, "HOLD!"

Stepping in front of Quid, his paralysis forgotten, Hohumph put his hand out to stop the Mautuk leader. Surprised, Quid lowered the spear. The fat Watinkee could speak.

Confidence started to build within Hohumph. He was not a brave man, but he was cornered. He would fight to stay alive. Even the smallest creatures fight when they have no choice.

His mind started to churn through the fear. The crafty Hohumph was back. Pointing to the fire, Hohumph made a large gesture to walk with him. Turning his back on the Mautuks and praying a spear would not find its way in his back, Hohumph strode over to the fire. Picking up his spear, Hohumph caressed the feather and put it to his ear.

All of their spears pointed in his direction, cocked and ready to throw. Seemingly unconcerned, Hohumph pretended to listen to his feather. He exaggerated his expressions so they could see what he was doing. A look of seriousness crossed his face as he continued to stroke his black feather. The Mautuks were engrossed by this and stood waiting for some sort of order. Finally, Quid took a step forward and impatiently asked, "What is the high priest, saying fat one?"

Hohumph held out his hand to stop him and pretended to pray to the gods of the black feather. Raising his arms up and dancing like a fool, Hohumph continued to keep the Mautuks guessing. His mind was working feverishly, trying to think of something when things started to go wrong.

Harroot grabbed Quid and said, "I don't understand a thing he is saying, do you?"

Quid looked curiously at Harroot and said, "You're right. Do you think it is some high priest gibberish?" Quid looked for reassurance," I think he's an imposter. Let's kill him now!"

The charade was up and Hohumph knew it. Preparing to run, everything broke loose and things started to happen faster than anybody could conceive.

The pink light of dawn started to brighten the sky. They had stayed too long in Watinkee territory and now felt vulnerable.

In the distance, the lone sound of hoof beats echoed like a stampede. A huge dark apparition bent low, with a spear pointed in their direction, was charging down on them with frightening speed. Superstitious horrors flooded their minds as they scattered from fear. The feather did talk to the warrior and now they would pay the price for being unbelievers.

Quid and Monchu ran for the lake. Stuffe and Harroot headed for the copse of trees near Monbeem, hoping to hide from the growing monstrosity. Hohumph found his chance to escape and ran for cover. Diving for a small bush, hoping to conceal his cringing body, Hohumph watched incredulously as Babtoo rode past them on the spotted zebra.

The earth shook with the nearness of the hoof beats. Each breath the animal took sounded like a charging Cape buffalo. The wicked looking spear tip reflected the pink dawn and seemed to drip red with blood.

Babtoo saw the first two run for the lake. Steering Enobi toward their fleeing forms, Babtoo closed the distance quickly. Monchu turned to look at the vision of death behind him. Horror creased his features as the demon rode him down. Turning back to run, he tripped over an exposed root and fell flat on his face. Rolling over to get back up, Babtoo's spear carved a path into his chest. Death came quickly as his spirit left his body.

Yanking the spear out of the unmoving Mautuk, Babtoo raced towards the other warrior and cornered him at the lake. Babtoo felt like a man possessed, allowing no room for fear. Leaping off Enobi to let him run free, Babtoo strode over to face Quid.

Quid stepped away from the water. The realization that Babtoo was a Watinkee warrior had restored a small amount of courage to his badly abused ego. Looking closely at Babtoo, Quid noticed he had a noticeable limp. He was a perceptive warrior and hoped to gain the advantage.

Circling one another like two stalking tigers, Babtoo wanted to end the fight quickly before the other two warriors gathered enough courage to rally round their leader. Quid concentrated on Babtoo's crippled leg. A stab down toward Babtoo's foot surprised the large warrior and he leaped back. Quid continued to attack the leg, backing Babtoo away from the water with every thrust. Working defensively, Babtoo back-pedaled and tripped over a large stone. Quid immediately leaped into the air, driving the spear down toward Babtoo's chest.

The spear dug deep into the earth as Babtoo rolled away. Grabbing the end of the shaft, Babtoo yanked the spear from Quid's hands and broke it in two. Surprised at his great strength, Quid drew his knife and jumped on Babtoo. Instantly he realized he was no match for the muscular youth. Babtoo grabbed his knife arm in an iron grip and squeezed his hand backwards.

Desperate to break Babtoo's grip, Quid punched down on Babtoo's ribs. Babtoo let out a gasp of pain and his grip loosened on Quid's arm. Punching the sore ribs again, Quid was able to twist his knife hand free. With victory close-at-hand, Quid raised his knife with both hands and stabbed downward.

To Quid's surprise, the knife never landed anywhere near Babtoo. Instead, he found himself flying through the air, landing heavily on his back. Struggling for breath, he stumbled to his feet. Babtoo was up and had his spear pointed in his direction. One hand held his ribs while the other hand lightly held the spear steady. Babtoo circled toward the Mautuk, forcing Quid back toward the lake.

Quid splashed in the ankle deep water waiting for Babtoo. He hoped the water in combination with Babtoo's crippled foot would slow him down long enough for him to gain the upper hand. Quid slowly waved his knife back and forth in front of Babtoo, teasing him to come fight in the lake.

Babtoo slowed as he watched. Relaxing his grip on his spear, Babtoo stood and waited. Puzzled by this, Quid realized why, but it was too late.

The sound of a splashing tail was all that alerted Quid to another, more fearsome enemy. Turning around in stunned silence, he watched in horror as the crocodile leapt out of the shallow water. Grabbing Quid by the leg, it pulled him down into the deeper portion of the lake. The big crocodile rolled and rolled until Quid no longer struggled and then slowly sank out of sight with his prize.

Almost collapsing from the effort, Babtoo gathered his strength and ran toward the campsite.

The distraction from Babtoo galloping down toward the camp had given Casteel a chance to slide down the small embankment and crouch in some bushes. Watching the Mautuks scatter gave him a sense of relief. He stealthily approached the tree where Monbeem struggled to escape her bonds. Sawing at her ropes with his knife, Casteel was not aware where Stuffe and Harroot had gone.

Monbeem turned around in surprise and saw Casteel, alive, freeing her from her bonds. A small gasp of elation escaped her as she struggled to free herself. Turning around she whispered, "Hurry Casteel, Hurry!"

Harroot and Stuffe, hiding in a nearby copse of trees, noticed Monbeem struggling to escape. Harroot turned toward Stuffe and pointed, "Kill her. Hurry before the demon comes back!"

Stuffe vaulted from his hiding place and ran from bush to bush toward Monbeem with an evil glint in his eyes that turned her blood ice cold. Taking his knife out slowly, Stuffe did not see Casteel behind the tree. Casteel placed his knife in Monbeem's hand so she could finish cutting the ropes and leaped from behind the tree, brandishing his tiny spear.

Surprised by the diminutive warrior, Stuffe's face quickly turning to glee. The smile on his face abruptly ended, however, when Casteel threw his spear, driving the point into his leg.

He howled in pain as he ripped the spear from his thigh. Blood trickled from the wound as he broke the spear in two. Casteel stood defiantly, hoping Monbeem would quickly free herself.

Stuffe charged at Casteel, but Monbeem stuck her leg out, tripping the big warrior. Slicing through the last of her bonds, Monbeem struggled to her feet to face Stuffe. She swayed on unsteady legs, but put herself in front of Casteel, holding the tiny knife.

Stuffe sprang up and backhanded Monbeem with a hard right hand. The force of the blow stunned her as she spun to the ground. Dropping the knife, she landed heavily on her back. Darkness closed in around her as she fought to stay conscious. Rolling to her hands and knees, she looked up to see Stuffe reach for Casteel. Grabbing the small boy, Stuffe's big hands encircled Casteel's throat. Stuffe raised Casteel's off the ground, his legs dangled, kicking in the air as he desperately tried to escape.

His swarthy skin turned blue and his struggles were getting less. Casteel desperately tried to breathe. Suddenly, Hohumph found some courage and out of nowhere plunged his spear into Stuffe's broad chest. The black raven feather fluttered in the big warrior's face, as if mocking him.

Dropping Casteel and falling back, Stuffe grasped Hohumph weakly. Hohumph drove his spear forward until Stuffe dropped to the ground. His eyes locked into Hohumph's in terror. His body relaxed, even as his hands clutched the raven's feather reverently.

Harroot jumped out of hiding as Hohumph broke from cover to engage Stuffe. Too late, Harroot could not make it in time and watched helplessly as Stuffe died under Hohumph's spear. With a running start, Harroot threw his spear at Hohumph, afraid to engage the fat Watinkee warrior up close.

Hohumph turned to help Monbeem as she struggled to her feet. Reaching his hand down to her, a look of surprise and shock, filled with pain, crossed his face. The tip of Harroot's spear pierced his back to emerge from his chest. Touching the point with his hand, he looked down at Monbeem and whispered with the last of his strength, "I'm sorry Monbeem. I just wanted you to like me. I hope you will find it in your heart to forgive me one day." With these last words, he toppled to the ground.

Harroot drew his knife to finish the job when he heard Babtoo coming up from the lake. He knew Quid and Monchu were dead if the demon man was returning. Dread filled his heart as the man-demon seemed unbeatable. Leaving his spear in Hohumph, Harroot decided to run. Panicking, he had to get back to his tribe to tell the high priest of the power the Watinkee warriors held. Perhaps Squanto was right after all. Fading into the bush, Harroot wanted no part of the fearsome Babtoo.

Babtoo half ran and half limped up to the camp. Looking around for other warriors and finding none, he noticed Monbeem bent over Hohumph, crying. Grim faced, he walked over to see what had happened. Casteel was trying to comfort Monbeem and stood uncertainly, not knowing what to do.

Tears streaked down her face as she cried shamelessly, falling on Hohumph's still form. She gently wiped his gritty face cradled in her arms. Babtoo stood stoically not sure what to do. He looked questioningly at Casteel whose eyes were red and puffy from trying not to sob. Casteel whimpered, "He saved my life Babtoo. He saved my life." Burying his head in Monbeem's shoulder, he started to cry.

Hohumph had told the truth in the end. Casteel was alive. Monbeem felt awful for not believing in him. She realized that everything he did was for her benefit. Unfortunately, he did the wrong things and paid with his life. She hoped his spirit was at rest now.

The time for grieving was not here or now. Babtoo gently pulled Monbeem away from Hohumph. She wrapped her arms around him and showered him with thankful kisses, finding it hard to let go. Burying her head in his chest, Monbeem shook with relief.

Her warm body pressing against his felt awkward. Casteel stood and wrapped his arms around Babtoo's leg, squeezing for all he was worth. Babtoo, unused to the affection, stood stiffly. Soon, he too, started to relax, and his arms fell around both Casteel and Monbeem, feeling the warmth of true love. He had never felt so needed and hoped the feeling would never end.

Slowly unwrapping her arms from around his body, Babtoo

whispered in Monbeem's ear, "We need to get out of here. Somewhere another Mautuk escaped and there might be more hunting parties out for him to meet up with. I don't know why you're out here with Hohumph alone, but we have to get back to the village for your father. I saw a shallow ravine where we can bury Hohumph. We can find plenty of rocks we can use for a cairn. I'll have Casteel get Hohumph's spear to bury with him to have in the spirit world. You can tell me why you were out here with him on the way back."

Monbeem looked up into Babtoo's eyes and felt safe. She had not felt safe in so long it seemed. Nodding, she said, "I saw the Mautuk run after throwing the spear at Hohumph. He saw you coming up from the lake and looked frightened."

Babtoo glanced around and said, "I know there were at least four. There is no time to look for him now. When we get back to the village, we'll alert Chief Bowhut. He'll know what to do."

They quickly dragged Hohumph to the ravine. Casteel placed the spear reverently on his chest. Babtoo folded his arms and placed the enemy's' spears around his body. Monbeem gently washed his face. Babtoo mumbled a short prayer to pave the way for Hohumph's spirit journey to the gods. A final last look and they hastily piled rocks on his body to protect it from marauding animals.

Babtoo found Enobi a short distance away, grazing on a green patch of grass. Walking up to the big animal, Babtoo praised him for his courage. Stroking his neck, he swung up on his back and offered his hand to Monbeem. She accepted timidly, not sure what to do. Awkwardly, she straddled Enobi's back. Casteel looked up at them and said, "I'll keep up. I'm well rested. You don't have to worry about me." Casteel's eyes darted around for his spear.

Babtoo shifted on the horse and said, "I'll not leave you behind, little warrior. If not for your courage, Monbeem would have faced the Mautuk by herself. We are all in this together now. When we get back to the tribe, we will make you another spear, a grown-up spear for a grown-up warrior. They will sing your praises around the campfire!"

Casteel could not smile any bigger. He stuck his chest out and started forward. He felt like he would do anything for Babtoo.

They started forward leaving the battle scene behind. Monbeem held Babtoo and rested her head against his back. Turning slightly, Babtoo asked the question that was perplexing to him. "Monbeem, why were you and Hohumph so far from home? There was evidence of Mautuks in the area. They are a very dangerous people and you put yourself at risk with Hohumph. Why would you go out with Hohumph anyway? He never was one to volunteer for anything."

A moment of silence followed as she tried to organize her thoughts. She spoke softly as she began her story, "Casteel had been missing and nobody knew where he was. You know how close I am to Casteel and his family. Hohumph approached asking me to help him find Casteel. I could not refuse. We even had the blessings of Chief Bowhut. Oh, I knew it was a mistake to go with him, but my heart went out to Casteel and I wanted to do something. I could no longer wait for your return and do nothing. Whutknot nursed Chintook constantly, making him comfortable and trying everything in his power to give him strength until you came back. It drove me crazy to be unable to help. Therefore, when Hohumph asked me to go look for Casteel, I did. At first, it seemed okay."

"But, as the time went on, I found him to be a coward. We ran into a large lion and before I knew it, I was alone, facing the beast, and he was safe in a tree. Fortunately, the gods were with us and the lion must have just eaten."

"Then strange things started happening. We found Casteel's shoes on the open savanna, and one was stuck on a high branch of a shrub. I was so excited about finding the shoe, I didn't think it was unusual at the time. Then there were two sets of Hohumph's tracks in the wildebeest crossing that led back to our camp. I didn't pay any attention to it until later."

"Not all of these things were adding up. I let him take first watch and pretended to sleep. He took off shortly and went back into the wildebeest crossing. I followed and caught him throwing Casteel's clothes around with blood on them. I thought he had killed Casteel. He, of course, denied the accusations."

She sighed and went on, "That is when the Mautuks caught us. It was not until Casteel was cutting my bonds that I believed Hohumph was telling the truth. Yes, I know he was a coward at heart sometimes, but he saved Casteel's life, and my own. He could have run. Hohumph has earned the right to be remembered as a warrior and as a hero. He knew the ruse was wrong and tried in the end to make up for it. I don't want the tribe to know anything beyond that he saved my life and the life of Casteel. I want this to be our secret, Babtoo, and I don't wish for Hohumph's name to be smeared. We will sing great songs about him."

Babtoo rode in silence thinking of everything Monbeem said. He did not feel bad for Hohumph, but realized the man proved to have found courage no one thought he had. Perhaps people can change for the better as Hohumph did in the end. He had no desire to speak poorly of Hohumph. It would serve no purpose for people to know the truth of everything that had happened. Telling the good parts of the story and leaving the bad out would not be a total lie. It would just be omitting a few small details that were unimportant compared with his greater deed in the end.

Babtoo turned his head to look at Monbeem and agreed, "No good would come of this if everything were told. You're right. The man has made up for a lifetime of mistakes. We'll let it go. Hohumph was a hero in the end and that's all anybody needs know!"

She squeezed him even tighter as they made their way across the plain.

CHAPTER 21

FAILURE

Harroot watched as Babtoo, Monbeem, and Casteel buried Hohumph. He found it amazing that a warrior with an injured leg could kill two competent Mautuk warriors. He watched Babtoo limping on his maimed foot, and yet, was afraid of him. The way Babtoo carried himself with confidence made him wary. There was something more about this warrior than met the eye. He was glad he didn't face him on the battlefield today or he too could be walking the spirit world with Stuffe, Quid and Monchu.

How was he able to control the beast with the speckled skin? What was this beast? Could it have breathed fire as Squanto said? He did not see any, but it could have. All he knew was this was a great warrior controlling a great beast. Only the high priest has the power to control a raven. Yet this crippled Watinkee has the power to control an even-larger magical beast. He was more afraid to face this warrior by himself than going back to the high priest with no prisoners. At least he would live, or so he thought.

Going back to the ravine where Hohumph's burial mound was, Harroot dug around to retrieve his spear.

He would not go after the big warrior. After all, there were three of them now and not just one. He would tell the high priest a war party of Watinkee warriors wiped out his companions and released the prisoners. He hoped the high priest would believe him as he had believed Squanto's story. After kicking the bodies of Stuffe and Monchu to be sure they were dead, Harroot headed back toward the forest.

The foliage enveloped Harroot within its dark comforting

confines. This was his home. Harroot breathed a sigh of relief. The darkness did not bother him, but soothed his tattered ego.

Harroot stopped by the cave for a moment to peer inside. There, the vivid memories of his scouting party seemed to come alive. He felt no sense of loss for Quid and Monchu. They were in the spirit world now with other great Mautuk warriors. He only felt a slight loss for Stuffe. He liked the superstitious warrior as much as any Mautuk could. Shaking his head of the memories, Harroot went on his way.

Glancing up into the umbrella-like canopy, Harroot could see only speckles of sunlight filtering through the leaves. Strange colorful large beaked-birds flew from branch to branch, bringing splashes of color to an otherwise drab world. Howler monkeys were busy chasing one another noisily, their cries sounded like expressions of grief. It would be at least another day before he got to the temple.

Walking confidently through the forest, blending in with the underbrush, Harroot went through his story again in his mind. He knew the high priest would not be happy losing three seasoned warriors and having no prisoners. He also wondered if it was wise for him to go back empty handed. The small warning in his subconscious went largely ignored. He was coming back with valuable information about the Watinkees. The high priest would be pleased after all, he convinced himself.

The large decaying citadel loomed ahead. Harroot felt elation at being close to home. He looked forward to seeing some of his friends from the last scouting party. Ugly black smoke stained the air, as he got closer to the pyramid. Sounds of misery coming from the slaves were like music to his soul.

Skirting around campfires and huts, Harroot walked toward the temple. Glancing at the many huts and campfires, he wondered why the other scouts he knew did not come to greet him. Approaching the stone structure in awe, Harroot made a small gesture of prayer to the leering skulls guarding the entrance. Stepping through, he waited patiently for the high priest and his twin abominations to appear. The gloom was menacing and only shadows barely glimpsed from the corner of his eye flitted here and there through the large chamber.

The red parrot feather on his knife was the first indication the high priest was emerging out of the dim interior. The next thing to appear was his bone white face with the matching skulls on his shoulders. His two henchmen standing to the side were dressed in black and were barely visible. The rustling of his raven's cape was all Harroot heard in the ethereal interior.

Instantly prostrating himself in front of the high priest, Harroot said, "I have brought important news Great One."

There was nothing but silence as his eyes tracked a roach traveling across the floor. Continuing to grovel, Harroot risked a peek up to see why there was no response. He had hoped for more of a reaction. His heart started to race as sweat began to pour from his pores. A thought suddenly occurred to him as to why his friends from the first scouting mission had not greeted him. He had seen no sign of them as he went through camp.

A booming voice that reverberated throughout the chamber and settled in his now churning stomach said simply, "You have returned and I see no prisoners. Where is the rest of your scouting party? You had specific orders and have failed me for the second time!"

Harroot squirmed like a bug on a stick. He started to talk and his story bubbled out of him in halting sentences. "We did everything you had instructed us to do. We came upon two lone Watinkees out in the plain. We captured them to take back to you. A war party of Watinkee warriors ambushed us and slaughtered our group. We had no chance! I was lucky to escape to warn you of a great warrior that was with the Watinkees. He was riding a great magical beast."

Silence followed. For several minutes, the only noise was Harroot's teeth chattering from fear.

Again, the booming voice said, "You have told me nothing new. This story is identical to Squanto's and you have no wounds to back up what you say. You let your brothers die without your help. There is no room for cowards here!"

Harroot screamed, "NOOOOO!"

Two beings separated themselves from the high priest. One planted his foot on Harroot's back to keep him down. The other grabbed his arms in a vice-like grip. Yanking him to his feet, Harroot was trembling so hard that his knees buckled.

The two huge Mautuk abominations dragged Harroot over to a large table. They lifted him up and slammed him down with such force he lost consciousness for a moment. Tying his feet and hands to the table, the two Mautuks guards stepped once again into the shadows. Looking more closely at the table, Harroot could see it was stained red and seemed sticky and damp.

Harroot started to plead for his life. All he could get out was gibberish. He could no longer pronounce simple words as he struggled to scream. His tongue became dry and stiff. Resistance was useless.

From far off, he heard the high priest praying. Harroot did not understand the words, but felt the power of the prayer. The shadowy gloom hid the high priest's skeletal features. The red parrot feather was all that was visible. It fluttered slightly with movement as it faded in and out of view. It reminded him of the parrots he saw flying in the trees when he entered the forest.

His mind went numb from terror as a disembodied skull detached itself from the darkness and floated toward him. The prayer became more intense. Somewhere he heard drum beats measuring out the cadence of his own thundering heart. Harroot opened his mouth to shriek. His scream echoed through the chamber as the knife dropped from the ceiling, striking his chest.

The serrated blade cut deeply into his chest, severing arteries and breaking ribs. Reaching in, the high priest grasped the erratically beating heart in the palm of his hand and raised it above his head. Harroot's eyes glazed over as his body twitched in death. In disgust, the high priest threw the pulsating heart on the floor, whispering "Coward. We cannot eat a coward's heart. It will weaken us."

CHAPTER 22

RETURNING HOME A HERO

The morning sun bathed the savanna in a soft light. This was the time when nocturnal predators were finished hunting and looking for some shade to rest from the heat of the sun. Animals that survived the night heaved a sigh of relief for the gift of another day of life as the sun rose to meet the sky. Prey and predator passed one another in peace for this brief moment before the savagery of the African savanna began again.

Babtoo was happy. Monbeem rested her head on his back as he guided the big horse toward the village. Casteel, in all his youth, was trotting alongside with his incessant chatter of the adventures they had encountered.

When Casteel talked about the snake and how large it was, she pulled away to examine his ribs. The thick ribbon of black and blue discolored his body like an ugly scar. She touched it with hesitant fingers. Babtoo flinched and could not contain a small wheeze. She looked at his broad back in silence and thought, "He has done things in a short time that many Watinkee warriors would have been proud to do in a life time. I would be proud to be his wife!"

The wood smoke from the cooking fires rose over the savanna in lazy columns to blend with the clouds in the sky. Casteel, excited to tell somebody of his adventures with Babtoo, ran to alert the village of their arrival. Before long, Babtoo and Monbeem watched as two Watinkee tribesman took shape in the shimmering haze.

Puku and Ukup were running toward them as fast as they could. There two silhouettes bobbed up and down like sticks in a lake. Out of breath, the two brothers waited on a hill for Babtoo to approach on the big animal. They could not control their excitement as their grins stretched their faces from ear to ear.

"Well met little brother. We didn't expect you for another week!" Puku said.

Before Babtoo had a chance to answer, Ukup, who could not contain himself any further, blurted, "Babtoo, you found Casteel and brought back Monbeem. How did you do all that and get the medicine too? I look forward to hearing your tale!"

Babtoo said with a tired smile, "Well met brothers. It is a long story for another time. Is Chintook still under Whutknot's care?"

Puku answered with downcast eyes and said, "Yes, but he continues to grow weaker. Now that you have the root, maybe he will get better."

Babtoo nodded and said, "Let's get back as fast as we can. Everything can wait until then."

Ukup said, "We are here to escort you in."

Babtoo replied, "If you have rested enough, we're ready to go!"

Puku excitedly said without false bravado, "We will lead but will you be able to keep up?"

A wry smile crossed Babtoo's face at that statement as he patted Enobi on the neck.

He saw the village first as Puku and Ukup led them over the small rise. The rich array of village life lifted his spirits. Children ran and played at their games as they dodged around tents and huts. Small fires danced merrily in the heat of the day as women were busy cooking and chatting about the latest gossip. Anxious warriors stood stoically waiting for the latest news of the Mautuks from the returning scouts. He was finally home and the tension of recent events slowly drained from his body.

Chief Bowhut stood patiently just outside his tent waiting to greet Babtoo, wondering on the success of his quest. Casteel jumped up and down by his side pointing in Babtoo's direction. Even from that distance, Babtoo could hear Casteel excitedly telling the Chief his part in their adventures together. The chief nodded now and then to acknowledge something Casteel said as he watched Babtoo ride closer.

Babtoo stopped a few yards away from them and slid slowly off. Offering his hand to Monbeem, she jumped lightly down. Patting Enobi, he sent him off to graze. Turning around, his grey eyes scanned the small group, picking up subtle details he may have not noticed before. Bowhut looked a little more haggard and tired with the stress of Mautuks trespassing on their land. The mantle of leadership is a heavy burden and one he took seriously.

Ohat jogged over to Chief Bowhut trying to peel Casteel away with little success. His clothes seemed travel stained and his features were drawn. He had little patience for Casteel's antics.

Chief Bowhut and Ohat saw Babtoo differently also. They no longer saw him as a boy. They saw confidence in his step. His eyes smoldered with passion and seemed to look deep into their hearts while his voice was strong and self-assured. Both men knew that Babtoo had passed the test into manhood and would never again be the maimed boy they once knew.

"Well met Babtoo! Your little friend has told us some amazing stories. I would like to hear them from you too! First, Whutknot has asked to give him the roots right away. Chintook's life hovers between the spirit world and ours." Chief Bowhut said.

Babtoo looked over to Casteel and said, "Casteel, take the herbs you collected to Whutknot. Chintook needs those right away. Be quick! Then go see your mother! She must be very worried!"

Casteel broke away from Chief Bowhut, grabbed the sack of herbs resting on Enobi, and flew toward Chintook's hut.

A look of amazement passed between Chief Bowhut and Ohat. Ohat stated, "That child has caused more trouble and has never listened to anybody, including his parents. You seem to have been able to get him to pay attention. How did you do that?"

"All he wanted was respect for what he can do. Because he is small does not mean he can't do what you or I can do." Involuntarily he looked at his own crippled foot. Chief Bowhut noticed Babtoo glance down at his foot and nodded in agreement.

Babtoo continued, "We have worked together and accomplished much. He will need a new spear - a warrior's spear. He has earned it!" Bowhut and Ohat looked at one another in disbelief. Babtoo's demeanor was now one of quiet confidence that left no room for disagreement.

You had to do a great deed to get a warriors spear. What could Casteel have done? What happened to Babtoo on this quest to have changed him into a man so quickly?

Tuning to Monbeem, Chief Bowhut said, "I'm sorry about Hohumph. I never knew you two were close."

Monbeem bowed her head and said, "He was a friend I was proud to have. He saved my life and the life of Casteel, with Babtoo's help." Monbeem looked into Babtoo's eyes and knew the story of Hohumph's bravery would be told around the campfires for many years to come. Instinctively she held Babtoo's muscular arm and laid her head on his shoulder.

Chief Bowhut looked curiously at Monbeem and wondered what had happened out in the savanna. He had known Hohumph since he was a child. Chief Bowhut thought, "The only thing Hohumph excelled at was to be a bully. There was never any bravery in that man. He would do as little as possible not to help anybody. Therefore, he was never counted on for anything. If he sacrificed his life for somebody else's, then that was worth talking about."

Ohat watched Babtoo move and said with concern, "You look injured. Those ribs still seem sore. As soon as Whutknot has given Chintook the herb, I will have him visit you."

Chief Bowhut nodded his head in agreement and said, "Yes, it looks like he's in need of some rest too. First, what happened out on the savanna with the Mautuk war party. Casteel talked so fast, I was only able to get about half of it. Let's get back to my tent. You can relax there over some food while we talk."

Babtoo entered Chief Bowhut's tent with Ohat. Monbeem left to help Whutknot and check on Chintook. Once inside the dim interior, Babtoo smelled the heady aroma of gazelle stew. Sitting down on the thick hides, his eyes closed for a moment, even though he was trying hard to stay awake. He felt safe here and needed this time to recharge.

Chief Bowhut saw this and quickly asked his wife for some stew. His wife bustled to the door and brought a large steaming plate. Grateful, Babtoo ate quickly as if he had not eaten for days. Embarrassed, he looked up and noticed that Chief Bowhut was smiling with great satisfaction.

Slowing down and remembering his manners, Babtoo said, "I'm sorry. Your wife makes excellent stew. Can I have more?"

Chief Bowhut laughed and in a deep booming voice said, "Of course you can have more. My wife will be pleased you like it so much. Have as much as you want!"

After Babtoo had finished the second plate of stew, Chief Bowhut became serious and said, "Babtoo, we need your help. Casteel said something about a scouting party of Mautuk warriors not far from here. What happened?"

Ohat said, "There are signs that Mautuks are about. I have found small things, but they were well camouflaged. Other trackers have noticed similar signs, but were not sure how recent they were. Nobody has come across a single Mautuk," pausing, "except you. Their high priest must have powerful magic to protect and hide his scouts. How is it that you are able to find them?"

Babtoo gathered his thoughts and said, "I was traveling into the night when Casteel spotted the campfire. We were traveling toward the watering hole where I had camped before anyway. Sitting on top of Enobi, I was able to see above the high grass but could not determine if it was a Mautuk or Watinkee campfire. However, after the fight with the Mautuks and the writings on the cave wall, I became very cautious. We went unnoticed and came around the waterhole from behind at the high point. We were surprised to see Monbeem and Hohumph captured by Mautuk warriors. Hohumph had convinced them to untie him and tried to distract the Mautuks from Monbeem.

"When Hohumph held their attention long enough it was time to attack. I rode down the hill on Enobi and killed two before got away they. Casteel crept up from behind Monbeem and set her free. A Mautuk warrior attacked Casteel and Monbeem and that's when Hohumph came to their rescue. In the confusion that followed, a spear came out of nowhere and struck Hohumph from behind, killing him. The remaining Mautuk fled, though we did not chase after him. We left swiftly after that to get Casteel and Monbeem back to the safety of the village with the medicine for Chintook."

There was a moment of silence as Chief Bowhut and Ohat absorbed the story. They looked at one another trying to decipher if any part of the story could be an exaggeration. Babtoo, a lone warrior, continued to impress with his bravery and ingenuity. Searching Babtoo's eyes, they quickly concluded it happened exactly as he said it did. Casteel had told the truth after all.

Ohat said, "I think Babtoo brought up a good point. Our scouting parties should be on high ground at night searching for their campfires. We don't have a magical beast, but we know this terrain better than any Mautuk warrior does. The Mautuk that got away will have scouted us and anything he has learned will take back to their tribe."

Chief Bowhut nodded and said, "Ohat, you're right. We'll have to split up the scouting parties between day and night. If we're lucky, we may get a prisoner out of this. Then we can find out more what they are planning to do."

Babtoo's eyes were slowly closing no matter what he did to try to keep them open.

Chief Bowhut glanced at Babtoo with concern and said, "Go get some rest. We'll plan from here."

Babtoo got up on legs stiff from sitting and said, "Thank you. Wake me up if you need me for anything." With those parting words,

Babtoo made his way to his tent and was surprised to see how neat and orderly everything was.

Monbeem came around the corner and said, "I tried to organize your tent a little bit. I hope you don't mind."

A grateful smile crossed Babtoo's face while he said, "Yes, this is perfect. Thank you." He disappeared into his tent and within moments was fast asleep.

The sun was up and the giant centipede was hungry and looking for food. It gathered its hundred legs and in a fluid motion started walking this way and that, searching for an elusive meal. Crawling out from under a tent, its hundred legs found an opening in the tent flap. It found a perfect hunting ground, digging its way between some skins and found a warm place to hide, wiggling its way between a brown leg and some pants....

Babtoo's eyes popped open. He jumped out of bed and hopped around on one foot trying to dislodge the centipede. It curled in a ball at this unexpected commotion, its antenna frantically tried to figure out what happened. Babtoo looked down at the centipede sheepishly and gathering it up in his hand threw it out of the tent.

Trying to compose himself and glad nobody had been there to see, Babtoo squinted into the sun. It was late in the day. Stepping outside, warily looking on the ground, Babtoo made his way to Chintook's tent.

Monbeem was outside the tent cooking dinner. Looking up at Babtoo, she said, "Welcome back from the dead! You slept for a long time. I checked on you to be sure you were o.k. I was going to send Whutknot in to check on your ribs, but he didn't want to wake you either."

"Thank you," Babtoo said gratefully. "I would have slept a little longer if not for an unexpected guest."

Monbeem looked up puzzled, but Babtoo said with a smile,

"It was just a centipede trying to make my tent its home! How is Chintook?"

"He's resting a lot more comfortably with the medicine. He still is very sick, but Whutknot thinks he'll recover soon. It will take him some time to get his strength back though."

"I would like to see him if he is strong enough to talk." Babtoo said.

Disappearing into the tent for a moment to check on Chintook, she called from inside, "Babtoo, Chintook is awake and wants to see you too!"

Stepping into the dark interior, Babtoo found Monbeem next to Chintook. Chintook was rail thin but his eyes were clear. His voice sounded ragged, "Babtoo, Monbeem told me you have saved my life. Thank you for that because any more of Whutknot's miracle cures and I would have died from those instead." A smile played across his features.

Babtoo smiled broadly and said, "You have been like a father to me. You taught me I could do anything even if I could not keep up. You had faith in me when others did not. I could not refuse to go!"

Chintook reached out and grabbed his arm with surprising strength, "You have also found the time to save my daughter from the Mautuks. That is courage I could not teach."

Embarrassed by the compliment, Babtoo simply said, "I have learned courage from a great teacher."

Chintook's smile faded and he dropped back down on the bed. His eyes closed and fluttered back open to say, "Well met Babtoo. You have made me proud!"

Monbeem gently took hold of Babtoo's hand and steered him toward the door. "He needs rest more than anything. He has wanted to talk to you ever since you got back."

Babtoo stepped into the sunlight blinking and said, "I wonder if Chief Bowhut has any more news on the Mautuks."

"Before you go, Babtoo, I have something to show you." Monbeem said mysteriously. Walking to the back of the tent, she unfolded the large black panther pelt. Holding it up, she said proudly, "I have finished this for you. You will now be the great black panther warrior! I hope it fits."

Babtoo gasped at its beauty. The black cape fit him perfectly. He felt the silky softness as it lay across his shoulders. The blackness of the fur gleamed in the sun reflecting back the colors of a rainbow. A tear fell from his eye as he turned around and gave Monbeem a hug and kiss on the cheek. Handing it back to her, he said, "I will wear it with honor, Monbeem. Thank you."

Turning away, he started for Chief Bowhut's tent. Before he had gotten very far, Casteel jumped out at him from behind the tent.

"It's about time you woke up. Nobody would let me see you until you were awake. I guess you are now. Are you going to see Chief Bowhut? Can I come with you? Do not leave without me next time!"

Babtoo looked down at the little warrior and grinned. "You didn't ask your parents about any of this, did you? I won't take you unless your parents say you can go. Part of being a good warrior is to follow the rules of your parents or chief. You will not let your parents worry about you anymore."

With downcast eyes Casteel said, "Yes, I know I disobeyed them, but without me, you would not have been able to get Monbeem free. I spotted the fire and I helped to set her free!"

Babtoo was not about to mention the times he had saved Casteel from the snake and crocodile. His ribs still ached from the large serpent but the pain was now bearable. Nor was he going to mention they were going to camp at that watering hole anyway.

Turning to Casteel, Babtoo said, "I have a big responsibility for you to do. I want you to be sure Enobi is well fed and has water. I'll check on him after I see Chief Bowhut."

Casteel's face became serious and said, "A great honor. I'll make sure the magical beast is well cared for." He scampered quickly away looking for Enobi.

Ohat, Puku, Ukup and other trackers circled Chief Bowhut as they compared what they had discovered on the savanna. Looking up from his work, Chief Bowhut stopped what he was saying and asked, "Babtoo! How are you doing? You look a lot better now that you have rested. Are your ribs still sore?"

Babtoo gave a slight nod to the other warriors. They parted for him to enter as a show of respect. Babtoo said, "My ribs will heal, but I still can help you hunt Mautuks."

The warriors nodded in agreement, yet none offered him a task.

Chief Bowhut said, "Babtoo you have done much already. These warriors have volunteered to go back out. We expect you to recover from fully from your injuries. There will be plenty to do later. Tonight, if you are ready, the tribe will hear your story. Everybody wants to know in your own words how you found Monbeem and Casteel on your quest for the healing flower."

Babtoo nodded and said, "Yes, I will be honored."

When evening fell, the glow of the council fire lit the sky for miles. It reached upward with long yellow fingers to rival the brightness of the moon. Sparks flew into the air swirling around the fiery tentacles only to settle back down to earth as black ash. Shadows of tribesmen danced back and forth as people jostled one another for a good space to sit.

Chief Bowhut stood waiting for the proper moment to summon the tribe's attention. Everybody was excited to learn of any new events that surrounded the topic of the Mautuks. By now, everybody had heard some version of the adventure Babtoo had but wanted him to tell his own story. Excitement ran rampant as everybody was talking about the latest rumors.

Chief Bowhut raised his arms for silence. It took several minutes for people to break away from their conversations and remain quiet.

Finally, when he had everybody's attention, Chief Bowhut began to speak. "Today is a special day. I'm going to tell you about our efforts to erase the Mautuk stain from our land. We have been sending out our best trackers to find any evidence of their foul presence. We have some idea they are here, but have not found any warriors until Babtoo killed two. He was not caught unaware and neither should we! At that, the people stood up and cheered. They loved Chief Bowhut and trusted he would keep them safe and find a solution to the Mautuks.

"I now present to you a new warrior to our tribe. BABTOO"

There was cheering followed by the chant, "BABTOO! BABTOO! BABTOO!"

Babtoo no longer walked into the circle of light a shy boy but walked with the confidence of a man. On his back, he wore the black panther cape made by Monbeem. People gasped in wonder at the sight. The cape shimmered in the firelight reflecting back the colors of the blaze.

Babtoo began, "My quest was to get medicine for Chintook which can only be found on Mt. Kikyomanjaro. I had not gone far when I received unexpected help. Casteel had followed and wanted to assist me in this noble quest. We traveled together as a team, and without his aid, I would not have been able to get the medicine so quickly. His spirit was indomitable and his courage served us well.

"On our way back, Casteel noticed the campfire at a watering hole where we had previously camped before. We approached the water hole with caution and on the high ground. There we saw Monbeem and Hohumph captured by four Mautuk warriors.

"The quick wit of Hohumph enabled him to get untied and to retrieve his spear. This distracted them from Monbeem. I then sent Casteel down to untie her while I charged down the slope on Enobi, scattering the Mautuks. Two went down to the watering hole. I ran those warriors down and defeated them." Babtoo glanced at Monbeem and continued, "Hohumph placed himself in great danger and killed a Mautuk before they could reach Monbeem and Casteel. The last Mautuk was a coward and could not face the great Hohumph in battle. With Hohumph's back turned, he threw his spear. We could not save Hohumph. The cowardly Mautuk fled into the savanna. Together, the bravery of Hohumph and Casteel against the Mautuks helped to defeat them. I only wish Hohumph were here to tell his own story."

Silence followed the story. Some of the women had tears in their eyes. Hohumph had never been a well-liked tribesman, but he still was a Watinkee. He had redeemed himself in the tribe's eyes and would now go down in Watinkee history as a warrior.

Monbeem smiled slightly, knowing the true story. She was happy for Hohumph and proud of Babtoo.

Kutlip was bored. Scratching some dirt from his nose, he placed it between his lips and sucked noisily, gazing across the darkening savanna. Hiding in a shallow depression, he lit a small fire to keep the animals away. He had been dodging Watinkee warriors for the past week.

These warriors were big, strong and very good at finding diminutive warriors like him. Several times during the past few days, he had to dodge or hide from the tall warriors and felt lucky to have escaped detection.

The skyline lit up with an orange luminescence caused only from a large fire. Wondering if this was a savanna fire, he looked around. It was not the right time of year for such catastrophic fires. The blaze came from the direction of the Watinkee camp. Something big was happening. He had to learn what they celebrated and then get out of this awful country. His high priest would be pleased.

Getting closer to the Watinkee gathering was tricky. It was dark, yet that's when he felt most comfortable in the surrounding blackness. What he saw and heard brought shivers up and down his spine. He heard chanting of a strange name. Babtoo, Babtoo, Babtoo.

"He must be a powerful high priest," Kutlip thought. A black panther stepped into the circle of light and started to talk. "Aiiiieee!" They must have summoned some very powerful spirits. This battle may not be a good idea." Sneaking back to his small hiding place, Kutlip shivered in fear. The high priest did not like bad news.

Arriving back at the Mautuk village, Kutlip was hesitant to cross beyond the skulls and bones of the high priest's great pyramid. Prostrating himself immediately, Kutlip waited for the high priest to appear. Sweat poured from his body, as a skull seemed to float out of the nothingness to stand over him. No word passed the lips of the high priest, yet Kutlip felt compelled to talk.

"Oh, great high priest, I have been to the Watinkee village. They made a great fire that lit the sky for great distances around. Their chief spoke a prayer and then they started chanting a name.

"BABTOO, BABTOO, they all screamed. Then out of nowhere, a panther man stepped into the circle of light. His fur was brilliant and I was blinded. I could not look directly onto his evil form. He spoke and the Watinkee people cheered and clapped. It was horrible. They are powerful and seem ready for war. What is your next order, Great One?"

A skeletal hand that smelled like black rotting flesh pointed out the door. An inhuman wail of anger welled from within the pyramid. Mautuks everywhere cringed at the sound. "I have heard about this Babtoo and he has yet to be killed! Do I not have warriors brave enough for that one simple task? Go and kill him. Go!"

Kutlip ran out the door and did not bother to re-supply himself, and headed back toward the empty savanna. The jungle beckoned Kutlip like a mother calls to a child. The comforting closeness of the trees and dim interior reminded him vaguely of his mother. Fear slowly drained from his body when Kutlip spotted Squanto as he reached the outskirts of the village.

"How goes Kutlip?" Squanto yelled to get his attention.

Kutlip turned toward Squanto sitting on a stump sharpening his spear. The jagged scar on his face gave him a permanent sneer as drool smeared his chin. Steering toward him, Kutlip said, "How goes Squanto?"

Squanto got up from the stump and asked, "What's the latest word out in the savanna?"

Kutlip quickly glanced behind him as he approached Squanto and said, "They are as many as the trees in the forest. I had a hard time trying to stay hidden. They are too big and strong for one scout to take back as captives. I got close to a village where they were having a big gathering. The chief said some kind of a prayer and then they shouted a name. It was terrible! I left soon after the spirit appeared in the firelight. It was a black panther man!"

Squanto looked closely at Kutlip trying to figure out if he was a coward or was being truthful. "What name did they shout?"

Kutlip's voice quivered as he spoke the name, "BABTOO!"

Squanto took a step backward. Babtoo was the same boy that gave his face this unsightly scar. Had this boy evolved into a spirit? Grabbing Kutlip's arm, his face twitched uncontrollably as he sputtered, spit flying everywhere, "That is the Watinkee that did this to my face! AAAeeeiiiii! I want that warrior's heart. We're going on the warpath just before the herds of wildebeest leave for their winter home. I will have my revenge!"

Kutlip shrank from Squanto's grip. Cowering, he squeaked, "He is powerful. He is part man and part panther. I fear him."

Squanto looked down on Kutlip with disgust. Hatred had blinded him of the fact that this same boy had almost killed him. He wanted vengeance for the suffering he had to endure and the disfigured scar he carried on his face. Letting Kutlip go, Squanto returned to sharpening his spear with monotonous precision.

Kutlip vanished into the forest leaving Squanto to his misery. The steady sound of the file on his blade did nothing to comfort him. With the last bit of patience used up, he threw the sharpening stone to the ground and peered into the forest. Without another thought, Squanto decided to follow Kutlip. He wanted to be sure Kutlip had not lied to save himself. "Fear this!" He thought as he hefted the sharpened blade.

CHAPTER 23

THE WAR

The Watinkee tribe was a flurry of activity for the next few weeks. Scouts were coming and going, but found little evidence of a Mautuk presence. Chief Bowhut was somewhat optimistic about the Mautuks not returning this year since two of their invading scouting parties had been discovered and defeated. Life in the Watinkee tribe was settling back down to a normal rhythm.

Babtoo and Enobi were grateful for the rest. His ribs started to heal with Whutknot's medicinal bandages and his breathing became easier. His health improved with each passing day.

Enobi also benefited from the rest. Whutknot experimented with different herbs and came up with a healing salve for his leg. Enobi was starting to feel like a colt again though he would always have a slight limp. Tossing his head up and down with anticipation, he waited for Babtoo each morning. Together, they became more and more comfortable with each other and their riding became more skillful.

On those days, Monbeem would watch the two riding with great pride. She was looking at a man that had limitless boundaries. He would not let his maimed leg be an excuse to do less. He was becoming a greater warrior than even Chintook.

Chintook was getting stronger every day. He was up and walking around. Still weak from the poison, however, Chintook still relied heavily on Monbeem and Babtoo for support. One more scar graced his already heavily disfigured body, but he wore them like badges of honor.

Monbeem and Babtoo became much closer. Babtoo's self-confidence grew with Monbeem as he began to realize she did not view him any longer as a boy. He smiled more often around her. She would brush against him often when they talked, their heads bent down close to one another as if they were telling each other secrets.

None of this went unnoticed. Chintook loved his daughter and wanted her to marry a great warrior. Babtoo could be that man. He watched as Monbeem would stare after Babtoo when he walked by and how she often made him special things to eat. Chintook was proud his daughter had chosen well.

Ohat, Puku and Ukup had been patiently watching Babtoo and Enobi practice riding in the open savanna. During one of those practice sessions, Ohat walked up to Babtoo and said, "Your skill grows everyday on this wonderful animal."

Babtoo nodded his thanks.

Ohat continued, "If you and Enobi are ready, we would like your help to scout for Mautuks near the forest fringe. We have not found any trace since the day you rescued Monbeem. I have an eerie feeling they won't let two of their scouting parties die and go unpunished. We think you can help us scout a few of the more remote areas. I think we should take a closer look near the forest. Maybe we can catch them off guard nearer their home."

Babtoo reached down and patted Enobi's neck. Squinting into the sun toward the direction of the jungle, Babtoo said, "I believe that's where they come from. Nobody has ever gone into the forest. I doubt the Mautuks would expect us so close to their home. We don't go near there very often and so that territory is unknown. This would be very risky. Does Chief Bowhut know about this?"

Puku said, "He brought the plan to us. We said we would go if you and your magical beast would come with us. It would give us an extra advantage. You are an experienced warrior now. Your spear and courage would be welcome if there is a battle. We know we can count on you."

Babtoo flushed with pride, "It would be an honor to be a part of this with three great warriors."

Ohat smiled and said, "This will be dangerous and we will be taking necessary risks, but we have to know if they are planning an attack. It's been too quiet lately."

Babtoo nodded, "When do we leave?"

Ukup said, "Two days from now. The moon will be hiding in the sky. The darkness will help cover our movements."

The two days gave Babtoo time to prepare for the journey. He rested Enobi and provided him with extra care for his leg. The long jagged scar was healing nicely with Whutknot's herbal remedies. The bond between man and magical beast grew stronger every day.

The relationship between Babtoo and Monbeem also grew. They now were finding ways to be together. Often they would brush up against one another and work in the same area so they could be close to one another, whispering soft words that only they could hear. Babtoo had lost the awkward feeling he had around her and was able to allow himself be vulnerable to Monbeem's advances. He knew he didn't have to be the fastest or strongest or the wittiest. In fact, around her, he often stumbled with his words trying to express himself. She, in turn, would laugh or giggle making him laugh at himself.

Darkness still blanketed the land the morning Babtoo was to leave with his three friends. Placing the panther cape on Enobi, Monbeem came up to him and said, "I have a present for your journey."

Babtoo stood awkwardly and asked, "What is it Monbeem?"

Pulling her hands from behind her back, she handed him a finely tanned skin pouch.

Stammering, Babtoo said, "Thank you. This pouch is very nice."

Laughing at his confusion, Monbeem said, "Silly, open it up. The present isn't the pouch but what is inside it!"

Babtoo looked a little sheepish and said, "Yes, of course, I knew that."

Opening up the pouch and pouring the contents in his hand, Babtoo inhaled sharply. The shark's teeth were polished and sharp on a beaded necklace. His eyes misted for a moment. He could not say anything because of the lump in his throat. Grasping her by the shoulders, he kissed her gently and said, "A great gift and I will wear it with pride."

Ohat, Puku and Ukup walked around the corner and stood watching this display with grins on their faces. Finally, Ohat said, "Babtoo, the day grows old. Hug her and let's get going!"

Babtoo looked up not realizing they had been standing there watching. His face turned a deep crimson as he quickly turned away to get Enobi.

Puku poked Ohat and reminisced, "Don't you remember when you were in love? Why I remember a time when..."

"We don't have to go there, Puku! But we do have to start our journey before the day is gone!" Ohat said.

Babtoo vaulted on Enobi and said, "I'm ready. I now wait for you!"

The three warriors looked at Babtoo and smiled. Ukup said, "Yes Babtoo, but not for long."

The three Watinkee warriors vanished into the savanna leaving Babtoo staring and wondering how far they thought they could go before Enobi caught up with them. Swinging the black panther cape over his shoulders, Babtoo followed them into the bush. Soon, all four warriors were on their way toward the jungle.

The strides of the three warriors were long and purposeful. They ate up the miles like hungry cheetahs looking for food. Their long spears wagged like fingers of death, thrusting forward with every stride, as if searching for that elusive enemy.

Babtoo rode behind directing them away from ravines and difficult terrain. Watching from Enobi, he was able to see the pitfalls and danger sooner.

There was little conversation as they conserved their strength in order to reach the jungle edge quickly. They continued to jog into the night with little rest. The moon was high in the night sky when Ohat signaled to stop. Puku and Ukup sank to the ground drinking greedily from their skins. Ohat looked toward Babtoo and said, "Babtoo, we'll rest here and leave early tomorrow. Will you take the first watch and wake me when you get sleepy?"

Babtoo nodded and slid off Enobi. "We've traveled far today and I fear tomorrow will be another long day."

Finding a small tree to stand by, Babtoo blended into the night like a forgotten spirit and watched over his sleeping companions. Two hours later, Babtoo woke Ohat and gratefully slid down the trunk of the tree and fell into a deep sleep.

The next morning Babtoo awoke to a cold wet nose and musty breath in his face. Startled, he saw two large cavernous holes in a whiskered muzzle nudging him awake. Chuckling to himself, he gently pushed Enobi away. Eating a quick meal, the four tribesmen started on their way.

Another grueling day and they could finally see the outline of the jungle on the horizon. The haze of the day cloaked the forest with a blanket of mystery. They were close and decided to spend the night safely away from the fringe instead of right next to it. There they sat and talked about what they were going to do.

Ohat said, "I think we'll explore the outer fringe of the jungle and get familiar with it. We'll locate any tracks or trails that lead out from there into the savanna. There's a good chance we'll be able to catch somebody leaving. We won't light any more fires from now on for secrecy. But if all goes well, we won't be out here long."

Puku groaned and said, "We could draw them to us. We could light a fire while one of us stays behind as a decoy while the other three hide. We could catch them sneaking up on the one warrior by the fire."

Ukup shook his head and said, "That would make it very dangerous for the man by the fire. You could be vulnerable to a spear throw. It is best we try to get them when they do not know we are around. What say you, Babtoo?"

Babtoo lowered his head in thought and said, "The Mautuks are clever and devious. I don't want anybody put in danger. Ohat is right. We'll scout during the day and find likely places they have been. We'll catch them out in the open."

Everybody agreed to the plan as the conversation died. Eating a cold meal, they would start tomorrow. Rolling in their blankets, three warriors fell fast asleep as one stood guard.

The sun crept over the horizon kissing the savanna in a soft warm light. The warm glow stretched toward the jungle, and seemed to stop abruptly, unable to penetrate the murky darkness. The trees swayed in the breeze threatening to extend their lightless interior by casting their shadows as far out into the savanna as possible.

The jungle was a giant maze with a seemingly endless amount of diversity. Trees, tall and stately, reached up to touch the sky. Lush green growth competed for space, extending their roots in the soft soil. Down below, animal trails zigzagged randomly between the boles of the trees, some intersecting with other, larger trails, while others faded into nothing.

Strange noises penetrated the quiet gloom, and at times seemed muted by the confining trees. Colorful birds flew amongst the treetops appearing like rich vibrant brush strokes on a dark, lightless canvas. Inquisitive monkeys jumped from branch to branch for a closer look at the unusual warriors before losing their nerve and screaming their unease.

All four warriors stood in awe at the immense size of the jungle. Standing near the outer fringe of the forest made them feel small and insignificant. A moment of uncertainty passed among them as they looked at the daunting task they had undertaken.

Ohat shook himself free from the overwhelming thoughts that entered his mind. Clearing his throat to get everybody's attention, he said "Enough! Let's get busy and do what we came here for."

Trying to appear unfazed, "What are a few big trees anyway? Puku and Ukup will scout along the edge of the forest going that way. Look for any animal trails going in and out. Pay closer attention to any signs of Mautuks using those same trails."

Looking at each in turn, "Be careful. We don't know if they are about now. Babtoo and I will search the other way and see what we can find."

Ohat paused to take a breath, "Remember, we are Watinkee warriors. Do not be intimidated. We'll meet back here when the sun is behind the tree line."

Puku looked at Ukup and said, "Come on brother. Let's be the first to find the Mautuk trail."

Ukup smiled and said, "Yes, Puku. Let's get started."

They stepped into the surrounding grass and gave the illusion of walking through a wall as they disappeared. It always amazed Babtoo at the skill the two brothers had. He had learned much from them.

Ohat looked up at Babtoo sitting atop Enobi and asked, "Are you ready, Babtoo? This way is closer to where I think they came out the first time. Remember when we had that skirmish with the Mautuks? This was the closest way back to the jungle."

Babtoo thought back at what seemed a long time ago and nodded his head in agreement. Urging Enobi forward, Babtoo scanned the ground for tracks, trails, or discarded items that would indicate a Mautuk might have passed that way.

The going was slow and tedious with trails that appeared to go nowhere. Babtoo and Ohat would follow shallow imprints or tracks that skirted around the trees but never entered the jungle. Frustrated at their lack of progress, they decided to take a break during the hottest part of the day. A large solitary tree shading a small ravine was a good place to stop.

Babtoo got down off Enobi, the panther cape billowing in the breeze. Enobi walked into the ravine for the lush green grass at the bottom. Talking softly between themselves, both men relaxed in the shade as the noon sun beat down unmercifully.

After a few minutes, Babtoo went to check on Enobi. He seemed restless and agitated. Walking over and talking quietly, Babtoo stroked his muscular neck, but that did nothing to ease his nervousness. Puzzled by this, Babtoo jumped on Enobi, his black cape billowed in the air. The ravine hid Enobi from prying eyes making it seem like he floated on air.

Ohat looked over and asked, "What's wrong with Enobi?"

Kutlip approached the edge of the jungle. The smell of the sweltering savanna made him sick. Several times during his trip, he had the feeling somebody was following him. Doubling back and hiding behind trees, Kutlip waited for the elusive sense to subside, but could see nothing behind him. He wondered if the Mautuk high priest made him paranoid.

Fear is the glue that holds the Mautuk tribe together. Without it, the village would slowly degenerate and vanish like the previous owners. Still, he could not shake the bad feeling as the hairs on the back of his neck stood at attention. Perhaps when he got into the open savanna and found a good hiding place, the fear would go away.

Squanto seethed with hatred. Saliva dribbled down his chin. Following Kutlip was demanding. The scout was very good at deception and hiding his trail. It was almost as if Kutlip knew he was following him. A couple of times, he was almost caught trailing the coward.

Reaching the edge of the jungle, Squanto hid behind a large leafy frond. Watching Kutlip creep out into the open brought a smile to his damaged mouth. He would wait here until evening to see where he went. Crossing the open savanna with little cover in the middle of the day was not wise.

Kutlip edged out into the open. Moving slowly and with great stealth, he looked up at the burning sun. His eyes watered, as he quickly looked away, spots filled his eyes, temporarily blinding him.

The buzz of the insects filled his ears with a monotonous drone, but as he moved forward, the insects stopped. His ears picked up another sound almost covered up by the whine of the bugs. There were voices that were barely perceptible.

Kutlip frowned in thought and wondered, "Who could be out here so close to home? Squanto never said there were other scouts out here. I wonder who it is."

Moving closer, he darted for a small tree. Looking at a large freestanding tree, Kutlip saw a Watinkee warrior talking to himself. Why this warrior was so far from home and alone made little difference to the Mautuk. This could be his big opportunity to bring back a Watinkee prisoner to the high priest. He could finally redeem himself and be elevated in the eyes of the tribe.

Sneaking forward, Kutlip got ready to run and throw his spear. The warrior still had not seen him and seemed to be talking to the tree. With a running start, Kutlip charged with spear cocked to throw.

In that instant, Babtoo swung over on Enobi's back. His panther cape flowed in the breeze as he looked over the ravine. All Kutlip saw was a black panther spirit rising from the earth. Screaming from fear, he threw the spear at Ohat. "AAAiiieee! BABTOO! BABTOO!" The poorly thrown spear arced in the air and landed with a thud between Ohat's legs.

Ohat was stunned for an instant as the spear thudded between his legs, sinking deeply in the hard dry soil. Recovering quickly, he stood and threw his weapon in the direction of the Mautuk. Running for his life, Kutlip dodged brush and small trees in his errant run toward the safety of the jungle. The Watinkee spear flew harmlessly by as Kutlip tripped on rock. He shuddered as the spear passed over his shoulder to shatter a small sapling, pinning it to a larger tree.

Babtoo already had Enobi out of the ravine and chased the swift Mautuk through the grass. Kutlip sprinted for his life, glad the forest was close by. The jungle reached out for the Mautuk to safely cloak him in her dark interior and hide him from Babtoo's spear.

Squanto was shocked as Kutlip leaped into the forest screaming about a "Babtoo" spirit chasing him. Then he saw a black panther man sitting on the magical beast running him down with a spear leveled at his back. Babtoo followed his every movement, but the elusive Mautuk reached the safety of the forest.

Squanto fumed with hatred, but the terror of facing Babtoo again froze him in place. The boy had gained animal powers and seemed bigger and more powerful. His lip quivered in terror as he disappeared in the jungle.

Babtoo turned Enobi around and raced back toward Ohat. He was retrieving his spear when Babtoo arrived. His voice shook with apprehension, "I should have been more prepared. I didn't expect to come across a Mautuk so soon. If you hadn't gotten on Enobi when you did, I might have been stuck to that tree by a Mautuk spear." Looking curiously at Babtoo, he remarked, "He seems to know your name. I wonder if you're gaining a reputation with the Mautuks."

Babtoo chuckled at this and said, "Perhaps he heard it from our conversation. We don't know how long he was there. Don't put too much stock in that."

Ohat shook his head and said, "I am not so sure. The Mautuk is gone but we'll follow him into the forest after we get Puku and Ukup. This is why we have come for to capture a Mautuk. The jungle is dangerous, but there is little alternative. Let's get Puku and Ukup to help us track. If were quick enough, we won't have to go too far in."

Babtoo nodded his agreement and they jogged toward the assigned meeting ground. Puku and Ukup were already there.

Ukup said, "We found some trails going in and out, but they were old and of little use."

Ohat quickly cut him off and hurriedly said, "We have been attacked by a single Mautuk and must get back quickly before he gets too far away. I'm lucky to be alive from his poorly thrown spear. This is our chance to catch him before he finds his way back home."

All four started back toward the lone tree with a new sense of determination. Reaching the tree a few hours before dusk, Ohat replayed the attack, praising the part Babtoo had in saving his life. The spear was still stuck in the soil and looked like a stunted sapling. Pulling it out of the ground, they noticed the tip, stained black, glistened in the waning light. Ohat said, "This is just a reminder of how careful we must be. These are a dangerous people."

Retracing the flight of the Mautuk, the four Watinkee started into the forest. Puku and Ukup took up the trail, followed by Ohat and Babtoo on Enobi. The smell of decaying vegetation was overpowering. Going in single file, they followed the faint prints of the Mautuk. A broken branch here, a toe print there, disturbed leaves and displaced fronds were the only signs of his passing.

The lightless interior compounded the difficulty of finding him. They soon became aware of the thousands of places any Mautuk could hide and fear of detection ate at the warrior's courage as they labored through the dense trees.

The dusky interior turned a coal black as the night sky hid the signs of the barely discernible trail, even for the competent Puku and Ukup. Stepping off to the side and squeezing into a small, secluded grassy area, the warriors settled in for the night. Conversation was very low and minimal. Using sign language, the warriors communicated their thoughts.

Babtoo took the first watch. Stepping by a large tree, he blended in with his cape. Jungle noises were unnerving, as life in the jungle never slept. Eyes appeared out of nowhere only to disappear somewhere else. Focusing on one unusual eye, he noticed it did not move, or blink, but wavered in the darkness. Squinting to see, he realized it was a solitary eye and not the normal two. He surmised it could only be a Mautuk campfire in the distance and decided to get Ohat to verify the distant light.

Excited, Babtoo stepped away from the tree and shook Ohat awake. Both men peered at the unmoving eye flickering in the distance and agreed to its origin.

Quickly Babtoo roused the others. Rubbing their eyes, Puku and Ohat came instantly alert. They checked to be sure that they had everything before stepping back out on the trail. Like hounds on a scent, they moved quietly forward.

Stalking their prey, the four warriors did nothing to disturb the forest floor. Moving slowly on a small animal trail that led to the cave entrance, the warriors could have been colorless shades on a moonless night. Slipping through the dark shadows, the animals of the wood heard only the soft hoof beats of Enobi on the moist ground. Creeping closer to the fire, they saw the occupant in the shadowy firelight and waited.

Kutlip was busy cooking some food over the small fire. Nervous and furtive, he continually peered out into the darkness. His movements appeared jerky and stiff and he often mumbled things to himself. The word, "Babtoo" said repeatedly carried into the still night air and sounded ominous as the four Watinkees closed in. Throwing bones out into the forest, Kutlip had finished his meal and disappeared into the depths of the cave.

Soon Kutlip had found a comfortable place to rest. He wrapped himself in a blanket and soon fell asleep. His harsh nasal snores blended in with other night noises.

Ohat waved Puku and Ukup forward. The three Watinkee warriors crept up to the cave entrance. Like angels of death, they slipped inside the rock entrance. Pointing their long sharp spears at his body, Ohat kicked the prone Kutlip awake. Startled, he became instantly alert, staring at the long pointed spears of the tribesmen. .

Rolling onto his back, he shook with fear. Their eyes were hard and unforgiving and their lean bodies born to the savanna stood like bronze statues. Still, he said nothing.

Babtoo entered the cave with Enobi, the black cape covering

his body like a second skin. Kutlip glanced at them and screamed, "AAAiiieeee! Babtoo! Babtoo! AAAAiieee!

A swift kick from Ohat sent the little Mautuk tumbling into the hard rock wall. Fear so intense made him ignore the spears from the other Watinkee warriors, and he bolted in an attempt to escape. Ukup tripped him as he went by and wrestled him to the ground. Swiftly they tied him like an animal and stuffed a rag in his mouth to shut him up.

Finally, Ohat, Puku and Ukup looked to where Babtoo had settled Enobi in the back of the cave. Ohat was the first to speak, "It seems you have a reputation with these Mautuks. We all heard it. They are afraid of you. Maybe you can help us find out what he knows. I think he's the one that tried to kill me." Glancing around the cave, Ohat continued, "I see no spear in the cave. That miserable Mautuk owes me his life. Let's see what he knows and get out of here before his friends find us."

Babtoo glanced down at the quivering Mautuk. Stepping toward the small hairy cannibal, Babtoo placed his body in front of the cringing warrior. Reaching out to grab him, Kutlip's eyes grew large as he tried desperately to chew through the binding in his mouth. With a muffled scream, Kutlip backed into the wall, hoping it would swallow him to disappear.

Stepping back, Babtoo said, "I'll not be able to get anything out of him. See how he cowers from me. Maybe I can help just by being close and pretending to be fierce."

Ohat chuckled at that, "Yes, that might work." Stay close, and try to be scary looking."

Puku and Ohat stood guard while Ohat tried questioning the Mautuk. There was little point in speaking directly to the cannibal. The languages were too different. Perhaps pictures could help. Dragging him toward the fire, Ohat untied his hands and gave him a small stick. Drawing a picture of the Watinkee village in the dirt, Ohat pointed to it.

A snarl escaped the lips of the Mautuk as he threw his tiny

stick down. Ohat glanced up at Babtoo as a signal to intimidate the warrior. With a flourishing of his cape, Babtoo strode toward the Mautuk with his spear raised. Quickly, Kutlip picked the stick back up and started to draw.

Squanto had made camp not far from Kutlip. Climbing a large tree, he sat on a branch overlooking the cave entrance. Exhausted from tracking the Mautuk scout, Squanto settled in and placed his spear across his legs. The hum of the night insects relaxed him from the stress of the day. Bugs flew lazily by as bats as big as parrots sliced through the air like guided arrows feeding on the unsuspecting insects. Animals casually walked underneath the tree looking for food or ran from some unseen predator. The chaos of the jungle made him sleepy.

Dreaming of a Watinkee raid, Squanto itched to drink Watinkee blood. He searched for the warrior Babtoo on the savanna. Across the battlefield, he imagined he saw the Babtoo on his magical beast with the flowing dark cape. Racing across the field to meet him in battle, Squanto yelled, "AAAAiiieee! Babtoo! Babtoo!"

Startled awake, Squanto was drenched in sweat. His heart pounded as he gasped for air. His hands were slick with moisture as he wiped drool from his face. Looking around furtively, he could not tell if it was a dream or if something else had awakened him.

Fully alert, Squanto silently berated himself for his own foolishness. Glancing toward the cave, Squanto lost his grip in surprise and crashed to the ground, twisting his ankle. A large animal and caped man had just walked into the cave. He thought desperately, "How could this be? Can this warrior travel the jungle like a ghost? How did he find Kutlip? What am I going to do?"

Pain washed over his face as he struggled to his feet. Limping toward the cave, Squanto cursed his luck. The darkness cloaked his movements as he approached the entrance. His blood ran cold when he saw the Watinkee warriors inside with Kutlip.

He almost didn't see the two Watinkee warriors standing like statues, blending in with the shadows guarding the entrance. The cowardly Kutlip drew something in the sand. A warrior stood with his spear pointing at his heart. The fierce warrior, Babtoo, with his panther skin cape would then raise his arms, and point his spear saying something unintelligible. Kutlip would shrink away from him and draw something more.

Squanto knew he could not save Kutlip. There was no remorse for what he was about to do. Instead, he felt he could ease Kutlip into the nether world before the Watinkee tribesmen killed him. The Watinkee warriors were too powerful for just him alone. Cocking his arm back, he let the spear go. Stumbling as he turned to run, Squanto took off for the deepest part of the jungle, hoping they could not follow.

The black shaft of the spear whistled through the air. It flew past the two warriors guarding the cave entrance. Like an arrow, it sped past Babtoo and went under Ohat. A surprised look crossed Kutlip's face as the spear threw him against the wall and rested in his chest. Death came quickly for the Mautuk and, with a final sigh, he stared sightlessly into the inky darkness.

Kicking the fire out, the Watinkee warriors waited and listened for the attacker. They heard leaves rustling and twigs snapping. The noise faded quickly away from them and soon was lost. On guard, the warriors waited patiently until dawn to leave the confining walls of the jungle behind.

The four men left the dank, dark interior of the jungle. Each man breathed a sigh of relief as the warm sunshine bathed their bodies. The mysteries of the jungle soon became dark memories as they jogged toward the lone tree by the ravine.

Ohat was the first to speak. "It feels good to be out in the sun again. We have accomplished what we came here for. Before that scout was killed, I think he gave us a good idea on some of their battle plans, thanks to Babtoo's reputation."

A chuckle went around the group along with looks of admiration. Being a young warrior the Mautuks feared was a great accomplishment.

Ohat continued. "A large force of Mautuks will attack us as we prepare to move with the wildebeest herd for their winter home. That's when we are the most vulnerable. It appears they have no remorse for killing their own people. That spear was meant for him and not for one of us."

Puku asked, "If he was the only one, why didn't we go after him?"

"We got what we came for." Ohat replied. "There would be no gain to chase down a Mautuk in his own territory at night. It would have put us in greater danger."

Babtoo peered into the forest and said, "I think it was only a single warrior. If there were more than just him, then the outcome may have been different." The others nodded in agreement. "We're not safe here. The lone Mautuk may try to organize a band of warriors to go after us."

Ohat looked at Babtoo and nodded at his wisdom, "You're right Babtoo. We just stopped here to make plans for ourselves once we left the jungle. Chief Bowhut can use this information to plan our defense. The wildebeest herd is already restless and beginning to show signs of their migration." With a backward glance toward the forest, the four Watinkee warriors quickly jogged off toward their village.

Casteel and Monbeem were the first to spot the returning warriors. Bending down to catch Casteel's attention, Monbeem pointed and said, "Casteel, run and get Chief Bowhut. The scouting party is returning!"

Casteel jumped up and said, "Chief Bowhut will be here before you know it!"

Turning, he ran for the village elders. Monbeem waited impatiently for the scouting party to get close. The black cape Babtoo wore shimmered in the noonday sun as it billowed in the wind. Her heart leaped for joy that Babtoo had come back unharmed.

Chief Bowhut and Casteel soon stood by Monbeem's side watching the warriors approach. Glancing at Monbeem, Chief Bowhut could see the excitement in her eyes. Touching her hand, he said, "Go ahead child. Let Babtoo know how much you care." Looking into Chief Bowhut's kind face, she sprinted off to meet him.

Babtoo noticed Monbeem running toward them. Urging Enobi forward, they met in a wild rush. Babtoo slipped off his mount and hugged her tightly. Monbeem showered him with kisses and held him in a warm embrace.

Ohat, Puku and Ukup finally caught up. Ohat breathlessly said, "Yes, yes, we brought him back safely for you, just like you asked!"

Babtoo frowned and asked, "Do you think me still a boy?"

Monbeem looked confused and shook her head. Biting her lip, she whispered, "No, I was worried you would do something heroic and get hurt."

Ohat realized it was a bad joke. He explained, "He kept us safe. He has a reputation with the Mautuks. They know who he is and are afraid of him!"

Babtoo looked away embarrassed. "Yes, one warrior knows my name and he is no longer!"

Chief Bowhut stood with arms folded watching the procession. A smile crossed his face as all the warriors came into view. None appeared to be wounded and all seemed in good spirits. He hoped they had been successful finding something out about the Mautuks. It was almost time to travel with the herds to the winter-feeding grounds. He didn't want to look behind his back when they were ready to leave. Worry lines seemed to have found a permanent home on his craggy face.

Stopping in front of Chief Bowhut, the four warriors were eager to speak all at once. Holding his hand up, Chief Bowhut said, "Well met brothers. There is a meal waiting for you at my tent. We will then talk of your successful scouting trip."

Babtoo reached for Casteel. "Casteel, could you make sure Enobi is well fed and watered? He has had a hard journey!"

Casteel jumped at the responsibility and glad he was the one chosen for such a high honor.

Babtoo walked hand in hand with Monbeem until they came to Chief Bowhut's tent. With a tender squeeze of her hand, he let go to enter the tent with the rest of the scouting party. Waiting for the chief to enter and sit down, their eyes adjusted to the dim interior when they spotted a shrunken head.

Chief Bowhut entered and noticed their discomfort. "Ah. You have noticed my little friend." Chuckling at their bewildered expressions, he reached for the head. Holding up the miniature skull, each warrior gasped in disbelief as he tossed it over to Ohat. Ohat almost dropped it as he juggled the small head. Looking closely at it, he passed it on to the others. Babtoo studied the head wondering what evil a person could do to deserve to get a shrunken head. Thinking back, Babtoo could not remember anybody he knew to have disappeared.

Chief Bowhut enlightened them. "It is not a Watinkee, but more likely a Mautuk sacrifice. I have no doubt they came to get sacrifices or slaves. This is how you would have ended up if you got caught." Tossing the skull in a corner, Chief Bowhut gave them each a long hard look. "Food will be coming in a minute. Sit down and get comfortable. We have a lot to talk about."

Breathing heavily, Squanto sucked in air through his scarred mouth and sounded like a bubbling pot of water. Spit dribbled down his chin as he crashed through the jungle to get away from the cave.

He watched Kutlip die by his own spear and silently congratulated himself on the accuracy of the long throw. He was no great friend of Kutlip, but decided he had done the Mautuk scout a favor. The Watinkees were fierce warriors and were unforgiving to their enemies. Chuckling to himself, he thought Mautuks were not gentle to their slaves either. Kutlip might never be missed, except by his wife. Kutlip was more of a coward than even he was. He just wished he had his spear back.

Leaning heavily on a tree, he looked down at his swollen ankle. The pain was excruciating as he examined his foot. As large as a small fruit, but hard as a nut, his ankle would no longer bend. Cursing himself, he grabbed a stick and limped back to the village.

The agonized cries of the slaves welcomed him home. Watching the workers toil always made him feel good. Looking out upon the Mautuk village reminded him of an ant colony. The soldier ants made sure the worker ants worked. If they did not, then they became food.

Passing by the cooking fires and heading to the stone pyramid, Squanto ignored the looks of his fellow tribesmen. Curiosity crossed their faces as they noticed his limp, though none bothered or cared enough to ask. His foot felt as if he had stepped in hot coals. Pausing at the entrance to the pyramid, the blackened stone beckoned him in. Glancing at the skulls before entering, Squanto thought they were smiling at him. Perhaps they knew he was bringing news to the high priest. Entering the dim corridor, Squanto looked around, letting his eyes adjust to the dim interior.

A voice like the clang of a bell sent Squanto down to the floor. "What is it that you want? I have not called for you!"

Squanto whimpered, "I have brought news mighty high priest. I have been following the scout Kutlip. The Watinkee warrior 'Babtoo' captured him inside the jungle with three other Watinkee scouts. I could not kill them all before they killed Kutlip. I got away but twisted my ankle. I have no spear now."

Squanto's devious mind allowed him to lie whenever it was convenient for him. He learned that telling the truth sometimes led to bad consequences. Shaking from fear, he awaited for the voice to speak.

"Babtoo! Babtoo! Babtoo! That name keeps coming back to haunt my dreams!"

There was a clatter on the hard stone floor as the high priest cast a spear down at him.

"I give you the task to kill this Watinkee warrior, Squanto. Do not fail me like the others before you! I will know when this spear drinks blood! AAAliiieee! Now be gone from me."

Squanto grabbed the spear and backed out of the stone edifice carefully. Reaching the entrance, he got up off his knees and turned to face the sun. Black smoke obscured the bright rays but was enough to see the ornate spear in his hand.

The spear was the color of the darkest ebony and had a smooth surface with an almost greasy feel to it. Hefting it in his hand, the spear seemed to undulate and writhe. Small scales imbedded in the shaft seemed to help the spear flex. The tip resembled a striking serpent head and seemed to hum with magic.

A soft whisper seemed to emanate from it. It talked to him in a soothing voice, wrapping itself around his very soul and stealing what little humanity he had.

Holding it closer to his body, Squanto limped toward his home. His foot would need to heal if he was to take on Babtoo. Perhaps in the confusion of the raid, he would find him on the open battlefield. The high priest had not put a timetable on when he had to kill Babtoo. This was a great gift and Babtoo would soon learn that it was for him. A thin lopsided smile cut across his face as he brought the spear closer to him. The spear continued to whisper more urgently.

CHAPTER 24

THE SAVANNA HAS MANY DANGERS

The stew bubbled in the pot sending aromatic odors wafting in the air. It permeated Chief Bowhut's tent, tantalizing the four warriors who now could barely concentrate on what the chief was saying. Furtive, uncomfortable glances at the shrunken head, however, brought back the seriousness of the meeting and the things they had learned.

Bringing the food and setting it in front of each warrior, Chief Bowhut's wife served her husband last. Waiting for his bowl of stew, the chief smiled and said, "Do not stand on ceremony here. Eat! Have as much as you like. I can vouch for my wife's cooking!" He gave her a little hug as she exited the tent. The four warriors ate as though it was their last meal. Hurriedly, they finished the stew, eager to tell the Chief what they had gleaned from the Mautuk warrior.

Ohat spoke first and said, "Chief Bowhut, we think we've found out when the Mautuks will attack. After capturing him, we convinced him to draw their battle plan. If what he drew is correct, and I believe it is, they are going to attack during the wildebeest migration back to their winter home."

Chief Bowhut silently chewed his stew for a moment and said, "Why do you think this is so? How do you know he told the truth?"

Ohat glanced at Babtoo and exclaimed, "Babtoo and I stopped to rest. We were unaware a Mautuk warrior was in the area. Enobi was restless and Babtoo went to calm him in a ravine, and so was unseen. The next thing I knew a spear quivered between my legs. Babtoo gave chase on Enobi, hoping to catch him before he entered the jungle. The only thing we understood was his screaming Babtoo's name as if he knew him. He eluded Babtoo and ran into the jungle to get safely away.

Taking a deep breath, Ohat went on, "We gathered ourselves together to follow him into the forest. Babtoo took first watch and saw his campfire glow inside a cave. We waited outside to see if there were others, but he was the only one. It was strange, but he continued to repeat Babtoo's name, as if he were a demon. We waited to see he was alone. When it was clear that he was by himself, we captured him. We wasted no time trying to question him. He was fearless and would say and do nothing, even at spear point, until Babtoo would threaten him. Then he would cringe as if looking at a demon. From what we were able to gather, the pictures in the dirt resemble the great wildebeest migration. We think that's when they will attack. Then, out of nowhere, a Mautuk spear was thrown and killed him."

The silence in the tent stretched for long minutes before anybody said anything. Chief Bowhut looked at each of his warriors with pride. Finally reaching over and playfully punching Babtoo in the arm, he said, "So, we have a demon in our midst." Smiling, he went on, "You have built a reputation in a short time, Babtoo. Maybe we can use this to our advantage. The Mautuks are a very superstitious people. They are also a very powerful enemy. For one so young, Babtoo, you may have to lead us all to victory. This could be the biggest attack the Mautuks will make since my father's time. We thought we had wiped them out in the last battle, but it looks as if they have gained much strength since then. They no longer fear us and that will have to change."

Sizing Babtoo up, Chief Bowhut smiled and said, "Babtoo, a great responsibility rests on your young shoulders. You will not be alone in this fight. I have an idea!"

It was late when they finally left Chief Bowhut's tent. Quietly saying their good nights, they headed in different directions toward their homes. The events of the past days weighed heavily on their minds but they all believed in Chief Bowhut's plan. They now felt they had a chance to defeat the Mautuks.

Babtoo was exhausted. Thinking back, it seemed like only yesterday when he found the cave at the seashore and the magical beast Enobi. His life from then on had forever changed. Becoming a man was easy, but the responsibility of being one was hard. He hoped for a day when things were lighthearted and the threat of the Mautuks was gone for good.

Taking a quick turn before he entered his tent, Babtoo went to see Chintook. Upon approaching Chintook's tent, light conversation floated toward him, beckoning him forward. His steps were lighter and a smile creased his travel stained face. A light shone from the tent and pleasant laughter filled his ears.

Babtoo announced his presence, "Chintook! Is that you I hear? I have come to visit."

"Babtoo? Of course, you can come in. Monbeem is with me." Chintook said.

Babtoo opened the tent flap and saw Chintook sitting up in bed. He smiled from ear to ear as he greeted Babtoo with a fierce hug.

Surprised, Babtoo said, "Last time I saw you, you couldn't get out of bed and complained about Whutknot. Your recovery has been amazing."

"Well, Babtoo, I'm still a little weak," Chintook replied. "Whutknot has done all he can. I am lucky to be alive with all that mumbo jumbo he does. I finally had to kick him out myself. Oh, he did leave me some of that medicine you got and said he'd be back to check on me. I told him not to bother me because I have Monbeem to help now!"

Monbeem smiled at her father's tirade.

Babtoo grinned at his spirit. It felt good to have the old Chintook back. He said, "I look forward to a hunt with you. When did Whutknot say you could get up?"

"Whutknot gave me a couple of weeks to get better. I say I can do it in a few days. I still feel a little weak, but with the care Monbeem has given me, it will be sooner. Nevertheless, forget about the hunt.

Let's hunt Mautuks instead. I have a debt I need to repay them for!" Chintook said.

Monbeem said quietly, "Father, do not overtax yourself. You need rest. There will be plenty of time to hunt Mautuks when you are feeling better."

Chintook looked wryly at Babtoo and said, "You see, son, I may never get out of here if Monbeem and Whutknot have it their way. You will have to save me from all this mothering!"

Babtoo smiled and got up to leave. "Sleep well, Chintook. There is always a place for a warrior like you!" With that, he left the tent for his own.

The sun was at its highest point in the sky, and yet it seemed it could not out race the tiny black smudge. The spot seemed to take great joy in racing the sun across the heavens. On closer inspection, when finally visible to human eyes, the speck seemed to sprout wings, which carried him down to the earth at dizzying speeds.

It was an eagle, fierce, proud and intelligent. His large eyes missed nothing on the Great Plains below. He took great delight in swooping down on the lesser birds, scattering them like windblown seeds.

His call was a challenge, striking fear in all that heard him. With nowhere to run, animals froze in place, waiting for the winged death to pass them by. He was master of the sky and none could challenge him.

Today, he was hunting for two. His mate had laid the most beautiful egg and when the eaglet finally broke free of the hard shell, was hungry. His tiny squawks for food triggered the need to feed the tiny ball of feathers. While searching for food, he felt something was wrong and streaked back toward the nest.

Babtoo woke up in a sweat. The dream was as vivid as real life. He wondered if he had gotten a glimpse of what would happen in the future. The memory of the dream was starting to fade but the reality of it was not. Could the dream of the eagles be his future with Monbeem?

Taking a deep breath to steady his nerves, he got out of bed. It was mid-morning when he opened his tent flap and looked toward the sun. A small dot appeared by the sun but was too indistinct for him to see clearly. Looking away, he decided to check on Monbeem.

Walking toward Chintook's tent, he noticed the women were gathering every scrap of material they could find. Large pots of blackened water were bubbling away with a pungent, unpleasant order. Women with large paddles were stirring the soupy looking mixture and putting scraps of material in the pots. Some had already come out and were drying in the sun. Ugly black strips hung on poles to dry, staining the earth underneath.

Babtoo looked curiously at the strips of cloth wondering why everything was the color of black. Finding Monbeem stirring a similar pot, Babtoo walked up and hugged her.

"Hello Monbeem. What are you cooking?" he asked jokingly.

She looked over at him lovingly and said, "It seems the black cape I made you is very popular. Since not everybody can go out and kill a black panther, we're making everybody a black cape to mimic you. This one is Chintook's cape. He insisted that I make his special."

Babtoo's face looked confused as he tried to contemplate what was going on. "Why the color change? Surely, this is not going to be permanent. They are....an ugly black."

Monbeem admonished him and said, "No silly. When the Mautuks attack, they will not know who you are. We will all be Babtoo. That should confuse them just like it is confusing you now." She laughed.

Babtoo smiled, now recognizing the most important part of Chief Bowhut's plan. Taking Monbeem's hands, stained black from the water, Babtoo looked deeply in her eyes and said in a halting, stumbling way, "Monbeem, I just wanted you know how much I care for you. I want to be your husband. I know I still have a lot to prove," glancing down at his maimed foot, "but I am strong and I think I can take good care of you. I will ask Chintook for your hand after we defeat the Mautuks, if you will have me."

The sun kissed Monbeem's face with a soft glow, giving her a flushed appearance. The breeze caressed her head as it blew lightly through her hair. Tears formed and slowly worked their way down her face. She caught her breath as she looked into his eyes.

Babtoo looked away, embarrassed. "I did not mean to offend you. What could I have been thinking?"

Jumping into Babtoo's arms, she showered him with kisses and almost lost her footing. She paused only for a moment and whispered, "Oh Babtoo, you don't know how long I have waited to hear those words from you. Of course, I will marry you. Let's tell Chintook now. I know he will be very proud."

Babtoo whispered back just as passionately and said, "No, not now. I will be a target for the Mautuks. If I don't make it back..."

"Why do you say such things? You will make it back and we will be together."

Wishing the feeling would never end, Babtoo finally disengaged himself from Monbeem and said, "You have made me very happy. I feel like I cannot lose you now." Stepping back and holding her hand, he said, "I need to check on Enobi now and see how he's doing."

Monbeem composed herself, wiping away tears of joy. "Casteel has not left Enobi's side. He won't leave until you tell him to. He takes his responsibility very seriously when you give him something to do."

"Yes, we've had a lot of adventures together and I respect his courage. He'll make a great warrior someday." Babtoo said.

Forcing himself to leave, he limped over to find Casteel and Enobi at the edge of camp. Sitting down next to the pint sized warrior, Babtoo asked, "How goes it Casteel? Has Enobi been a bother?"

Casteel turned toward him and said, "No, Babtoo. He has been no bother. I think he likes me. We seem to get along well."

Babtoo picked up a piece of grass and sat there chewing while watching Enobi. Casteel nonchalantly picked up a similar piece of grass and put it in his mouth. Casteel's face winced from the sour taste as he bit down on it. He continued to chew, however, wondering why Babtoo found this so enjoyable. Maybe it had something to do with Enobi. He would just have to get used to it. Together they sat and talked, looking across the savanna, wishing for a more peaceful future.

Chapter 25

Battle Preparations

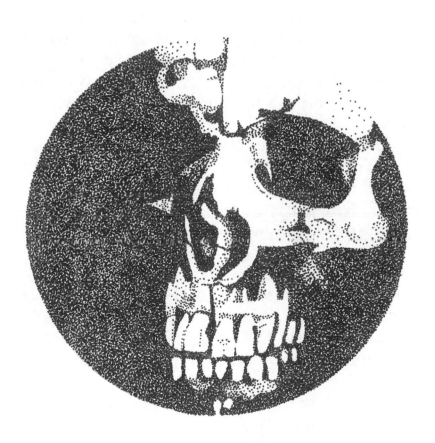

The mysterious mist blotted out the sun and covered the jungle like a giant suffocating blanket. It rolled over the trees, muffling the cries of even the noisiest monkeys. Birds that would normally welcome the new day with loud and raucous songs perched huddled together, fluffing out their feathers against the oppressive cloud. Nocturnal animals hurried home to burrows or dens, uncomfortable in the clinging mist.

His dull brown eyes opened from a sleep only exhaustion could induce. His bones ached from sleeping on the hard packed earth. Muscles stiff from fatigue screamed in agony as he shifted his position. Sores and scabs cracked and opened with each twist of his body. His stomach rumbled for food, but the revulsion of eating the cold thin gruel made him ill.

It was just a few minutes before dawn and Moab was looking through eyes that were sleep encrusted slits. He watched as some slaves feigned sleep and others too emaciated to move. In a few minutes, the Mautuk slave master would use his cruel whip and club to beat people and begin the day's toil. Moans of pain greeted his ears as the day began.

Thinking back just one short year ago, Moab remembered happier times. He had a wife and an only son. His family had lived on the outskirts of the great forest, moving from place to place.

His tribe had not been large and consisted of a few families that banded together after the great fire eighteen years prior. They had no chief, but coexisted as a large, extended family. There was a counsel formed of the elders and they decided on the day-to-day things that ran the tribe. The biggest thing ever to be decided was when they should move to a different hunting ground. Life was good.

One year ago, Moab's life changed dramatically. They had just moved to a new section of the savanna next to the jungle, foraging from the fruits of the forest and meat from the plains. The place they settled into was serene. It had a beautiful meadow that abutted the fringe of large tree's that seemed to reach the sky. Here, large red berries and fruit grew in abundance. Water was close by with herds of antelope and gazelle grazing nearby.

It was early morning and the sun was not yet up when he and fifteen other hunters departed for the day's hunt. They had to go a little further than usual that day as the herds had migrated to a different section of lush grass. They were expert hunters and by the end of the day had more than enough food for the week. Turning back toward the village, they noticed a black streak floating up into the air. Even from that distance, screams and yells filled the air.

Dropping everything they had, the hunters sprinted toward the village. A swarm of small hairy black men with wicked looking spears had attacked the village. The women picked up anything they had to protect themselves but were quickly overwhelmed. Small children cried loudly as they desperately clung to their mothers. Mautuk warriors struck them down without mercy or compassion. Old men picked up spears and stood valiantly trying to defend the tribe, but soon they were overwhelmed and fell to the pointed spears of the Mautuks.

Moab and the rest of the hunters rushed in to save the remainder of the village. Spears flew from their hands with unerring accuracy, pinning the Mautuks to the ground. Drawing knives from their belts, they slashed and stabbed, killing anything they could catch. The Mautuks vastly outnumbered them and they soon dwindled to just a few remaining warriors.

A horrifying scream that stood the hairs straight up on the back of Moab's neck caught his attention. His wife was fending off three of the warriors as his small son cringed at her feet. She clumsily held a spear and waved it in their direction. Blood flowed from multiple wounds as the Mautuks surrounded her. His son picked up a stone and threw it at one of the hairy warriors, pelting him in the head. There was a howl of anger and a Mautuk spear quickly pierced his small body as he crumpled to the ground.

Rage gave her strength beyond her drained endurance. Attacking the three Mautuks, she managed to stab down at one, slicing through his body. A look of surprise crossed his face as he clutched at the spear with hairy fingers. Trying to pull the spear free, she whirled to face the other two. Together, they closed in on her.

Moab ran to her side. Picking up a spear left in a Mautuk body, he threw on the run. The spear hit the closest Mautuk, propelling him off the ground. The last warrior disengaged Moab's wife and quickly threw his spear, missing him, and then ran into the forest. Gathering his wife in his arms, he started running. He didn't know where to run, but just that he had to run.

It seemed like he ran for hours until his legs would no longer carry him. His breath came in ragged gasps and his arms strained from the weight of his wife. Exhaustion finally got the best of him as he finally stopped to rest.

The Mautuks were like jackals for scraps of food. They were relentless in their pursuit, waiting until he could go no further. He slid down next to his wife, shocked at what just happened. Looking up, small fierce warriors suddenly surrounded the exhausted couple.

His wife, grieving over their child, screamed insanely and ran at them with a small knife. They quickly dispatched her and waited for Moab to attack. He got up on unsteady legs. Catching and holding a Mautuk in his hands, Moab choked him as a swarm of the hairy warriors engulfed him. There were too many and he was quickly overwhelmed. The last thing he remembered was the overpowering stench of death filling his nostrils.

Waking up in the dark, the nightmare was just beginning. His face was stiff and swollen from the pounding he received in the battle with the Mautuks. Blood had dried from his nose and lips. Bruises and welts covered most of Moab's body, and his movements were jerky and stiff.

Looking across the encampment, he noticed other people bound up like himself. Some of the people were his friends and others he did not recognize. All bore the signs of a recent battle or some kind of abuse. Some were still bleeding from recent wounds and still others harbored signs of past cruelty. The fear and humiliation of defeat were evident on their faces. Downcast eyes spoke of the shame they felt, as their once proud shoulders slumped forward and their heads, once held high, lay buried in their hands.

Hundreds of small squat warriors surrounded the group poking at them with spears and shouting insults to motivate them. The gloomy jungle loomed ahead like a vast empty hole. Single file, they entered the darkness of the jungle and finally the oppressive shadows swallowed them never again to see the open savanna.

It had since been a year and still he wondered why death had not claimed him. Looking around at the other captives, Moab was curious why they still embraced the life of a Mautuk slave. He wondered if they still had some hope of escape, or if they clung to life with no spirit or will, but as empty shells. Moab believed their spirits were long gone or shattered by the merciless cruelty of the Mautuks. He could not help to think that they resembled walking corpses.

The slave masters were busy rousing the captives for the new day. The crack of the whip preceded the moans and screams as the captives struggled to their feet. The skeletal captives rocked on trembling legs. Some leaned on one another for support.

Black smoke from the campfires discolored the fog making the encampment surreal. The cloud shrouded the top of the pyramid structure hiding it from view. Everything it touched had a greasy dirty feel. Breathing seemed difficult and labored.

Today, despite the fog, there was excitement in the air. Mautuks were busy preparing for some great festival. Moab waited for the slave masters to herd them to their appointed tasks. Breakfast consisted of a greasy mash with chunks of meat. His gut knotted as the slimy meat hit his shrunken stomach. Some retched at the rancid meat, and then beaten, had to swallow the rotten mash again.

A steady drumbeat heard through the air gradually got stronger and more pronounced. Slowly, in single file, the slaves, led by their taskmasters, shuffled one by one toward the pyramid. Moab was one of the last to go. He noticed every slave ceased to struggle and obediently followed the next in line. He wondered if the Mautuks had drugged them, but was past the point of caring. The steady drumbeat continued until he anticipated every beat.

Reaching the pyramid door and seeing the leering skulls seemed comical to him. Moab almost laughed aloud but could manage only a croak. They seemed to tell him to run, but his feet would not obey him, his will sapped.

Looking up toward the long stairs dimly lit in the pyramid, the line of slaves climbed. Moab heard a loud roar and then the line would move another step closer to the top. He knew he should run, but where? His thoughts could go only as far as moving up one more agonizing step after another.

At last, he was out on the platform located at the pinnacle of the pyramid where an odd-looking Mautuk with two skulls on his shoulders held a jagged knife. Two huge ape-like creatures came and dragged him by the arms, throwing him on a sticky platform wet with blood.

Too late, the realization came to him that he was about to die. Quietly mumbling prayers to his god, a small spot in the mist cleared giving him an unobstructed view of the bright sun. There, an image of his wife and child waited for him with open arms. The priest held the jagged knife high screaming guttural words and phrases. Moab was no longer afraid. His body relaxed as peace settled over him. He looked forward to his death. His only regret was that he had lived so long.

◈◈◈

The sacrifices took most of the morning. Hundreds of Mautuk warriors scrambled over each other like maggots over rotting flesh to get the best view. Looking into the concealing mist, they imagined what the high priest was doing with every syllable he spoke. The cries of pain were an added delight as the dying bodies tumbled down from the apex of the pyramid to land unceremoniously in a pile at the bottom.

Squanto, caught up with the excitement of the ceremony, shook his foul spear in the air. The limber scaled weapon hissed with each wave of his hand. The tip turned blood red with anticipation as if it had already tasted blood.

They had used all their slaves for the sacrifices. Their god would be pleased with the generosity of their people. Faith in their malevolent deity gave them courage. The great migration of the wildebeest herd was just beginning. It was time to go to war. They would attack the Watinkee tribesmen and get more slaves. Like a disturbed ant mound, the warriors assembled in small groups and took off for the trees. Soon they would be in Watinkee territory.

CHAPTER 26

THE FINAL OUTCOME

The old bull wildebeest was just past his prime. He stood proud and defiant, snorting his challenge into the wind. This year he had successfully defended his herd of females against other, younger, stronger bulls. During one of those battles, a horn had broken off leaving him at a distinct disadvantage. Long scars on his poorly defended side had weakened him.

Sniffing the air, the smell of the changing season assailed his senses. Flaring out his nostrils to catch the scent, instinct told him to herd his group of females in the direction of the winter grazing grounds. Joining thousands of other wildebeests, they blended into the herd of several hundred thousand. The journey would be perilous, but food was getting scarce. This was a time when old grudges of competing bulls were laid to rest and in a single-minded purpose, they all headed for greener pastures. To get to their destination, the herd had to swim a large swift river.

The river held many dangers to the wildebeest herd. Hundreds of large crocodiles hid in the murky waters waiting to ambush any that were too slow. Strong currents often swept a wildebeest downstream to drown. Others scrambling on the opposite bank would slip and get trampled from behind if they could not get out of the way fast enough. These unlucky few paved the way for the rest of the herd.

Babtoo and Casteel sat on Enobi. They saw the restlessness of the herd and knew they would soon be migrating. They needed to help move the village toward the river where they would wait for the wildebeest to assemble on the bank to cross.

Time was running out for the Watinkee tribe. Moving an entire village was a complicated task. They were many days from the river and still they had to be ready for the Mautuk assault. Babtoo and Casteel rode back to report the progress of the herd.

Chief Bowhut was in the center of the village directing his people as they prepared to move. Tents were packed away and put on litters so able-bodied tribesmen could drag them. Food was being smoked and stored. Everybody from small children to older adults carried a pack. Warriors laid down their spears to pick up heavier items.

Everybody was nervous and continually looked back in the direction of the jungle. A few warriors guarded the retreating tribe, quick to give an alarm if needed.

Puku and Ukup stepped out from behind a small grove of stunted trees, stopping Babtoo and Casteel. Blending in perfectly with their surroundings, Babtoo was unaware they were around until they suddenly materialized in front of him.

"Whoa there, Babtoo!" Puku raised his hands to halt Babtoo's progress, "How much time before the herd starts its migration? I can smell the change of seasons in the air and I know they can too." Puku said.

Babtoo thought before answering, "They are restless and ready to move now. I think they're waiting for one to take up the lead. More importantly, how is the camp disbanding?"

Ukup looked back. "Things are going a little slower because many of the scouts are out searching for Mautuks. But I think Chief Bowhut has everything moving as quickly as possible."

Puku emphasized this last statement, "Babtoo, the people are nervous and afraid. They are distracted from their tasks and keep looking toward the jungle."

Babtoo nodded, "Yes, I can see why. However, we have two of the best warriors guarding our backs in you and Ukup. I'm on my way to help Chintook now. He can't make the move by himself."

Both warriors grinned from the compliment and stood a little straighter as they waved Babtoo on.

Casteel looked back and piped in, "I want to be as brave as they are when I am old enough to be a warrior."

Babtoo turned around and said proudly, "You already are Casteel, you already are."

Riding through camp with the flurry of activity, Babtoo and Casteel headed for Chintook's tent. People noisily went about packing up their belongings, getting ready for the big move toward the river. Chief Bowhut was busy giving instructions and taking reports from the scouts as they filtered in from the field.

Chintook was on his feet and waved as Babtoo approached. Monbeem was busy disassembling the tent and putting things on a litter to drag. Casteel jumped down and said, "If you don't need me anymore, Babtoo, I go to help my parents now. I'll come back to help you if they are done." With those parting words, Casteel jumped off the horse and ran to help his mother, Floret.

Babtoo slid off Enobi and offered his help to Chintook who was watching Monbeem struggle with the heavier items. Chintook was pale with sweat dripping from his body as he tried to help her. Still too weak from his ordeal, his breathing was heavy and labored.

Babtoo admonished, "Chintook, if you allow me to help we can get done much faster. You need to rest for the upcoming battle."

Monbeem whirled around and said, "There will be no upcoming battle for Chintook. You can see he is still weak and not himself."

"Now, Monbeem, we have talked about this," Chintook chided. "I am going to go with the rest of the warriors. There will be no argument from you that can make me stop. I feel fine."

Babtoo saw the determination of Chintook and also the fear Monbeem had of losing her father. Struggling with an answer that would accommodate both of them, Babtoo said, "Monbeem, I need your father at my side. He is a great warrior and I can use his vast knowledge of the savanna."

Monbeem conceded. "Babtoo, he can barely stand, but if you promise not to leave him alone, I will trust you two will both come back." Tears streamed down her face as she turned away.

Babtoo came up behind Monbeem and tenderly put his arms around her. "Monbeem it is important we both go. You cannot stop your father. He is a great man and to keep him back with the women and children will break his spirit. We need each other and will look after one another in the upcoming battle."

Turning around she wiped the tears from her face and whispered, "Oh Babtoo. I am so scared of losing both of you when I feel like I have just found you."

Babtoo leaned close to her and said, "I will be back. Nothing can keep me away from you. I'll bring Chintook back with me too. I promise!"

She buried her face in his muscular chest and cried.

The day went quickly for Babtoo as he helped Monbeem and Chintook get ready. If not for the nagging fear of the Mautuk attack, they would have been joking and laughing as they worked together. Finally finished and organized, Babtoo bid farewell for the night.

Exhausted, Babtoo walked toward his own tent. Falling onto his mat, he quickly fell asleep. Tomorrow they would begin the trek toward the river.

The eagle screamed his defiance as he raced back toward the tree where his mate and eaglet waited. His shriek froze animals in place and his shadow blotted out the sun as he sped on by. Breathing sighs of relief, his prey ran towards burrows or concealing cover quivering in fear. Searching the skies for signs of the bird, they remained there for hours afterward.

The eagles continued to call for him and he feared he would be too late.

Babtoo woke up to the same recurring dream he had before. His body was bathed in sweat and he felt a sense of an unnamed urgency to do something. Disturbed by this, Babtoo got up and searched for Whutknot. He hoped he had some insight to these disturbing nightmares and that it was not Monbeem's cooking.

Whutknot sat on a stump smoking a pipe. The smoke lazily drifted into the air as he playfully blew smoke rings. Glancing at Babtoo, he said, "I did not mention this before, but you saved Chintook's life. That was an incredible journey you took in so short of time. Then you save Casteel and Monbeem from Mautuks on the way back. You have a powerful totem my friend. How is the old bird anyway?"

Seeing the confusion on Babtoo's face made him chuckle. Babtoo suddenly realized he was not talking about his dream, but about Chintook. "Oh, he's fine. You know, feisty, but still a little weak. I have come to talk with you about something that disturbs me greatly."

Whutknot peered at him and sat a little straighter on the stump. "What's bothering you, Babtoo?"

Babtoo looked in the sky as if searching for something. Then he sat down next to Whutknot and explained, "I am having a recurring dream. It is about an eagle and it seems like it is flying toward something, but I can't see what it is. I just know I need to go and look for it. It seems like it's in trouble and that maybe I can help."

Whutknot blew several smoke rings in the air thinking about what Babtoo had just said. Finally looking at him, he said, "Babtoo, that dream could be your true totem. Every warrior has one. Most are small, a feather, a claw, or a tooth. You, on the other hand, do nothing small. You need to search for that eagle. I believe the feather on your spear is an eagle feather, most likely your father's totem. Perhaps you will follow in your father's footsteps."

Relieved it was not Monbeem's cooking, he got himself ready to travel toward the river thinking about Whutknot's revelation.

The water in the river was fast and deep. Churning mud from the banks kept it muddy and dirty. Flowing out into the savanna a small stretch of river widened out into a shallow lake. The water moved sluggishly until it narrowed down again to a fast flowing river. Over hundreds of years, the banks on either side had grown steep, making it a daunting task for animals to climb down to the water. Yet this was the same place every year for centuries the wildebeest herd gathered to cross.

On the bank, the reptile stretched its heavy body gathering the heat from the noonday sun. Mud adhered to his scaly hide, drying to a fine crust camouflaging him from unwary eyes. His jaws were open to cool his body showing off rows of pointy teeth. Eyes the color of rotting fruit barely opened. Enjoying the hot sun, he and others waited for the wildebeest to cross.

The bull croc was close to twenty feet long. He had long scars on his body from previous fights for dominance and territory. He found the best place on the bank to rest and wait. Coming here for decades, like clockwork, he anticipated the feast to come. This meal could be his last for several months.

Babtoo and Monbeem walked toward the river. The tribe moved the village to the banks of the river several hundred yards away from the wildebeest crossing. Looking at the crocodiles sent a shiver down Monbeem's thin frame. Babtoo chuckled and picked up a stone tossing it into the water. Several smaller crocodiles raced from the bank gliding into the water and diving where the stone sent circular ripples echoing out in the water.

Babtoo held Monbeem close. This was the last few moments he would spend with her before the battle. Tomorrow, he and the other warriors would meet the Mautuk hoard. Whispering to her, Babtoo said, "Tomorrow I leave with Chintook. I won't see you until I get back. That may be for a few days. We'll leave some of the older warriors behind. If something were to go wrong, cross the river to safety. Leave everything behind. Cross over there," he pointed in the distance, "around the bend downstream is a narrow place. Most of the crocodiles will be here feeding on wildebeest. You should make it across safely."

Monbeem snuggled against him and said, "I will not leave without you!"

Babtoo held her closer and said, "If things go wrong, Chintook and I will not be able to save you as we may already be dead. You must cross and live. Do that for me."

Looking into his eyes she whispered, "I will only do that if you promise me you will live and find me someday." She kissed him on the lips and they held one another for a long time watching the setting sun.

That next morning, Chief Bowhut gathered all the warriors. Each warrior's angular face was smudged black with white lines. All warriors donned a black cape. Hundreds of tall hulking plainsmen looked like shifting shadows in the near darkness. Chief Bowhut smiled and looked toward Babtoo.

Sitting on Enobi, Babtoo wore his black panther cape. The sharks tooth necklace gleamed in the early dawn light. His spear with the single feather fluttered as if eager to go. Enobi stomped his foot, infected with the excitement around him. By his side, Chintook stood proudly wearing his lion's mane cape. The black cape Monbeem made for him sat around his shoulders covering the brown lion's mane fur.

Chief Bowhut looked proudly at his men. Fear gnawed at his stomach even though a smile touched his face. He was not afraid for himself. He was afraid for every man woman and child in his tribe. His plan hinged on deception and if that did not work, they were facing incredible odds. He hoped the information Ukup and Puku had given him was accurate.

Every man waited for Chief Bowhut to say something. His mind was at first blank. He could not think of anything they did not already know, and yet, they expected something. Clearing his throat, he began, "I am proud of each and every one of you. Many of you I have known since we were children. Others I am getting to know as you grow into men and women. I am honored to be the chief of such a great tribe. Today, going forward, we will be facing a terrible enemy that has plagued us for centuries. We will end that plague and cleanse the soil of their pestilence!"

A roar of cheers erupted with a great clatter of weapons.

Chief Bowhut continued, "Many of you are untested in battle. Remember, you are fighting for your home, your family, your friends and yourself. There will be many great stories to tell around the campfire when this is over. I look forward to seeing each and every one of you when this day is done!"

A wild cheer again went up. They were ready. Chief Bowhut gripped his spear tightly and turned his back to begin the journey out on the plains. Choking back emotions as he passed by old friends, he let the excitement of the coming battle overtake him. This was the time to be strong. They looked for him for leadership. Together they would wipe out this scourge for the last time.

The army of shadows headed out to the savanna toward the wildebeest herd. There they would await the Mautuk warriors. Hopes were high that they could effectively turn the massive attack back.

The silence was unbearable. The air was stagnant and not a leaf moved as the army passed through the dense undercover. The birds were quiet and insects stopped their raucous chirping and humming as the black hairy phantoms passed by. Monkeys nervously squirmed and jumped to higher branches as glimpses of warriors flooded the jungle. Animals fled quickly on the forest floor, quick to escape the advancing Mautuk army.

Abruptly the gloominess of the forest ended leaving the vast open savanna immersed in the dazzling morning sun light. Hundreds of pairs of eyes watered in the unaccustomed bright light as they blinked back tears. Several long minutes dragged by as if waiting for a signal.

Squanto, impatient to find Babtoo, was the first to step out. Sprinting like a rabbit from cover to cover, he found shelter behind a tree. Soon, many warriors were filtering out of the jungle in ones or twos looking for cover. In unfamiliar territory, many warriors were unsure how to proceed. The high priest's generals, cruel and unyielding, prodded the last warriors forward.

The wildebeest herd milled about uncertain what to do. Finally, the old bull started walking in the direction of the river. Swinging his head from side to side, he bellowed out a forlorn note. Others turned and listened and one by one began to follow the old bull. Soon the massive herd headed toward the water. Other herds joined his as thousands of animals gathered for the migration. A dust cloud billowed in their wake camouflaging the herd in grime.

The Watinkee tribesmen positioned themselves on the outskirts of the herd. Sinking into the ravines, copses of trees, and behind termite mounds, they watched the herd slowly begin their migration. Each tribesman concealed himself expertly to await the Mautuk army.

Babtoo rode ahead and positioned Chintook in a well-concealed ravine. Riding toward the jungle on Enobi, Babtoo could see the surrounding savanna and the encroaching army of Mautuks. He wanted the Mautuks to notice and focus on him. He would be the center of their attention, drawing them forward into a trap. Biting back fear, Babtoo rode forward into danger.

The exodus of the Mautuk hoard from the jungle spread like an ugly black stain radiating outward from the jungle. Soon the small hairy cannibals competed for the limited cover, giving the savanna a blotched, diseased appearance. Occasionally a fight would occur over certain prime spots.

At first, it was only a slight discoloration at the edge of the forest, which could have been the shadows of trees or shrubs swaying in the breeze. The continuous shifting of those shadows soon made it obvious to Babtoo that the Mautuk army was on the move. Soon, the tidal wave of warriors spilled from the forest pushing the leaders in front to move on out.

Babtoo's breath caught in his throat. The sheer number of warriors far exceeded the Watinkee tribesmen. Babtoo's only hope was that Chief Bowhut was right and that their superstitious natures would work against them.

Massing at the edge of the forest, Squanto drooled with excitement. His black fingers clutched the spear, giving him a false bravado. The intoxicating power of the spear overwhelmed him as he pushed forward. It seemed to whisper the name of Babtoo in his head. His one focus was to find the boy warrior. Sprinting to the next clump of cover, Squanto scanned the landscape for the figure in the black cape.

Babtoo headed for cover to watch wave after wave of Mautuk warriors spread into the savanna. Trying to remain hidden for the time being, Babtoo observed the Mautuks as they exited the forest. He had to wait for just the right time to appear in front of them.

A single Mautuk led small pockets of warriors. No single leader directed and organized the vast army. Looking disorganized, they spilled onto the savanna. One group would move ahead as other groups followed or mimicked their movements. A look of hungry anticipation collectively crossed their features as they anticipated the pillage and destruction of the Watinkee tribe.

Babtoo felt evil emanate from them as the plains animals fled in terror. Their sheer numbers were overwhelming to the young warrior. Small shrunken heads attached to belts of more than a few warriors and spear tips blackened by poison glittered in the sun. Guttural sounds from their harsh language broke the silence. He wondered if Chief Bowhut's plan would work with what seemed a limitless Mautuk army. He decided to let the chief know what he had observed before continuing with his part of the plan

Watching the wildebeest plod by, Chief Bowhut hid in a small copse of trees. He watched as Babtoo rode up. Stepping out from their leafy embrace, Chief Bowhut waved him down. "How goes it, Babtoo?"

Babtoo, deep in thought, almost rode past Chief Bowhut's hiding place. Smiling to himself, he was reminded of the hours of hide and seek he had played as a child. He had to be one of the best at concealing himself because he could not keep up with his maimed leg. Often times the other children eventually gave up looking for him.

Babtoo slid off Enobi and asked, "Chief Bowhut, is everything in place? There are hundreds of them sneaking out of the forest. It seems like there is no end to them. They're using the wildebeest herd for cover, just as we thought."

Chief Bowhut answered, "Babtoo, everything is in place. It does not matter how many there are. They'll fall like overripe fruit before the day is over. The important thing is to remember your part. You have the most important role of this plan. They need to believe you are invincible. Are you ready?"

Babtoo nodded his head in acknowledgement.

Chief Bowhut gripped his arm, "I expect to be hearing about your exploits in this battle by you and you alone around the campfire. Be careful, Babtoo!"

Getting back on Enobi, Babtoo declared, "I will make them believe!" With that last statement, he rode back into the teeth of the enemy.

The dust cloud hung in the air making it difficult to see. The Mautuk army followed the massive herd as it moved toward the river. The wildebeest nervously watched the advancing army. Occasionally, a bull would charge a Mautuk and hook him with wicked looking horns. A scream would abruptly end, as the Mautuk became air born to bounce on the ground amid a flurry of hooves.

Babtoo sat unobserved on Enobi watching the advancing army. It looked like a giant plague was infecting the savanna. He watched and waited until he saw a small group of Mautuks ahead of the others. They had not seen him and were eagerly pushing forward. So intent on keeping away from the wildebeest herd, they never saw him approach.

Babtoo encouraged Enobi to run and with a blood curdling scream, galloped toward the lone group. The Mautuks were startled and turned to see an apparition materialize out of the dust. A black panther sat on a mighty animal they did not recognize. The cape billowed around Babtoo making him appear far larger. Fear struck their hearts as they turned to run. Riding hard, Babtoo picked the fattest and slowest and dispatched him as he rode past. His cries ended quickly as his spear passed through his body.

The lead Mautuks, now wary, looked around searching for the magical creature that could kill at a moment's notice. Bewildered by what they had just seen, the nearest Mautuks turned to go back. This was a bad omen. Primal superstitious thoughts tormented them and they became distracted. The Mautuks from the rear unaware of Babtoo, moved forward, pushing the first ones further ahead.

Babtoo rested for a moment a short distance away. Observing the confusion his attack had made brought a bitter smile to his face. Blood ran down the length of his spear and dripped slowly into the dusty earth. Babtoo looked for another target and waited a moment to let his reputation work for him. Undoubtedly, rumors of his attack would be carried toward the rear of the army.

Another group of Mautuks took the lead. This group was a bit more cautious. Babtoo followed them until their attention wandered back toward the wildebeests. Suddenly, from out of the dust, he came charging at them again. Enobi neighed a challenge as he galloped forward, tossing his head. Babtoo screamed a curse as the cape streamed out behind him, startling the small group of Mautuks.

The group turned and stared in disbelief as the dust parted revealing a creature running toward them with a large pointed spear already red with blood. Frozen for a moment, they turned and ran toward the back. Babtoo chased them down until they came too close to the main body of warriors before he veered off. Other Mautuks saw him as an apparition, or demon, and turned back toward the jungle. Soon the milling army was a mass of confusion. Babtoo rode on the outskirts of the Mautuks creating mayhem and fear wherever he could.

Squanto continued to close on Babtoo. The whispering from the spear in his head drove him forward, telling him Babtoo was the warrior he had come to kill. Stabbing a warrior who got in his way, the spear seemed to come alive in his hands. Quenching its thirst in Mautuk blood, the scaly spear drank deeply, driving Squanto forward.

Oblivious to anything else, Squanto's single-minded purpose had eroded his mind as he lost his sanity to the spear's incessant whispering. The spear took what little humanity he had, leaving only the crazed shell of a cannibal. Holding his head for a moment, the voices only got louder.

The spear's power gave him inhuman strength and stamina. But the high price he paid for that strength was to be merely the high priest's puppet. A budding demon in his black heart was taking root and every time Babtoo appeared, he would charge in that direction.

Riding back toward Chief Bowhut's concealment, Babtoo approached with caution. Dismounting and walking toward the copse of trees, Chief Bowhut stepped out to meet him.

"Chief Bowhut, I have created the confusion, but maybe it will not last for long. Do we attack now?"

Chief Bowhut nodded, "Yes, it is time. Precious moments will be lost if we wait any longer."

"They're getting close to Chintook's hiding place and I need to get back there. I promised Monbeem nothing would happen to her father!" Babtoo said as he jumped back on Enobi.

Chief Bowhut produced a big horn out of his sack. Blowing three short bursts and then three more signaled the Watinkee warriors. The wildebeest herd stopped and listened, sensing danger. Then the Watinkee tribesmen in their black capes emerged from their hiding places, running and screaming at the herd.

The wildebeest, alerted by the horn, saw hundreds of black panthers running toward them. Eyes wild with fear, they stampeded in the opposite direction toward the Mautuk army.

Mautuk warriors hearing the horn also rose out of the grass looking for the enemy. What they saw struck fear in their hearts as they sprinted to get out of the way. Thousands of wildebeest were running in their direction trampling everything in their way. The Watinkee tribesmen chased after the herd, turning it toward the Mautuk army.

Mautuks scattered like leaves in a windstorm. Screams of the dying filled the air, as the wildebeest caught the Mautuks by surprise. The lucky ones died instantly while others suffered grievous wounds as the herd passed on by. Animals, dust and noise filled the air as both the Mautuks and wildebeest tried to escape the confusion.

Soon the exhausted animals regrouped and headed once again toward the river, trampling any remaining Mautuks that were left in their path. Moans of pain that filled the air were cut short by slashing hooves or curved horns.

Squanto, at first, was one of the lucky ones. Jumping into a well-hidden ravine, he was surprised to find a Watinkee tribesman. Astonishment crossed his face when he recognized who he was. The flowing lion's mane the Watinkee wore had to be the leader of the warriors that attacked his scouts. This man was in the same hunting party as Babtoo. Squanto was confused for only a moment as to why this man still lived. A spear poisoned with the dart frog was lethal and few people survived a spear thrust tipped with that poison.

His new spear hummed with anticipation. Possessed as he was, Squanto knew no fear and attacked without abandon. The whispers in his head drove him forward.

Chintook watched the Mautuk jump into his ravine over the clumps of grass. Shifting his feet so he was square with the Mautuk, he threw his spear. As if an invisible force shielded Squanto, the spear sailed over his head. Drawing his knife, Chintook waited for the shifty Mautuk's next move.

Hefting the snake spear in his hand, Squanto poised to charge. Chintook planted his feet waiting for the attack. Sprinting toward Chintook in the narrow ravine, he thrust his spear toward his heart. Spinning counter clockwise, Chintook used his lion mane cape to wrap the spear and deflect it from his body. Snatching the spear, the sacrilegious feel of it made him drop it immediately as the Mautuk brushed by, tripping over a root.

Getting up, his eyes were blood shot and slobber dripped from his lopsided face as he made grotesque sucking noises. Squanto searched for his spear but not before Chintook fell on him with his knife and stabbed down. Gripping Chintook's knife arm, Squanto pushed back. Surprised at the strength the little Mautuk possessed unnerved Chintook and his knife went wide. Desperately grabbing onto Squanto's knife hand, Chintook tried forcing the weapon down, but his strength was rapidly fading. The little warrior had turned his own knife back toward him. Chintook's vision swam and his breath came in gasps as his struggles became feebler.

Babtoo rode through the scattered Mautuk army. Single warriors or groups avoided him or fled in the opposite direction. Babtoo was concerned the confusion so close to Chintook's hiding place could be disastrous and he would be found the disorganized army. Bent low over Enobi, he hurried to the ravine.

Sounds of the struggle reached Babtoo as he rode up to the ravine. Looking down, fear twisted in his belly thinking he was too late. Chintook fought for his life. His face was pale as sweat rolled down his body. His eyes were intense with concentration as the long Watinkee blade pressed against his chest. Chintook gasped as he struggled to keep the knife from penetrating his body, and yet, he knew no fear, only courage of a man that cannot accept defeat.

Babtoo dropped beside the struggling warriors. They were too close to use his spear so he grabbed the Mautuk around his body and threw him to the side. The little warrior flew through the air and bounced off the wall of the ravine. Getting up slowly, Squanto hesitated, recognizing the boy who had badly disfigured him. The voices in his head screamed their urgent message of death for the young warrior

Babtoo looked down on the hairy cannibal, and recognized his scarred face. He smiled slightly when he saw his handiwork on Squanto's face. Resolve that he would not get away again hardened his young features and with a grimace of determination, pulled out his knife.

Chintook lay on the ground, winded and gasping for air. Weakly he struggled to get up but fell back against the side of the dry gulch, his energy spent.

The crazed Mautuk was the first to attack. Seeing Babtoo smile sent a lightning bolt of hate coursing through his body. The voices in his head screamed at him demanding him to sacrifice his own body to rid his people of this nemesis. Leaping forward, a wild ear-splitting shriek forced itself from his gaping mouth as spittle flew everywhere.

Babtoo leaped back to get out of the way of the charge and tripped over Chintook. Frantically rolling to get back on his feet, his hands closed on the snakehead spear. Without thinking, he lifted up the spear and braced it against the earth as Squanto fell toward him. The razor sharp spear pierced Squanto's chest and a hiss sounded as blood stained the spear's shaft.

His eyes, once blood shot, turned back to the smoky black of a forest dweller. A serene look crossed his face for only a brief moment as death claimed him, before returning to a look of utter terror. Grabbing feebly at the spear shaft, Squanto tried desperately to dislodge it from his dying body.

The spear seemed to writhe in Babtoo's hand. He let go of it instantly and watched in disbelief as the magical spear took the life and spirit from Squanto's shuddering body. The black, scaly spear had trapped Squanto's spirit for eternity, always thirsty and always hungry, but never satisfied. Squanto took his last breath as the spear seemed to writhe out of his body and fall to the ground.

Babtoo uttered a prayer for their safety. Shaking from the depraved act he witnessed, he looked over to Chintook who also was visibly shaken.

Chintook sounded troubled, "I have only heard of such spears of power from stories told to me by my parents. Mautuks make a spear like that for their most feared enemy. It will capture their enemy's spirit inside the shaft for the high priest to torment at his leisure. It seems you have turned the table on this warrior. This spear must be destroyed before it falls into the wrong hands."

Babtoo stood apprehensively, looking at the quivering weapon. It seemed to pulsate with malevolent energy. The black scaled shaft was so dark; it looked like a gateway to the underworld. Looking closely, he could almost see Squanto's spirit struggling to get out. Shaking his head, he gingerly picked it up and wrapped it in Squanto's bloody shirt. Repulsed by the evil radiating from the spear, Babtoo placed it on Enobi.

Babtoo said, "We can't let another Mautuk take this spear. It's cursed. Chief Bowhut will know how to destroy it."

Chintook nodded and said, "It is evil! The sooner we destroy it, the better everyone will sleep!"

The ghoul, huge and ugly stood like a pillar as the Mautuks gathered around him. He was one of a pair of creatures created by the high priest and given special powers of strength and leadership to command the Mautuk army. The power that emanated from him drew the straggling army to his side. He was the eyes and ears of the army relaying visual messages back to the high priest. Poised as if listening, he received the next set of orders.

Groups and individuals found their way to the small rise and rallied where he stood. Bewildered, and looking around warily, they waited to learn what to do next. All stood watching the Mautuk ghoul on the hill.

Chief Bowhut looked out from his hiding place wondering what they were planning. He already had his warriors spaced around back to prevent them from reentering their forest stronghold. The day was getting late and the time to attack was getting close. He knew he had to kill the ghoul on the hill before he could organize the remaining warriors. Without this creature, the rest of the Mautuks would fall quickly.

Chief Bowhut gathered Puku and Ukup to him. Putting his hands on their shoulders he said, "The time has come. Tell our people to separate into pockets of about fifteen to twenty warriors. Be sure to wear their capes. We want to appear as Babtoo, spirits or panthers. Show yourselves briefly and then disappear back into the savanna. They will break away and follow you. Attack them then, when they are in small groups, away from the larger force.

"Their confidence is shattered. I believe they will not put up much of a fight. The wildebeest herd trampled a large part of their horde. They will see that as a dangerous omen and their superstitious natures should make them easy targets. While you do this, I'll take care of the ghoul. This will make them leaderless. Drive them toward the river and let the crocodiles do our dirty work. I want no survivors."

Puku and Ukup looked at one another in concern. Puku spoke for both of them, "Let us help you defeat the ghoul warrior. You take a big risk by yourself."

Chief Bowhut, touched by their concern said, "I need you need to lead our men. I have to do this by myself. Now go! We have little time."

Without saying another word, the two brothers left, running in opposite directions, and trusting in the strength of their chief.

Chief Bowhut watched the two warriors vanish into the savanna with their orders. Observing the Mautuk ghoul on the hill gave him some trepidation. This warrior was unusual and unlike the others. His frame was huge and his muscles rippled in the sun. The head was devoid of hair and was skull-like in appearance. His hairy body was the color of charcoal, dull and lifeless. Mautuk warriors cringed around him or scurried to get out of his way. Like a general, he directed the attack from the safety of the hill.

The Watinkee tribesmen broke up into small groups. Black capes flowed in the wind as they charged forward. Phantoms could not have been more believable. Three or four groups would suddenly appear and disappear as quickly as they could get Mautuks to follow. Then three or four more groups would appear somewhere else to distract the army. The Mautuks were effectively separated into small groups and led toward the riverbank. Chief Bowhut wanted to take no chances with any of his warriors. The savanna held many dangers he could use to do the battle for him.

Like a statue, the ghoul stood alone on the hilltop. Gusts of air swirled around him, as if not wanting to caress his evil malevolence. As the last of his warriors charged after the retreating Watinkee warriors, he turned to leave. Long strides down the hill quickly ate up distance.

At the bottom of the hill, Chief Bowhut stood waiting. His long hair touched by the breeze played along his shoulders. His sun kissed face brimmed with confidence and determination. This was why he was chief. Not a young man anymore, he still had the strength of someone half his age. He would not put other warriors in danger. This was for him to do alone.

The ghoulish warrior spotted him when he was half way down the hill. Recognizing him as the chief, he quickly changed direction to intercept Chief Bowhut. Not slowing down to assess his adversary, the ghoul quickly closed the distance.

With a running start, Chief Bowhut threw his spear as the gap closed. His spear flew true to its mark and sailed through the air toward the ghoul's beating black heart. The creature moved with remarkable speed and stepping to the side, snatched the spear out of the air, reversed it, and threw it back toward Chief Bowhut.

Stunned at the speed of the Mautuk, Chief Bowhut stood almost a second too long as the spear sped toward his chest. Leaping aside, he rolled into the grass as the spear flew inches from his head. Grabbing his knife, he circled the Mautuk looking for some sign of weakness as the beast continued to stride forward, eating up the distance between them.

The two met with a clash. Chief Bowhut slashed with his knife, cutting the Mautuk deeply. To his surprise, very little blood appeared from the deep wound. Without flinching, the cannibal grabbed his arms and head butted him. Stars exploded in Chief Bowhut's head.

Fighting to stay conscious, he twisted away and stood on wobbly feet.

A laugh from the Mautuk sounded like a tortured soul and almost unmanned him as he fought to get his senses back. Swaying on unsteady feet, he faced the Mautuk ghoul.

Babtoo rode Enobi with Chintook by his side. Atop Enobi, he spotted the battle between Chief Bowhut and the Mautuk beast. As the spear flew from Chief Bowhut's hand, Babtoo was certain it would hit its mark. Amazingly, the Mautuk reached for the spear and casually plucked it out of the air. Then with startling accuracy, reversed his grip and threw it back toward Chief Bowhut. For a split second, he thought the spear would hit Chief Bowhut before he nimbly dodged out of the way. Astonished at what he just saw, Babtoo knew he was not a common Mautuk warrior. Realizing the chief was in trouble, Babtoo rode hard to help.

The Mautuk heard the drumming of Enobi's footsteps. Turning from Bowhut to face Babtoo, he stood with his arms spread. His skull like face leered and seemed to welcome the challenge.

Babtoo grasped his father's spear and bore down on the Mautuk. Veering off at the last minute, Babtoo threw the spear as hard as he could. The Mautuk ghoul had no time to react as the spear pierced his chest and continued out his back. The blow from the heavy weapon should have dragged the cannibal down. Instead, he stood on braced feet as if a feather had blown into him. Not once did his gaze leave Babtoo. Reaching with both hands he slowly pulled the heavy spear from his body hand over hand until it finally clattered to the ground.

Taking this opportunity, Chief Bowhut attacked the Mautuk from behind. Slashing the back of the beast with his knife, he was stunned by a heavy backhand. Spinning to the ground, Chief Bowhut spit out blood from his mouth as he fought for breath. Struggling to gain his footing, he watched incredulously at what happened next.

Babtoo saw his spear had no effect on the ghoul. The wound should have been fatal and yet he stood as if nothing had happened.

Thinking better of not getting into a hand-to-hand battle with the Mautuk, Babtoo instead reached for the magical spear.

The sacrilegious feel of it made him nauseous as obscene voices whispered in his head. His hand closed on the vile scaly black shaft. It was cold and heavy to the touch. The whispers grew louder as ghastly horrors crept into his mind. Straining to remain in control, Babtoo fought the vile suggestions and corrupt thoughts.

Turning Enobi around, Babtoo attacked again. The cape billowed behind him and made him look like a black angel of death. The sun glinted off his cape almost blinding the Mautuk. The evil weapon flew from his hands with unerring accuracy. Grateful to be rid of the repulsive spear, Babtoo's mind cleared as he watched it soar through the air.

The Mautuk stepped aside and grabbed for it as it flew toward his heart and yet the spear seemed to follow his every movement pinning his hand to his chest. A cloud of black dust billowed in the air as a frightening howl filled the air. Grabbing at the spear, the Mautuk could not get it out of his body. The spear latched into his body and would not let go. The grisly wound got bigger and bigger, absorbing the Mautuk, until only a greasy red spot on the soil remained.

The shaft lay on the ground fat and swollen, pulsing with the undead life it held. Black oily smoke escaped from the tip seeking to reform as a ghoulish image in the air. A small black cyclone took shape while a terrible shriek filled the air. Swirling in a haphazard fashion toward the jungle, the cyclone lost its momentum to finally dissipate and die. The shaft of the spear lost its power and started to crack and dry, turning to ash.

Visibly shaken, Babtoo slid off Enobi and stumbled toward Chief Bowhut. Reaching down, he offered his hand to the fallen Chief. Even though Chief Bowhut was still groggy, he looked at Babtoo gratefully. His grip was strong as Babtoo helped him to his feet. The side of his face was swollen and already turning black and blue. Blood still trickled from his mouth, but despite his injuries, he smiled at Babtoo.

"Well met Babtoo! I was just about to finish him off before you came." The smile in his eyes told Babtoo he was joking and that Chief Bowhut was going to be all right.

"Well, I just happened by and wanted to try out my new spear," Babtoo chuckled.

Huffing and puffing, Chintook finally arrived. "Are you telling me I ran all the way here for nothing?" He said sarcastically as a smile creased his face.

All three men stood staring at the ugly black spot where the spear had disintegrated. Shaking their heads, nobody could express themselves at that moment. Chief Bowhut knew they had just fought a Mautuk ghoul. Powerful and almost invincible, he could not have killed him with his mortal weapons. Glancing at Babtoo, he silently wondered where he got the powerful spear to kill it. He turned away; it was a story for another time.

The respect in the eyes of both warriors told Babtoo how they felt about him. His chest almost burst from pride because they considered him a warrior and a man.

Looking in the air, an eagle soared.

The bush was stout and strong yet had few branches to support its existence. Roots long and tough tapped into the earth for moisture supporting the few leaves remaining on its branches. The breeze danced through the leaves as they struggled to be free, barely concealing the figure behind it.

Crouching down behind the plant a Mautuk waited. He was one of a very few that had survived the Watinkee attacks. The sun blazed down on him drying the perspiration before it had a chance to cool his body. His black hair absorbed the heat raising his body temperature even more. He was on the verge of heat exhaustion.

They should have defeated the tall warriors by now. He was not sure if he was fighting apparitions, spirits, or Watinkee tribesmen. Out of nowhere, they would attack. Their long wicked spears were deadly accurate. The black caped ghosts would appear out of nowhere and before they could react, several of his friends would be dead.

Although the breeze was slight, it carried with it a long terrifying wail that seemed to seek him out and sent shivers of fear through his body. He was not brave, but its resonance reached deep inside him groping for his life's essence. His eyes rolled up in his head, and for a moment, he fought a battle to survive. His heartbeat became erratic and his breath came in gasps. The wail finally grew weaker and died within leaving him mentally exhausted.

His mind became clear once again. He knew the high priest's pet Mautuk ghoul sent to lead them was dead. They were now leaderless. He wondered if he should go back, or continue to fight. Bringing no prisoners would result in almost certain death. Better to die in battle or, better yet, to hide than to go back empty handed. A rustle next to him brought him out of his reverie. His group leader had come to find him.

Looking up at the Mautuk, he noticed the leader was uncertain and he could read a look of defeat in his eyes. Afraid and unsure of what to do, he said, "The ghoul is dead. His undead spirit searched for me. He tried to take my body."

The Mautuk from the bush said, "He tried to take mine too! What do we do now?"

The leader looked around, expecting at any moment to be attacked, and said, "We have to get back to our home in the jungle. It's safe there and the Watinkee warriors won't follow us there. But every time I circle back, Watinkee warriors are there searching for us. Our only way is to get to the river. I can smell the water from here."

The warrior crouching behind the bush slurred his words with a swollen tongue thick from thirst, "I need water. I cannot go on without it."

Looking down at his companion, the leader whispered, "I need water too. That's where we'll go."

With a backward glance to see if all was clear, the two Mautuks started toward the river. On their way, they met up with several other groups heading in the same direction. Soon, what was left of the army was scattered along the banks of the river.

From the rear, the Watinkee tribesmen continued to herd them like cattle, trapping the Mautuks against the river. After the high priest's ghoul death, the long undead moan carried by the wind desperately searched for a new body to inhabit. Every Mautuk warrior felt the loss of his leader and the unholy violation of his body. Some milled about not knowing what to do. Others fought to get back to the jungle, but a forest of Watinkee spears prevented their escape. Black caped men struck fear into the Mautuk army and many ran from their own elongated shadows as the evening sun started to set. The net of Watinkee tribesmen slowly tightened around them.

The smell of the water was intoxicating. The wildebeest, thirsty from the dust and dirt, picked the pace up to get to the river. The younger wildebeest, inexperienced with the dangers of the river pushed forward to lead the herd. Large, living, floating logs alive with hunger waited in the muddy water for the first animals to enter the water.

The young wildebeests approached the bank with little caution greedily drinking the water along the bank. Animals from the rear of the herd continued to move forward creating a huge press that forced some of the younger animals into the river. Great snapping jaws and a lunge barely missed a young wildebeest as it jumped back frantically. Struggling to regain the bank among the tightly packed animals, the wildebeest finally succumbed to the hungry crocodiles.

Contagious fear spread through the herd. Confusion reigned as the animals instinctively wanted to move ahead, but fear of the lurking dangers in the river kept them from crossing. Thousands of animals grunted and called to one another as the drive to get to the opposite side of the river became more intense.

It was dusk and the remaining Mautuk army gathered by the bank of the river. Not far away, the wildebeest herd milled about stirring up dust obscuring the sunset. Leaderless, they waited for somebody to take charge. Crouching among the reeds and bushes by the river, they waited for an opportunity to escape into the night.

Chief Bowhut, Babtoo and Chintook brought up the rear of the Watinkee warriors. Finding Puku and Ukup, Chief Bowhut asked, "Are all the Mautuks on the banks of the river? Did we get them all contained, or did any of them get past us? Most importantly, was anybody hurt?"

Puku help up his hand at the Chief and said, "I think we got all of them. We were very effective with these black capes in creating fear and confusion among them. They didn't put up much of a fight and everybody is safe. Your plan work perfectly! Everybody goes home to their families!"

Peering closely at the chief, Ukup said, "Looks like you got in one, though. I hope you did more to him than he did you!"

Chief Bowhut said wryly, "The gods were smiling on me. I got help when I needed it the most." Looking at Babtoo and Enobi, Chief Bowhut smiled faintly. "Babtoo, I want you to go where you can be seen by the Mautuks. Ride your magical beast back and forth and distract them. You will be a decoy. I'll gather the warriors and attack when you have their full attention. I hope to force them into the water and let the crocodiles do the work for us. We'll deal with any stragglers trying to escape over land."

Everybody nodded in agreement. So far, Chief Bowhut's plan had worked well. Everyone had survived the battle so far. This was a great success and would be over before nightfall.

Babtoo slid down off Enobi and checked his rear leg. Babtoo noticed that the wound would need time to heal. Patting Enobi on the neck, he whispered, "We're almost finished big boy. Soon you'll have the rest you deserve." Getting back on Enobi, Babtoo rode toward the riverbank.

Chief Bowhut watched him go. Admiration and respect for Babtoo touched him. At one time, he didn't think Babtoo would amount to much and this changed his outlook on people forever. He now realized everybody had a gift to give and no one should be judged by his or her disability. For him, Babtoo was a great lesson learned.

Chintook looked at Chief Bowhut and knew in his heart what he was thinking, "He saved my life. I owe him my respect. He is more of a man than are others that I have fought with. His bravery is unquestioned for one so young. He has proven to be considerate and thoughtful despite what Hohumph and others did to discourage him. He has sacrificed much for those honors. If he asks for Monbeem's hand, I will give it to him with all the blessings I can."

Chief Bowhut looked at him and said, "He has done more in this one year than many will do in a life time. We both are indebted to him for our lives."

Chintook turned to say, "I'll follow Babtoo in case he gets into trouble. His magical beast limps from the long day. Maybe he can use my help."

Chief Bowhut said, "Yes, he has done enough for one day. Look after him Chintook. I will lead our people for the final blow and I hope we can end this battle tonight."

With those parting words, he strode away leaving Chintook to go after Babtoo.

Bachton was terribly thirsty. The Mautuk cannibal could not seem to escape from the sun wherever he tried to hide. The savanna shimmered with heat waves even with the dying sun. Dust caked in his mouth making it hard to swallow. His dirty fingers rubbed blood shot eyes that no longer produced tears.

The river looked very inviting. It reflected the evening sun with bright colors of orange and red. Small waves lapped lazily on the bank begging him to take a drink. The reeds along the bank beckoned him to cool off as they lazily swayed back and forth in the cool breeze.

Bachton cautiously crawled down to the river. Parting the reeds, he tentatively reached out a cupped hand to sample the refreshing water. Greedily sucking the water down his parched throat, Bachton edged closer. Splashing water on his body to cool down and drinking to satisfy his thirst, he failed to notice the reflection of two eyes glimmering from the retreating sun.

The crocodile alerted to a potential meal, slipped into the water and swam toward the Mautuk on the bank. Sinking down into the water to allow only his eyes and nose to show, he used his powerful tail to propel him closer. Looking at his victim, his tiny brain could not figure out what it was. It appeared bigger than a monkey but smaller than a wildebeest. It was too complex for him and so instinct took over.

Bachton had finished drinking and was making his way out of the river. Hearing a small splash like a stone thrown in the river, he turned to investigate. Looking closely at the water, he did not notice the giant crocodile heading in his direction at a ferocious speed. Bachton had no time to react. The large crocodile leaped out of the water, grabbing the Mautuk's body.

Bachton's last saw a giant cavernous maw that suddenly appeared before him. The blackness was so deep, it could have been a pit to the underworld. Breath that smelled of decay and rotting fish enveloped his senses before he realized he was caught. The crocodile clamped down and sank back into the water with his prize. Bachton barely had a chance to struggle before he felt his body pulled in different directions from other crocodiles. Blood pooled momentarily before being carried downstream to dissipate into the peaceful river. The flowing water lapped lazily on the banks once again carrying away the violence as if it had never happened.

Babtoo rode toward the trapped Mautuk army. He knew Enobi was limping and yet the proud animal would still do anything he asked of him. Not wanting to aggravate the healing wound, Babtoo was reluctant to run him back and forth. He approached a large hill overlooking the banks of the river. There he could clearly see in the waning light the disorganized Mautuk army milling about hoping that a leader would emerge.

Raising his spear above his head, Babtoo yelled a challenge to the army. His cape caught the breeze and in the fading light, appeared like a wraith ready to drift down upon the army.

The Mautuks froze at Babtoo's battle cry. Their nemesis had returned. Searching for an escape route, many turned toward the river.

Glowing eyes dotted the surface only to disappear and then reappear somewhere else. Masters at stealth, the crocodiles waited patiently. They knew a meal would eventually come to them.

A loud battle cry echoed from the Watinkee warriors as they charged toward the bewildered Mautuks with spears leveled, chasing the disorganized Mautuks toward the water. Confusion, panic, and fear ran rampant in the Mautuk army.

Hundreds of black caped men charged down toward the surviving Mautuks. Some Mautuks turned to fight, only to face overwhelming odds. Others braved the rushing river. Throwing their weapons down and running toward the river, they hastily jumped in hoping to avoid the deadly spears of the Watinkee warriors.

The water soon boiled with activity as the first warriors entered the water. The attack from the crocodiles was instant and vicious. Some had not eaten for months and the Mautuks had no horns or hooves to harm them. The carnage was over quickly as screams of the dying filled the air. Soon, Babtoo heard a ragged cheer from the Watinkee warriors. He was grateful the battle was over. Sliding off Enobi, he decided to walk toward the village. He looked forward to seeing Monbeem and felt a great weight lifted from his shoulders. Exhausted, he led Enobi away from the sounds of victory.

He soon came upon a small ravine that was well hidden and shallow with small rocks and bushes making it almost invisible.

The sun had already set with the stars beginning to dot the sky.

The breeze had died with the last light and soon warriors from the Watinkee tribe were making their way home to their families.

Thus, the attack from the ravine came as a complete surprise to Babtoo. Enobi had not caught any scent of the two cannibals, and with the lack of light, Babtoo did not see them. The two Mautuk warriors burst from the shallow depression and charged at Babtoo. Eyes wild with fear, they attacked with knives drawn. They were desperate to escape the fate of their brothers and wanted to avoid capture. Babtoo blocked their only escape route into the open savanna.

A twig snapped and small loose stone cascaded down as the Mautuks scrambled out of the depression. Babtoo turned to see two warriors sprinting in his direction. Startled, Enobi backed away. They barreled into Babtoo, as they fell in a tangle of limbs, each searching for an opening to bury a knife in his flesh.

Strong hairy arms encircled his body and the stench of their foul breath gagged him. Stabbing downward, the Mautuks desperately tried to end the fight quickly. Panic gave Babtoo the extra strength he needed to flip the hairy cannibals from him. A sharp pain in his side and Babtoo felt the bite of the Mautuk knife. Breathing heavily, he drew his own knife and glanced down at the burning sensation in his side. Blood flowed freely between his fingers as his hand clamped down on the wound.

Circling Babtoo, the Mautuks sensed they had the advantage. If they could wait just a few minutes more, Babtoo might collapse from his wound. Feinting back and forth, they took turns distracting him, hoping for an opening to deliver the final blow.

Babtoo's reflexes were slowing. The hairy cannibals were getting nearer with each feint. Fighting to stay conscious, Babtoo changed tactics and took the fight to them.

Charging at one of the Mautuks, Babtoo closed easily with his long strides and caught the cannibal off guard. Struggling to overpower him with his waning strength, he chopped down with his fist. The satisfying sound of crunching bone as he splattered the

Mautuk's nose across his face stunned the Mautuk. Grabbing weakly for Babtoo's knife hand, the Mautuk labored to stay conscious. Struggling to end the fight quickly, Babtoo expected an attack by the other Mautuk warrior at any moment.

Darkness was building inside his head as his own strength slowly ebbed away. Afraid he would lose consciousness, Babtoo fought desperately. Turning, he saw a spear protruding from the other Mautuk warrior. Screaming vulgarities, the Mautuk fell to the ground, cursing as he died.

With the last of his strength, Babtoo thrust down hard feeling the knife bite into Mautuk flesh. Rolling away, the dying warrior feebly tried to get up, only to fall to his knees. Chintook strode over making sure he would no longer rise.

Lying on his back, Babtoo stared into a friendly, compassionate face with a lion's mane spilling off his shoulders. Chintook said, "I wish I had come back sooner, Babtoo. I thought we had routed the Mautuks and had them all trapped by the river."

Babtoo whispered hoarsely, "Thank you my friend. I could not have done it without your help. They caught me off guard when they attacked. I, too, thought the way home was safe."

Chintook, trembling from the exertion, looked closely at Babtoo's wound. Shaking his head, Chintook smiled. "Babtoo, must I look after you all the time? You were supposed to watch out for me! Let's take a look at the wound."

Upon closer examination, Chintook bound the wound tightly and said nonchalantly, "You will live. The knife was not poisoned. It will be a few days before you can do anything. Monbeem will be thrilled you live and now she can take care of you. This is good, because I need a break from her incessant mothering!"

A slow weary smile played across Babtoo's face.

CHAPTER 27

MARRIAGE PROPOSAL

The sky was a dazzling blue stretching from the horizon to the sea. Ocean and sky seemed to be various shades of blue melding into each other creating limitless boundaries to the eye. The sun felt warm as the clouds floated by changing shapes in their race across the heavens. The moving shadows they cast on the savanna looked like countless images of animals and birds and with a little imagination, faces of friends. They struggled to hold their shape as the breeze transformed them into something completely different in their mad dash to the ends of the earth.

The breeze blew across the savanna in waves crashing against the shores of the jungle where it could not penetrate. The grasses swayed back in forth in a hypnotic dance revealing unseen life temporarily exposed, and then hidden again by the next wave.

Rabbits hopped from hole to hole nibbling on the succulent grass as they reached safety. A grasshopper feeding on a stalk of grass rubbed its back legs together letting the whole world know he was alive.

Flocks of birds flew through the air. Their shrill calls to one another were music to the Watinkee people. Cape buffalo moved slowly forward, bawling at one another about some perceived aggression. Lions sprawled out on a rocky bank absorbing the heat of the day, content only to flick their tails at annoying flies. Cheetahs sat on a hill observing the passing gazelle with interest eager to hunt. Wild pigs grunted to one another as they rooted up the soil looking for grubs and roots.

The lakes and rivers across the savanna reflecting the sun appeared like blue sapphires and sparkling diamonds. Large, flexible crocodiles swam back and forth across the surface in their constant search for food. A hippopotamus grunted and showed a massive mouth with hooked teeth warning everybody that he was the king of this stretch of river.

These things the eagle saw and more. He was young and strong and reveled in the gift of life. He was the master of the sky and his large eyes large missed nothing.

Drifting on air currents, he spotted a young man. The man called for him to come down with a sharp whistle. Tucking his wings to his side, he dived down at the young man with remarkable speed. Wind buffeted his feathers as his streamline body parted the air, plummeting like an arrow shaft toward the muscular man. He screamed loud and fierce drawn to the man's irresistible call.

The man had leather bindings wrapped around his arm. His smile split across his face watching the big bird in its joy at being free. At the last moment, the eagle spread its mighty wings to slow down extending wicked looking talons. The man reached up with his leather wrapped arm and gasped...

Babtoo woke up to intense pain. His arm was reaching out as if to grab something when the stitches in his side pulled free. Looking down at his wound, he fell back into bed wondering how he got there. The last thing he knew was Chintook had helped him to the village. Closing his eyes to ward off the pain, he reopened them to gaze at an angel.

She was beautiful with olive skin and large brown eyes. Her breath smelled of peppermint as she whispered softly to him. Her voice was like the song of birds, clear, delightful and musical. Her touch was light and smooth and where her fingers touched, the pain would go away. Monbeem smiled down at him.

Blinking again at this mirage, he realized he was not dead but that Monbeem was leaning over him rewrapping his wound. As she kissed him lightly on the lips, Babtoo felt like he could fly. Reaching for her, he pulled her to him.

"I love you Monbeem. I will ask Chintook to marry you now. Please say yes!"

Tears flowed freely from Monbeem's eyes as she buried her head in his shoulder. "Oh, Babtoo, how long I have waited for you to ask me. I love you so much!"

Holding each other closely, Babtoo felt strength return to his broken body. Life was so worth living!

Pulling away from his gentle embrace, she gazed into his eyes and said, "I'll get Chintook now before you change your mind!"

"I will not change my mind. I have always loved you and until I could prove to you I could be a worthy husband, I had to wait to ask." Babtoo whispered, afraid this was only a dream

"Babtoo, if you only knew there was never any doubt in my mind what kind of man you were going to be. You allowed your foot to hold you back and yet you could fly with the eagles!" She admonished.

Babtoo lay there for a moment remembering the frequent dreams of the eagles. Deep in thought, he looked at Monbeem and said, "Yes, yes, go get Chintook! I have an important question to ask him. If he says no, I will take you for myself anyway!" He laughed.

Monbeem jumped up and ran toward the tent door; her feet barely touched the ground. Left alone with his thoughts, Babtoo still wondered if this was all a dream as he lay back down on the bed exhausted from the strain. The throbbing pain from the knife wound brought the reality back and he realized he was not sleeping. Staring at the ceiling of the tent, silhouettes of eagles flew in concert with the dancing flame of the fire.

Chintook entered the tent with a flourish. He was wearing his lion's mane cape over his thin frame and his face was stern and unsmiling. Clenched between his teeth was a pipe puffing smoke to match his formidable features. Hands and arms folded across his chest, he abruptly said, "Babtoo, I understand you have something to ask me. For some odd reason Monbeem can barely contain herself.

What good news have you been keeping from me?" Puffs of smoke circled his head to drift toward the ceiling collecting in a big cloud at the top.

Babtoo's heart dropped like a stone in a cold pond. Chintook's demeanor was not good, but too much had happened to him since his first hunt. He hoped Chintook would not say 'No'. Struggling to sit up without taking his eyes off Chintook he said, "I have come far, Chintook. I want to ask for the hand of your daughter Monbeem!"

Silence in the tent followed. Chintook could barely stand it. The ends of his mouth kept twitching upward. His eyes laughed merrily. Smoke poured from his pipe like a chimney to hide his fondness for the boy. Babtoo stared hard at Chintook.

All of a sudden, Chintook could not hold it back any longer. Almost choking on the pipe, he accidentally inhaled the blue smoke. "Of course, you can marry Monbeem and I give you my blessing! If you did not ask soon enough, I would have given her for you to keep. I am tired of her bad cooking and mothering ways. Maybe you can teach her proper manners and to respect an old man like myself." Slapping Babtoo on the shoulder, he strode out of the tent telling everybody the wonderful news.

Wincing from the slap, Babtoo fell back down in the bed. Excitement would not let him sleep. His heart raced with happiness. This had worked out better than he had hoped.

CHAPTER 28

BABTOO'S TOTEM

A week had gone by and Babtoo felt he needed to stretch his legs. The wound was tightly bandaged and healing well. It hurt to stretch or turn his body, but the stitches held the pink scar tissue together. Getting up stiffly on unsteady legs, he made his way to the door.

The bustle in the Watinkee camp over the wedding of Babtoo and Monbeem was exciting. Everybody wanted to get involved in one way or another. Hunters gathered rare meats and berries. Women were busy making clothes to wear to the big event. Everybody smiled or congratulated him as he walked by.

Limping over to Whutknot, Babtoo sat down on a log across from him. Whutknot glanced at him as he continued to stir some odd concoction in a bubbling cauldron.

He was the first to speak. "Congratulations, Babtoo, on your soon impending wedding."

Babtoo picked up a stick and haphazardly drew something in the dirt. "Yes, thank you."

Peering closely at Babtoo, Whutknot said, "You did not come here to hear me congratulate you. What is on your mind, Babtoo?"

Babtoo looked up at Whutknot, but his mind seemed elsewhere. "Whutknot, I still have dreams of eagles. They are getting more intense. I feel I have to leave soon to find my totem. I dream of a bird flying in the air. I can see what he sees no matter how small. Wherever he flies, I feel my spirit soar with him. I see lakes, streams, and animals. I feel what he feels as he climbs the air currents. I cannot get married until I do this final thing. I don't know how long it will take and I do not mean to disappoint anybody. But I feel I must go." Babtoo said this last with a heavy sigh.

Whutknot looked closely at Babtoo. Glancing down at his doodling in the sand, a bird was drawn and redrawn as he erased it and started over.

Reaching out to Babtoo, he quietly said, "Babtoo, you must go and find your totem. The wedding can wait. This will shape your life forever. I had at once thought the spotted zebra to be your totem. Instead, it has enhanced not only your life, but everybody else's life too. As we speak, little Casteel has taken it upon himself to look after Enobi when you were wounded. All the children come to him to help with the care of your spotted zebra. He has gained great stature for his small size in the eyes of the children. When you feel it is time to go, then you must go. A totem only comes around once. If you miss it, it will be gone forever."

Looking up at Whutknot, Babtoo held his head high. "Thank you Whutknot for your advice. I will leave tomorrow. I hope Monbeem will understand."

The morning dew had not evaporated from the grass. Two sets of footprints left a trail in the field toward Enobi. The Watinkee camp was still asleep as the blanket of peacefulness settled over the early morning hours. The darkness kept the sun at bay as Babtoo and Monbeem walked hand in hand. They said nothing to one another letting the stillness of the morning speak for them.

Babtoo had talked with Monbeem the day before. He asked her if they could postpone the wedding. He had talked with Whutknot about the urgency of his dreams and he was convinced he had to leave immediately.

Monbeem cried softly during the conversation. She had seen throughout the summer the toll his responsibilities took on him. His strength was more than in his body, but of his character and spirit.

She felt lucky to have him. She wanted him to stay and hold her and never leave again but knew how important it was for a warrior to gain his totem.

They stood looking deeply in each other's eyes. The love they shared for each other flowed through their bodies as they held each other tightly. An intruding ray of sunlight cut short the passionate kisses they both had hoped would never end.

Babtoo looked down on her beautiful tan face and said, "I have to go now. I wish I could stay but I feel compelled to go. When I get back, the first thing we will do is get married. I love you and do not want to leave you."

Monbeem gazed into his intense grey eyes and knew this was something of great importance to him. She forced herself into agreeing with him even knowing how significant it was to have your personal totem, but she desperately hoped the journey would not take long.

Wiping a tear from her face he said, "I have to go now. Do not fret. I will be back before you miss me!"

Sniffling she whispered, "I already miss you my husband to be. Hurry back before dinner gets cold."

Knowing he would be gone for a time, he played along and said, "Who could miss a meal prepared by you? I will be there promptly for supper. Chintook says he cannot live without your cooking. Your gazelle stew is the best!"

Turning quickly before a tear fell from his own eyes, he jumped on Enobi. The animal, sensing the emotion, snorted softly and nodded his finely chiseled head. His large brown eyes seemed to speak to Monbeem letting her know he would bring Babtoo back safely. Turning away, Babtoo led Enobi out into the savanna. Monbeem watched him fade into the emerging morning light. He was just a speck on the horizon before she shook herself free and walked back to camp.

◈◈◈

The old Baobab tree was centuries old. Its long branches pointing to the sky had just a few leaves left on individual twigs. The only shade the ancient tree could provide anymore was from its large trunk and its few remaining branches.

The plains animals had once used it to escape the hot noonday sun but with the lack of foliage, they preferred other trees or bushes. Few animals really used it for shade anymore and so it stood as a sentinel of days gone by. The young and inexperienced animals still came by, but became annoyed at having to move to keep the glowing orb on the opposite side of the trunk.

The root system had long since lost its capacity to take up water and so had shrunk significantly through the years. The old tree clung to life only by the underground stream still nourishing it. It too was centuries old and was slowly drying up.

With little water and the blazing sun, the arteries in the tree became rock hard. It was a testament of a living petrified statue of the magnificence of days gone by. Clinging to life, it had only one important purpose yet to fulfill.

In the upper branches, a vast nest built of sticks was precariously perched. Many of those sticks came from the Baobab tree itself. Others came from the jungle not far away. Every year it seemed to get bigger and heavier. Pairs of eagles had nested in this same tree for decades. They may not have been the same pair over the years, but fathers, daughters, mothers and sisters had claimed the nest at one time or another.

A single egg had hatched and a small eaglet was born. There was little difference between him and any other eaglet. A tiny ball of fluff with dark piercing eyes, talons and a hooked beak gave the bird a regal look. A small defect in one of his toes prevented it from completely grasping a twig. It stood at attention with a tiny nail pointing to the sky. He did not know there was anything wrong with his talon. He just used it a little differently and it did not slow him down.

The big bull elephant was a loner. He remembered when this

ancient tree in its younger days had offered shade and food. He made his way across the plains seeking the shelter of the once great Baobab tree.

Hungry and thirsty, he approached the tree with caution. The tree was not how he remembered it. Instead, he found the husk of what once was a giant among trees. Animals in the vicinity slunk away, distracted by the constant rumbling of the elephants stomach, afraid of what it might be.

Looking up with tiny eyes, he saw a branch with some foliage that still clung to the tree. Raising his trunk, he reached for the succulent branch. Higher and higher, his trunk went but it was teasingly out of reach. The small branch waved at the big bull elephant in the wind as if mocking him to reach it.

Aggravated at his predicament, the elephant did what only elephants can do. Using his great strength, he grasped the tree with his trunk and started to push. Two titans in a wrestling match could not have been greater.

The elephant dug in with his toes and rocked back and forth shaking the tree. The root system, old and dry, slowly lost its grip on the dry soil and pulled free from the hard earth.

Distracted by a mother eagle diving at him, he waved his trunk in the air trying to knock her down. His large ears flapped furiously as his aggravation grew. With a final push, the large tree toppled to the earth with a resounding crash spilling the nest and the tiny eaglet to the ground.

Ignoring the screams of the eagle, he reached for the succulent branch and munched contently not realizing the lives he had changed.

Babtoo heard the shrill piercing shriek in desperation, anger, and a challenge rolled into one. The echoes in his mind continued long after the eagle flew from his sight. Babtoo had spotted the eagle around the fifth day of his journey and followed doggedly behind knowing he would eventually come upon his totem.

He was confident the bird would somehow be able to tell him what his dreams meant. He continued to travel north following the bird. Losing sight of it at the end of the day, he would find him the next morning wondering where he was taking him.

Today he watched the eagle soar in the air. His spirit seemed to soar with the large bird. The joy he experienced watching the eagle lifted his heart and felt like a freedom beyond anything he had ever experienced. The scream of the bird today was different, though, and sent shivers down his spine as he encouraged Enobi to hurry through the grasslands.

Trying to keep from losing sight of the bird, he came upon a large elephant tearing into an uprooted tree. Two eagles were swooping down on the pachyderm with little success.

Babtoo approached with caution. The bull elephant finished with its meal and turned to look at the horse and boy. Weary from the exchange of the birds and now from a new nemesis, the bull elephant lifted his trunk and bellowed a challenge to everybody.

Babtoo swung wide of the beast hoping to draw him away. The elephant charged but drew up at the last moment. Old and tired, he wanted nothing to do with Babtoo. Ambling away, he looked for a more peaceful place to rest.

Babtoo slid off the horse and walked toward the tree. The two eagles drifted down toward a branch of the fallen tree to sit and watch. The elephant had destroyed the nest, trampling it to get at the food. Babtoo walked closer to where the proud birds sat as if beckoning him to come closer.

A sudden shrill squawk came from underneath a branch and startled Babtoo. Hidden by dry leaves and twigs, the eaglet tried to free himself. Reaching down, he removed the debris from around the small bird and waited.

The two eagles sat on the branch and waited patiently watching Babtoo carefully. Slowly picking up the eaglet from the ground, he cradled it to his chest. The bird was just a ball of fluff with few feathers on his shivering body.

Was this his totem? Where was the feather he would carry on him? Confusion started to sift into his mind as he wondered what to do. Picking out a small piece of gazelle meat Monbeem had given him for the journey, he poked it into the small hooked beak. Swallowing the food seemed to revive the bird and he flapped his bald wings and squawked harshly. This was a good start to like Monbeem's cooking and it put a smile on his face.

The eaglet's eyes were fierce and indomitable matching his spirit to survive. At that moment, Babtoo knew what he had to do. His spirit seemed connected to the little bird. Glancing at the two eagles sitting on the branch, the birds spread their wings and flew in the air. Swooping down toward Babtoo, their cries were of relief, as if giving Babtoo permission to raise their baby. Together, they flew off toward the sun as if sensing everything would be all right.

Babtoo continued to feed the hungry bird and for the first time saw the connection to his totem. He looked into the eyes of the eaglet, fierce and indomitable, free and powerful. He stared back, equally indomitable.

His spirit soared.